CW00863231

THE GHOSTS OF PUNTA MORRO

A Run for the Devil novel

J. J. Ballesteros

iUniverse®

THE GHOSTS OF PUNTA MORRO
A RUN FOR THE DEVIL NOVEL

iUniverse books may be ordered through booksellers or by contacting:

iUniverse
1663 Liberty Drive
Bloomington, IN 47403
www.iuniverse.com
844-349-9409

ISBN: 978-1-6632-0315-1 (sc)
ISBN: 978-1-6632-0317-5 (hc)
ISBN: 978-1-6632-0316-8 (e)

Library of Congress Control Number: 2020914040

Print information available on the last page.

iUniverse rev. date: 08/07/2020

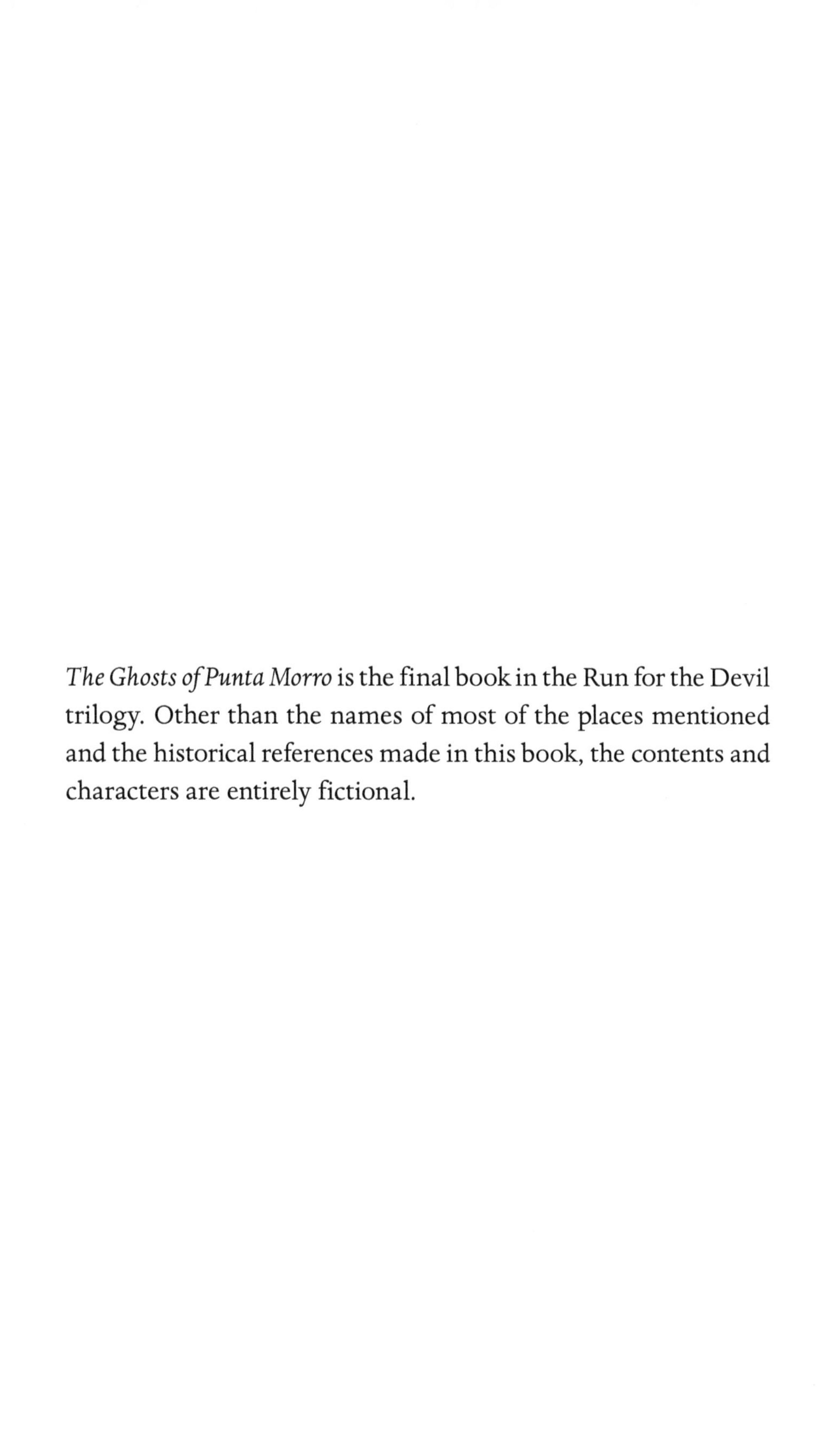

The Ghosts of Punta Morro is the final book in the Run for the Devil trilogy. Other than the names of most of the places mentioned and the historical references made in this book, the contents and characters are entirely fictional.

Dedicated to

Ramiro M. Ballesteros

January 28, 1933—August 28, 2019

Prologue

A long time had passed since this part of the island had seen this many people walking on its shore. Only a few outside of the rattlesnakes and coyotes had ever seen the sun rise over the Gulf of Mexico or listened to the gentle rolling of the surf from the pristine sands and rolling dunes of the Devil's Elbow on Padre Island.

Special Agent Jack Lyons stood on the beach next to a burned-out Lincoln Navigator, staring pensively at the empty space between three stacks of tightly wrapped bundles on the high-tide line, mesmerized by what it meant. One stack sat by itself, separated from the other two by two rows of footprints leading from the empty space between the stacks to the water's edge.

He looked out to sea at the rising sun shining through the storm clouds gathering ominously on the horizon, illuminating their swollen bellies with shades of purple and crimson. He gazed at a sloop sailing perilously toward the storm as he listened to the surf's soothing murmur whispering gently in his ear. He had never known a place where such tranquility and foreboding could coexist.

"Beautiful," he heard someone say behind him.

He turned to look at Deputy Noah Sykes and Chief Ranger Wilkes. "I didn't see you standing there."

"We noticed," the detective remarked. "What are you looking at?"

"That sailboat out there," Jack replied as a helicopter engine started to whine.

They turned to look at a paramedic closing the cargo bay door after loading Ranger Cummings, wounded in the firefight of the previous night, into the Bell 407 medevac helicopter. Jack thought the air ambulance looked small compared to the Coast Guard MH60T Jayhawk helicopter sitting just beyond it.

"Cummings did a pretty gutsy thing going up against an automatic rifle," Jack commented.

"Jerry has a lot of problems, but courage isn't one of them," the chief ranger replied.

Jack recalled how Ranger Cummings balked when Wilkes assigned him to take his team down island to look for a caravan of Chevy Silverados led by a Lincoln Navigator carrying prohibited weapons. They didn't have much daylight left when they set out to look for the gunrunners. Jack rode with the malcontent park ranger in his government Durango while the rest of his team rode in Sykes's county Expedition. They had no idea that a lookout had spotted their vehicles and tipped off the gunrunners, who set up to ambush them.

The whine increased in pitch as the helicopter's blades started to turn slowly. As the blades went faster, the whining turned to a chopping sound and then to a dull hum. As the helicopter rose vertically, it turned gracefully, raised its boom, and then dashed over the water along the beach toward the trauma center in Corpus Christi.

Jack gazed at the five body bags lying in a row by the Coast Guard helicopter as the crewmen started to load them into the cargo bay. He looked at the scene of the ambush between him and the Coast Guard helicopter, at the smoldering hulks of the pickups by the water's edge, the cindered shell of the one by the dunes, and the two bullet-riddled vehicles that brought his team to the Devil's Elbow and thought how it reminded him of the road out of Kuwait during the first Gulf War.

"That could have been us," Deputy Sykes remarked. He cocked his head as he looked at the cindered wreck by the dunes in front of the shot-up government vehicles. "If somebody hadn't blown up that pickup with an antitank gun when they did, we would have rolled into their ambush, and that would've been it."

"They didn't use an antitank gun," Jack commented. He walked over to the burned-out Lincoln Navigator and pointed out a neatly cut half-inch diameter hole in the front of the vehicle between the left headlight and the grill. "That was made by a fifty-caliber round." He pointed at the burned-out pickup by the dunes behind the Navigator and then up the beach at the hulks of the truck by the dunes and the three by the water. "They all have similar, well-placed holes."

"What made them explode like that?" Ranger Wilkes asked.

"My guess is explosive incendiary rounds," Jack replied. He turned to look at the sloop sailing into the storm. "Fired from out there."

"By whom?" Sykes asked.

"I don't know," Jack replied pensively as he watched the sailboat heading for a gray haze joining the sky with the water. In his mind's eye, he recalled seeing a molten glob streaking toward the Navigator from offshore. "Someone aboard a ship … with masts."

Sykes looked out to sea at the sloop Jack had his eye on.

"You mean a sailboat?"

"Maybe," Jack said as he turned to him. "I saw a tracer streaking in from offshore before the Lincoln went up in flames. I thought I saw a couple of masts, but I couldn't get a good look through all the smoke."

"You don't think the people they came out here to meet fired on them?" Sykes asked.

"I don't know," Jack replied. "The informant said they were meeting a ship."

"But why would they fire on them?"

"Don't know." Jack shrugged his shoulders. "Rip-off, maybe. Deal gone sour."

"Well, at least you got the guns," Ranger Wilkes commented.

Jack turned to look at the wide, empty space between the bundles stacked on the high-tide line.

"Not all of them," Jack retorted. "There're over a hundred AK-47 rifles missing."

"How you figure that?" Sykes asked.

Jack pointed at the burned-out pickup behind them. The blast had blown the lid off the secret compartment built into the bed.

"All five pickups had similar hidden compartments built into them," Jack explained. "If you look at the bundles stacked on the beach, they wouldn't fill two-thirds of the available space in all the compartments."

"That's not conclusive," Ranger Wilkes remarked.

"Look at the stacks of bundles," Jack added. "See how one is sitting alone, apart from the other two?"

"Yeah," Sykes said.

"Now look at the two sets of footprints leading from the empty space to the water."

"There are two stacks missing," Sykes concluded. He turned to Jack. "Good eye, Jack, but how do you figure they contained AK-47 rifles?"

"I opened a couple of the bundles on each stack before you got here," Jack said as he pointed at the first stack. "There are fifty-five bundles in that stack, each containing two Beretta nine-millimeter pistols."

"That's a hundred and ten pistols," Sykes said.

Jack pointed at the stack next to it. "That stack contains 9-millimeter and 7.62-millimeter ammunition."

"Seven-six-two—that's what an AK-47 fires," Sykes commented.

"That's right," Jack said as he pointed at the stack sitting apart from the other two. "And that stack contains fifty-five bundles packed with two AK-47 banana-shaped magazines each."

"For one hundred and ten AK-47 rifles," Sykes concluded.

Jack looked at the two sets of footprints leading away from the empty space between the bundles. "My guess is that the missing stacks contained a hundred and ten AK-47 rifles." Jack turned to watch the sailboat disappear into the haze. "I think there's a sailboat out there with a fifty-caliber rifle and a hundred and ten AK-47 rifles headed for Mexico."

"It's too bad none of the traffickers survived," Chief Ranger Wilkes remarked. "You'll never know if your theory is correct."

"Not all of them were killed," Jack said. He turned to look at the Coast Guard crew loading the last body bag. "Five bodies and six vehicles—someone got away."

CHAPTER 1

Among the most important things Donovan had learned in the cargo business included how to blend in with the crowd. Standing out always drew unwanted attention, especially from customs officials and nosy port policemen. He had hoped that mingling in with the yawls, ketches, cutters, and sloops participating in the Corpus Christi to Tampico yacht race would get him safely into Mexican waters without attracting the US Coast Guard's attention. However, the white hardwood hull; freshly stained teak deck, masts, and cabin tops; and plain white sails on his vintage schooner, the *Siete Mares* stood out like a prima ballerina on an indigo-blue stage among the brightly colored fiberglass hulls and painted sails of the other ships participating in the regatta.

His ship had the wind, her fore and main sails swinging their booms well beyond the starboard side. Her jib sails pulled on her bowsprit like runaway kites on a summer day as she glided across the Tampico shipping lanes on a broad reach. Soon, she would cross into Mexican waters and leave the relative safety of the regatta to make a run for her home waters in Campeche.

Donovan's mind drifted to the incident at the Devil's Elbow and how easily it could have ended badly. Everything happened so quickly, like dominoes tumbling before he had a chance to stand them all on their ends. He could still see in his mind's eye the swirling billows of smoke rising from the burning hulks of the vehicles he destroyed as his ship headed out to sea under a full moon. He had taken back his ship, foiled an ambush, and saved the lives of his crew but not without consequences. He made it impossible for any of them to go back to the lives they had before, not just because he had crossed a ruthless narco-terrorist but because he had also broken up a family. His thoughts turned to the day that set everything in motion.

He had just taken on a charter for the National Institute of Anthropology and History and needed a deckhand to complete his crew. Working the deck of a schooner required skill, good physical condition, and stamina. Finding anybody who knew anything about sailing in a fishing village like Seyba Playa proved more difficult than he had thought. After placing an ad in the local paper and hanging flyers around the port, only Benício, a part-time minister and artisanal fisherman, had put in for the job.

He knew the moment he met him at the Cocina Maya restaurant that the little man couldn't handle the work. His weight far exceeded his size, and he looked tired and in ill health. He only went ahead with the interview to spare the old man his feelings. He had just turned him down for the job when Itzél walked into his life.

She had hair the color of a raven's wing and the face of an angel. Her eyes sparkled like emeralds, and her skin looked as smooth as mocha. She had just come from the bank after failing to secure a loan to pay off a debt Benício owed for an outboard motor forced on him by El Demonio, the local drug lord.

He had mistaken her for Benício's daughter and had hoped that she could drive the demons that haunted him away just as he had hoped that buying the *Siete Mares* would fill the emptiness he felt in his life. He recalled how she had dashed that hope when she introduced him to her sixteen-year-old son, Poli, and told him of her marriage to Benício. Still, he had to have her in his world somehow.

As he listened to her son tell him about his dream of having his own ship someday, a stringy-haired man came to the restaurant to see Benício. Itzél told him that the man had come to collect for the motor and explained that El Demonio would forgive the debt if her husband agreed to go to the Seyba Reef and pick up a package for him.

Then the debt collector got rough with Benício and started to push him around. Without thinking, Donovan stepped in and stopped him, humiliating him in the process just as El Demonio and Dario, his cousin, walked into the restaurant.

Both men stood as tall as Donovan and looked as formidable as a pair of heavyweight prizefighters. As Donovan prepared for a fight he believed he would most likely lose, El Demonio called him by his name and brought up his job as a shipping agent in Panama. He realized then that he couldn't run from his somewhat undeserved reputation as a smuggler.

He should have walked out of the restaurant after declining El Demonio offer to hire his ship, but instead, he paid off Benício's debt and inserted himself between him and the trafficker. He liked to believe he did it out of outrage, but deep down, he knew he did it just so that he could see Itzél again. He even hired her sixteen-year-old son as the crewman he needed just so that he could.

In the weeks that followed, Donovan took every opportunity to see Itzél, lavishing upon her the attention she obviously enjoyed. Encouraged by that, he foolishly took a chance and asked her to leave Benício, promising to shower her with diamonds. She rebuked him for his offer, referring to a diamond as just a rock. He remembered the sting he felt, not because of what she had said but because of what it made him remember.

Xóchitl's Apartment near Old Town Veracruz
Three Years Ago

Xóchitl held her hand out to look at the diamond on her engagement ring.

"I love my ring," she said enthusiastically. "The diamond's almost as big as my eyes."

Donovan chuckled softly. "But not nearly as brilliant," he said softly as he brushed back the lock of rich black hair that always seemed to fall over her right eye.

The two lovers sat quietly on an antique Italian sofa in Xóchitl's apartment, watching the flickering lights of Old Town Veracruz through the open french doors to her balcony as they listened to the romantic sound of a jazzy saxophone playing.

The neighborhood Xóchitl lived in looked like it belonged in the French Quarter in New Orleans instead of Veracruz. The buildings all had a brick-and-mortar facade with small wrought iron balconies. Her apartment dated back to the early years of the previous century. It had hard plaster walls, antique french molding, and a long metal conduit that ran along the floor and up the walls connecting the metal boxes housing the light switch and electrical sockets. The apartment came furnished with antiques from stem to stern, including an antique refrigerator and stove in the kitchen.

Donovan chuckled when he saw Xóchitl hold out her hand again to admire her ring. "You're going to wear out the stone looking at it so much," he remarked.

She slapped him on his arm. Donovan smiled as he caressed her dainty shoulder with his hand and recalled the look on her face when he proposed to her earlier that evening.

"Do you promise to love me forever?" she asked as she laid her arm across him. "Until death do us part?"

"Until the end of time," Donovan said softly.

"Legally, the church only obligates you until one of us dies," she commented.

"I don't think of it as an obligation."

Xóchitl snuggled her head deeper into his shoulder as she stared at the lights in the distance. "If I were to die first, would you remarry?"

Donovan scoffed. "What brought that on?"

"I was just thinking." She looked at him. "About what would happen if one of us was to die before the other."

He caressed the side of her face. "We're going to live forever."

"I could never marry anybody else," she said as she laid her head back on his shoulder.

"Neither could I."

"Liar," she said playfully. "You'll find someone else."

He kissed the top of her head. "Where am I gonna find another you?"

"You shouldn't try to find another me," Xóchitl replied. "You should find a woman to love for who she is and not because she reminds you of me."

Donovan pulled her in tighter. "Enough with the death talk."

"Seriously," Xóchitl said, raising her head, "I want you to find somebody you truly love."

"What about you?"

"We'll meet again in another life." She rested her head back into his shoulder. "Until then, I'll be your guardian angel."

"What if I die first? Can I be your guardian angel?"

"You have to go to heaven before you can become a guardian angel."

"You don't think I'm going to heaven?"

"Not right away." She chuckled mischievously. "You'll have some serious time-out to do in purgatory first."

As hard as he tried, he couldn't keep Xóchitl from entering his thoughts. He wondered if she would continue to haunt him after he and Itzél had begun their life together. He had other things he could think about to get her off his mind, like having a wanted narco-paramilitary aboard, over a hundred illegal rifles in his hold, and the US Coast Guard and Mexican Navy looking for his ship. He also had Benício, Itzél's husband, below deck with a bullet in his side, but he didn't want to think about any of that either.

Instead, he chose to think about the day Itzél offered to make lunch for him at her restaurant to thank him for all he had done for Benício and Poli. He went reluctantly, the sting of her rejection still fresh in his mind. He had asked Poli to come with him and recalled the panic he felt when he took off unexpectedly, leaving him alone with his mother. She quickly allayed his discomfort by taking his hat and teasing him coquettishly with it. The next thing he knew, she took him to her room upstairs and made passionate love to him.

He turned to look at the hatch when he heard the slider rolling back on the runners as Dario Róbles, El Demonio's cousin, came on deck. The big man went to sit on the starboard bulwark by the stern. Donovan gazed pensively at him as he sat quietly staring into the wake. He didn't know what to make of the vigilante turned narco-paramilitary.

He had protected and befriended Itzél during her brief abduction by El Demonio's men before Donovan agreed to make the voyage to the Devil's Elbow. He had also befriended Augie and Benício and kept the other *sicarios* in check on the run to Padre Island. He expressed a longing to leave his past behind and try his hand at making a living as a fisherman. Donovan thought he could play on that, offering him a chance at a new life in exchange for helping his crew take back the ship. He not only refused Donovan's offer; he threatened to stop him if he tried only to come through when he needed him to most.

"I haven't thanked you for what you did back there," Donovan said to Dario.

"I told you I wouldn't let them hurt you or your crew."

"You also said that you'd stop us if we tried to take back the ship."

"If Nacho hadn't tried to shoot you," Dario added, "I would have."

It happened when Donovan and Beto returned to the ship with the rifles. Donovan had just tied the *Rona* next to his boat when Nacho came down the ladder to help bring the rifles aboard. As Beto tried to step into the *Mona*, Donovan took his pistol from him and knocked him back into the *Rona*. When he turned to face Nacho, he slapped Beto's pistol out of Donovan's hand and would have shot him if Dario hadn't intervened.

"If you hadn't pulled up on Nacho's rifle when you did, he would've killed me," Donovan added.

"If I hadn't lost my pistol when your crewman rushed me, I would have shot you."

Sandy tried to tackle Dario when Donovan made his move but only managed to knock his pistol to the deck.

"Sandy told me you could have picked it up," Donovan said as he looked at him curiously. "Instead, you chose to run down the ladder where Nacho and I were fighting for the rifle."

Donovan continued to stare at Dario, waiting for him to admit he chose to help him and not Nacho.

"I didn't mean for you to kill him," Dario said reluctantly.

When Dario pulled up on the rifle, Donovan pulled Nacho's knife from his scabbard and shoved it into his sternum.

"I felt I didn't have a choice," Donovan said sincerely. "You saved my life."

"If you're looking for someone to thank for saving your life, thank Itzél's husband."

After Donovan killed Nacho, Benício saw Beto threatening to kill Donovan with an AR-15. He picked up Dario's pistol and shot Beto, killing him.

"I was never in any danger," Donovan said. "Beto's rifle was empty."

"Benício didn't know that," Dario responded. "And by the look on your face, neither did you."

Donovan couldn't deny that. When he removed the bullets from Beto's rifle on the beach, he had lost count and didn't know if he had gotten them all. He recalled the shock he felt when he heard Benício fire the pistol, believing for a split second that Beto had gotten off a round.

The obnoxious shrill of the satellite phone blaring interrupted the conversation. Augie came halfway up the companionway and rested his forearms on the sides of the cabin top.

"You gonna answer that?" Augie asked.

Donovan did not reply as the deafening shrill continued.

"What do you want to do?"

"If you don't answer, Fausto will kill Señora Itzél," Dario advised him.

"He'll have to find her first," Donovan retorted. "Don Macario moved her and Poli beyond his reach."

"We're gonna have to talk to him eventually," Augie commented over the shrilling.

"Let's get a plan together first," Donovan retorted.

The satellite phone finally stopped ringing. Donovan looked at Augie and Dario.

"It's obvious none of us can stay in Campeche," he said. "But we have to go back for Itzél and Poli."

"How are we gonna do that without getting our throats cut?" Augie remarked.

Donovan sighed. "I don't know."

"How 'bout using the guns to make a deal with El Demonio?" Dario suggested.

The wind suddenly dropped off as it changed direction slightly. Donovan glanced at the telltales dancing erratically overhead and turned the ship into the wind until the telltales resumed their gentle horizontal flutter.

"Is that why you stopped us from throwing the rifles over the side?" Donovan asked Dario. "So that Fausto can get his guns?"

"No, I thought we could use them to bargain with Fausto if we had to, *and* it seems that we do."

Donovan didn't like the idea of delivering the guns to Fausto, but he had to consider it at least as a possibility if he wanted to get Itzél and Poli safely out of Campeche. He didn't want to think about what happened to Xóchitl the last time he delivered weapons to paramilitaries.

"Do you think Fausto will deal with us?" Donovan asked Dario. "Safe passage out of Campeche for all of us, including Itzél and Poli?"

"I can almost guarantee it."

"Will you set it up?"

"It's better that I don't," Dario replied. "By now he's heard about what happened at the Devil's Elbow and assumes I'm dead. If he hears from me now, he'll expect me to take the guns to him immediately. He won't trust me if I don't."

"I didn't think about that," Donovan said. He stared at the ship dead ahead of him in thought. "I don't want to deliver the guns to his beach at Lorenzo like he wants. I need a more public place."

"What about the port in Seyba Playa?" Dario suggested. "There's a warehouse there Don Rodrigo lets him use as an office."

"Don Rodrigo? The Campechano?"

"Sí," he replied. "Fausto might agree to accept delivery there."

"I don't know," Donovan responded. "The port might be a little too public."

"The back of the warehouse extends over the water with a small dock behind it," Dario added. "The Campechanos built a trapdoor in the floor so that they could bring their drug loads to the warehouse in pangas without anybody noticing."

"That's a little too private," Donovan said.

"How about the dock behind the warehouse?" Dario countered. "It faces the beach at Payucán. There're always people there, mostly *pangueros* working on their pangas or mending nets. You could deliver the guns there."

"Wait a minute," Augie interjected as he stepped onto the deck through the hatch. "You're not seriously considering giving the guns to El Demonio?"

"I'm just bouncing ideas around," Donovan responded. "It might be the only way of getting Itzél and Poli out of Campeche alive."

"There's got to be another way," Augie insisted.

"Capitán Dónovan is right," Dario added. "Fausto has people watching for your ship to come back. He has *halcones* everywhere. He even has a spy in the Armada."

Donovan stared at Dario suspiciously. "It sounds like you want Fausto to get the guns."

"What I want is to see Señora Itzél out of danger," Dario retorted. "It's her I care about."

It bothered Donovan to hear Dario say that. Since that day he went to get Itzél at Fausto's plantation house, he suspected that Dario might have romantic feelings for her. It didn't help that Itzél thought highly of him as well.

"All right, you said he'll deal with us," Donovan began. "But will he keep his word?"

"I can't answer that," he replied.

"That's it, then," Augie concluded. He looked down through the hatch into the main cabin. "Sandy," he called to his nephew.

A young man on the lee side of twenty came to the foot of the companionway. Unlike his crusty old hippie throwback uncle, Sandy looked like a '60s era California beach boy.

"Yes, Mister Fagan?" he replied in keeping with onboard protocol.

"Start bringing the guns topside," Augie ordered.

"What are you doing?" Donovan asked.

"I'm throwing them overboard," he replied. "No use keepin' them any longer."

"Belay that order, Mister Trelis," Donovan yelled into the main cabin. He glanced at Dario and then turned to Augie. "I'm not ready to throw away the only option we might have."

Don Macario sat quietly sipping hot tea and working a crossword puzzle on the patio facing the lagoon outside the Paradise Lounge. He listened to a saxophone playing samba over the sound system as he took in the new day. A mourning dove cooing lethargically somewhere nearby seemed to sing a refrain to the song much as in a Martin Denny piece.

The storied Don Macario, the internationally renowned adventurer, scholar, and man of action had aged gracefully and kept in top physical condition. He looked like a movie star from Mexico's golden age of cinema, although he never appeared on the silver screen. He reemerged after many years of self-exile to resurrect the crumbling family hacienda, converting it into a five-star hotel called the Hotel Paraiso, more commonly known as the Paradise Inn in the American, Canadian, and European travel brochures.

He set the crossword puzzle down when he heard Dr. Conrado Ventura, the eminent anthropologist and marine archeologist call to him as he walked out of the lounge to the patio.

"May I join you?" the professor asked Don Macario.

"Please do, Professor," he said as he removed his reading glasses and set aside the crossword puzzle. "Did you have any luck?"

"I'm afraid no one has seen Itzél," Dr. Ventura replied. "I tried the restaurant, the community center, and several of her neighbors."

"Did she leave word at the convent?"

"Only that she was going after her son."

"Maybe she's still in Campeche City."

"No," he said as he shook his head. "I gave her description to the ticket agent at the bus terminal. She got on the last bus to Seyba Playa."

"How sure was the ticket agent?"

"The ticket agent was a man."

"Hmm," Don Macario nodded. "I suppose that answers that question quite aptly."

"What about Poli?" the professor asked. "Has he turned up?"

"Not yet," Don Macario replied. "I've had Quino watching for him."

"The note he left for his mother said he was coming here."

"Might he've gone to the restaurant to get some things from home first?" Don Macario suggested.

"I don't think so. Somebody would have mentioned it when I asked about Itzél."

They both turned to look toward the lounge when they heard several pairs of hard-heeled shoes on its hardwood floor coming toward them. Quino, Don Macario's concierge, stepped out of the lounge, leading El Demonio and two of his minions to the patio. The young man remained by the door, keeping a watchful eye on the infamous narco and his henchmen as they went to Don Macario's table.

Fausto López, alias El Demonio, stood over six feet tall and had a build like a prizefighter. He had another distinguishing feature that many equated with witchcraft. He had one blue eye and one brown eye. His ghoulish behavior during the recently concluded drug war on the northern border only added to the horrors associated with his name.

Unlike most drug traffickers, who dressed like retro-era drug runners of the 1970s, El Demonio chose a less stereotypical image, preferring the country club look to the country and western attire worn by his counterparts.

The narco-paramilitary and his men stood menacingly over the table looking down on Don Macario and the professor.

"Your men are obstructing my view," Don Macario said calmly.

The crime boss glared angrily at him before motioning his men to move.

"You're too bold, old man," Fausto remarked.

Don Macario sipped from his tea. "Is there something I can do for you, Señor López?"

Fausto pulled up a chair and sat between Don Macario and the professor.

"You've heard about what happened on Padre Island?"

"I saw something about it on the morning news," Don Macario replied. "You don't believe they were involved?"

"Almost certainly," Fausto retorted. "That's where they were headed."

"There was no mention of a ship."

"Which leads me to believe Dónovan got away," Fausto retorted. "Since I haven't heard from any of my men, I'm presuming they're dead."

"You're also presuming they were there," Don Macario countered. "What if they never made the rendezvous?"

"They got there," Fausto argued. "The news said that the police recovered a hundred pistols but made no mention of rifles. Dónovan was supposed to pick up a hundred and ten pistols and a hundred and ten rifles. No mention of a ship. No mention of rifles. Dónovan must have gotten away with the rifles."

"You can't be sure of that. News reports aren't always complete. If your men are dead like you presume, what makes you think Donovan or any of his people survived?"

"Because Donovan has a way of doing things like that," Fausto replied. "He's famous for it."

"You're taking a lot for granted."

"I don't think so." Fausto stared at him intensely. "I expect he'll be contacting you soon. When he does, I want you to tell him to bring me my guns, or I'll kill the woman."

Don Macario put his teacup down and looked at him sternly.

"Did you really think you could hide the woman from me?" Fausto added. "You don't know who you're dealing with."

"I want to see her," Don Macario insisted.

"When I get my guns."

"Donovan will want to know you really have her."

"I'll send him an ear to prove it," Fausto said sinisterly.

"What if he never contacts me?"

"He will," Fausto insisted. "For the woman's sake, he'd better."

Don Macario glanced at the professor, whose face betrayed his concern.

"Tell Dónovan that I'm giving him a week to bring my guns if he wants his woman back." El Demonio stood and buttoned his blazer. "After that, I'll start sending her to him a piece at a time." He turned to his sicarios. "Vámonos."

Don Macario watched López and his minions walk past Quino as they went into the lounge. He waved Quino over as the clip-clop of their hard heels faded quickly on their way out of the lounge.

"¿Sí, señor?" Quino said as he got to Don Macario's table.

"I want you to keep trying to reach Capitán Donovan," Don Macario said. "Tell him López has Señora Itzél."

"Yes, I heard everything."

"Tell him that I'm available to help any way I can."

"Sí, señor."

"That goes for me too," the professor added.

"Sí, señor."

Poli lay on the bed in the back of the dive shop with his hands behind his head, looking at the ceiling. At sixteen years old, the handsome young man with the jet-black hair and green eyes had come a long way since signing on as the newest crewman on the *Siete Mares*. He had come to regard the ship as his second home and the crew as his second family. He especially felt that way about the skipper, Simon Donovan, whom he compared to the father he barely knew.

He felt that Donovan and his first mate, Augie, had guided him into manhood—not that he did not appreciate the love and guidance given to him by his stepfather, Benício, who had taken in him and his mother, Itzél, after his father's untimely death on an offshore oil platform eleven years earlier. He owed him for giving him a loving home and a strong moral compass to guide him through life.

Benício and Donovan could not have differed more starkly. His aging and rotund stepfather barely stood over five feet while Donovan's slimmer and younger six-foot-two frame towered over the little panga fisherman and weekend minister. Whereas his stepfather lived by the tenets of his faith, turning the other cheek and avoiding confrontation, Donovan met his problems head-on and at times with his fists. Donovan sailed his schooner across the open sea while Benício seldom took his sixteen-foot fiberglass panga beyond sight of the shore.

It hurt Poli that he could not make the run to Padre Island with his crew because of the beating he had suffered at the hands of El Demonio's men. He didn't like the idea of hiding in a convent while his stepfather made the hazardous run for him. Don Macario arranged with the distinguished professor Conrado Ventura to hide him and his mother at a nunnery in Campeche City to keep El Demonio from finding them.

Since he could not make the voyage, he believed he should at least wait for his crew to return at the Paradise Lagoon. Knowing that the mother superior, the professor, and above all, his mother would oppose his decision, he sneaked out of the convent like a thief in the night and went to hide in the dive shop to wait for his ship.

Poli heard someone unlocking the door and went to look, hoping to see Captain Donovan or Mister Fagan walking into the dive shop. Instead, he saw Quino, the concierge at the Paradise Inn. He ducked into the back room before the young man dressed in the hotel uniform could spot him. He looked anxiously for a place to hide and then slipped under the bed when he heard the slamming of the screen door.

Quino walked into the back room where Augie had his bed and a small office equipped with antique furnishings, including a metal oscillating fan, an antique radio, and a Smith Corona manual typewriter. He also had a modern computer and a fixed satellite phone installation with a microwave antenna set to automatically track satellites mounted on the roof.

Poli watched Quino's feet as the concierge sat in the old oak wood swivel chair and pulled himself up to the satellite phone terminal. He listened to him take the handset from its cradle and to the musical progression of numbers dialing. Poli could hear the phone ringing on the other end as Quino waited for someone to reply. After a while, he heard the concierge put the handset back in the cradle and watched him push back on the swivel chair and leave.

Then, the satellite phone began to ring loudly. He heard Quino running back into the back room and picking up the handset as he sat in the swivel chair.

"Bueno," Quino said, answering the phone like they did in Mexico. "Ah, Capitán Dónovan. We've been trying to reach the ship. Is everything all right?"

Poli listened to the muffled sound of the skipper speaking on the other end but could not make out the words. He cupped his hands around his ears but to no avail.

"¡Madre de Díos!" Quino muttered under his breath. "How bad is Señor Benício hurt?"

Poli covered his mouth as tears welled up in his eyes.

"I have bad news too," Poli heard Quino say. "El Demonio has la Señora Itzél. He's threatening to kill her if you don't give him his ... property right away. Don Macario and the professor told me to tell you they're ready to help however they can."

A tear trickled down Poli's face as he listened to the one-sided conversation.

"They *were* moved," he heard Quino say. "Dr. Ventura took them to the convent in Campeche City, but Poli snuck out to come here and she went after him."

Poli waited for Quino to continue as he listened to Donovan's muffled voice on the other end.

"He hasn't shown up. Dr. Ventura has been out looking for him," he heard Quino say. "He checked La Cocina Maya and talked to the neighbors. No one has seen him." Quino paused for a moment. "Un momento, Capitán."

From under the bed, Poli watched Quino turn the swivel chair toward the other side of Augie's desk and then turn back toward the terminal.

"Go ahead," he heard Quino say and then listened to him scribbling on a pad of paper and muttering, "Um-hmm," periodically.

"Sí, Capitán," he heard Quino say as the scribbling stopped. "When do you want Dr. Ventura to meet you in Sabancuy?"

Quino continued to scribble on the notepad frantically as Poli held his breath.

"Sí, Capitán. I'll pass your instructions to Don Macario right away," he heard Quino say, and then he hung up the handset.

The concierge continued to scribble for a moment longer before tearing the page from the notepad. Poli watched his feet as he hurried out of the room. When he heard the screen door slam, he slid out from under the bed and went over to the desk, where he saw the notepad Quino had used to take notes. He took a pencil from the tin can on Augie's desk and carefully began to shade the page, using the side of the lead point. He sniffled, wiping the tears from his cheeks as he read what Quino had written.

Donovan returned the handset to its cradle and closed the cabinet door, stowing the satellite phone. He stood alone in the main cabin below deck dressed in the same faded green brushed cotton shirt and khaki pants he wore the night of the incident at the Devil's Elbow. The lines on his bronzed face seemed deeper and his gray eyes distant as he thought about losing Itzél. He couldn't bear to lose her like he had lost Xóchitl. He looked at the specks of blood on his clothes and wondered if they belonged to the man he stabbed to death or to Benício.

"Coast Guard fast approaching off the port beam," he heard Augie call down into the main cabin.

Chapter 2

It never made Jack Lyons happy having to drive to the Drug Enforcement Administration's Houston Division Office during morning rush hour. He used to do it quite often when his group worked joint investigations with the single-mission agency. Dope dealers commonly carried weapons and hid their gun acquisitions as carefully as they did their drug trafficking and money laundering operations. Jack's agency specialized in gun and explosives-related crimes, from unlawful possession to gun trafficking to arson and bombings. The DEA only had a peripheral interest in those crimes and gladly referred them to Jack's agency.

The DEA's division office had a lot in common with a modern-day corporate office. It shared commercial space with private businesses in a high-rise located along a long line of office buildings. Unlike a corporation, it did not have a showy marquee with the company name or logo on it. Instead, it had the agency's name listed subtly on a plaque at the entrance to the building among the other offices doing business there. It occupied the top two floors of the building with a reception desk and a security post like any major corporate office.

He had come there to meet Agent Thomas Gebhardt, the agency's assistant attaché assigned to the US consulate in Mérida, Mexico. Gebhardt had come to Houston to attend a conference hosted by the DEA to discuss the evolving drug trafficking situation in the Isthmus of Tehuantepec and the Yucatán Peninsula.

After clearing the metal detector and x-ray machine at the security station, Jack signed in with the reception desk and received his official visitor's badge. A young agent then escorted Jack down a maze of corridors to an anteroom outside the conference room.

"I'll get Agent Gebhardt for you," the agent said.

As the agent disappeared into the conference room, Jack sat in a leather sofa across from the beverage station. He looked at his watch and sighed. He had a meeting at the US attorney's office downtown to discuss the gun seizure on Padre Island in just under an hour. He stood when he saw the conference room doors open and Agent Gebhardt walk out holding a bottle of water.

Thomas Gebhardt stood over six feet tall and had a build like an NFL defensive back. He had dark hair, dark eyes, and the rugged good looks of a Hollywood leading man of the film noir era. Jack had met him at a major bombing investigation in the Midwest several years before.

"Good to see you again, Jack," Gebhardt said to him. "Glad you could make it."

"Good to see you, Tom," Jack replied as they shook hands. "How're you enjoying Mexico?"

"It's marvelous. I get in a lot of sightseeing. There're a ton of pyramids, old Spanish colonial buildings, forts, and churches. Cancún and Cozumel are not that far away. I'm loving it."

"It sounds great," Jack said as he glanced at his watch. "You said you might have some information about the guns we seized at Padre Island?"

"I do," Tom said. "Have a seat."

The two agents sat on the sofa facing each other.

"There's a drug war simmering in the isthmus," Tom began as he undid the cap of his water bottle. "And we believe the guns you intercepted were destined to arm one side of it."

"Didn't a war just end on the other side of the border?"

"That's what we all thought, but it looks like all it did was move to the other end of the country." Tom took a sip of water. "One of the key players, a man called El Demonio, is trying to set up a do-over with the Thunderbolts."

Jack frowned. "The Thunderbolts?"

"The Norteño cartel's paramilitary wing," Tom explained. "They get their name from their commander, Colonel Aníbal Barca Rayos, alias El Rayo—the Thunderbolt."

"I remember now," Jack said. "They're the ones that deserted from the Mexican Army."

"They're not just any deserters, Jack. They're elite special forces. Hombres malos."

"What about this El Demonio character?"

"His real name is Fausto López. He's a piece of work," Gebhardt remarked. "He's supposed to be some kind of satanic priest turned narco-paramilitary hired by the Frontera cartel to fight the Norteños."

"I love it"—Jack scoffed—"a warrior priest."

"I'm telling you, Jack. You can't make crap like this up." He took another sip of water. "Everybody thought he was dead until he showed up in Campeche."

"Where's Campeche?"

"It's on the west side of the Yucatán Peninsula by the Gulf of Mexico," Tom explained, using his finger to draw an imaginary map. "The Thunderbolts are on the other side of the isthmus, getting payback on another bunch of narcos called the Commission."

"Now you're starting to lose me."

"With what, Jack? The players or the geography?"

"Both."

Jack glanced at his watch as Tom looked at him curiously.

"The isthmus is where Mexico necks down separating the Gulf of Mexico from the Pacific before you get to the Yucatan Peninsula," Tom explained using his hands. "The Commission are a bunch of crooked cops turned drug traffickers in the state of Chiapas on the Pacific side."

"How do you keep up with so many players?"

"It's not easy, Jack." He took another sip of water. "Every time the Mexican government breaks up a cartel, a whole slew of others springs up."

The conference room doors swung open as the conferees came into the anteroom to take a break. An especially attractive DEA agent with flowing hair and a big purse slung over her shoulder, dressed in tight jeans tucked into a pair of knee-high brown leather boots and a partially unbuttoned orange top over a white scoop neck camisole went to sit in the matching leather chair next to the sofa where Jack and Tom sat. She smiled at them as she crossed her legs and got her cell phone out to look at it.

"I'm working for the wrong agency," Tom muttered under his breath.

Jack scoffed as he grinned. He looked at his watch again.

"You got somewhere else to be?" Tom asked.

"I got an appointment with the AUSA downtown, and if I don't leave soon, I'm not gonna make it on time in this traffic."

"I'll try to be brief," Tom said as he screwed the cap back on his bottle of water. "We believe the guns you intercepted were ordered by El Demonio to arm the Campeche gangs."

"Another cartel?"

"No—not yet anyway."

"If they're not a cartel, then what are they?"

"Good old-fashioned organized crime," Tom replied, setting the bottle aside. "They're into everything from prostitution to protection. In a way, Mexico's like China used to be a hundred years ago with some strongman carving out a piece of the country for himself, but instead of calling themselves warlords, they call themselves plaza bosses."

The meeting Jack had with the US Attorney had to do with the guns he had recovered at the Devil's Elbow. Thanks to the forward tracing work done by the inspections side of his agency's house, Jack already had the names of the straw purchasers who had bought the pistols he had recovered. They also gave him a list of Romanian AK-47 rifles bought by many of the same people he suspected might have gotten away in the mystery ship he saw.

Ordinarily, the US Attorney had little to no interest in prosecuting straw purchasers who falsified the gun forms unless the person they bought the gun for could not legally buy it or if the gun turned up in a violent crime scene. Gebhardt's information would make his case a lot easier to sell to the prosecutor. If he could learn who masterminded the acquisitions, he could even put together a decent organized crime conspiracy case.

"The US attorney can wait," Jack said. "Tell me more about these Campeche gangs, like who's on top of the food chain."

"Nobody, really."

"Somebody's gotta be." Jack frowned. "You said they were organized. Somebody's got to call the shots."

"Here's where it gets interesting," Tom commented as he angled his body to better see the attractive DEA agent. "The gangs are made of countless smaller gangs that used to be at each other's throats until they were organized by the state police."

"That's insane."

"That's Mexico," Tom remarked. "A corrupt state police commander named Sánchez, heading of all things the antinarcotics task force, got the idea that he could do what the cops did in Chiapas."

"You mean the Commission."

"You catch on quickly, Jack." Tom glanced at the DEA agent. "He persuaded the governor to organize an antidrug task force, handpicked the commanders, and started making drug seizures but instead of destroying the drugs, he sold them to the Commission, who in turn sold them to the Frontera cartel."

"Whose drugs were they seizing? The Norteño cartel's?"

"No," Tom said with a shake of his head. "They targeted a regional organization known as the Campechano Growers Association, a.k.a., Los Campechanos. They're low key, so the government pretty much leaves them alone. They run their business like a Fortune 500 company. They don't believe in violence. They'd rather negotiate and make payoffs to settle their problems. In fact, they've passed on some of their profits to the community, building low-rent apartments, schools, hospitals—that sort of thing."

"Like Escobar did in Colombia," Jack said.

"In a way, but with no quid pro quo. Anyway …" Tom said as he watched the DEA agent scrolling on her cell phone. "Back to Sánchez. He needed somebody to take the drugs to Chiapas, so he had his comandantes pick up all the gang leaders in their jurisdictions. They gave them two options: align their gangs under a new gang headed by the police commander or go to jail—or worse."

"How did the police commanders get the smaller gangs to stop fighting each other?"

"How else?" Tom said as he looked at him cynically. "By making money. The smaller gangs had never seen the kind of money they were making taking the seized drugs to the Commission. It was a hell of a lot more profitable than fighting over turf."

"Pretty ingenious of Sánchez," Jack remarked.

"Yeah, but it backfired on him," Tom said with a sly grin. "The Campechanos paid off Sánchez by giving him a sizeable monthly stipend to leave their loads alone. They even made him the head of their security. Where Sánchez went wrong is keeping the lion's share of the money, alienating the comandantes. When the drug seizures stopped, so did the money that kept the gangs working together."

The attractive DEA agent put her cell phone back in her purse and stood to go to get a bottle of water from the beverage station. Both Jack and Tom couldn't help but admire her rhythm as she walked away from them.

"How were the comandantes able to keep the gangs from breaking up?"

"That's where El Demonio comes into the picture." Tom smiled at the agent as she walked back to the leather chair. "We're not sure how he got close to the comandantes, but he showed them how to use the gangs to extort protection money from the legitimate and illegal businesses operating in their plazas—everything from leaning on pimps and prostitutes to getting a piece from street-level drug dealers and pirated disc sales. They're even leaning on the street vendors selling candy. They've gone from humping drugs across the Campeche jungle to the Commission to becoming the independent criminal organizations they are today."

"So, getting back to the guns ..." Jack said.

"El Demonio's convinced the gangs that the Norteño cartel's coming to take their plazas away from them," Tom said.

"Are they?"

"Not according to DEA or anybody else in the intelligence community," Tom said as he made eye contact with the pretty DEA agent.

Jack checked his watch as Tom and the pretty DEA agent smiled at each other. He grinned as he shook his head softly.

"So, how are you linking the guns I recovered to all this?" Jack said, redirecting Tom's attention.

"El Demonio's trying to get the gangs to work together so that he can get a rematch with the Thunderbolts," Tom explained. "But he needs guns to do it."

"And you think my guns were destined for this El Demonio."

"There's a Mexican naval infantry lieutenant I work with that thinks so," Tom said as he turned to look at the DEA agent, who had gone back to reading the screen on her cell phone. "He's the Mexican Navy's point man when it comes to drug intelligence. It was his work that helped bring down the Domínguez brothers and the Frontera cartel."

"Do you trust this guy?"

Tom let out a long sigh. "I know the Mexican authorities have a long history of corruption, but the Mexican Navy, especially the marines, are the DEA's go-to guys when it comes to passing intelligence on the cartels." Tom drew a breath. "I'd like you to come down and meet this lieutenant. I think he can help you with your gun case."

"I'll have to run it by the SAC first," Jack said, meaning the special agent in charge. "I'm sure it won't be a problem."

"Good, I'll let the lieutenant know you're coming," Tom said. "By the way, I read your preliminary report. In it, you mention that you believe that one hundred and ten AK-47 rifles got away." He scrunched his brows. "What makes you think that?"

"The traffickers stacked the guns in several piles on the beach to load into two boats sent by the larger ship to pick them up." Jack smiled cleverly. "A couple of piles were missing."

"And you think those piles had a hundred and ten Romanian AK-47 rifles?"

"We found a hundred and ten nine-millimeter Beretta pistols, a hundred and ten Beretta nine-millimeter pistol magazines, and a hundred and ten AK-47 magazines but no AK-47 rifles." Jack raised his brow. "Based on how a hundred and ten seems to be the magic number, I figure they got away with a hundred and ten AK-47 rifles."

"Does the forward trace information you got from industry operations tally up?"

"So far, they've only identified just under seventy Romanian AK-47 rifles, but they're still on it," Jack explained.

"What about the ship you mentioned in your report, the one you saw leaving?" Tom turned to watch the conferees returning to the conference room, especially the attractive agent. "You didn't say what kind of ship it was."

Jack turned to his mind's eye to recall what he saw that night. He remembered the thick billows of black smoke rolling across the beach from the wrecks of the three pickups by the water's edge, some with the flames still burning like firepots, and then the bright light streaking from offshore toward the beach like a small glob of molten lava before the last vehicle burst into flames. He remembered turning his head to look from where it came, only seeing a pair of masts swaying in the moonlight before the smoke obscured his vision.

"That's because I wasn't sure," Jack said.

"The reason I ask is because that lieutenant believes he knows whose ship it might have been," Tom explained. "Could it have been a sailboat?"

"I thought so at first, but I can't be sure," Jack replied. "It was hard to see through the smoke."

"But it could have been?"

"Yes ... I suppose. There was a sailboat race from Corpus Christi to Tampico," Jack said as he shook his head softly. "But they would have been way offshore. I don't see how a sailboat could have dropped out of the race, picked up the guns, and rejoined the regatta."

"That's too bad," Tom explained. "It was all coming together so nicely."

As the crew watched the Barracuda-class coastal patrol boat approaching the regatta from the northeast at about fifteen knots, Donovan came on deck and joined Sandy at the helm. He stared at the broad bright red band and narrow blue stripe on the all-white hull forward of the superstructure that made her instantly recognizable as a US Coast Guard ship. He looked at Dario, who stood by Augie by the boom crutch, watching the ship close in on the regatta.

"You'd best go below, Dario," Donovan said to the wanted narco-paramilitary. "We can't have them taking your picture."

"I understand, Capitán," he said as he started for the hatch.

Donovan stared at the big man as he made his way to the hatch. He didn't know whether he should tell him that his cousin had taken Itzél, but he needed to know where he might have her.

"Where did your cousin keep Itzél that time he kidnapped her?" Donovan asked him.

He watched Dario stop suddenly and turn to look at him curiously as he got to the hatch leading into the cabin.

"At the plantation house," he replied.

"Why not at the warehouse?"

"What are you getting at, Skipper?" Augie inquired.

"Fausto's got Itzél," he replied reluctantly. He turned to Dario, who had a genuine look of concern on his face. "Any chance he'll keep her at the warehouse this time?"

"He could," Dario replied. "But I doubt it."

"Why?"

"Like you said, the port is too public, and he doesn't have enough people to watch her around the clock," Dario explained. "That's why he kept her at the plantation house the last time, so his housekeeper and her husband could watch her."

"What's in the warehouse?" Donovan asked. "Any beds he could tie her to?"

"There's nothing like that," Dario replied. "It's empty, except for some crates in the back."

Donovan looked at the Coast Guard ship closing in on the ketch trailing the *Siete Mares.*

"You'd better get below," he said to Dario.

"Sí, Capitán."

The Coast Guard ship turned to port to fall in behind the ketch and followed it for several minutes before increasing her speed to close in on the stern of the *Siete Mares.* The oblong radar antennae mounted above her wheelhouse rotated ominously below the imposing microwave antennae-infested tower that rose high above her superstructure and eighty-seven-foot-long deck. On her foredeck, she had twin Browning fifty-caliber machine guns mounted on the port and starboard sides with the barrels pointing harmlessly skyward. The officers on the bridge looked through their binoculars at the *Siete Mares* as the ship reduced speed to fall in behind her.

"What are they doing?" Augie asked.

"Looks like they're reading our transom." Donovan looked back at Sandy. "Don't let that ketch catch us, Mr. Trelis. Make it look like we're racing them."

"Aye, Skipper," Sandy said as he turned the wheel and adjusted the trim on the mainsail.

Donovan watched the Coast Guard ship increase speed and ease up slowly until it paralleled his ship's course and speed off the port side. Several crewmen stood at the stern of the craft by an orange rubber dingy powered by an impressive outboard motor. Donovan lifted his arm over his head and waved at them.

"What are we gonna do if they board us?" Augie asked as he also waved at the coasties.

"Get a good sea lawyer," Donovan replied calmly.

"That's not very reassuring."

"Relax," Donovan added. "If they were gonna board us, they'd've dropped the launching ramp by now."

Donovan looked up at the bridge at a comely woman of about forty dressed smartly in a blue uniform and wearing a blue baseball cap with "USCG" embroidered in gold block lettering. He could tell by her demeanor that she commanded the ship as she looked at him through the starboard panes of the bridge. She had steel-blue eyes as hard as the sea and an expression just as welcoming as she looked down on the afterdeck of the *Siete Mares*. Donovan locked eyes with her and then raised his right hand and issued her a casual salute. The hard expression on the Coast Guard captain's face gave way to a barely suppressed smile as she returned his salute and winked.

The crews watched each other as the patrol vessel slipped past the *Siete Mares* and closed in on the sloop ahead of them.

After performing the same dance with the single-masted ship, the Coast Guard vessel turned to port before heading in the opposite direction.

"We must be entering Mexican waters," Donovan commented. "I think we can safely say goodbye to the US Coast Guard."

"And *hello* to the Mexican Navy," Augie retorted sharply. He stared assertively at Donovan. "I still say we ought to dump those guns overboard. I don't fancy doing time in a Mexican jail."

"We don't have a choice anymore," Donovan said somberly.

"What do you think happened?" Augie asked. "Wasn't Don Macario supposed to move them to a safe place?"

"The professor moved them to a convent in Campeche City," Donovan explained. "But Poli snuck out, and Itzél went to look for him." Donovan sighed. "He's demanding I take him his guns right away, or he'll kill her."

"Why is he talking to us?" Augie said softly. "Shouldn't he be sending a message to Dario or one of the others?"

"He might have tried, but since we haven't been answering the phone, he probably assumes that his people are no longer in control."

"What are we gonna do?"

"First of all—get Benício to Doña Estér so she can patch him up," Donovan replied.

"You put a lot of stock in her," Augie remarked. "How do you know she can get that bullet out without killing Benício?"

"Don Macario believes in her," Donovan explained. "She's trained as a paramedic or something like that."

"What makes you think she'll help us?"

"She'll help us," Donovan replied confidently. "Don Macario told me she cut her teeth treating wounded civilians during the Central American wars." He thought about the day he met Doña Estér at her restaurant by the Sabancuy Channel. She brought up the time he helped some of her friends in the Venezuelan resistance. "She's been down this road before."

"Sounds like quite a gal."

"She is," Donovan said as he watched the Coast Guard ship fading into the distance. "The Coast Guard will be out of visual range before long. We'll change course as soon as we get to Mexican waters."

"Good idea," Augie remarked. "I was starting to get tired of this parade."

Sandy had taken Donovan's order to take part in the race to heart. He had not only increased the distance between the *Siete Mares* and the ketch trailing the ship but had also closed in substantially on the sloop ahead. He looked at Donovan and Augie as they joined him at the helm.

"Good job, Sandy," Donovan said to him. "That took real skill to catch that sloop."

"I don't think the helmsman knows what he's doing," Sandy commented.

"Or is not paying attention," Augie remarked as he looked at the two figures at the stern of the single-masted vessel. "Looks like they're arguing about something."

"What could they be arguing about?" Sandy inquired.

Donovan took the binoculars from the binnacle to look at the stern of the sloop. The north wind blowing across the deck pressed the clothing on the two-man crew tightly against their bodies. Both wore loose-fitting matching jackets and slacks. Donovan smiled when he sighted in on the curves and roundness of the helmsman's rump.

"I wonder if they got a couch aboard," Donovan remarked. "She looks pissed."

Augie put his hand on the wheel. "Why don't you go below and check on Benício?" he said to Sandy. "Me and the skipper gotta talk business."

"Tell Dario to stay below until we get clear of the regatta," Donovan added.

"Aye, aye, Skipper," Sandy said as he went below.

"Are you gonna tell Benício about Itzél?" Augie shaded his eyes with one hand to look down into the cabin and then turned to Donovan. "After all ... she is his wife."

Donovan put the binoculars down. "I don't want to upset him in his condition."

"Don't you think that ship has sailed?"

"If you're talking about what happened between Itzél and me," Donovan began, "he had to know it was coming. She would have eventually left him for somebody else if not me."

"You know she means the world to him."

Donovan put the binoculars back in the binnacle. "He'll get over it."

"Like you did with Xóchitl?"

Augie's remark bit deeply into Donovan, giving him a sick feeling in the pit of his stomach that gnawed at him like a cancer. He got that bitter feeling every time he thought about how he lost Xóchitl. He looked at his partner but couldn't think of anything to say to explain himself.

"I'm sorry, Skipper," Augie said remorsefully. "That was uncalled for."

The bitterness on Donovan's face had nothing to do with Augie's acerbic remark, though it did help put it there. Augie had held up a mirror to his face, and he didn't like what he saw.

"You don't get over someone like Xóchitl," he said softly.

"I've never had anyone I loved die on me," Augie began. "I can't imagine what it's like."

Thinking about Xóchitl always came with a price. It always took him back to that misty day in the rainforest by the river.

"It's a living hell," Donovan muttered almost inaudibly.

Donovan closed his eyes to purge the image of Xóchitl's lifeless body lying under a blood-soaked bedsheet in a row of dead bodies next to the river.

"You never told me how she died."

He had never told anybody how it happened. Until he met Augie and got to know him, he didn't believe he had anyone he could tell.

"She was working with Doctors without Borders in Colombia," he began.

The memory of the bloodstained bedsheet made into a makeshift banner by the right-wing paramilitaries accusing the mobile hospital of helping the guerrillas still festered in his mind. So did the stench of wet, smoldering canvas rising from the remnants of the tent they used to shelter their patients.

"She was killed in a mortar attack," Donovan said dolefully as he stared at the sloop dead ahead of the ship.

He couldn't tell Augie, as much as he wanted to, about his role in providing the mortars to Xóchitl's killers. He turned to Augie, who thankfully knew better than to ask him to revisit the incident any further.

As the *Siete Mares* continued to close in on the sloop, neither Donovan nor Augie spoke a word. Donovan stared at the sloop without seeing it as he tried to think of anything but Xóchitl. He tried thinking about Itzél and the afternoon he shared her bed, but the thought of losing her like he had his last love kept him from savoring that precious moment.

"You know we can't put in at the Sabancuy Channel with those guns aboard," Augie commented, breaking the awkward silence. "Remember what happened the last time."

"You mean the Mexican gunboat," Donovan replied.

"You know they'll probably be sniffing around." Augie turned to him. "That lieutenant's taken a big interest in you."

"We can use that to our advantage. Fausto won't dare try anything with that gunboat hanging around."

"What if Lieutenant Baeza boards us?"

"Let him," Donovan retorted confidently. "We have a permit to dive on that wreck for the institute, remember?"

"Yeah."

"I asked Don Macario to pass a message to Conrad to meet us at Doña Estér's restaurant in a couple of days. If we get boarded, we'll show them the stabilization tank in the hold to preserve the wreck's bell."

"What if they find the guns?"

"They won't find them."

"What do you mean they won't find them?" Augie asked skeptically. "There's got to be over a hundred rifles, never mind that antitank gun you used to blow up those trucks."

"It's not an antitank gun. It's a Barrett Bullpup fifty-caliber antimateriel rifle."

"Whatever," Augie said, cutting him off. "There's no way some *marinero* is not gonna find them."

"They won't find them because they won't be on the ship," Donovan said confidently.

Augie looked at him curiously, waiting for an explanation. Donovan ignored him as he often did when he had a scheme working.

"Are you gonna make me guess what you're gonna do with 'em?"

"It's best you don't know," Donovan replied.

"Like with what happened at Cayo del Centro?"

"Something like that."

The incident Augie referenced had happened several weeks earlier on Dr. Ventura's initial charter to dive on the wreck in the Sabancuy Channel. Donovan used a squall that had blown in to divert the *Siete Mares* many miles in the opposite direction to an islet called Cayo del Centro in the Arcas chain. When confronted by Augie and the professor, all he would tell them was "It's better that you don't know."

"You ever gonna tell me what you did when you swam ashore?"

"Like I told you then, I went to make sure Fausto wouldn't bother anybody else about making a run to get his cocaine."

"By planting it on the pirates we saw beached by the lighthouse?"

The pirates Augie referred to had come to Cayo del Centro to escape the same storm that had blown in that night. They had terrorized the Yucatán coast from Holbox Island to Isla Aguada like the pirates of long ago.

"What makes you think I planted it on them?" Donovan countered. "They could have brought the cocaine with them."

"Come on, Simon," Augie said. "They denied having anything to do with that coke."

"Naturally," Donovan said. "Wouldn't you do the same thing in their place?"

"Why deny the cocaine was theirs when they confessed to being the pirates everybody's been lookin' for? They even admitted to killing the lighthouse keeper. It doesn't make any sense."

"It's a crazy world," Donovan remarked. "It's a good thing that beacon went out like it did or they might've got away with it."

"That's another thing," Augie said suspiciously. "That beacon was working fine before you swam ashore."

"Was it?"

"You know damn well it was," Augie retorted sternly. "I guess the next thing you're gonna tell me is that the pirates cut the fuel lines to their own outboard motors."

"That was probably poor maintenance," Donovan remarked. "You know how fuel lines get brittle if you ignore 'em."

"They'd've been out of there long before the Armada sent someone to check on that beacon," Augie added.

"Well," Donovan said dismissively, "thank God for small miracles."

He turned the wheel to port to avoid running into the sloop that had until then led the group. A tanned woman of about thirty-five, wearing a ponytail and oversized sunglasses, manned the helm of the fiberglass sailboat. An older man stood next to her in the cockpit holding a travel mug in his hand. They wore matching sailing jackets and white captain's peak hats, suggesting that they shared more than just a love for sailing. She waved her hand over her head at Donovan and Augie as her companion looked at them jealously.

"I just thought of something," Augie said. "What are we gonna do about Dario? He's just as hot as those guns."

"I realize that," Donovan replied.

"We owe it to him to at least get him to a safe place."

"I don't think he has any intention of leaving the ship," Donovan said. "I think he's determined to deliver the guns to his cousin."

"That doesn't sound right," Augie retorted. "He saved your life and helped us take back the ship."

"He didn't help us take back the ship," Donovan countered. "All he did was stand aside."

"He kept Nacho from shooting you."

"He told me he wouldn't have pulled up on his rifle if he had known I was going to kill Nacho."

Augie looked confused. "What about helping us stop the gunrunners from ambushing those cops?"

"He knew the gunrunners would start shooting at the ship once they realized we had taken it back," Donovan explained. "He didn't want to get shot any more than we did." Donovan looked at the Coast Guard vessel fading into the distance. "I think he did it to make sure we got away with the rifles."

He looked at Augie, who didn't seem convinced about his suspicions.

"I think you're wrong about Dario," Augie said.

"Remember how quick he was to stop us from dumping the guns overboard?"

"As it turns out, he made the right call."

"He couldn't have known his cousin would find Itzél," Donovan argued.

Donovan turned to look at the sloop across the water. The woman turned away when her companion tried to kiss her on the cheek. The man stomped angrily away and went below, leaving her alone in the cockpit.

"I still think you're wrong about Dario," Augie concluded.

"Right or wrong, he can't stay with us when we put into the Sabancuy Channel."

"What are we gonna do with him?"

"I'm putting him on the beach in Veracruz," Donovan replied. "He said he wanted to try his hand at fishing. Here's his chance."

"Veracruz is in Norteño territory," Augie commented.

"He can catch a bus in Coatzacoalcos and go anywhere he wants," Donovan retorted. "Oaxaca's not too far and out of the way enough to get lost in. There're plenty of fishing villages on the coast he can choose from."

"I wish there was more we could do for the guy," Augie said.

"Yeah, well ..." Donovan glanced back across the water at the woman in the sloop.

They both watched her as she locked the wheel and took a message board out of stowage. Her oversized sunglasses and blond ponytail protruding out the back of her hat made her look like a model at a boat show.

"What's she up to?" Augie asked curiously.

They continued to look at her, waiting for her to finish scribbling on the message board with a grease marker as the wind puffed her jacket up like a balloon.

"I don't know," Donovan replied. "Maybe she needs assistance."

As the woman held the message board over her head, the wind blew her jacket open, revealing the ampleness of her bosom.

"What's it say?" Augie asked.

Donovan grinned and held a thumb up, acknowledging the message.

"She wants to meet us at the Hotel Tampico for happy hour tomorrow," Donovan replied.

The woman returned the board to stowage and unlocked the wheel. She turned to look at Donovan and Augie and flashed a wide smile as she waved her hand enthusiastically over her head. The wind pressing her jacket against the side of her body sculpted her female form deliciously.

"Let's go home, Mister Fagan," Donovan said.

"Why does something like this always happen when there's a load of illegal weapons in the hold?" Augie remarked as he waved at the voluptuous blond sea nymph one last time.

The *Siete Mares* heeled sharply to port as she broke away from the regatta and set off for the Sabancuy Channel. The booms on the main and fore swung out well beyond the starboard side as she gave her back completely to the wind.

Rancho Noche Buena
Near Monterrey, Nuevo León

Casimiro Mendiola loosened his tie and tugged on the coat of the expensive suit he wore as he followed the manservant to the enclosed cobblestone-covered courtyard behind Don Anastasio's sprawling Spanish-style estate. The sound of thunder rolling off the canyon walls around the mansion echoed in the distance.

A large expertly pruned shade tree dominated the center of the courtyard. Beyond that sat a stable made of stone, built against the back wall of the enclosure, where an old man dressed in western clothing, wearing a straw cowboy hat, brushed down a horse with a shiny ebony coat.

"Looks like rain," Casimiro said to the servant.

"Sí, señor," he replied politely.

The servant led Casimiro to a clay-tile patio laid around the base of the tree and offered him a seat at one of several pairs of wrought iron chairs connected to each other by a small table.

"Gracias," Casimiro thanked the servant.

"Por nada, caballero," the servant replied graciously. "Would you like an agua fresca?"

Casimiro turned to look at the table on the other side of the patio. On it sat several pitchers of refreshing ice-cold beverages made with fruit, sugar, and water.

"Maybe later," he said.

"Don Anastasio will be with you in a moment," the servant said to him.

"Gracias."

He bowed graciously, dismissing himself before returning to the house. Casimiro wiped the sweat from his massive forehead with his handkerchief. He ran his hand carefully over his thinning comb-over as he admired the Mediterranean-style stone house with sweeping archways and a Spanish-style red-clay tile roof.

A sharp thunderclap startled him, causing him to look at the sky.

"It's not going to rain," the old wrangler brushing the horse reassured him. "It always thunders like that this time in the afternoon, but it hardly ever rains."

"That's a fine animal you've got there," Casimiro commented. "What breed is that?"

"Paso Fino."

Anastasio Noches Treviño, the Norteño cartel leader, kept a string of champion Paso Fino horses. He also kept a fine remuda of quarter horses to ride around the canyon.

"I've heard of that breed," Casimiro remarked. "They're the ones with the peculiar gait."

"They sound like a typewriter when they walk," the wrangler remarked.

With his back to the house, Casimiro did not notice Anastasio walking toward him. The founder of the Norteño cartel did not look well. His skin looked gray and his face gaunt. The hair on his head showed signs of graying. His clothes hung on his thin frame like an anemic scarecrow's. The suspenders he wore to hold up his linen pants hung loosely from his shoulders. He wore the collar of his pricey white linen shirt open and had his sleeves rolled up to the middle of his forearms.

"What do you think of my horse, Macadú?" the Norteño kingpin asked Casimiro.

"Buenas tardes, Don Anastasio." Casimiro stood as he greeted him. "He's a fine animal."

"Would you like to mount him?"

"No, gracias." Casimiro chuckled. "I'm afraid I'll break his back," he said, alluding to his size.

Anastasio chuckled softly as he signaled the wrangler to leave. The old man took the horse by the reins and led him into the stable.

"Can I offer you an agua fresca?" he offered Casimiro.

Casimiro joined Anastasio at the table. "Por favor."

"What would you like? Lemonade, tamarind, cantaloupe, or horchata?"

"I have a very sweet tooth."

"Horchata, then."

He watched Anastasio fill a glass with the sweet rice drink and hand it to him.

"How was your flight?" Anastasio asked.

"As comfortable as it could be for such a small airplane," Casimiro replied. "Thank you for sending your driver to pick me up."

"It was the least I could do," Anastasio said as he filled his glass with lemonade.

The men went to sit on the patio and set their juice drinks on the wrought iron table connecting their chairs.

"Thank you for agreeing to see me," Casimiro said.

"I'm glad you came."

The two men sat quietly for a moment enjoying their drinks as another thunderclap resonated off the canyon walls.

"How is Don Arturo?" Anastasio asked.

"Well. He sends his regards." Casimiro took a sip of horchata. "You look well."

Anastasio scoffed. "The war against the Frontera cartel has taken a toll on me." He pulled on a loose-fitting suspender strap. "Fortunately, it looks like Colonel Barca will be done soon in Chiapas."

"About that—I keep getting disturbing reports about your man, Cisneros, in Ciudad del Carmen." Casimiro set his drink down. "He's talking like he means to stay."

Anastasio sighed as he shook his head. "Cisco is brash, ambitious, and likes to talk. You shouldn't take anything he says seriously."

"There's talk that he plans to move on Champotón," Casimiro added.

"Nonsense," Anastasio retorted. "He was told to sit on the Ciudad del Carmen plaza until Colonel Barca is done in Chiapas. Nothing more."

"My associate, Rodrigo De León insists he plans to raid Champotón."

Anastasio frowned. "Where is he getting such nonsense?"

"Fausto López."

The sickly drug kingpin sank into his chair. "We heard he was in Campeche."

"Against Arturo's wishes, Rodrigo retained him to train the gangs to fight like an army," Casimiro explained. "I'm afraid of what will happen if Cisco moves on Champotón."

"I don't want to see that any more than you do," Anastasio said. "None of the Norteños do."

"Can you recall Cisco?"

Casimiro watched Anastasio draw down the corners of his mouth as he stared at his lemonade.

"That might prove difficult," Anastasio replied. "He has too much support in the cartel. Without proof, I'm afraid I'm powerless. The best I can do is have Colonel Barca rein him in."

"Has the colonel established a timetable for his withdrawal from Chiapas?"

"He has persuaded most of the independent traffickers working for the Comisión to align with us," Anastasio responded.

"Only a small faction is still resisting. They can't expect to hold out much longer without help." He looked firmly at Casimiro. "The only help available in the region is the Campeche gangs."

"If you can keep Cisco out of Champotón, we can keep the gangs in Campeche."

"What about this training you say López is giving them?"

"It won't amount to much without a reason to use it," Casimiro replied. "The gangs aren't interested in a war but will fight if their plazas are threatened. No threat—no army."

"You sound confident."

"The comandantes running the gangs are interested only in keeping their plazas and could care less about whether any of their compadres keep theirs. If you'll recall, not one of them came to the aid of El Cosario when the Thunderbolts attacked last Easter," Casimiro explained. "They won't unite unless there's a common threat, *and* even then, they won't do it without guns."

"Yes, we've heard about their efforts to arm," Anastasio said cautiously.

"They won't succeed," Casimiro insisted. "Don Arturo and I are making sure they don't. We stopped a shipment from coming through at Punta Morro not too long ago."

"Are you referring to the guns taken by the marines?"

"That's right," Casimiro replied. "We have a well-placed source inside El Demonio's circle that keeps us informed of his every move to arm the gangs. So far, we've succeeded in blocking him every time he's tried."

"What about Comandante Sánchez? Are you doing anything to keep him from arming the gangs?" Anastasio inquired. "I hear he's been talking to the Commission about trading guns for drugs."

"He won't succeed. Sánchez has lost his stock with the Comisión, and the gangs are satisfied with the money they make from their respective plazas. They won't go back to hauling drugs."

The two men sat quietly in thought, staring at the ice in their otherwise empty glasses.

"More horchata?" Anastasio asked as he stood.

Casimiro followed the Norteño cartel leader to the table, where he poured the sweet rice drink into his glass.

"I'm sure you heard about the incident at Padre Island," Anastasio commented as he poured himself another lemonade.

"Of course," Casimiro replied. "We warned you that Fausto might force Donovan to go to Texas to get a load of guns for him."

"It appears he did, and it looks like Donovan may have gotten away," Anastasio added. "We can't take a chance he got away with any part of that load."

"My source is keeping me up to date," Casimiro said. "We've already alerted the Armada to watch for Donovan's ship."

CHAPTER 3

The horizon looked dark and ominous as Fausto López and his lead sicario, Felipe, sat on a pair of weather-beaten Adirondack chairs on the beach behind his plantation house, watching the squall encroaching on the until-then clear blue skies over the ocean. The low, eerie rumbling of distant thunder grew louder as the sky yielded to the rising mass of darkness. Fausto turned to look when he caught a glimpse of San Juana, his housekeeper, and Comandante Sánchez coming toward them after emerging from the coconut palms.

The old, gray-headed woman looked like a plump little munchkin next to the tall, burly state police commander. It surprised him to see his housekeeper on the beach. He knew she had a terrible fear of the *sendero*, the narrow path that meandered through the coconut palms behind the house.

The former vigilante turned narco-paramilitary rose to his feet. He stood as tall as the corrupt police commander but had a more formidable build. He turned his heterochromatic eyes on San Juana.

"Es todo, San Juana," he said, dismissing her. "You can go."

The old woman took two steps toward the sendero and then stopped to stare apprehensively at the coconut palms. She took another step and then went to cower behind the comandante.

"The woman is obviously afraid of something," Sánchez commented.

Fausto clicked his tongue. "She thinks the coconut palms are haunted."

"She works for a devil worshiper"—the comandante chuckled—"and she's afraid of a bunch of trees."

"Why don't you wait for the comandante with me?" Felipe said to her.

As Felipe sat the old housekeeper in Fausto's Adirondack chair, Fausto walked past Sánchez, leading him a few steps up the beach.

"Why did you come here?" he asked Sánchez.

"I was wondering if you saw the news about the gun smugglers on the Texas coast."

"What about it?"

"Those weren't the guns you were expecting by any chance?"

"Of course not," Fausto lied. "My guns will be here in a couple of days."

"Are you sure?" The comandante looked at him skeptically. "It seems unlikely that there would be another illegal gun shipment of that size coming from Texas."

"Anything's possible," Fausto retorted angrily. "My guns will be here in a couple of days." He looked at Sánchez's uniform. "Why are you dressed like that?"

"I'm working today," Sánchez replied. "There's a drug shipment arriving at an airstrip near Simochac."

Fausto scoffed. "Aren't you biting the hand that feeds you?"

"What?" Sánchez feigned surprise. "The Campechanos didn't say anything about expecting a shipment today."

"Who else flies cocaine into Simochac?" He looked at him suspiciously. "I thought the Comisión turned down your proposal to reinstate your arrangement."

"Since the Thunderbolts came to Chiapas, their suppliers have abandoned them like rats on a sinking ship." Sánchez chuckled smugly. "Soon, they won't have a choice but to do business with me."

"Aren't you concerned about the colonel?" Fausto asked. "When he learns you're trading with the Commission, he'll come after you."

"Let him," Sánchez said defiantly. He smirked obnoxiously. "With the guns I get from them, we'll be more than ready for him."

"You'll need more than just guns to take on Colonel Barca." He looked at the comandante. "You need an experienced leader."

"I was in the army. I know about leading men," Sánchez countered.

"The gangs aren't ready. They need more training that only I can give them. They won't stand a chance against professional soldiers like the Thunderbolts."

"They're ready," Sánchez said. He turned to the housekeeper. "Vámanos, señora."

Fausto glared at the comandante as he started back to the plantation house with the little housekeeper struggling to keep pace with him. Felipe walked up to his side.

"We'll see how ready the gangs are," Fausto said under his breath. He turned to Felipe. "Call Villegas. Tell him to set up what we planned for Champotón. Remind him that I want the Campechano businesses targeted, especially the dealerships and the container warehouse."

"Sí, jefe," Felipe responded. "Should I warn El Chino?"

"No," Fausto said bitterly. "Comandante Briones has been acting like he doesn't need him. Him and that *pinche* little naco, Tápia."

As he had done the last time he took Itzél against her will, El Demonio put her in the care of San Juana and her husband, Adán, who lived in the tiny two-bedroom Spanish-colonial-style cottage across the lawn from the old Mireles plantation house in Villa Lorenzo. Like the main house, it too had a white stucco facade and a red-clay tile roof but lacked the marble columns and sprawling verandas.

Itzél hung her head as she slept fitfully bound to the chair in the kitchen of the little cottage. She jerked suddenly when she felt someone pulling on the cord that bound her hands to the arms of the chair. She looked up at San Juana, who put her finger to her lips to quiet her as she struggled to loosen her bindings. They both jumped when the screen door slammed suddenly. The old housekeeper stepped away from Itzél, looking as guilty as a child caught with her hand in the cookie jar when her husband walked into the kitchen.

"What are you doing, old woman?" he asked.

"Help me loosen these ropes," she replied.

Itzél looked at Adán, who shook his head as he reached for his pocketknife.

"What are you going to do?" San Juana asked.

"The knots are too tight," he replied. "I'm going to cut them off."

"Felipe wants her tied to the chair when no one's here to watch her," she whispered. "He'll get mad."

"I've got some more rope," he said as he cut through the first cord. "I'll retie her hands after she eats."

"Can't you just let me go?" Itzél pleaded as he freed her other hand.

"We'd love to, *mijita*," San Juana replied. "But they're watching too closely, and you won't get far."

She turned to Adán, who looked at her sympathetically.

"They'll move you to the main house, and I can't protect you there," he added.

"How are you going to protect her?" San Juana remarked sarcastically.

"With my fists, of course," he replied proudly. He smiled at Itzél. "I used to wrestle in the Lucha Libre."

"Bah! One match." San Juana scoffed. "And you lost."

Itzél smiled at the loving couple as they jousted playfully with each other.

"Newcomers always lose the first match," he explained.

"Is there any way out of here where they can't see me?" Itzél asked.

"There is," Adán replied. "If it was just you and me, I would take you myself."

"How?" San Juana asked skeptically.

"Through the coconut grove." Adán leaned closer to Itzél with an eye on San Juana. "She's afraid of the *cucuy* in the coconut grove."

Itzél turned to look at San Juana, whose eyes and expression made it difficult to refute his assertion.

"I'm not," San Juana responded meekly. "There's no such thing as the cucuy."

"Then come with us."

Itzél looked up at San Juana, who made no effort to argue the point.

"I thought so," he said.

"Why are you afraid of the coconut grove?" Itzél asked San Juana.

"Because it's a doorway to the underworld," she replied softly.

"What are you talking about, *vieja tonta*?" Adán chided her lovingly.

"It's true," she said earnestly. "Sometimes in the morning, the fog swirls close to the ground but never goes beyond the trees. It always stops when it gets to the lawn."

"That's because the ground drops off," Adán said disparagingly.

"At night, little lights go off and on like spirits slipping between the world of the living and the world of the dead."

"Those are fireflies," Adán said.

"They use the fireflies like lanterns to see at night."

"What kind of spirits?" Itzél asked, intrigued by the old woman's conviction.

"The spirits of the coconut grove," she replied anxiously. "The Alux."

San Juana believed the Alux, a sort of Mayan goblin, haunted the coconut palms like they did other natural settings, such as forests, fields, rivers, and beaches. She believed they also watched senderos like the one through the coconut palms, bridges, and lonely roadways, waiting for a passerby to extort candy and cigarettes from.

"Not that again." Adán turned to Itzél. "Do you believe in the Alux?"

"I did—when I was little girl."

"You see." Adán looked at his wife. "You're too old to believe in the Alux."

Itzél turned to San Juana like a frightened child listening to a spooky bedtime story and wanting to hear more.

"We shouldn't be talking about them," San Juana said nervously. "They'll leave the grove and come into the house."

Itzél looked at Adán as he clicked his tongue and muttered something under his breath.

"Suppose you do go without me," San Juana said. "How would you get away?"

"I'd swim to Playa Bonita. It's not far."

"What if she can't swim?" San Juana countered.

"Then I would take her on my back like Tarzan."

"Tarzan?" She scoffed.

"You don't think I'm like Tarzan?" Adán asked playfully. Itzél smiled at him as he rolled up his sleeve and flexed his bicep. "Eh?"

"Stop showing off," San Juana said.

The old man winked at Itzél. "She gets like that when there's a pretty woman around. She gets jealous."

"You're loco," San Juana said, barely suppressing a smile.

Itzél watched Adán roll down his sleeve as he looked at her.

"She used to be a beautiful woman like you, señora. Of all the men that were after her, she chose me."

Itzél turned to San Juana.

"You know what they say." San Juana interjected. "The mangiest dog gets the juiciest bone."

"I'm not talking to you, old woman," he grumbled playfully as he winked at Itzél. "It's true. I was skinny when I was young. I had no money and no prospects." Itzél watched him look adoringly at his wife. "But she married me anyway. That was over fifty-one years ago."

"It's been fifty-seven years," she said. She turned to Itzél. "I could have married a rich man."

"But you chose me," Adán said proudly. "She knew none of the others would last."

"Youth and beauty fade away like the shine on a new peso," San Juana said.

"True love is like an old pair of shoes," Adán added. "The leather may be worn, but they feel good when you put them on."

Itzél smiled as she watched San Juana and Adán look at each other adoringly. Adán turned to Itzél.

"Did I tell you I used to be a wrestler?"

Former Ciudad del Carmen police officer Alonso Andrade owed much to Doña Estér, the owner of the Tucán restaurant in Sabancuy. She took him in last Easter after having found him bleeding by his overturned patrol car, the victim of an ambush perpetrated by Cisco Cisneros of the Norteño cartel and Comandante Norias.

Doña Estér stitched the gash on his face and gave him a job as a waiter at the Tucán, where he worked until the day Comandante Norias came and nearly recognized him despite his shaven head and the beard he had started. Since he could no longer work there, the doña had arranged with an old friend to give him a job working as a handyman at a motel in nearby Isla Aguada.

Two weeks had passed since he had seen Doña Estér when she called to invite him to dinner at the Tucán. Since then, he had started growing his hair back and his beard had filled in nicely, except for the thin scar on his cheek. He took the short motorcycle ride from Isla Aguada to the restaurant, looking forward to sharing a hot seafood dinner with the always delightful Doña Estér. Alonso arrived at the Tucán just in time to catch the sun setting over the emerald-green waters of the Sabancuy Channel.

As Alonso parked his motorcycle, he saw Doña Estér standing at the entrance waiting for him. She was wearing a silk blouse and form-fitting slacks. She typically wore her luscious auburn hair resting on her shoulders, but that evening, she had it tied neatly behind her head in a bun. She didn't wear expensive perfume to speak of but somehow always managed to smell as fresh as the ocean spray.

"I like your new look," the doña said as he walked up to her. "Very Steve McQueen."

He brushed back his short-cropped hair and fluffed his beard over his scar. "I've been trying to lose weight."

"Not tonight," she said as she took him by his hand. "Come in and tell me what you've been up to."

Alonso followed her into the open-sided restaurant with an unobstructed view of the sunset over the ocean. He looked at the odd assortment of dinner guests dressed in touristy tropical shirts or T-shirts, shorts, or swimming trunks or one-piece bathing suits. Some had skin as pallid as a bedsheet, while others looked like pink flamingoes. Some wore hats, and others went bareheaded as they sat under the large thatched roof chatting quietly or laughing boisterously. One especially loud woman wore a large neon-colored sombrero while a puny man, most likely her husband, wore a small Frank Sinatra–style straw hat.

As Doña Estér led him to a table away from the crowd, Alonso noticed Fernando, the maître d', standing on the beach next to the sixteen-foot fiberglass launch the restaurant used to bring in the daily catch of red snapper. He had two busboys scrubbing the interior of the boat vigorously with detergent.

"I see Fernando's washing out the panga," Alonso commented. "Most people just run a hose on 'em to clean them."

"It needs to be extra clean for what we're using it for tonight," Doña Estér said.

"What's going on?"

"I'm expecting a man with a bullet lodged in one of his lungs to be brought to me tonight," she said matter of factly.

"Why isn't he being taken to a hospital?"

"For the same reason I didn't take you to a hospital when I found you last Easter."

Alonso just looked at her, not knowing what to say.

"I have fresh *huachinango* the boys brought in only an hour ago," she said, ignoring his obvious concern. "I put the largest one aside for you."

"Who is this man?"

"He's a member of Capitán Dónovan's crew," Doña Estér replied.

"Capitán Dónovan—the smuggler?"

"He's not a smuggler."

"The Armada would disagree with you," Alonso remarked. "They put out a bulletin on him and his ship, the *Moonlight Runner*."

"They're wrong about him," she said. "He's a good man, and he helps people."

"I don't know about that," Alonso responded skeptically.

"But I do," she retorted. "I saw him risk his freedom, maybe even his life, to bring a shipment of computers to Venezuela to give the oppressed a voice."

"Regardless of the reason, that's still smuggling."

"He's taken medicine to the marginalized people in Venezuela, Panama, Colombia, and Mexico."

"You mean smuggled medicine behind the backs of the governments."

"The proper channels take too long," Doña Estér explained. "Oftentimes, the medicine never gets to the people who need it and ends up on the black market."

Alonso knew better than to try to argue an indefensible point. It was not uncommon for officials in a third-world government to divert humanitarian aid meant for the people to line their pockets. What did get to the people often got delayed by a heavy-handed bureaucracy.

Doña Estér had put him in a quandary. If the man had received his wounds as a result of a shootout with police, helping her would make him complicit in a crime.

"How did the man get shot?" Alonso inquired. "Never mind—I don't want to know."

"Then you'll help me?"

Alonso smiled, not minding that the lovely doña had asked him to dinner with an ulterior motive behind it. She had stuck her lovely neck out for him, and now it fell upon him to return the favor.

"Tell me what you want me to do."

"Be here at midnight tomorrow."

A woman like Linda Ochoa could have any man she wanted. The stunning brunette with the charcoal eyes, creamy skin, and smoky voice had long legs, a bottom you could bounce a quarter off of, and a bosom busting to break loose. She only dated Billy Chávez, the pockmarked, horse-faced, mid-level drug dealer to upset her father, the once-famous gangster known as "El Ocho."

She enjoyed driving to Billy's house in her champagne-colored BMW convertible with the top down past the Tudor-style homes and the tall pines. She made the slow-going trek from stop sign to stop sign through the upscale middle-class neighborhood in North Houston as she listened to dance music on her radio.

As usual, Billy left the garage door up, but she stopped short of driving into it when she spotted a white Toyota Corolla parked in front of the house. Although she didn't love Billy, she couldn't stand the idea of him touching another woman. As she stared at the car, she pictured him making love to some bimbo on the living room floor. So, she took her can of pepper spray from her purse and went to catch him in the act.

She hurried through the garage and opened the door carefully to go into his kitchen. As soon as she entered, she heard moaning coming from the living room. As she looked at an empty wine bottle sitting by a half-eaten pizza on the kitchen counter, she put her finger on the pepper spray button and prepared herself to rush into the living room. She stopped suddenly when she heard a man's voice speaking sternly.

"Wake up, *pendejo*," she heard him say.

She jumped when she heard a resounding slap followed by Billy whimpering.

"What else did you tell the police?" she heard the man ask.

"I didn't tell them anything, José Luis," Billy replied weakly.

"Liar!"

Her eyes teared up as she listened to José Luis backhanding Billy in the face.

"Your friend Elton told me all about your deal with the police," the Mexican trafficker countered. "You sent him down to Corpus to spy on us."

Linda peered around the doorjamb and saw Billy, dressed only in his briefs, tied to a wooden chair in the middle of the living room. She covered her mouth when she saw his eyes swollen shut and blood oozing from his nose and the corners of his mouth.

"No, I didn't," Billy said as he wept. "He went down there on his own."

"He told me you snitched me off to keep from going to jail."

"That's not true," Billy replied.

The tears streamed down Linda's face as she watched in horror from the kitchen. She saw José Luis go down the hall and ducked her head back when she saw him reappear shortly afterward with Billy's white suit in a cellophane bag in one hand and a roll of duct tape in the other.

"I see you took your Scarface suit to the cleaners," she heard José Luis say.

She leaned her head carefully to look around the doorjamb. She watched José Luis take the suit out of the cellophane bag and drop it on the floor, holding on to the bag.

"You know, I was halfway to the border when I decided to come back to Houston."

"What … what made you come back?" Billy asked weakly.

"You did, amigo," José Luis said as he tied a knot at one end of the cellophane bag. "I couldn't leave Texas without saying goodbye."

Linda watched as Billy cocked his head back to see out of the narrow slits of his swollen eyes. She covered her mouth as she watched him struggle to breathe.

"Do you know what it's like being stuck way out on Padre Island with the police looking for you?" José Luis asked as he crunched up the open end of the bag with both hands. "I ran behind the dunes for a couple of hours before I came across some campers sleeping on the beach."

"I had nothing to do with that," Billy cried.

"Shut up, pendejo!" José Luis barked. "I had to get out of there before the sun came up, so I had to settle for a pickup with big tires and fishing poles mounted in the back like radio antennas. I stood out like a sore thumb."

"I'm sorry you went through that, but I had nothing to do with it."

José Luis just glared at him as he finished crunching the bag into the shape of a cap.

"I drove all the way to Kingsville wondering if the campers had reported their truck stolen. It took a while before I found an old Toyota behind some apartment buildings I could take." He glanced at the Scarface movie poster hanging over Billy's fireplace. "What do you think Tony Montana would do to a filthy snitch like you?"

"I'm not a snitch," Billy whimpered.

"You're the only one that knew we were meeting a ship at the Devil's Elbow," José Luis said. "How else would the police know where to find us?"

"Linda," Billy said, weakly.

"What?"

Linda's eyes widened with horror as she listened to her lover deflect José Luis's rage at her.

"It could have been Linda," he replied. "She must have overheard us talking about it the last time you were here."

"Impossible," José Luis countered. "She was at the liquor store when you guessed where we were taking the guns."

"She must have snuck into the kitchen from the garage after she got back to listen to us talking. I've caught her doing that before."

"She wouldn't have known where to tell the police we were going," José Luis said.

"You drew a map in the dust on the coffee table, remember?" Billy explained. "She must have seen it when we went to my study to smoke cigars."

"Nice try, amigo," José Luis said as he slipped the open end of the cellophane bag over his head.

"No!" Billy said as he shook his head vigorously. "Don't!"

"Sorry, amigo. I'm going to miss your hospitality," José Luis said as he pulled a long strand of duct tape off the roll. "But somebody has to pay."

Billy squirmed and kicked violently as the vengeful narco wrapped the tape around the wannabe Tony Montana's neck, sealing the bag. Linda gasped as she jerked her head back, knocking down the empty wine bottle. She ran to open the door to the garage when she felt José Luis's hand dig into her left arm. She screamed and shot a stream of pepper spray blindly over her shoulder.

"¡Puta!" she heard José Luis cry.

She ran as fast as she could to her car and backed it out of the driveway, nearly running into a furniture truck. She gunned the BMW convertible down the street, racing past the stop signs until they looked like fence posts along a country road. She reached into her purse for her cell phone and almost ran into a police car at an intersection.

CHAPTER 4

The wind blew across the ship from the portside as she skirted across the northern limits of the Bay of Campeche on a beam reach. A day had passed since the *Siete Mares* had left the Tampico shipping lanes on their way back to Campeche. Donovan had changed the ship's heading from due south to southeast on a course for the Sabancuy Channel, taking her well into blue water far from the Mexican coast. If the wind held up as it had since leaving Padre Island, the ship would make it to home waters in the next couple of days or so but not before making a brief stop at Coatzacoalcos on the coast of Veracruz.

Putting a man on the beach never came easy, especially when driven by little more than suspicion and perhaps a little jealousy. Donovan knew that but for Dario, things could have turned out badly back at the Devil's Elbow. Still, he couldn't help but feel that the former vigilante turned narco-paramilitary might have a hidden agenda. Donovan returned the map to its slot under the chart table after plotting the new course and headed up the companionway.

When he came topside, he found Dario at the helm standing the afternoon watch. He turned to Augie, who stood at the stern with his elbow on the boom crutch. The look on his face reflected his disapproval of what Donovan came on deck to do.

"I've been thinking about the guns," Donovan said to Dario. "I've decided we can't give them to your cousin."

"What about Señora Itzél?" Dario asked as he relaxed his hold on the wheel. "If you don't deliver the guns, Fausto will kill her."

"We'll find another way."

Dario releasing the wheel caused the sails to lose the wind. He looked up at the telltales and turned the wheel until they fluttered horizontally.

"I hope you know what you're doing," he said solemnly.

"So do I," Donovan said under his breath.

Itzél meant the world to Donovan, and he didn't want to lose her like he had Xóchitl. He had learned a bitter lesson the last time he delivered a cache of weapons. Not only had it resulted in the death of his love but of other innocents as well. He couldn't justify delivering the guns to save Itzél if it meant innocents would die.

"Change your course to due south," Donovan said to Dario.

Dario looked at him curiously. "Where are we going?"

"Coatzacoalcos," Donovan replied. "I'm putting you ashore."

The color left Dario's face. He looked at the binnacle as he turned the wheel to bring the ship to a heading of due south. He raised his head to look dead ahead.

"May I ask why?"

"It isn't safe with you aboard," Donovan explained. "The Armada could board us at any time before we get to Sabancuy."

"What about Señora Itzél?" Dario turned to look at Donovan. "You need my help to rescue her."

"The best way for you to help is by not being aboard if we get boarded."

Donovan stared at the former vigilante. He had expected him to get angry or put up an argument, but he didn't. He just stood at the helm staring blankly at the horizon like a man waiting on the hangman to do his job.

"Coatzacoalcos is not safe for me," he said. "I might be recognized."

"You can catch an express bus across the isthmus and be in Salina Cruz in a couple of hours," Donovan suggested. "There's a score of fishing villages all up and down the Pacific coast I'm sure have never heard of you. You can take up panga fishing like you always wanted."

"We can give you some money to hold you up," Augie added. He turned to Donovan. "Until you get settled."

"Sure," Donovan agreed. "Whatever you need."

"I can get money." Dario scoffed. "That's not the problem."

"Would you rather we drop you off somewhere else?" Donovan asked.

"No, Coatzacoalcos is as good a place as any," Dario replied dolefully. He let the air out of his lungs. "I knew it would eventually come to this."

Donovan felt bad for him. While his reasons for putting him on the beach had merit, deep down, he knew the real reason behind his decision. The way Augie kept staring at him made him feel worse. He looked toward the hatch when he heard Sandy running up the companionway.

As the least senior member of the crew, it fell on Sandy to care for Benício. He had stayed by his side for most of the voyage to make sure the wounded man didn't do anything that might open his wound.

"There's something wrong with Benício," he said anxiously. "He's sweating badly, and I can't keep him still."

"I'd better go take a look at him," Augie said as he started to go below. He turned to Donovan. "If he starts bleeding again, we'll need to get him to a doctor."

As Donovan watched Augie go down the companionway, Sandy bolted suddenly for the companionway.

"Let me go with you," Sandy called to his uncle.

"San—" Donovan called, trying to keep Sandy from leaving him alone with Dario to no avail.

He didn't know what to say to him after basically giving him the boot. The minutes that followed felt like hours as they ticked off like drops leaking slowly out of a faucet in the dead of night. Neither he nor Dario looked at the other nor did they say a word until Donovan could no longer stand the awkwardness and blurted out the first thing that came into his mind.

"Why does Fausto need guns so badly?" he asked Dario.

"Fausto wants to start another war with Colonel Barca," Dario replied. "He's convinced the Campeche gangs that the Norteños want to take over Campeche."

"Do they?"

"I don't think so," Dario replied. "War is bad for business. The Norteño cartel made it clear they're interested only in settling accounts with the Commission."

"Then why take Ciudad del Carmen?"

"Knowing the colonel, he probably wanted to protect his back," Dario replied as he adjusted the trim with an eye on the telltales. "The Cosario gang was in Carmen. They, like the other Campeche gangs, have a history with the Commission. He didn't want to go into Chiapas with a potential threat sitting so close."

"So, he took 'em out," Donovan said as he looked at Dario.

Dario nodded as he stared dead ahead.

"He left Cisco Cisneros and his *soldados* to keep the other gangs from moving into the city."

Donovan looked at the sun's position. He went over to glance into the binnacle and then went back to stand on the starboard side of the steering station.

"Due south," Dario said. "Like you ordered."

"So, if what you say is true," Donovan said, not wanting to explain his lack of confidence in Dario. "El Demonio's not goin' to get another war with the Thunderbolt."

"Except that Fausto has a plan to lure Cisco to Champotón to start that war." Dario turned to Donovan. "He was setting it up just before we left Campeche."

"Do you think it'll work?"

"Cisco likes being the plaza boss of Ciudad del Carmen," Dario said. "He doesn't want to give it back when the colonel is done in Chiapas. He's been trying to persuade the cartel to take Campeche, but the cartel isn't listening."

"War is bad for business," they both said in unison.

"Do you think Cisco will defy the cartel?"

"I have no doubt he will," Dario replied as he turned to Donovan. "He's that arrogant and would have by now if it wasn't for Colonel Barca. The colonel is not interested in another drug war any more than the cartel is. He's tired of fighting and wants to start enjoying the money the Norteños paid him."

"And Fausto thinks that luring Cisco into a trap will draw the colonel into a fight."

"Definitely," Dario responded as he glanced at the binnacle. "It's a matter of honor. Cisco, whether he likes it or not, is part of the cartel's military wing. He would have to settle accounts."

Donovan stared at Dario as he thought about Don Macario, the professor, and all the good people he had met since coming to Seyba Playa. The future looked bleak for the good people of Campeche.

"Do you think Fausto's plan will work?"

"Almost surely." Dario emptied his lungs. "Cisco's too impulsive. He doesn't have the experience, and his sicarios are untrained and undisciplined." He scoffed. "It wouldn't take much to lure him into an ambush and wipe his people out."

Donovan had run into people like Cisco before across the Americas. They always seemed to rise to positions of authority. He had counted on their arrogance and ignorance to baffle them with a little sleight of hand when it came to import documents, bills of laden, and licenses. Having to ask somebody or check the rule book to determine the veracity of his paperwork would mean losing face, and they would rather let the cargo pass than do that.

"Do you think Fausto's already set his plan into motion?"

"I don't think so," Dario replied. "He was waiting on the guns."

Now more than ever, Donovan knew he couldn't let Fausto get his hands on the guns. He liked living in Campeche. Everyone treated everyone else like family, even outsiders like himself. He had made friends all along the coast from Campeche City to Ciudad del Carmen. He couldn't stand to see them suffer a drug war.

"So, if Fausto doesn't get the guns, there'll be no war."

"Not necessarily," Dario said. "There's a state police comandante named Sánchez working a deal to trade guns for drugs with the Commission. If he succeeds or if the cartel even hears about what Sánchez is doing, they'll see that as an alliance and send the colonel to Campeche to neutralize the gangs."

Guns, Donovan thought to himself. It all comes down to guns. He'd do his best to keep Fausto from getting the guns he had in his hold but with Sánchez dealing with the Commission, Campeche's future looked dim.

"Do you think Sánchez will succeed?"

"So far, he hasn't, and he won't without the gangs' support," he explained as he turned to look at Donovan. "The gangs make too much from their plazas to start running drugs to the Commission again." He looked up at the telltales. "They don't want a war either." He turned to Donovan. "It's bad for business."

It occurred to Donovan that if Fausto failed to lure Cisco into a trap, the gangs wouldn't have a need for guns and Sánchez wouldn't have any drugs to trade for guns with the Commission. The colonel would wrap up his business in Chiapas, and a war in Campeche could be avoided.

"So, all we have to do is keep Cisco from raiding Champotón," Donovan concluded.

"I don't see that happening," Dario said cynically. "Cisco is too eager, and Fausto has a good plan. To stop Cisco, you would first have to stop Fausto."

An idea came to Donovan as they often did. For it to succeed, he had to work out all the details, but he had to test the water first.

"What if the colonel learned of Fausto's plan? Do you think he'd try to do something to stop it?"

Dario stared at the horizon, obviously in thought. He looked warily at Donovan.

"Like what?"

"I don't know," Donovan replied. "He could head off Cisco, spank him publicly, snitch him off to the cartel—any number of things."

"How are you going to find the colonel to tell him about Fausto's plan?" Dario inquired. "Even if you could somehow find a way to get a message to him, he might not believe you. He might think you were sent by Fausto to drive a wedge between him and Cisco."

Dario didn't know that Donovan had the colonel's contact number or about his standing offer to protect him, especially against El Demonio. He had no intention of letting him know about it either.

"Say that someone found a way to contact him and convince him. Do you think the colonel would try to stop him?"

Dario seemed reluctant to answer. He glanced at the binnacle and then at the telltales and then turned to Donovan.

"He might."

"What if someone was to show him a way to stop him permanently?" He looked keenly at Dario. "Like taking him out."

Donovan waited to see how Dario would respond. He wanted to gauge his loyalty to his cousin before he probed any further. He didn't want to tip his hand about what he had in mind. Again, Dario seemed reluctant to respond. He stared at the horizon pensively before turning to Donovan.

"I fought alongside the colonel in Michoacán," Dario began. "I was Fausto's liaison officer when we joined forces against the traffickers. I also fought against him on the northern border. He's a tactical genius and not afraid to take chances if the opportunity is right." Dario nodded his head slowly. "If he sees a chance to kill Fausto to stop a war, he'll probably take it."

They both turned to look at Augie as he came up the companionway.

"He's not bleeding," Augie announced. "But he's running a fever. I quieted him down, but if he starts up again, that bullet could move, and he'll open that wound for sure."

"Did you ask him if he's changed his mind about seeing a doctor?" Donovan inquired.

"I asked," Augie replied. "He still insists on going home."

"I've seen men with lesser wounds bleed to death. He needs help as soon as possible," Dario interjected. "Taking me to Coatzacoalcos would be an unnecessary delay."

"He's right, Skipper," Augie added.

Donovan looked at Dario, who stared at him like a batter waiting on a pitch. A good captain always considers the lives of his crew over the life of just one man. In this case, he had to weigh Benício's survival against spending the next thirty years in a Mexican jail. He made the only decision his conscience would allow him to make.

"Put us back on course for Sabancuy."

The next day, Alonso went about his business, tending to the needs of the motel owned and operated by Doña Estér's longtime friend, Doña Matilde. Alonso liked the good-hearted doña, who shared the delightful disposition of her friend in Sabancuy but lacked her well-kept form, having gained weight over the years. He didn't recognize her at first, but after a few chats over a glass of wine, he remembered her.

In her youth, she had enjoyed an hourglass figure and collected a fistful of tiaras after winning several beauty contests around the Yucatan. She caught the eye of a very successful businessman fifteen years her senior and six inches shorter. After a whirlwind romance, they married. For many years, he wined and dined her. He loved showing off his trophy wife in public. However, slowly and inevitably, the good life caught up with Matilde, and her figure went from looking like an hourglass to a bowling pin.

Matilde took over the motel in nearby Isla Aguada after her husband died suddenly after many years of marital bliss. Several rumors about how he met his demise had come to Alonso's attention, none of which carried any weight except maybe for the one about his succumbing to a heart attack brought on by her insatiable sexual appetite. One rumor going around went so far as to claim that she accidentally crushed him to death in her sleep. In truth, the poor devil's heart just gave out from the stress of his declining business ventures and mounting debts. Doña Matilde had no choice but to sell off their palatial home and what remained of his businesses until only the notorious motel remained.

The motel had once enjoyed a reputation as the best place for lodging for vacationers who came to Isla Aguada to enjoy the beaches. Her husband had worked feverishly to maintain the single-story collection of cottages with adjoining carports to avoid that rundown look often associated with roadside motels. When the economy took a downturn, the occupancy rate did as well. Matilde's husband adapted by converting the roadside motor inn into a love motel, catering to lovers looking for a discreet place to indulge their carnal desires. He renamed it "La Concha" and so saved it from going out of business.

He kept the roadside kittens who peddled their virtues to truck drivers and men with lascivious tastes from using the motel by refusing to charge by the hour and arbitrarily imposing a two-night minimum. Under his watch, La Concha developed a reputation as a respectable place for decent people to conduct a discreet romantic liaison. After his death, Doña Matilde moved in and ran the motel with an iron hand, ensuring her husband's legacy.

Working as the unofficial maintenance man at the La Concha motel did not require much of Alonso. The owner's late husband had kept up the roadside inn requiring little attention from the former Ciudad del Carmen municipal police officer. The most common tasks he had to do involved clearing toilets of debris not meant for them and dismantling traps to recover wedding bands dropped carelessly into the washbasin by philandering husbands or unfaithful wives.

Alonso had just cleared the toilet in the cottage across from the motel office when he heard Doña Matilde speaking to a man whose voice he immediately recognized as that of his nemesis, Comandante Norias. He looked through the curtains of the bathroom window and saw him standing by his patrol car, talking with the indomitable doña. He couldn't make out the conversation but could tell that she dominated it, barely allowing him to get a word in edgewise. He watched him hand her a card as he excused himself to leave. He waited until he saw Norias drive his patrol car out of the walled hotel before he went across the way to speak with Doña Matilde.

"What did he want?" Alonso asked her.

She took Alonso by the arm and dragged him into the office, locking the door and closing the blinds behind her.

"Comandante Norias knows you're alive," she said in a barely contained whisper. "He showed me your picture and said that he had an order for your detention for dereliction of duty."

"Only that bastard would think of bringing charges against me after shooting me off the road," Alonso remarked bitterly.

"How do you think he found you?"

"I don't know. Someone must have recognized me."

"Let's check the register," she suggested.

She handed the bound book to Alonso, who shuffled through the pages until he came to a sudden stop.

"That's how," he said as he showed her the name. "He's a member of the municipal president's staff. He must have seen me when he was here."

"Him?" Doña Matilde sounded surprised. "He came here with a man."

"There's a rumor that he and Norias are ... friends," Alonso commented.

"Oh," she said in a singsong tone. "That kind of friend."

"It's the worst-kept secret in the police force."

"Oh, that reminds me." She went to her desk to get a yellow sticky note and handed it to him. "Somebody named Camilo called for you. He said he was a policeman."

Alonso chuckled softy as he read the note.

"Who are the Rickshaw Romeos?" she inquired.

"Just a bunch of horny old men," he replied. He put the note in his pocket and headed toward the door.

"Alonso," Doña Matilde said anxiously, "it's not safe for you here anymore."

"I know," he said as he opened the door. "I think that's what Camilo wants to talk to me about."

The building the Major Offenders Unit worked out of looked like an old warehouse during the Prohibition era. The two-story building had a red-brick facade and a crushed-rock parking lot and sat in the shadows of the Houston skyline by a railroad track. Nothing about the building would lead anybody to suspect that it housed the Houston Police Department's elite unit.

Sergeant Steve Grimes waited by the door to let Agent Lyons into the building. The Major Offenders Unit often targeted the same people Jack's agency did, and the two outfits routinely worked investigations together.

"Thanks for the call, Steve," Jack said to the ace investigator, who was dressed in jeans, a black sweatshirt, and a Houston Astros baseball cap.

Grimes led Jack through a maze of cluttered desks occupied by plainclothes policemen and women, talking or cussing into their phones or to each other. He stopped at his desk to pick up a case file and then led Jack to the break room where he closed the door. Grimes handed the file to Jack and went to pour two cups of coffee.

As Jack sat at the table, he opened the file and took out a picture of a half-naked man sitting with his hands tied behind his back and a cellophane bag wrapped around his head.

"I take it this is the late Billy Chávez," he remarked.

"He had a pretty good thing going for him," Grimes commented as he set a Styrofoam cup of coffee in front of Jack. "Until somebody gave him a cellophane facial."

"And that somebody's name is José Luis."

"Same as your suspect in the murder of your informant."

"You think it's the same guy?"

"That's my guess. Billy and Elton go way back," Grimes explained as he sat. "Billy's been using Elton's body shop to move drugs from Mexico to Houston for years."

"Have you ever known them to move guns?"

"Never," Grimes responded. "That's why I never told you about Billy."

"That's the same reason I didn't think to run Elton's name past you," Jack commented. "The highway patrol nailed him for DUI and found a sawed-off shotgun and a stolen gun with the serial numbers scratched off when they inventoried his car." Jack scoffed. "I figured him for being either a burglar or an armed robber."

"We weren't looking at him either," Grimes admitted. "Not until Intel told us that Billy might be moving money for a Mexican trafficker."

"José Luis?"

"Nah," he replied. "Some mope named Saenz—goes by the handle 'The Magician' or something like that."

"Hmm, can't say I heard of him. Did you check with DEA?"

"They haven't been playing nice lately," Grimes remarked. "ICE was no help either."

"That doesn't surprise me," Jack commented. "They're not interested in anything that doesn't roll over dead for them." Jack took a long sip of coffee. "Tell me more about this woman you have in protective custody."

Grimes took the file from Jack and handed him another picture of Billy dressed in a white suit wearing a black shirt with an open collar. He had his arm around a beautiful, well-endowed dark-headed woman.

"Her name is Linda Ochoa—Billy's girlfriend."

Jack looked at Billy's gaunt, pockmarked face and thinning hair.

"She's way out of his league," Jack remarked.

"In more ways than just looks," Grimes added as he slid a black-and-white photograph toward him. "Her dad's the infamous 'El Ocho,' a.k.a., Federico Ochoa."

"I can't say that name rings a bell," Jack said as he glanced at the picture.

"He was a bigtime gangster in Houston up till about the middle seventies," Grimes explained as he put the picture back in the file. "He had a hand in everything from loan sharking to protection to hijacking. The companies doing business at the ship channel used to pay him just to leave their stuff alone."

"What about drugs and guns?"

"Never heard anything about guns. He might've dabbled a little in drugs, but I don't think he needed to." Grimes scoffed. "That's what I don't understand. What's a gangster princess like Linda doing with a gaudy, two-bit drug dealer like Billy?"

"Maybe she just wanted to piss off her old man," Jack suggested.

"Think so?"

"You have any teenage girls?"

"I got a nine-year-old."

"Give her a few years, and you'll see what I mean," Jack commented. "When can I talk to her?"

"Now, if you want. She's in the interview room."

"How did you get her to come in?"

"One of our traffic units pulled her over for driving like a bat out of hell," Grimes replied. "She walked in on Billy getting murdered and barely made it out alive herself."

"Does she know the killer?"

"Not very well. Only that his name is José Luis and that he's a sharp dresser." Grimes took a sip of coffee. "How well does your witness in Corpus know your suspect?"

"I'm afraid not much better," Jack admitted. "All she could tell us was that Elton was dragged out of the bar where she worked by a couple of Mexican men the night he was killed. She heard Elton call one of them José Luis." Jack nodded his head slowly. "She also said he was a nice dresser."

"It sounds like it might be the same guy," Grimes concluded.

"That's what I'm thinking."

"Was Elton tagged by the killer in any way?"

"You mean as an informant?"

"Yeah," Grimes said as he nodded. "You know how Mexican drug dealers like to do that with snitches."

"Yeah." Jack sat back. "After they cut off his head, they cut off one of his hands and stuffed it in his mouth with a finger pointing out."

"That's a classic," Grimes remarked as he cocked his brows. "The hand in his mouth marks him as a 'big mouth' while the finger marks him as a *dedo*."

"Dedo?"

"A finger," Grimes explained. "The cellophane bag is another favorite they like to use to tag informants."

"What's the significance of the cellophane bag?"

"From what I understand, Mexican slang for snitch is *'soplón.'* I'm told that roughly translates to blowhard or someone full of hot air." Grimes downed his coffee. "I guess the plastic bag symbolizes a balloon or something like that."

"Poor bastards." Jack sighed. "Do you think he's still in the area?"

"He's long gone. He took Billy's Charger and is probably halfway to Mexico by now." Grimes pointed at Jack's cup. "You want some more coffee before we go talk to Linda?"

"I'm good."

Grimes pushed his chair back and led Jack back through the maze of desks in the squad room, past an ill-tempered officer barking at his ex-wife on the phone, to the opposite side of the building. Grimes opened the door to the interview room for Jack, who glanced back at him after setting eyes on the very attractive, big-busted young woman dressed in a low-cut white blouse and blue jean cutoffs.

"Can you get me a coat or something?" she asked Grimes. She hunched her shoulders, causing her cleavage to swell. "It's freezing in here."

"Sure thing, Linda," Grimes said as he closed the door. "There's someone here I want you to meet."

"Hello," Jack said as he sat across from her at the table. "I'm Special Agent Jack Lyons."

"Hello, Jack," she said, smiling flirtatiously.

Grimes opened the door and motioned a uniform officer to the room. He whispered something to the young officer, who glanced into the room and then nodded his head. He closed the door and sat next to Jack.

"If it's all right, Linda," Grimes began as he tucked in his chair, "Jack here has some questions he'd like to ask you about Billy's business with José Luis."

"Can I have a cigarette?"

"It's against a city ordinance to smoke in a public building."

"God," Linda complained. "Who's it gonna hurt if I smoke a cigarette?"

"Jack's a gun cop," Grimes said. "Can you tell him what you told me?"

"Sure." Linda crossed her arms and brought up her shoulders to warm herself. "Billy and this cute guy named Elton bought a whole lot of guns for this Mexican named José Luis. One day, José Luis and Billy were getting drunk at his house. Billy wanted to smoke some cigars but was out of brandy, so he sent me to the store to buy a bottle. When I got back, I overheard Billy and José Luis talking about taking the guns to Mexico in a boat."

"Tell them about the coffee table," Grimes said, prompting her.

"Oh, yeah," Linda said. "There were some lines in the dust. It looked like a map."

"Do you remember what you saw?" Jack asked.

"I got a picture of it on my phone," she said as she rubbed the sides of her arms.

The door opened as the young officer stepped into the doorway holding a police jacket.

"That policeman's very rude," Linda remarked as she pointed at the uniformed officer.

Grimes thanked the officer, took the jacket from him, and closed the door.

"You have to excuse him, Linda," Grimes said as he handed her the jacket. "It upsets policemen when they almost get clobbered by someone running a stop sign like a bat out of hell. They're funny that way."

"He had no right to talk to me like that," Linda said as she draped the jacket over her shoulders. "Even if he is kind of cute."

"Can I see the picture?" Jack asked, trying to get Linda refocused.

Linda nodded her head and reached into her purse for her phone. She opened the gallery and scrolled through it until she found the picture she wanted. Jack held his fist to his mouth to cover a yawn.

"Tired?" Grimes asked.

"It's been a long week," Jack replied as he took the phone from Linda.

Jack looked at the screen, running his finger up and down it after enlarging the image. He nodded his head as he glanced at the abbreviations, stopping at the devil-like stick figure image.

"This looks like a map of Padre Island," Jack commented. He showed the image to Grimes, pointing at the stick figure. "This probably represents the Devil's Elbow, where the shoot-out occurred."

"I also have a recording of Billy talking to José Luis," she commented as she picked her purse off the floor. "I made it when Billy sent me to the liquor store."

Jack watched Linda rummage through her purse until she finally located the microcassette tape. She put it on the table and slid it toward Jack, who picked it up to look at it. He turned to Grimes.

"You got anything that'll play this thing?" Jack asked.

"I think our tech guys might have something stored away in the dungeon."

"Have you listened to it?" Jack asked Linda.

"Nope," she responded in a childlike voice. "To tell you the truth, I forgot I had it."

The sun had just started to set as Carmen municipal police officer Camilo García sat at his usual table by an old Airstream trailer parked at the entrance to the RV park at Isla Aguada. The proprietor of the makeshift café dragged his plus-sized wife across the Puente de La Unidad bridge from Ciudad del Carmen in the old Airstream trailer he had converted into a mobile kitchen and had yet to find a good reason to leave.

The thirty-year veteran had the build of a Mexican wrestler and the sagacious eyes of an owl. The color of his hair had faded, as had the blue of his uniform. His years of experience and gentlemanly manner had earned him the respect of the people he policed. His reputation for fairness, kindness, and that rarest of traits among his brethren, an unwillingness to accept gratuities or take bribes distinguished him from his fellow officers. This made Camilo the poorest policeman on the force, but it also made him the richest in the way that mattered most to him.

Beyond the entrance to the park sat a dozen or so recreational vehicles parked side by side and row by row under the coconut palms on the white sands of Isla Aguada. In between the motor homes, huddled comfortably in their lawn chairs with their ice chests next to them, sat an odd mixture of aging American and Canadian tourists waiting on yet another majestic sunset over the emerald-green waters of the Bay of Campeche. The aroma of chicken grilling drifted in the sea breeze, as did the sound of laughter and the caustic twang of country and western music.

Camilo liked taking his afternoon breaks at the café to enjoy the cool sea breeze and watch the retirees at play. He liked to watch the old beachcombers swinging their metal detectors over the sand as their blue-haired wives basked in the tropical sun so heavily covered in sunblock that they looked like sun-bleached beached whales. He especially enjoyed watching the old men riding in the motorcycle-towed rickshaws, leaving the park for a night on the town in pursuit of a May-December romance. Almost invariably, the doddering Casanovas dressed in outrageous Hawaiian shirts, plaid Bermuda shorts, and knee-high socks. Those whose white manes had retreated to the back of their heads generally wore cheap straw fedoras or Irish tweed flat caps.

Camilo took a sip of his soft drink as he watched Alonso park his Japanese motorcycle in front of the beachside café. He turned to look at a motorcycle-drawn rickshaw emerging from the RV park, ferrying two over-the-hill beach boys wearing straw cowboy hats and puffing on counterfeit Cuban cigars. He chuckled as he watched the seagulls hovering around the rickshaw, cawing incessantly as if mocking the old-timers.

"I see the rickshaw Romeos are starting early," Alonso remarked as he joined Camilo at the table.

"That's Steve and Charlie," Camilo said as he waved at them. "They come here every year about this time to do some fishing."

"Do they ever catch anything?" Alonso asked as he waved at the cowboy Casanovas.

"I don't think they want to."

"Of course not," Alonso said with a chuckle. "Why would they?"

They smiled as they watched the motorcycle-pulled rickshaw roll down the road toward the small hotel strip in the tiny village of Isla Aguada.

"Norias knows you're not dead," Camilo commented.

"I know," Alonso responded. "He came by La Concha today looking for me."

Camilo waved at the café owner's wife and ordered two more soft drinks.

"It's not safe for you here," Camilo remarked.

"So, I've been told."

"Why are you sticking around?"

"I have a score to settle with Norias and Cisco," Alonso replied.

The owner's wife set two ten-ounce soft drinks on the table and left.

"That could take some doing," Camilo said.

"Will you help me?"

A foreboding shadow rolled over the rustic table as a pod of pelicans glided past the seaside café like a squadron of Catalina PBY Flying Boats. They came in for a soft landing on a derelict wharf that reached out into the calm waters off Isla Aguada. A forgotten storm had swept most of the wharf out to sea, leaving only a smattering of twisted planks clinging to some of the pylons like wooden crosses in an abandoned cemetery.

"I don't know what I can do, but I'll try," Camilo replied.

"Do you still have that informer close to Norias?"

"You mean the gay?" Camilo smiled playfully. "You know, I think he likes you."

Alonso's face turned red. "I can't believe he asked me out."

"I hear he cried when he heard you were dead," Camilo added to tease his friend.

"I'm touched," he said, playing along. "Is he still close to Norias?"

"Norias wants to get in his pants," Camilo replied. He scoffed. "What do you think?"

"So, the answer is yes."

Camilo took a long swig of his soft drink.

"What do you need from him?" he asked Alonso.

"I don't know yet," Alonso replied. "All I know is that I have to do something about Norias before he succeeds in getting me killed."

The two men sat quietly as they looked at the pelicans perched motionless on the pylons like the Queen's Guard at Buckingham Palace.

"You might have to kill him first," Camilo suggested coolly.

Alonso turned to Camilo. "That would be an act of murder."

"It would be an act of self-preservation," Camilo retorted.

He could tell by Alonso's demeanor that it made him uncomfortable, so he decided to drop it.

"Why did you decide to work at La Concha?" Camilo asked. He snorted as he chuckled. "Thinking about becoming a peeping Tom?"

"You know why I had to leave the Tucán."

"Yes, but that place?"

"Beggars can't be choosers," Alonso said as they watched another motorcycle-pulled rickshaw leave the RV park with another pair of aging Casanovas. He frowned as he turned to look at Camilo. "What's the deal between Colonel Barca and Cisneros? Cisco didn't look happy to see him that time he and Norias came to the Tucán."

"That's an understatement," Camilo said. He scoffed. "Cisco wants to stay in Ciudad del Carmen after the colonel is done in Chiapas."

"The Norteños aren't staying?"

"That's what the gay hears," Camilo replied. "He overheard Cisco complaining to Norias about it."

"Why aren't they staying? The colonel went through a lot of trouble last Easter to get rid of Los Cosarios," Alonso reasoned. "It doesn't make any sense that they'd abandon Carmen after doing all that work."

"According to what the gay hears, the only reason the Thunderbolts came to Carmen was to neutralize the Cosarios to keep them from helping the Comisión," Camilo explained.

"I didn't realize the gangs were still working with the Commission," Alonso commented.

"The colonel is obviously a very careful man," Camilo explained. "Cisco was left behind to keep the other Campeche gangs from claiming the plaza but only until the Thunderbolts are done in Chiapas. Then, it's back to Nuevo León for him."

"Does the colonel know that he wants to stay?"

"How could he not?" Camilo asked rhetorically. "Cisco's been talking openly about taking Champotón for the 'New Order', as he calls it."

"Does he mean to start his own cartel?"

"Who knows?"

"What has the colonel to say about that?"

"According to what Norias told the gay, the colonel put Cisco in his place and told him to shut up."

"So, it's just talk then," Alonso surmised.

"It may not be," Camilo said. "Norias's been bragging to the gay that Cisco's going to make him the plaza boss in Champotón."

"And defy the cartel?"

"That's what it looks like."

"I don't see the cartel sitting still for that," Alonso commented. "The colonel'll stop Cisco before he gets started."

"According to what Norias has been saying, Cisco is waiting for when the colonel is too tied up to do anything about it."

Camilo took a napkin from the holder on the table and started to write his informer's number on it as Alonso sat quietly digesting what Camilo had just told him.

"I don't know what you're going to do about Norias," he said as he wrote. "I'll break the news to the gay that you're not dead." He chuckled softly. "I'm sure he'll be glad to hear that." He handed the napkin to him. "He'll help you however he can."

"Thank you, old friend," Alonso said as took the napkin and stood to leave.

"Are you going back to La Concha?" Camilo asked.

"Just to get my things." Alonso dropped several coins on the table. "Hasta luego."

"Vaya con Dios, mijo," Camilo replied.

Camilo remained at the table as Alonso got on his bike and rode away from the café, turning down a side street as a dark blue Chevrolet Tahoe turned left from a different side street and drove toward the café.

Camilo finished his drink and went to get into his patrol car as a large recreational vehicle drove slowly out of the park. Camilo noticed the Tahoe creeping by the café. The heavily tinted windows made it impossible to see inside. As the motor home drove by blocking his view, he looked behind it, expecting to see the Tahoe drive into the park. He heard a horn honk and turned to look in the other direction, where he watched another Carmen municipal police car creeping up to the café until the RV again blocked his view.

Camilo turned his head when he heard a pair of car doors opening across the street. His eyes widened in horror when he saw the gunmen standing outside of the Tahoe with their machine guns pointed at him.

CHAPTER 5

The *Siete Mares* dropped anchor at the mouth of the Sabancuy Channel just after midnight as Donovan had figured it. Fernando met the ship in Doña Estér's panga soon afterward with a stretcher to bring Benício ashore. Augie rigged the davits to lower the stretcher carrying him gently into the panga. Benício had spent a restless night tossing and turning, so Augie and Dario rode with him to keep him from opening his wound.

Donovan followed the panga in the *Mona*, leaving Sandy alone to watch the ship. Fortunately, the wind blew gently from the south, making the water lap lazily against the boat's hull. The soft blue light of the waning moon made the water glimmer like tiny broken pieces of glass rippling softly under a cloudless sky. The bioluminescent glow of the wake flowing away from the stern of the panga ahead of him made him think of a flock of geese flying high in the night sky. He turned to look at the beach, which looked like a long band of sugar in the dim moonlight under the coconut palms.

As he got closer to the beach, he saw Doña Estér and a man step out of the shadows to meet the panga carrying Benício. He cut the outboard on the *Mona* and let the boat slide onto the beach next to Doña Estér's panga. It didn't make him happy to see Alonso, the ex-policemen who as much as called him a crook the time they met at Doña Estér's restaurant.

"How is he?" Doña Estér asked.

"Stable," Augie replied. "Your man did a good job bringing us ashore."

She pulled the blanket covering Benício aside and checked his bandages. She felt his face and chest and then put two fingers against his neck as she looked at the luminescent dial on her watch. Donovan went to stand next to Alonso.

"How did he get shot?" Alonso asked Donovan.

Donovan looked at him warily. "With a gun."

"I can see that," Alonso retorted bitterly.

"You two really have to get over what's bothering you," Doña Estér said to them.

"I don't appreciate some two-bit ex-cop calling me a crook," Donovan said.

"What am I supposed to think about someone who rubs elbows with drug traffickers?" Alonso asked sarcastically.

"That's enough," Doña Estér said. She turned to Fernando. "Why don't you and Dario take Benício to the truck?"

"Sí, señora," Fernando responded. "Vamos, Señor Dario."

Dario stared fiercely at Alonso for a moment before going with Fernando.

Doña Estér and Augie walked with them as they got Benício out of the panga and took the stretcher through the restaurant out to Fernando's truck. Meanwhile, Donovan and Alonso remained on the beach, glaring at each other like dogs waiting for the other to lunge first. Doña Estér returned shortly afterward with Augie.

"You're wrong about Capitán Dónovan," Doña Estér said to Alonso.

"Am I?" Alonso replied as he pointed into the restaurant. "Pardon me if I'm wrong, but isn't that Dario Róbles, El Demonio's right-hand man?"

"It's not what it looks like," Donovan responded.

"I'll tell you what it looks like to me," Alonso said. "You accepted El Demonio's offer and were involved in that shootout on the Texas coast."

"Things aren't always what they appear to be," Doña Estér interjected.

"Then what's he doing with Dario Róbles, a wanted man?"

"You could ask me the same thing about yourself," Doña Estér retorted. "Aren't you also wanted?"

Donovan cocked his brow, amused by the revelation as he watched Alonso's face turn red.

"That's different," Alonso said uncomfortably.

"What d'you do?" Donovan asked sarcastically. "Get caught taking a bribe?"

Alonso glared at him angrily.

"Stop it," Doña Estér said sternly. "Neither of you know what you're talking about."

"I think I do," Alonso said. "He went to Padre Island to get a shipment of guns for El Demonio but didn't count on the police being there." He looked distastefully at Donovan. "Tell me, how'd you manage to get away?"

"I helped him," Dario said as he walked up on them. He turned to Doña Estér. "Fernando sent me back to get you."

"Is Benício all right?" she asked.

"He's sound asleep," he replied. He turned to Alonso. "Capitán Dónovan did go to Padre Island like you said but not by choice." He glanced at Donovan. "My cousin kidnapped Benício's wife and threatened to kill her if Capitán Dónovan didn't go get his guns."

"See?" Doña Estér said. "Capitán Dónovan is a victim just like you."

Making snap decisions comes with a badge, and policemen often take things at face value or risk getting hurt if not killed. Soldiers fighting a guerrilla war face the same challenges. Pride also comes with a badge, and policemen often find it difficult to admit their mistakes.

"I didn't know," Alonso said awkwardly. "I'm ... sorry."

Donovan had also made a snap decision about Alonso. His experience with corrupt customs officials and policemen across the Americas made him suspicious of anyone carrying a badge. Like Alonso, he too found it difficult to swallow his pride.

"So ..." Donovan cleared his throat. "Why are the cops looking for you?"

"It's not the *cops* that are looking for me," Alonso replied. "It's Cisco and Comandante Norias."

"What do they want with you?"

"They think I'm a threat. They tried to kill me when the Thunderbolts raided Ciudad del Carmen last Easter," he replied. "They would have succeeded if Doña Estér hadn't found me and took me in."

"Somehow, Comandante Norias found out where he was hiding," Doña Estér explained. "Now we have to find another place to hide him."

"He can hide on the ship with us," Augie suggested as he turned to Donovan. "Right, Skipper?"

Donovan glared at his partner and then glanced at Doña Estér, who looked at him like a nun after breaking up a fight in the schoolyard.

"Sure," Donovan said clumsily. "There's plenty of room."

"Thank you, Capitán, but I think I'll look for somewhere a little less conspicuous," Alonso said.

"We won't be conspicuous at all," Donovan said. "We have a charter to raise an artifact from the mouth of the Sabancuy Channel for the institute. You'll be safe once we take care of a couple of ... issues."

"What kind of issues?" Alonso asked suspiciously.

"Well," Donovan said as he gathered his thoughts, "I have to find a place where Dario'll be safe first."

"Now *he's* conspicuous," Augie added.

"He can stay with me and help me care for Benício," Doña Estér suggested.

"Are you sure that's wise, señora, with the Norteños so close?" Alonso asked.

"I've hidden refugees before," she explained. "I won't make the same mistake I made with you."

After she had found him and treated his wounds, he wanted to pay her back for her kindness and took a job as a waiter at her restaurant. He hid in the open much like what Donovan wanted to do until the day Comandante Norias showed up with Cisco Cisneros.

"You couldn't have known Comandante Dientes would come to the Tucán," Alonso responded. "He seldom leaves Ciudad del Carmen."

"Who's Comandante Dientes?" Augie inquired.

"That's what they call Comandante Norias," Fernando explained as he walked up on them. "He has two large gold teeth in the middle of his mouth."

Like many people in the Yucatán, Comandante Norias adorned his mouth with gold teeth as a form of status symbol. Unfortunately, he chose to have his two front teeth adorned with the precious metal, which made him look like a gilded beaver.

"What are you doing here, Fernando?" Doña Estér asked him. "Why did you leave Benício alone?"

"I came to get you, señora," Fernando replied. "He's asking for water. I didn't know if I should give him any."

"I'd better get my patient home," she muttered to herself as she turned to Fernando. "Can you get my medical bag out of the panga?"

"Sí, señora," he said as he went to get it.

"Dario'll be safe with me," Doña Estér said to Donovan. "What other issue do you have to take care of?"

A thought came to Donovan as he watched Fernando go to the fiberglass launch and return with the medical kit. He sized up the length of the boat as he recalled how quietly the outboard motor performed.

"Nothing I can't handle if I had a panga to take care of it," Donovan said as he played the idea out in his head.

"Why don't you use my panga?" Doña Estér offered.

"Thanks, Doña Estér. I'll have it back by morning."

"What have you got in mind, Skipper?" Augie asked him.

He looked at his partner warily. "We got to move those"—he glanced at Alonso—"things."

"You can speak openly, Capitán," Doña Estér said. "You're among friends."

"He won't do that," Augie interjected. "It's for our own protection."

"It's all right," Donovan said, surprising Augie. He turned to Alonso. "We took on some weapons before we could take back the ship. I need them as insurance to keep Fausto at bay, but I can't take a chance the Armada will find them if they board us."

"You're not going to give them to El Demonio?" Alonso asked. "Are you?"

"Of course not," Donovan replied. "I just need him to think I am. I'll get rid of them as soon as I get"—he glanced at Dario—"Benício's wife back."

Alonso stared at Donovan. "I can't be a party to that."

"With any luck, you won't have to," Donovan retorted. He turned to Augie. "Take the *Mona* back to the ship and bring the guns topside. I'll need the big cargo net, a block pulley, and some rope."

"Where are you taking them?" Doña Estér asked.

"Now *that* I know he won't answer," Augie interjected.

"It's all right, Augie," Donovan said. "Like Doña Estér said, we're among friends." He turned to her. "There're some caves at Punta Morro."

"I know those caves," Dario said. "They're very treacherous."

"And they flood during high tide," Donovan added. "The municipality posted warning signs to keep people out of them. I'm counting on those signs to keep anybody from finding the guns."

"You're not afraid of the ghosts, Capitán?" Fernando asked.

"Ghosts?"

"I told you about that, Skipper," Augie reminded him. "Remember?"

"I remember you telling Sandy about buried treasure, but I wasn't paying attention." Donovan scoffed. "I thought you were just trying to scare him."

"Uh-uh, Skipper. The stories are real," Augie responded. "Don Macario told me the pirates always killed one of their men when they buried treasure so his ghost could protect it."

"People have died looking for treasure in the caves," Doña Estér added.

"Tell him about the witch," Fernando added. "Sometimes, at night, you can hear her groaning."

"There isn't time, Fernando," Doña Estér said. "We have to care for Benício."

"You can't do that alone," Augie said to Donovan. "Let me go with you."

"I need you here to take care of the ship," Donovan said. "I'll be all right."

Augie looked at Donovan disconcertedly, obviously unhappy with his decision.

"You're gonna have to stay clear of the coast," he said as he exhaled sharply. "You might run into a patrol boat."

"I plan to."

He looked at Augie, who turned away, looked down, and twisted the ball of his foot in the sand.

"You'd better take the spare fuel cans," Augie added. "It's a long way to Punta Morro."

To save time, Donovan set a course from the Sabancuy Channel to Punta Morro rather than follow the coastline. With only a compass heading, he took the gun-laden panga north by northeast from Punta Varaderos out to the open sea.

The nearly flat bottom boat slid across the calm water like an empty beer can on a wet countertop. The light of the waning moon sparkling off the gently rolling waves made it easy for Donovan to find his way. He lost view of the coast within the first half hour of the run but had a sense of his position using dead reckoning. He used the soft glow of the Champotón city lights, shining over the eastern horizon, as his reference point. The coast came back into view as he approached Sihoplaya Point. He smiled when he saw the lights of Seyba Playa just beyond it.

He thought about Itzél as he stared at the city lights. He recalled the warmth of her body and the feel of her skin against his as they lay together in her bed above her restaurant. He thought about her eyes, which gleamed like jade and the way her raven hair framed her delicate face. He thought about the way she took his Panama hat from him earlier that day, coquettishly holding the brim with her fingertips as she cocked her head to smile at him.

As he pushed the panga closer to the Port of Seyba Playa, Donovan could see the limestone hill perched over Punta Morro. He thought about how he would get Itzél back from El Demonio. He went over what he knew. Dario said that his cousin would most likely hold her in the small cottage on the plantation grounds. He remembered Itzél telling him about the first time El Demonio had her kidnapped. She spent most of the time alone with an old housekeeper and her husband in the cottage, and they did everything possible to make her comfortable. If he only knew for sure she was at the cottage alone with the old couple, he could go and get her at that very moment.

He looked at the bundles containing the Romanian rifles gathered on the deck. He would have to throw them over the side before he made the attempt. If he did that and failed to find Itzél, he would lose the only bargaining chip he had if it came to that. He thought about hiding them somewhere and immediately thought about the Paradise Lagoon just on the other side of Punta Morro. However, if he hid them there, he would put Don Macario in jeopardy. He looked at his watch and realized he had a limited window of opportunity before the coming of the dawn. None of that really mattered if he didn't know where they had her for sure.

Then he thought about the life he would have with her and Poli after he got her back. As much as he didn't like the idea, they would have to leave Campeche. He thought about where they would go and decided on South Florida. He could set up a charter business to the Bahamas, and she could get a job as a cook until they saved enough money to open her own restaurant. Poli would continue to crew for him while he graduated high school and went to college.

He liked the idea of having Poli by his side—not as a crewman but as the son he didn't realize he wanted until then. He would do the things fathers did with their sons and guide him into manhood. He looked forward to cruising the Bahamas with Poli and coming home to Itzél. Then, out of the deep recesses of his memory, Xóchitl came calling.

Galveston Bay, Texas
Three years ago

Xóchitl sat in the cockpit of the sloop Donovan had rented to take her out for an afternoon cruise. He looked at her and chuckled to himself when he thought about spending most of the morning with her shopping for an outfit to wear for the outing. He had given her a ball cap with his shipping company's logo, and she had to find a windbreaker with a yachting theme to match it. She gathered her jet-black hair into a ponytail and pulled it through the opening in the back of the cap, tying it with a veil-like aquamarine scarf. To complement her version of a sailor's ensemble, she wore a pair of large sunglasses to handle the Texas sun, hiding her almond-shaped eyes.

Donovan sat next to her with a hand on the wheel.

"So, what do you think?" he asked her.

"The water in Veracruz is prettier."

"About what we talked about."

She sat quietly watching a pod of dolphins swimming along the starboard side.

"I need more time to think about it."

"What's there to think about?"

"It would be great living here," she said. "I just don't feel like I'm needed."

"People get sick in Texas all the time."

"That's not what I mean," she said. "Texas doesn't need doctors like the Indians living in the mountains of Veracruz."

"But my company doesn't have a position for me in Veracruz," Donovan explained. "It's either here or Panama."

"Why don't you retire?" she suggested. "We can live off what I make."

"What would I do?"

"You can buy a boat like this one and take people out for rides like you're always talking about."

Donovan chuckled. "That's just a dream, and this is not the kind of *ship* I've been telling you about."

"Tell me again," she said as she rested her head on his shoulder.

"First of all, I would get a schooner with two masts, able to sleep at least six passengers"—he kissed her on the top of her head—"and I'd be taking people on long cruises, not just afternoon outings."

"Why don't you do that?"

"I told you, it's just a dream. I'm tired of being away from you." He looked beyond the bow. "That's why I brought you here. I was hoping you'd get a job around Houston so I can work out of the home office."

"But I'm not needed here."

He looked at her. "I need you."

A chill shot through Donovan as she buried herself deeper into his chest.

"Couldn't you find a shipping company to work for in Veracruz?"

Donovan stared pensively at the dolphins swimming along the starboard side as they weaved in and out of the water, matching the sloop's speed.

"I'd settle for a job at a car wash in Veracruz just to be near you."

Donovan kept his distance as he ran the panga around the end of the long pier at the Port of Seyba Playa, putting him well off the coast off Payucán Beach. He didn't want to risk drawing the interest of the preventive policeman stationed at the port, who would send a launch to intercept him.

He turned the panga toward Punta Morro and headed for the caves. The surf made a thunderous roar as it crashed against the massive overhang that once overlooked the caves before falling into the ocean ages ago. The sea breeze blowing into the caves reminded Donovan of Fernando's witch as he listened to the wind swirling into the caves, making a sound not unlike the tormented moaning of an old woman.

The water began to churn, tossing the panga like a toy boat as he neared the coast. He looked over the side and saw a rock in the clear water just below his boat. He then turned his head from side to side and saw other rocks jutting in and out of the water as the swells rose and fell. He felt a chill run through him when he realized he had wandered into a boater's version of a minefield. Donovan realized he had to get out of there or risk losing the panga. He turned the fiberglass launch gently to starboard, weaving through the rock outcroppings until he had cleared the angry water.

Shaken but undaunted, Donovan stared at the lights of the Port of Seyba Playa and the silhouettes of the warehouses sitting on the pier. In the dark, they looked like a long, segmented worm with a big flat head and a spiny back or a square-shaped locomotive pulling a line of triangle-topped cars. He wondered if the square-shaped building was the Campechano warehouse Dario described on the voyage home and if El Demonio might have Itzél hidden there. Then he remembered what Dario had said about Fausto not having enough men to watch it properly.

He looked to his left at the pangas moored along Payucán Beach, bobbing gently in the water. He raised his eyes to look at the *palapa*-covered shelters lining the high-end of the beach. In the darkness of the early morning, they looked like squatting giants with straw hats staring eerily at him.

He looked over his shoulder at the limestone hill overlooking Punta Morro as he listened to the torturous moan coming from deep within the caves. In his haste, he had forgotten to check on the tide. He didn't know how much time he had before the tide would roll in, filling the cave with water and trapping him or worse.

As much as he hated the idea, he had to consider depositing the guns in the cabañas on the bluff overlooking the Paradise Lagoon. It would take some doing to sneak the guns up the steep incline to hide them, and he might not have enough time before the sunrise. Then he thought about Lieutenant Baeza, who by then would have learned about the incident on Padre Island and would naturally suspect him. He had no doubt that the nosy marine would probably think to search his cabaña or the ruins of the other cabañas. If he discovered the guns, he would have no choice but to charge Don Macario unless he took responsibility.

He throttled down the outboard motor and turned the panga to starboard to reevaluate the approach to Punta Morro. He wondered if he had enough time to beach the panga as near to the caves as he dared go and manhandle a hundred and ten rifles into the dark grotto before the tide washed ashore.

He saw a light flicker to his left, and he turned to look toward the port. He saw a search beam dancing between the silhouettes of the warehouses coming from a police car patrolling the docks. The light from the streetlamps along the pier shining down through the predawn mist looked like a row of halos hanging in the void. A sea fog rising low along the water had started to roll in around the port, giving Donovan a wild idea.

CHAPTER 6

Comandante Villegas sat in his Champotón transit police car on the side of the coast road smoking a cigarette as he watched the seagulls hovering over several broken-down pangas scattered along the narrow beach. Most of the fishermen had already set out in search of the day's catch. The streets looked like those of a ghost town, empty but for an old man sweeping the dirt from his sidewalk into the gutter and a lone jogger running along the seawall. The sound of his feet on the pavement carried in the stillness like the quiet thumping of the second hand on a clock. On the horizon sat a line of clouds with imposing towers rising ominously over them like silent harbingers of the day to come. A mild sea breeze blew ashore so faintly that even the seagulls had difficulty staying aloft as they scavenged the coast for something to eat.

Villegas tossed his cigarette out the window when he spotted a string of compact cars coming toward him. He locked eyes with the drivers as the cars crept by slowly before turning into a small parking lot across the street from him. Each car had at least one passenger, who, along with the driver, had short-cropped hair and tattoos on his face and neck. He turned to look at the last car in the string as it drove across the road to park beside his police car. Comandante Norias flashed his gold teeth at Villegas as he put the car in park.

"¿Como estás, Villegas?" Norias said, greeting him.

Villegas stared at Norias, who looked ridiculous wearing a straw cowboy hat that was far too small for his head. He had never seen the Ciudad del Carmen police commander out of uniform, and it didn't suit him.

"Have you got my money?" Villegas asked dryly.

Norias turned to get an envelope off the passenger seat and handed it out his window to him. The corrupt Champotón transit cop opened it and ran his thumb across the bundle of crisp thousand-peso notes.

"Señor Cisneros is very generous," Villegas remarked as he slipped the envelope into the inside pocket of his uniform jacket.

"He appreciates your assistance," Norias replied. "He hopes he can continue to rely on your cooperation."

"I'll be here," Villegas said as he glanced at the men sitting in the cars across the street. "Where did you find these rejects? They look like refugees from a methadone clinic."

"That's because they are," Norias said candidly.

"How do you think they'll do against Los Chinos?"

Los Chinos were the local Campeche gang headed by Comandante Antonio Briones, alias "El Chino." Like Villegas, he too was a transit police commander who came to head the gang through his association with Comandante Sánchez and his task force.

"They won't be going up against Los Chinos," Norias said harshly. "Cisco decided he wants to firebomb the municipal building, the newspaper, and the radio station."

"But they're supposed to hit the dealerships and the warehouse on the river," Villegas protested.

"After they bomb their assigned targets—if there's time."

"But there won't be time," Villegas protested. "The Marina will respond as soon as the first explosions go off."

"That's what Cisco is counting on. He wants to see how they react." Norias scoffed. "A little trick he picked up from the colonel."

"What about Los Chinos?"

"Cisco's not worried about them."

"But you agreed to hit the dealerships ..."

"I agreed to pass your recommendation to Cisco," Norias countered harshly. "That's all."

Norias looked out his passenger window and whistled sharply at the drivers of the compact cars. He made a motion with his hand like a cavalry officer ordering a charge. One by one, the compact cars filed out of the hotel parking lot and headed into town. Norias turned to Villegas as he put the car in gear.

"We'll be in touch," he said sardonically and drove off.

As Villegas watched Norias turn his car around and head back to Ciudad del Carmen, he wondered what he would say to Fausto about the Norteños' decision not to attack the Campechano businesses. He sighed as he got out his cell phone to make the call.

When Don Macario first set out to convert the old family plantation into a five-star hotel, he did so with the beautiful scenery in mind. He wanted to showcase the magnificent views from every possible angle, for the old stone-and-stucco building literally sat in the middle of a paradise.

The hacienda itself stood as a shining example of Spanish colonial architecture. The two-story rectangularly shaped building with a sandstone stucco facade and a flat roof sat on a rise over the parking lot. It had a green concrete veranda that wrapped around three sides of the building covered by a portico with a red-tile roof supported by massive stone columns. A series of ceiling fans spaced evenly between the columns ensured the comfort of the guests sitting in the white wrought iron patio furniture situated around the veranda to take in the magnificent views.

On the north side of the hacienda, Don Macario built a sprawling patio facing the lagoon and the bluff that overlooked it from the opposite bank. Behind the hacienda, he had a red crushed-stone walkway that meandered lazily across the putting-green-like lawn to the bluff overlooking the Bay of Campeche. There, the guests could take in the spectacular sunsets or the view of the old lighthouse sitting on top of the limestone hill at Punta Morro.

Don Macario sat at a table perched near the top of the white stone staircase leading to the entrance of the Paradise Inn, watching Dr. Ventura park his BMW. True to his image, the professor dressed in his field outfit, which included a cotton shirt, canvas pants, and hiking boots topped off by an Australian-style Outback hat and a photographer's vest.

Neither he nor the professor noticed Poli moving stealthily through the maze of cars parked behind the BMW as the professor hurried up the staircase to sit with Don Macario. Neither saw Poli open the driver's side door to pop open the trunk, nor did they see him go to the back of the car and get into the trunk, pulling on it gently until it shut.

"How did your talk with El Demonio go?" the professor asked the illustrious proprietor of the Paradise Inn.

"Like talking to a bitter ex-wife."

"I wouldn't know what that's like. Mine refuses to leave me," the professor said as he sat. "What did López say about the exchange?"

"He's agreed to accept delivery at the warehouse but refuses to release Itzél until he inspects the rifles."

"Simon's not going to like that."

"It gets worse," Don Macario said as he looked at him grimly. "He insists that he pick her up at the plantation house after the exchange."

The professor looked thunderstruck as he sat back slowly.

"López was adamant," Don Macario added. "He was livid about Donovan refusing to bring the rifles to his beach like he wanted."

"What am I going to tell Simon?" the professor asked softly.

"I'll revisit her release after he calms down."

"Let's hope he'll be more reasonable," the professor remarked as he stood. "Do you have anything else for Donovan or Augie before I go meet them?"

"Just let them know that I'm ready to help in any way I can."

The previous night couldn't have gone better for Cisco Cisneros. He had set his plan to seize the Champotón plaza in motion and finally persuaded the municipal president's daughter to go home with him after a long night at Ciudad del Carmen's premier dance clubs. It didn't matter to him that the big-bosomed, brown-eyed beauty had paraded him by the nose from club to club until the break of dawn just as it didn't matter to her that the puny plaza boss had the face of a dehydrated weasel.

People like Cisco Cisneros, who rise to the apex of the drug trade often have ignoble beginnings but none like his. He came into the world the bastard son of a barfly with the morals of an alley cat and a face that could not only stop a clock but make it go backward. Not even the dim light of a seedy bar or any amount of alcohol could get a man past her face. Only a witch's spell could have clouded a man's mind enough to get past her gorgonian features.

Unfortunately for Cisco, he did not inherit any of the physical attributes of the man who recklessly donated his life-giving essence to his birth. He had a scrawny stature and the same bony facial features and bulbous eyes of his mother, who abandoned him soon after his birth. She left him with her sister, who despised men but relied on their generosity to survive.

He may not have inherited his father's looks or other manly attributes, but he did come away with a knack for handling a business, a trait he must have inherited from his nameless genetic donor since his mother couldn't even balance a checkbook. This ability allowed him to rise in the Norteño cartel such that when the war for control of the trafficking routes into the United States on the northern border broke out, the cartel turned to Cisco to run the business while they fought the war.

As a reward for his service, the cartel installed him as the temporary plaza boss of Ciudad del Carmen while Colonel Barca and his Thunderbolts settled accounts with the Commission for hijacking their drug loads as they focused their attention on winning the northern border war. He believed he deserved better, and he meant to change that.

Cisco shaded his eyes as sunlight burst suddenly into his bedroom after Sergeant Reséndez threw back the curtains and pulled the sheets off him and the municipal president's daughter. He put both hands down to cover his nakedness when one would have done as the sergeant dragged the half-naked girl dressed only in scarlet hipster panties out of bed and threw her into the bathroom. Cisco held a hand up to shade his eyes to look at

Colonel Barca and Major Zamora standing at the foot of the bed as he heard the sergeant turn on the shower.

"What are you doing here?" Cisco asked the colonel.

The leader of the band of special forces deserters stared at him stoically as Sergeant Reséndez walked out of the bathroom.

"Get Cisco something to wear," he said to the sergeant.

The sergeant picked up a pink pair of pants off the floor and threw them at Cisco's face.

"These aren't mine," Cisco said as he covered himself with the pants.

"Put them on," he heard the major say unsympathetically.

Cisco got out of bed and slipped into the pants the best he could. He looked bitterly at Sergeant Reséndez who had a smile on his face.

"What's so funny?" Cisco snarled at the sergeant.

"The zipper goes to the back," he replied.

Cisco turned to the colonel. "Why aren't you in Chiapas?"

"Really, Cisco?" the colonel replied. "You conduct an unauthorized operation in Champotón, and you have to ask me why I'm here?"

"I saw an opportunity—"

"You're not here to seek opportunities," the colonel replied sternly. "You're here to keep the Campeche gangs out of Ciudad del Carmen until I'm done with the Comisión. Nothing else."

"But it's a mistake to let go of Ciudad del Carmen," Cisco argued.

"Don Arturo was gracious enough to allow us to temporarily occupy Carmen while I completed my mission," the colonel said. "It would upset Anastasio if we betrayed that confidence by overstaying our welcome."

"It's only a matter of time before the gangs take over the drug trade from the Campechanos."

"That will never happen," the colonel retorted. "Don Arturo will never give them the chance to organize."

"Have you forgotten about El Demonio?" Cisco countered. "He's already worked his way into the gangs. How long before he turns them against the Campechanos?"

"He won't get anywhere without guns."

"What about the guns Dónovan went to Texas to get?" Cisco commented wryly.

Cisco grinned as he watched Colonel Barca turn to Major Zamora, who nodded his head subtly.

"The Armada has been alerted to watch for Donovan," the major responded for the colonel.

"So, it's true," Cisco surmised. "Dónovan did go to Texas. I told him I'd torch his boat if he did."

"Leave Donovan to me," the colonel said sharply. "I'll take care of him. In the meantime, I want you to stay out of Champotón. I will not tolerate another stunt like what you did today. Is that understood?"

Cisco looked at the colonel resentfully. "I still say it's a mistake giving Carmen back."

"Enjoy it while you can," the colonel responded. "We'll be back in Monterrey by the end of the month."

The door to the bathroom opened suddenly. The girl stepped out wearing only a smile as she fluff-dried her hair vigorously with a towel.

"Have you forgotten your modesty?" Major Zamora commented. "Where are your underclothes?"

"They're wet," she replied as she stopped drying her hair. She turned to the sergeant. "He didn't give me a chance to take them off before he threw me into the shower."

"Put something on," the major said.

She looked at Reséndez as he went to the nightstand, tore a Kleenex out of its box, and handed it to her. She sneered at him and then turned to the major. She took her time wrapping the towel around her hourglass body, tucking the end in the gap between her impressive cleavage.

"This girl has no shame," the major remarked as he turned to Cisco. "And poor taste in men." He looked at the colonel. "I guess it's true what they say about the mangiest dog getting the sweetest bone."

The sun had already made it well into the sky over the Sabancuy Channel when Donovan rounded Varaderos Point in Doña Estér's panga on his way back to the restaurant. He smiled when he saw the *Siete Mares* sitting in the waters off the beach. The reflection of the jade-colored water undulated softly against the white of her hull. Her brass fittings, freshly stained deck, and polished hardwood masts gleamed in the sun like a new penny. He turned to look at the beach and saw Augie standing with Fernando under the coconut palms and Doña Estér waving at him from under the palapa roof of her open-air restaurant with Alonso standing by her side.

First impressions are sometimes hard to get over, and Alonso had not made a good one with Donovan. The former policeman lived in a black-and-white world of right and wrong, and Donovan had made a living navigating the gray that existed in between. Donovan always believed in not judging a man until he'd walked a mile in his *huaraches*, and he would give Alonso the benefit of the doubt. Doña Estér liked him, and he agreed to get along with him if only for her sake.

He cut the outboard motor as the bow of the panga slid onto the wet part of the beach. As Fernando took the bow line to tie it to a post sunk into the ground, Donovan went to talk to Augie.

"Did you have any problems?" Augie asked Donovan.

"It took some work, but I got 'em all stashed in a safe place."

"Not all of them," Augie said. He lowered his voice. "You forgot to take that antitank gun with you."

"It's not an anti—"

"Yeah, yeah, I know. You told me," Augie said impatiently. "It's a Barrett Bullpup antimateriel rifle. I get that, but it's dangerous having that thing onboard. I was going to throw it over the side but couldn't find it." He glared at Donovan. "Where'd you put it?"

"It's in a safe place," Donovan whispered.

"What if the Armada finds it?"

"They won't." Donovan grinned at him cleverly. "Not where I put it."

He looked up the beach at Alonso walking toward him arm in arm with Doña Estér.

"I see Joe Friday's up early," he said sarcastically.

"Try to play nice," Augie said.

"I don't see Dario," Donovan remarked as Fernando joined them. "Tell me he's not here."

"He stayed at Doña Estér's house to watch Benício," Fernando explained. "Doña Estér said it was not safe for him to come to the restaurant."

"Smart call," Donovan said as Doña Estér and Alonso came closer.

"Remember," Augie said softly. "Play nice."

"I can be nice—watch," Donovan whispered as he smiled broadly at Alonso. "You're up early."

"I had to see if you made it back," Alonso said. "I must admit, I didn't expect you would."

"Your concern is touching," Donovan remarked.

"Did you see the Punta Morro witch?" Fernando asked.

"Fernando," Doña Estér said, admonishing him like a mother.

"That's all right," Donovan said as he recalled the eerie sound the wind made as it swirled around the interior of the caves. "I can see how the legend got its start."

"It's not a legend," Fernando argued. "The caves are truly haunted."

"Ya basta, Fernando. Enough haunted talk," Doña Estér chided him. "Go get breakfast ready. Ándale."

"Sí, señora," he said as he left.

The relationship Doña Estér had with Fernando and all her employees for that matter went beyond that of a mere employer. She treated them like a mother treats her children, and her employees responded in kind.

"Welcome back, Capitán," Doña Estér said. "I trust everything went well?"

"Well enough, I guess," he replied. "You're looking especially radiant this morning."

"Did you have any trouble with the boulders blocking the run up to the caves?" Augie inquired. "Some of them are underwater."

Donovan glanced briefly at Alonso before responding.

"I put in on the north end of Payucán Beach."

"That's a good twenty-five yards from the caves," Augie remarked. "That's a long way to hump a hundred rifles over rocky ground."

"Not if you do it a few at a time," Donovan said, hoping his partner would drop it and change the subject.

"That would've taken you all night," Augie remarked skeptically. "The tide would have started rolling in before you were done."

"I had plenty of time," Donovan responded as he watched Augie walk past him toward the panga.

"I'd like to hear all about it over breakfast," the doña interjected. "Come. Fernando will have it served soon."

Donovan didn't respond as he watched his partner staring pensively into the panga. Augie reached into the bow and pulled out the block pulley he had given him.

"I'll be with you in a minute," Donovan said to Doña Estér as he started for the panga.

"Don't be long," she called to him.

The wheel on the pulley squeaked sharply as Augie gave it a hard spin.

"Doña Estér's got breakfast waiting for us," Donovan said.

"I see you didn't use any of the stuff you asked for." Augie dropped the pulley. "Not the net, the pulley—you didn't even use the rope."

"I didn't need to."

"What'd ya do? Find a place high enough to keep the tide from washing the bundles out to sea?"

"Something like that," Donovan said.

"What are you up to, Skipper?" he asked suspiciously. "It's not like you to talk openly, especially in front of people you hardly know. You're up to something. I just can't figure out what it is."

"All right," he said as they started walking to the restaurant. "I think I know how we're going to get Itzél back and finally be done with El Demonio."

"I'm almost afraid to ask," he remarked apprehensively.

Donovan looked at Augie as the seagulls overhead cawed down on them.

"I'm gonna set up El Demonio."

Augie scoffed. "And here I thought it was going to be something complicated."

"It's a fairly simple plan," Donovan added. "But I'm gonna need a little help to make it work."

"Do tell," Augie remarked sarcastically. "I don't see how you plan to do it with just our help."

Donovan stared at Fernando seating Alonso and Sandy by the beach reentrance. He turned to Augie. "That's why I'm going to the Thunderbolts for help," he said as they got to the Tucán.

The tourists who trickled into the Tucán for breakfast never numbered over a handful at a time before ten o'clock in the morning. Since most of the wait staff didn't come in until eleven, Fernando, Doña Estér's maître d' and driver, confined seating to the section directly in front of the kitchen to better serve them. On those occasions when a group like the Sabancuy Rotary Club wanted to meet at the restaurant for breakfast, Fernando would seat them in the section away from the other diners to afford them some measure of privacy. Knowing that Doña Estér's special guests would need privacy, he seated them at the large round table by the beach entrance.

Donovan and Augie walked into the Tucán and went to sit at the table across from Alonso and Sandy. Fernando served each of them a mixed plate of diced watermelon, cantaloupe, honeydew, and cottage cheese. Donovan removed his white captain's peak hat and hung it on the back of his chair as he watched Doña Estér floating from table to table, attending to her other guests like a butterfly in a flower garden.

"She's quite graceful, wouldn't you say, Capitán?" Alonso remarked.

"Enchanting," Donovan replied as he admired the seductive sway of the delightful doña's dancing derrière.

"She turned down a chance to be a model in Europe," Fernando commented. "Instead, she decided to study medicine."

"Lucky for us she did," Augie remarked. "Benício would have been up a creek if she hadn't." He turned to Fernando. "I've never known anybody to have blood available to them like that outside of a hospital."

"Doña Estér knows people who help her with such things," Fernando explained. "Very quietly."

"Did she say how long Benício would be laid up?' Donovan asked.

"Maybe a week, if that." Augie scoffed. "She didn't think it was bad."

"That's because she's seen a lot worse," Donovan remarked.

"What are you caballeros talking about?" Doña Estér asked as she walked up on them.

"We were just commenting on your expert medical skills," Donovan replied.

"I do what I can," she said modestly. "Dr. Ventura is here."

"Good. I was hoping he'd get here early." Donovan craned his neck to look for him. "Where is he?"

"I saw him in the parking lot talking to a young man," the doña replied. She looked toward the entrance. "Here he comes now."

Donovan turned to look as the professor came toward him with Poli walking one step behind him.

"Well, look at who's coming to breakfast," Augie remarked.

"What's Poli doing here?" Donovan asked the professor.

"I'm sorry, Simon," he replied. "He snuck into the trunk when I wasn't looking."

"He seems to have developed a habit of sneaking in and out of places lately," Donovan remarked.

"How's my father?" Poli asked.

The question seemed to knock the wind out of Donovan. He had never heard Poli call Benício anything other than by his first name.

"He's going to be fine," Doña Estér responded. "He's resting at my home."

"I want to go see him," Poli said impatiently.

"Of course, *mijito,*" Doña Estér said as she turned to Fernando. "Take him to his father. I'll take care of things here."

"Sí, señora." He turned to Poli. "Ven, muchacho."

"Put a cot in Benício's room," Doña Estér added. "See that he has everything he needs."

"Sí, señora."

As Donovan watched Poli follow Fernando out of the restaurant, a waiter set a tray of food on a folding table next to him. He continued to stare with glazed eyes, oblivious to the clatter of the plates and the tinny clanking of silverware as the waiters exchanged the plates of fruit for larger plates with hot food.

"Are you all right, Skipper?" Augie asked him privately.

"Um," Donovan muttered and then cleared his throat. "Yeah. I'm just a little tired, I guess."

"I wonder if I could have a word with you," the professor said to Donovan. He glanced at Alonso. "In private."

"It's all right, Conrad," Donovan replied. "Alonso's onboard. He's agreed to help us." He turned to Alonso. "Right, Alonso?"

"Within reason," the former policeman said warily.

"Of course." Donovan looked at everybody around the table. "Before we go on, I don't think I have to tell anybody how important it is that we don't talk about what we discuss here with anybody else." He turned to Augie and Sandy. "Especially Dario."

Donovan could tell what he said bothered them. Augie and Sandy had gotten close to him on the voyage to Padre Island.

"All Dario wants is to help get Poli's mom back," Sandy commented.

"We can't take a chance he'll tip off El Demonio," Donovan explained.

"He would never do anything to jeopardize Itzél," Augie added. "He really cares about her."

As much as Donovan tried not to let his jealousy show, he could feel his face getting red. He looked at his plate to hide it.

"If you don't trust him, why is he still with you?" Alonso inquired.

"There wasn't time to find a safe place to put him ashore," Donovan replied.

"He saved our lives," Augie added. "We owe him."

Alonso had a suspicious if not skeptical look in his eye as Donovan stared back at him wanting to slap that look off his face.

"Tip El Demonio off about what?" Alonso inquired.

The moment had come for Donovan to lay out his plan, something he had never needed to do in the past. He had always worked alone and handled any problems, however unforeseen, by himself. What he had in mind required the help of others, some reluctant and others unwitting. It relied on human nature, perfect timing, and a lot of luck. It required a steady hand to get all the parts to fit together, however tenuously, much like building a house of cards, and like with a house of cards, one slip, and it would all come crashing down on him.

"I'll get to that," he replied. Donovan turned to the professor. "Did Don Macario talk to El Demonio?"

"Yes," the professor responded. "He's agreed to accept delivery at the warehouse."

"I thought you said you weren't going to give him the guns?" Alonso said sternly.

"I'm not," Donovan replied. "I just need him to believe I am." He resumed his conversation with the professor. "What did Fausto say about trading Itzél for the guns?"

He watched the professor squirm uncomfortably in his chair.

"He insists on holding on to her until after he sees the guns."

"That's not unreasonable."

"At his house in Lorenzo," the professor added reluctantly. "He said you can pick her up there after he inspects the weapons."

The mood at the table turned somber as they all turned to Donovan.

"That's perfect," Donovan said.

"How is that perfect?" Augie inquired dubiously.

"It tells us where she'll be and buys us time," Donovan explained. He turned to Doña Estér. "I need to get a message to Don Macario. Do you have something to write with?"

"Of course," she replied. "I'll go get it."

"I'll also need an envelope and some Scotch tape!" he called to her as she left the table.

"Buy time to do what?" Alonso asked curiously.

"Set up El Demonio and a rescue," he replied.

"How do you plan to set him up?" Alonso asked.

"I'll get to that," he replied as he waited for Doña Estér to return to the table.

He pulled a chair out for her as she looked at him curiously and handed him the tape dispenser and the writing materials. Donovan sat down and began writing as he explained.

"The last time I was here, I got braced by some weasel-faced punk and an ape with a gold-plated smile in a police uniform," Donovan began.

"That would be Cisco Cisneros and Comandante Norias," Alonso commented.

"Somehow they knew about El Demonio hitting me up to bring a load of guns to him from Texas and threatened to burn my ship if I did," Donovan continued. "I was in the middle of telling him he had nothing to worry about when the Thunderbolts burst into the restaurant and disarmed Cisco's men."

"It was really quite exciting," the professor added. "These masked men dressed in black sprang out of nowhere and …"

The professor stopped when he noticed everyone staring at him. "Sorry."

Donovan used the distraction to go over what he had written. After a brief pause, he continued to lay out the groundwork for his plan.

"The colonel also knew about El Demonio's desire to use my ship. He wanted me to help him take the guns from him," Donovan said as he finished writing his note. "He was disappointed when I told him I had already turned El Demonio down."

"He'll think you lied to him when he finds out you did it after all," Alonso commented.

"He already knows," Donovan said as he folded the paper and slipped it into the envelope. "I told him."

"When did you get a chance to talk to him?" Augie inquired.

"I put in at Huayahaca on the way back from Punta Morro and called him," Donovan explained. "He told me when he gave me his card to call if I ever needed his help. Well"—Donovan paused as he sealed the envelope with his tongue—"I need his help."

"I hope you're not thinking about giving *him* the guns?" Alonso said cautiously.

"Of course not," Donovan retorted as he wrote Don Macario's name on the front of the envelope.

"What did the colonel say?" Alonso asked.

"He wants to see me this afternoon to talk about it."

"He's going to want something in return," Alonso warned.

Donovan flipped the letter over and signed it across the V-shaped edge of the flap.

"I'm gonna serve up El Demonio on a silver platter for him," Donovan responded. "What more could he want?"

"Ha!" Alonso blurted. "Just how do you intend to do that?"

"By sneaking his men into El Demonio's warehouse—Trojan Horse style," Donovan replied.

Donovan stared across the table at Alonso, who looked back at him curiously. He turned to his shipmates, who had the faces of a pair of barn owls. He glanced at the professor, who looked catatonic and then at Doña Estér, who looked as cool and lovely as Emma Peele waiting to learn her part in the scheme.

"Suppose you succeed in sneaking the Thunderbolts into the warehouse—Trojan Horse style like you say. How are you going to get them out? The Armada is just up the coast. They'll have a gunboat and a platoon of marines at the port"—he snapped his fingers—"like that."

"Good." Donovan retorted unexpectedly. "I'm gonna need them to crash the party. They shouldn't have any trouble taking El Demonio and the Thunderbolts."

"What about your ship and crew?" Alonso asked.

"By the time the Armada gets there, Augie'll have the ship home at the Paradise Lagoon, and I'll be well on my way to Lorenzo to get Itzél."

"A double double cross," the professor remarked softly. "How delightfully … insidious."

"It'll never work," Alonso said. "The colonel will never go for it."

"I think he will," Donovan said as he ripped a strand of tape from the dispenser. "Dario told me the colonel is not above taking a chance if he sees an opportunity for a big payoff." He taped over his signature. "He'll go for it."

"What about the guns?" Alonso inquired.

"I'm not telling him about the guns."

"What if he knows you have them?" Alonso countered. "He's going to want them."

"I'm betting he'll be more interested in taking out El Demonio. I got the sense he wanted to do that personally the last time we talked."

As Donovan waited for Alonso to fire the next volley of questions, it appeared to him that the cynical former municipal policeman had his eyes on something behind him. Donovan glanced over his shoulder but could not see anything that could possibly attract his attention. He looked back at Alonso, who continued to gaze blankly into the void.

"Something on your mind?" Donovan asked him.

"Hmm?" Alonso said as he looked at him. "Oh, nothing."

"You seemed distracted."

"I was just thinking about your plan," Alonso explained. "You seem to have everything figured out."

"Not everything," Donovan countered. "The Federal Preventive Police at the port could spot my ship dropping anchor and send a launch to check me out. I need to make sure that nobody crashes the party unexpectedly."

"That could be a problem," Alonso commented.

"Another thing," Donovan added. "Fausto is short of men, and he could recruit one of the gangs to help him with the guns."

"Most likely Comandante Briones and Los Chinos," Alonso speculated. "Seyba Playa is part of his plaza. He's nearby and would have an interest in seeing the guns delivered."

"That's what I'm afraid of," Donovan commented. "I need a diversion, something to keep them occupied so that they don't show up unexpectedly and cause the colonel to call off the operation."

"That makes sense," Alonso agreed.

"Can you help me?"

"How? "Alonso scoffed. "By starting a fire?"

"In a way," Donovan retorted. "El Demonio's got the gangs convinced the Norteño cartel wants to get take over Campeche. He's been using Cisco's trash talk about taking Champotón to do it. I need you to make it look like he's coming."

Donovan saw that faraway look return to Alonso's face and gave him time to work out whatever he had on his mind.

"Simon, if I may," the professor said. "There were several fire-bombings in Champotón early this morning."

"Did they say who was behind it?" Donovan asked.

"The public safety director blamed the Norteños for the attacks at a press conference."

"There you go," Donovan said to Alonso. "The stage's already been set. All you have to do is get Comandante Briones to believe Cisco's coming in full force."

Alonso didn't say anything as he continued to stare contemplatively into the void. Donovan glanced at his shipmates and then at Doña Estér and the professor.

"Do you know Comandante Briones?" Doña Estér asked Alonso.

"No," Alonso responded. "But I know Comandante Sánchez. I think he still has influence over him."

"Any chance you can convince Sánchez that Cisco's raiding Champotón in the next night or two?" Donovan asked.

"Won't that compromise your plan?" Alonso inquired. "What if Briones goes to El Demonio for help against Cisco? He could put off the delivery."

"He could, but I don't think so," Donovan responded. "From what Dario tells me, El Demonio's desperate to get the guns."

"What's gonna happen when Cisco doesn't show?" Augie proposed.

"Hopefully, it'll be all over by then," Donovan replied. He turned to Alonso. "What do you say?"

Alonso sat with the corners of his mouth turned down and his arms crossed as he stared at Donovan. Donovan stared back at him as he waited for an answer. Up to that point, the cynical ex-policeman had only expressed his skepticism and pessimism and didn't seem inclined to want to get involved.

"You'll need to do something about the federal police at the port," Alonso commented. "I can help with that."

"Then you'll do it?" Donovan asked eagerly.

"Sure. When do you want to do it?"

"Let me get a few things lined up first," he said as he hung his elbow on the back of the chair. He turned to Doña Estér and handed her the envelope. "Can you see that Don Macario gets this?"

"Of course," she said.

"Well," Donovan said as he stood and looked at his watch, "I'd better try to get a little shut-eye before I go see the colonel."

CHAPTER 7

As Fausto López sat behind his desk in the small office at Don Rodrigo's warehouse waiting for Felipe to bring Comandante Villegas to him, he thought about how his plan to lead the Campeche gangs in a war against Colonel Aníbal Barca Rayos had started to unravel.

Not everything had fallen into place for him like he had hoped. He had succeeded in duping Don Rodrigo into retaining Comandante Sánchez and the police commanders controlling the gangs as the Campechano's security wing. He had successfully driven a wedge between the comandantes and Sánchez by showing them how to extort money from the legal and illegitimate businesses in their plazas but had not expected that to dissolve their cohesiveness. Only the threat he fabricated of a hostile takeover by the Norteño cartel had kept them from completely severing ties with each other. Many did not believe it and had adopted a wait-and-see attitude. He needed something to make that threat more real to unite them under his command. He had hoped that luring Cisco Cisneros into launching a raid against the Campechano holdings in Champotón would do that. However, it fell far short of what he wanted.

Fausto stood when he heard Comandante Villegas protesting boisterously as Felipe and Daniel brought him into the office and forced him to sit in a chair across from his desk. Felipe handed the policeman's revolver to El Demonio, who put the gun into a drawer in the desk.

"Why was I brought here this way?" Villegas said angrily. "You don't realize who you're dealing with here."

López stared at him coldly as the comandante pointed his thumb proudly at his badge.

"Take a good look at this," Villegas said proudly as he tried to stand. "I'm not just anybody. I *am* a comandante in the Champotón transit police."

Daniel shoved him rudely into his chair as Fausto looked at him unimpressed.

"What you are—*comandante*—is a thief," Fausto said sternly. "I paid you good money to arrange for Cisneros to raid Champotón, and you failed miserably."

"I did what you asked," Villegas countered. "I can't help it if the Norteños didn't hit the targets you wanted."

"You told me you could get Cisco to attack the dealerships and the warehouse."

"I told you I could get him to attack Champotón," Villegas argued. "I didn't guarantee he would attack anything specific."

"That's not what you said," Fausto said sharply. "You told me that you could get them to hit the Campechanos' businesses."

"I told you I would suggest it to Norias. It's not my fault he didn't pass it on to Cisco." Villegas eased himself back into his chair. "Why are you complaining?" he said calmly, toning down the pitch of the conversation. "The raid accomplished its purpose."

Fausto had counted on having the Norteños firebomb the Campechano holdings to shake the gangs' sense of security and to shock them into believing that they needed his leadership to defeat the Thunderbolts.

"He's right, jefe," Felipe interjected. "El Chino's called a meeting with the other comandantes to discuss the raid."

"It looks like they believe the Norteños are coming now," Daniel added enthusiastically.

"It won't be long before they ask you to lead them, jefe," Felipe added.

Fausto looked at his yes men curiously, sensing that they had left something out they didn't want to tell him.

"Where are they meeting?" Fausto inquired.

Felipe's eyes danced from side to side as Fausto stared at him intently with his odd-colored eyes.

"At the cantina," he replied reluctantly.

"Sánchez's cantina?" Fausto asked.

Felipe swallowed apprehensively. "Sí, jefe."

The vein on Fausto's forehead began to swell as his rage started to rise. The swivel chair screeched sharply as Fausto sat in it gently. He closed his eyes and pinched the bridge of his nose to calm himself.

"Is Sánchez going to be there?" he asked calmly.

Felipe licked his lips.

"That's my understanding," he replied reluctantly.

"I don't understand," Fausto said to himself softly as he put his elbows on his desk and held his head in his hands. "They should have come to me. I trained them. I showed them how to raise money to buy guns. I'm the one with experience fighting the colonel."

"Don't you mean you have experience losing to the colonel?" Villegas asked sarcastically. "As for showing them how to raise money to buy guns"—he scoffed—"where are the guns?"

Villegas either didn't know of or ignored Fausto's reputation for his bouts of rage. He foolishly continued to taunt him.

"The gangs have lost confidence in you," Villegas added as El Demonio raised his head to look at him. "You've become a joke."

"Where are you getting this?" Fausto asked him. "How would you know what they're thinking? You're an outsider."

"You're the outsider," Villegas retorted. "I'm a comandante like them. They talk to me."

"What else are they saying?" Fausto asked as he struggled to keep from losing control.

"Some are saying maybe it's better to go back to the old arrangement Comandante Sánchez had with the Commission," he replied. "At least they know he can get guns from them. He's done it before."

The vein on Fausto's forehead seemed ready to burst as his face turned crimson and his odd-colored eyes glowered angrily at Villegas.

"The guns Sánchez gets from the Commission are junk," Felipe interjected. "Half of them don't work."

The guns at issue originated in Central America, primarily surplus AK-47 rifles left over from the civil wars in Nicaragua and El Salvador during the 1980s. Most had spent decades underground wrapped in plastic and newspapers, others squirreled away in attics and closets, and others in government armories where they saw little to no maintenance.

"Those that are beyond repair are stripped for parts and used to fix the others that only need a part or two to work," Villegas argued.

"But for how long?" Fausto commented skeptically. "The guns are worn out. The ones I can get them are brand new."

"You keep saying that, but so far you haven't produced a single one," Villegas retorted. "You've failed every time you've tried to get a shipment through. First at Punta Morro and now with the shipment you sent Dónovan to Texas to get."

El Demonio glanced angrily at Felipe, who shook his head and hunched his shoulders. He turned to look at Villegas for an explanation.

"Chino told me about the shipment you were expecting," Villegas added.

Fausto stared bitterly at Villegas. "Briones talks too much."

"Too bad. Comandante Briones was looking forward to getting a brand-new Cuerno de Chivo," he remarked, using Mexican slang for an AK-47 rifle. "He really believed you were going to succeed this time." He stood and held out his hand. "My sidearm, please."

"Where do you think you're going?" Fausto asked sternly.

"I'm going to the meeting, of course," Villegas replied. "Now, if you'd be so kind as to give me my revolver."

"When is this meeting?" Fausto asked as he opened the drawer to get Villegas's revolver.

"Later this afternoon," he replied with a smirk on his face. "If you want, I'll see if I can get you invited."

"No, thanks," Fausto said as he pointed the revolver at Villegas. "I have other plans."

A shot rang out as Fausto pulled the trigger. Villegas looked stunned as he stumbled back, knocking over the chair on his way to the floor. Daniel stood over him and rolled his body over with his foot. Villegas's body shook like a bowl of jelly, his eyes gazing emptily at the sicario.

"He's dead," Daniel said unsympathetically.

Fausto put the revolver on the desk and went to stand over Villegas's body. He squatted over the dead comandante, tore the badge from his shirt, and wedged it into his mouth.

"This is me taking a good look at your badge, Villegas," Fausto said. "You *were* a comandante in the transit police. Now you are a sacrifice for the Santa Muerte." He looked at Daniel. "Take him to the coconut grove and get him ready."

When Dr. Ventura chartered Donovan's ship to survey the shipwreck at the mouth of the Sabancuy Channel, he had no idea that it would take him where it had so far. Besides the stated purpose of the charter, he had had a brush with pirates on a small island, nearly gone on a run across the Gulf of Mexico to pick up a load of illegal weapons, and now was on a collision course between two notorious narco-paramilitaries. He had met some interesting people, some dangerous and some adventurous, but none as lovely and adventurous as Doña Estér.

After breakfast, the professor took Fernando to go get his pickup for Donovan to use. Fernando lived with his wife in the servants' quarters behind Doña Estér's house on the outskirts of town not far from Santa Rosalia beach. As he drove up to the colonial-style stucco house, Fernando told him that it had once belonged to a drug trafficker who had built secret rooms and a small bunker-like basement beneath the house. The house had a walled courtyard attached to it and a covered entrance with high columns.

Dr. Ventura waved at Poli, who sat on a concrete bench just outside of the courtyard as he drove up the crushed-rock driveway and parked under the covered entrance.

"Thank you, Professor," Fernando said as he got out of the car.

The professor looked at Poli in his rearview mirror as the boy sat quietly and stared sadly at the ocean. He decided to go try to cheer him up.

"Hola, Poli," the professor said as he walked up to him. "Why so glum?"

"I'm worried about my mother," he replied as he looked up at him. "Is she going to be all right?"

"Sure, mijito," the professor said as he sat next to him. "Captain Donovan is working on getting her back. She'll be home in the next day or two."

They both turned their heads when they heard Fernando rumbling out on the road in his pickup truck.

"Where's Fernando going so fast?" Poli asked the professor.

"He's taking his truck to the restaurant for Captain Donovan to use before he takes Doña Estér to see Don Macario."

"Where's the skipper going?"

"He's going to ask a very important man to help him get your mother back."

The professor turned to look when he heard the gate to the courtyard open and saw Dario walking toward them.

"Is there anything I can do to help get Poli's mother back?" he asked.

The professor stood and faced him. The famed marine archeologist stood six-foot-three but looked puny standing next to the former vigilante.

"I'm sorry, Dario," the professor said awkwardly. "Simon's asked me not to discuss it with anybody."

"That's okay. I think I know what he's going to do," Dario said. "He's going to trick my cousin to get la señora back."

"I … uh …"

"He needs my help, Professor," Dario added. "If he does what I think he's going to do, he's going to need somebody on the inside to protect her—I can do that."

"I'm afraid Captain Donovan was firm when he said not to involve you."

"He doesn't trust me. I know that." Dario sighed. "He doesn't have to worry about me. I only want to make sure no harm comes to la señora."

"The skipper should let him help," Poli said to the professor. "My mother trusts him."

"I'm sorry, Poli," the professor said before turning to Dario. "It has to be this way."

Dario hung his head and nodded softly. "I understand."

The professor watched him as he returned to the courtyard. Never could he remember seeing a sadder-looking man than Dario at that moment. Poli seemed to believe in his sincerity, as did Augie and Sandy. Still, he had to trust Donovan's instincts, and it concerned him that Dario had guessed that Donovan planned to trick his cousin to get Poli's mother back. He felt he had to warn Donovan.

The professor waited until he saw Dario close the gate behind him before he leaned over to whisper to Poli, "I have to go back to the restaurant and catch Simon before he leaves."

The road north from Sabancuy to Champotón didn't have much to offer in terms of scenery, but it did give Alonso a chance to take his motorcycle on a long ride and clear his head. He thought about his meeting with Comandante Sánchez as he rode down the highway that straddled the Bay of Campeche like an asphalt ribbon separating the ocean from a tangled landscape of shrubs, brush, and high grass that seemed to go on forever. One spot looked very much like the other with nothing of interest to occupy his eye except for the occasional gypsy seaside eatery that sprang up along the beach every few miles or so.

The eateries all looked alike. They had thatched roofs made from dried palm leaves, dirt floors, and no walls except maybe for a skeleton-like divider made from irregularly shaped branches separating the camp-style kitchen from the dining area. They all had portable tables with white plastic chairs that attested to the impermanence if not the portability of the eatery.

Alonso had eaten at *El Cangrejo Loco* before. It served the best grilled fish, shrimp tacos, and steamed blue crabs in that part of the country. Besides the food, Alonso found the husband and wife who ran the gypsy eatery entertaining. The husband, a slender little man with a receding hairline, worked as the waiter, busboy, and dishwasher. His wife, a plump woman of little humor with the tongue of a longshoreman, worked the kitchen as well as the poor man's patience with her incessant nagging.

It amused Alonso to watch the docile little man bolt out of the restaurant when he heard a car approaching, no doubt to escape the constant cacophony of snide remarks. He smiled as he watched him run to the edge of the highway to wave a red flag over his head like a sideshow hawker, spinning the flag slowly at first and then increasing the tempo as the car got nearer. Then suddenly, he saw him snap the flag down sharply and walk briskly back into the eatery, making eye contact with Alonso.

"Policía," he said softly to Alonso as he disappeared into the kitchen.

Alonso watched the two state police cars park beside his motorcycle outside the Cangrejo Loco. He immediately recognized Comandantes Sánchez and Prieto as they got out of their respective cars and came into the restaurant. They barely gave him a glance as they walked past him to the far end of the eatery by the beach. It didn't surprise him that neither man recognized him. He had shaved his head, grown a beard, and put on weight.

As he watched Sánchez and Prieto sit at a portable table, he thought how different they looked despite wearing the same uniform. Comandante Prieto wore his well-pressed, minding the tuck of his shirt and aligning his buttons with the buckle of his gun belt. His boots glistened like patent leather, and he kept his white policemen's peak hat well-formed and spotless. In contrast, the notoriously irascible Comandante Sánchez wore his uniform like an overweight bus driver on a hot summer's day.

He turned to look when he saw the owner run out of the kitchen to attend to the comandantes. The sea breeze blowing in from the ocean carried their voices so that he could hear almost everything they said.

"Dos Cocas, por favor," Prieto said to the nervous bootleg restauranteur.

"Sí, jefe. Con mucho gusto."

Alonso continued to watch them as the owner rushed off to get them their soft drinks. He watched Sánchez test the table for sturdiness by shaking it and then turned away when he saw him looking at his surroundings.

"How much do you think this pendejo makes in a week?" Alonso heard Sánchez ask Prieto.

"It can't be very much," Prieto replied.

Alonso watched the owner return to the table with their drinks.

"¿Algo más?" he heard the little man ask.

"No, gracias," Prieto replied.

The little man scurried back to the kitchen, and Alonso continued to listen in on their conversation as he stared into the kitchen through the gaps in the makeshift wall.

"I bet he has a good little business going here," he heard Sánchez say.

"Leave him alone," he heard Prieto reply. "He's not hurting anyone."

"Cabrón probably doesn't even have a permit."

"He probably can't afford to give you a bite. You might as well close him down."

Then, as he had hoped, Alonso heard Prieto and Sánchez begin to talk about him.

"What do you suppose Andrade wants?" he heard Prieto ask.

"He said he had information about the fire bombings in Champotón."

"Why is he coming to us instead of the AFI or the PFP? He's always kissing their asses."

"Quién sabe," he heard Sánchez reply. "Could be he's afraid the *federales* have lost confidence in him since he abandoned his post."

Alonso turned to look at them, as he couldn't help but glare distastefully at Sánchez. He looked away when he saw Prieto turning his head in his direction.

"Somebody shot him off the road," he heard Prieto say. "I'd hardly consider that abandoning his post."

"If he had any balls, he wouldn't have gone into hiding," he heard Sánchez remark. "Norias filed on the coward for failure to report for duty."

Alonso hung his head to hide his rage as he continued to listen to the conversation.

"I heard it was Norias that set him up."

"That doesn't surprise me. He's been sucking up to Cisco like a two-dollar whore since the Norteños came to town," he heard Sánchez say. "Did you know he complained to the director when I didn't choose him for my task force?"

"Lucky for him you didn't," he heard Prieto say. "It would have been him instead of El Cosario lying on the concrete with his throat cut last Easter."

Alonso raised his head and glanced at the two comandantes sipping from their drinks. He turned his head when he saw Sánchez begin to turn in his direction.

"Do you trust Andrade?" he heard Prieto say.

"He's part of the new breed," he heard Sánchez reply. "He actually wants to serve the public. How can you trust someone like that?"

The owner came out of the kitchen unexpectedly as Alonso finished his soft drink.

"Will you be eating today, Señor Andrade?" the owner asked him.

"No, gracias," he replied as he turned to look at the comandantes.

Both Sánchez and Prieto stared at him intently as he set the empty bottle on the table and got his helmet off the chair next to him. He reached into his pocket as he stood and handed the owner several peso coins.

"Andrade?" he heard Prieto utter in disbelief.

"I'll be joining my friends now," Alonso told the owner as he walked across the dirt floor to sit with Sánchez and Prieto.

Sánchez glared at Alonso as he set his helmet on an empty chair and sat. Prieto looked slightly unnerved as he stared at him curiously.

"Why did you let us walk by you without saying anything?" Sánchez chided him.

"I didn't want to interrupt you," Alonso said as he brushed his beard to cover the scar on his face. "You looked like you were talking about something important."

"Were you eavesdropping on us?" Sánchez asked sternly.

"How could I in this wind?" Alonso asked as he lowered his brow. "I was across the room from you."

"Where have you been?" Prieto asked. "Nobody has seen you since last Easter."

As much as Alonso wanted to let Sánchez know he had heard him call him a coward, he didn't want to antagonize him and ruin what he came there to do.

"I decided to take a leave of absence."

"By deserting your post? That's not very professional," Sánchez said sarcastically. He clicked his tongue repeatedly and shook his head slowly. "Some might even call it cowardice."

Alonso felt the rage rising in him again. He had to resist Sánchez's taunts even if they insulted his sense of honor.

"Let them call it whatever they want. Cisco Cisneros tried to kill me with the help of my shift commander," Alonso said, barely able to keep from raising his voice. "I didn't want to give them another chance to finish what they started."

"So, you decided to hide like a mouse."

"I decided that I couldn't watch my back and do anything about it," Alonso retorted bitterly. "That's why I asked to meet with you."

"I thought it had something to do with Champotón?" Prieto interjected.

"It does," he said as he turned to Prieto. Looking at Sánchez, he continued, "Cisco is planning a raid on Champotón."

"Aren't you just a little late with that?" Sánchez scoffed. "His people hit the city this morning."

"That was just a probe," Alonso explained. "He's coming in full force in the next couple of days."

The two comandantes looked at each other.

"How do you know this?" Prieto inquired.

"Let's just say I know and leave it at that," Alonso replied.

"How?" Sánchez asked.

"You don't need to know that."

"What do you expect us to do with this?" Sánchez asked skeptically.

"That's up to you," Alonso replied. "All I ask is that I have a hand in it."

"Why?" Prieto inquired.

"Cisco and Norias tried to kill me." Alonso looked at him. "Do I have to explain any further?"

"Why are you telling us?" Prieto asked. "Why not go to the AFI or the PFP?"

"Because they'll cut me out," Alonso replied. "I want to be there when you stop Cisco and his sicarios."

Sánchez folded his arms and sat back. "Stop them how?"

"You're the leader of the Campeche gangs," Alonso replied. "Surely, with your experience and cunning, you can come up with something."

Comandante Sánchez just stared at Alonso, not knowing whether to take his remarks as a compliment or sarcasm.

"There's only one road into Champotón from Ciudad del Carmen," Prieto pointed out to Sánchez. "We can set up an ambush—at Villamar."

"My thoughts exactly," Sánchez agreed.

Prieto turned to Alonso. "We'll have to know when they're coming."

"My guess is in the next day or two during the night or the predawn," Alonso responded.

"Your guess?" Sánchez remarked skeptically. "Can't you find out?"

Alonso swallowed as he looked at the cantankerous comandante.

"What's the matter? You don't look so confident anymore," Sánchez remarked brusquely. "Do you know for sure Cisco's coming, or is it just speculation?"

"He's coming," Alonso retorted confidently as he took his helmet off the chair. "If you choose not to believe me, I can pass the information to El Demonio." Alonso reached into his pocket for a couple of coins and tossed them on the table. "I'm sure he won't squander the opportunity."

"Can you find out when?" Comandante Prieto asked.

"I can do better than that. I'll call you when they're leaving for Champotón." Alonso glanced at Sánchez as he started to leave. "Just be ready when I call."

"If you're lying to me, muchacho, there'll be hell to pay," Sánchez said menacingly.

Alonso glared at him for a moment and then left.

The waterfall where Donovan agreed to meet the colonel sat in the middle of the Chiapas jungle, about twenty kilometers south of the ruins at Palenque. The drive in Fernando's pickup from Sabancuy around the backside of the Laguna de Terminos and across the narrow strip that separated Campeche from Chiapas went smoothly; he had run into only one checkpoint as he left the state of Campeche. That all changed as soon as he entered the Free and Sovereign State of Chiapas.

The region hadn't seen any violence since the Zapatistas laid down their arms and settled into a peaceful coexistence with the Mexican government. However, the fighting between the Comisión's sicarios and the Thunderbolts had destabilized the area, prompting the US State Department to issue a travel advisory. Those sicarios not dispatched by the Thunderbolts turned to banditry, compelling the Zapatistas to dust off their weapons and don their guerrilla uniforms once again to defend their autonomous communities.

At each checkpoint, the soldiers searched Donovan's pickup, using canines trained to detect explosives and mirrors attached to the end of a pole to inspect the undercarriage. They checked his passport and work visa, questioning him only about his destination and purpose for traveling in Chiapas. He found that refreshing in contrast to his meanderings around the Campeche coastline.

From Palenque, he drove south on the road to San Cristóbal de las Casas for about twenty kilometers until he reached a sign pointing the way to the waterfall. He drove down the side road for a mile or so to a small area cut out for parking. The recent trouble in Chiapas had driven off the normal flow of tourists visiting the natural wonder, causing the souvenir shops and eateries to close.

Donovan heard the waterfall as soon as he got out of the pickup and started down a path toward the sound. He followed it through the jungle until he came to a clearing where he saw the water cascading over a limestone cliff, dropping over a hundred feet into a clear pool of water with a thin veil of mist drifting surrealistically across it.

"Beautiful," Donovan heard someone behind him say.

He turned and saw Colonel Barca standing with Major Zamora to his right and a hard-jawed, ill-humored man to his left. All three men dressed in street clothes but in no way resembled common tourists.

In all his years delivering cargo across the Caribbean and Central and South America, Donovan had developed a sense for telling the difference between the true tourist and people who wanted to look like one.

He could spot a businessman the easiest. They had wandering eyes and behaved saucily, particularly in bars and restaurants.

A few had better control of their libidos. Those who did seemed withdrawn or uncomfortable with their surroundings. Most seemed ignorant or oblivious to the local customs and demonstrated a disrespect for the local culture. Very few spoke the language, most drawing from their high school Spanish or French, which they spoke poorly with thick gringo accents.

The American military had personnel across the region, and he could spot them more easily. They generally traveled in pairs, had tight haircuts, and exuded a distinct military bearing. They all seemed to have a working knowledge of the local language and behaved professionally if not courteously. However, when they let their hair down, *saucy* didn't even begin to describe it.

He had even developed a knack for spotting intelligence operatives. They tended to pass themselves off as mature, unassuming businessmen; they dressed low key and generally kept to themselves. The older ones tended to drink too much but always kept themselves under control. They didn't mingle much, kept their conversations shallow and brief when they did, and refrained from commenting on current events, especially politics. They pretended to ignore who came into or left a room or to show an interest in their surroundings, their biggest tell. They always seemed to have a mastery of the language and more than a passing familiarity with the local culture.

"You remember the major," the colonel said. He glanced at the hard-jawed man. "This is Sergeant Reséndez."

"Mucho gusto," Donovan said to him graciously. The hard-nosed sergeant did not reciprocate the gesture.

"Don't mind the sergeant," the colonel said. "It takes time for him to warm up to people."

"Reminds me of a pit bull I had to put down."

"An interesting comparison," the colonel commented. "But I must warn you, he can be twice as vicious."

"That must explain why he's twice as ugly," Donovan remarked.

The sergeant contorted his face angrily as he glared at Donovan.

"Tell me more about this trip you made for Fausto López," the colonel said.

Donovan turned to look at the waterfall. "Like I told you when I called, I was forced to make it." He looked at the colonel. "He threatened to kill somebody very important to me."

"Yes, I know," the colonel responded. "Itzél Canek."

Donovan looked at him curiously.

"I know all about it," the colonel added.

"Then you understand why I had to go."

"Oh, I understand," he replied. "What I don't understand is why you waited so long to call me."

"There wasn't time," Donovan explained. "El Demonio strapped me with three goons to make sure I made the voyage."

"Felipe, Beto, and Dario Róbles," the colonel said, again surprising Donovan with what he knew. "I agree to your characterization of Felipe and Beto as goons but not when it comes to Dario."

Donovan cocked his brows. "I understand you worked with him in Michoacán."

"I'd like to think we were friends," he responded unequivocally. "I've never known a man as loyal as Dario." He sighed regretfully. "Unfortunately, it's misplaced with Fausto López." He looked at him bitterly. "Is he among the dead you left on the beach at Padre Island."

"Look, Colonel," Donovan said, taking exception to the question. "I don't know how you're getting your information, but I didn't have anything to do with killing those men on the beach."

"What happened to the men Fausto sent with you?" Colonel Barca countered. "I can't imagine a scenario short of you killing them to take back your ship."

Donovan just stared at the exceptionally perceptive colonel.

"Was Dario killed?"

Donovan was no great hand at reading body language, but he did see genuine concern in the colonel for the gentle narco-paramilitary.

"No," Donovan responded.

"Arrested?"

"No."

"If he wasn't killed or arrested, how is it you were able to take back your ship? The Dario I knew would have stopped you or died trying."

"I guess he just decided to sit this one out."

"I find that hard to believe."

"In fact, he even helped us escape."

"Why would he do that?"

"It's simple really," Donovan began. "When he realized he literally was in the same boat we were, he knew he only had three options. He could either join his compadres in Davy Jones's locker, do time as a guest of the state of Texas, or help us get away."

The colonel looked curiously at Donovan as he waited for the next barrage of questions.

"Where is Dario now?" Colonel Barca asked.

"I don't think he wants you to know."

"I'd like to talk to him."

"I'm not sure he wants to talk to you."

"He will when he learns what I have to offer him," the colonel said confidently. "If he did what you say he did, Fausto will kill him if he goes back to Campeche."

Nothing would have satisfied Donovan more than getting Dario off his hands. Despite all he had done to help his crew get away from the Devil's Elbow, he couldn't help but not trust him. He still worried that the gentle giant had a hidden agenda. His presence also jeopardized not only him and his crew but Doña Estér as well. It could mean a long jail term if the authorities discovered any of them hiding him. Dario had expressed a desire to lead a normal life, and Donovan felt he owed him at least that.

"Dario's changed," Donovan said. "He told me he wants a normal life. He's through with your world."

"Nonsense," the colonel retorted. "He is as much a part of my world as you are a part of yours."

Donovan chose to ignore the colonel's remark. He knew what he meant but didn't want to discuss it.

"Anybody can change," he responded.

"You say that like you really believe it, Capitán," the colonel remarked.

"Why shouldn't I?"

He looked at the colonel as a twisted smile came to his face gradually.

"That's right," the colonel conceded, albeit sarcastically. "You're just a simple schooner captain, and the *Moonlight Runner* is just a simple charter boat."

"She's the *Siete Mares* now," Donovan responded. "And despite what you may believe, I was never anything more than a shipping agent and not the smuggler you make me out to be."

"Just like the *Moonlight Runner*—I'm sorry—the *Siete Mares* was never a smuggling vessel? Really, Capitán Donovan. Have you never read Shakespeare?"

"You mean that thing about roses?"

"A smuggler by any other name ..." the colonel added.

"Like I told you before, I'm no smuggler," Donovan said firmly. "And Dario wants to live a normal life."

"He'll never live a normal life," the colonel said bluntly. "He's too well-known and made an untold number of enemies when he was a vigilante. He'll be discovered and dead within a year."

"That's his choice," Donovan countered.

"I'll be the judge of that," the colonel said confidently. "I know him infinitely better than you do. Let me talk some sense into him."

Donovan couldn't help but feel a little sorry for Dario. He too had his doubts about his chances alone in the world.

"The best I can do is pass along a message."

The colonel inhaled deeply and released it slowly as he gazed at Donovan.

"Now that that's settled, let's get back to the matter at hand," Colonel Barca said. "Do you still insist you didn't come away with any guns?"

The art of interrogation has a basic premise: to filter through the deception, omissions, and half-truths to get to the truth. A skilled interrogator never goes into an interview without knowing the answers to as many of the questions he plans to ask as possible. The way that the colonel posed the question left little doubt in Donovan's mind that he knew he had.

"I got a few rifles."

"I'm told somewhere in the neighborhood of a hundred Romanian AK-47 rifles."

"A hundred and ten," Donovan retorted. "Who've you been talkin' to?"

"I'm a professional intelligence officer," the colonel retorted. "Where are the guns now?"

"In a safe place."

"Where?"

"I'd rather not say."

"I'll get it out of him," Sergeant Reséndez said aggressively.

"Give it your best shot, sugar cheeks," Donovan said as he clenched his fist.

"Stand down, Sargento," the colonel ordered. He turned to Donovan. "I understand your reluctance to tell me. You want something in exchange for them. Is that the proposition you wanted to make?"

"Not exactly."

The colonel sat on a boulder on the side of the path. "Tell me then—exactly."

Donovan listened to the sound of the water crashing into the pool. He glanced at Major Zamora, who looked at him attentively, and then at Reséndez, who glowered at him like a vicious dog through a chain-link fence.

"Fausto is holding Itzél at his plantation house in Lorenzo. He's threatening to kill her if I don't deliver the guns to him," Donovan explained.

"I can't let you do that," the colonel commented.

"I don't intend to," Donovan countered. "I was thinking that instead of delivering the guns, I could deliver a team of your men to take him out."

The colonel glanced at the major. "Where is he expecting you to deliver the guns?"

"At the old Campechano warehouse at the Port of Seyba Playa."

The colonel turned to Major Zamora, who resumed the questioning.

"Have you been to this warehouse?" the major asked.

"No, but I know someone who has."

"Dario?"

Donovan didn't answer as he removed a paper from his shirt pocket, unfolded it, and handed it to the major, who looked at it briefly.

"This looks pretty detailed," the major remarked as he handed the diagram to the colonel.

"There's a dock at the back of the building and trap doors on the roof and in the floor over the water," Donovan explained. "You can use them to sneak your men into the building."

"Where will Fausto be?" Colonel Barca asked.

"There's an office in the southwest corner of the building. He'll probably be in there with his goons."

"Why not in the warehouse?" Major Zamora asked.

Donovan remembered what Dario had told him. "He doesn't have any reason to go in there."

"Does he keep anything in the warehouse?" Colonel Barca inquired.

An idea came to Donovan that could help him convince the colonel to go along with his plan. However, he didn't want to seem too eager and risk spooking him instead.

"As far as I know, he doesn't," Donovan replied. "Except ..."

"Except what?" Major Zamora bit.

Donovan looked at the major and then at the colonel. "There're some crates by some old containers at the back. I've heard he sometimes keeps guns and explosives in them."

"Does he have anything in there now?" Colonel Barca asked.

"I don't know, but I can try to find out," Donovan replied.

Colonel Barca turned to Major Zamora. They looked at each other as if conferring telepathically. Donovan listened to the sound of the water crashing into the pool from above as he waited for their decision.

"How many men does López normally have around him?" Major Zamora asked.

"I've never seen him with more than a few."

"Weapons?"

"I've only seen handguns," Donovan replied. "But that doesn't mean they won't have anything heavier."

Major Zamora knelt by the colonel to discuss Donovan's proposal privately. Donovan waited for his decision, betting on Dario's assessment that the colonel would take a chance to pull a coup if he saw an opportunity. If Dario had it right, his plan to rescue Itzél had a greater chance of working. Not only that, the Thunderbolts would bring an end to El Demonio's presence in Campeche, leaving him to pursue his dreams with Itzél and Poli at his side. If not, he would have wasted a day and had to go it alone.

"Your proposition is ... *intriguing*, but I feel I haven't heard all of it," the colonel said as he gave the diagram back to the major. "You obviously came here to get help to rescue your woman."

"I think I know where Fausto's keeping her at his plantation house," Donovan began. "It's just up the coast from the port. I figured I could get her while you're taking him out."

"I can't spare any men," the colonel commented.

"I wasn't going to ask for any," Donovan retorted. "I shouldn't have any problems getting her out on my own."

The colonel and the major again looked at each other without saying anything. After a moment, Colonel Barca looked at Donovan.

"When is Fausto expecting the guns?" he asked.

"Whenever I tell him I'm ready."

"Tell him you'll be ready tomorrow at midnight."

"I can do that."

"I want to launch the operation by sunset," the major added. "To allow for contingencies."

"The tide'll be up, so that shouldn't be a problem."

"Where do we meet the boat?"

"Ship," Donovan said, correcting the major. "There's a pier in Isla Aguada near the bridge. I'll be there right at sunset."

"Can your ship handle a ten-man team?" Major Zamora asked.

"They'll have to ride on the deck. There isn't room enough below."

He watched the major turn to the colonel as he waited for his decision.

"Any last thoughts, mí Coronel?" the major asked him.

The colonel stood and looked at the waterfall. Donovan watched the mist rising slowly from the pool before the light breeze dispersed the vaporous veil.

"What are your plans for the guns?" the colonel asked Donovan.

"I'm getting rid of them."

"Any chance I can persuade you to sell them to me?"

"Sorry, Colonel, I'm not in the gunrunning business," Donovan replied. "I only kept them this long as a last resort. Once I get Itzél back, I'm deep-sixing 'em."

CHAPTER 8

As a matter of practice, Comandante Norias always came to the café on Ciudad del Carmen's Norte Beach in the late afternoon for a cup of café con leche, which basically involves a cup of strong joe with a healthy helping of cold milk. He didn't go there for the coffee or the milk. He didn't like either. He went there to flirt with a twenty-one-year-old waiter, who waited on tables by day and danced in drag by night.

The comandante started coming to the café when it first opened as a Cuban sandwich shop. The owner bought it to keep his new wife busy while he toiled offshore on an oil platform. The dark-eyed Cubana with long legs, a plump posterior, and a love of dancing had no skills other than a knack for making Cuban sandwiches. Unfortunately, the doe-eyed dancing darling knew as much about running a business as she did about fidelity.

To the comandante's delight, a group of businessmen bought the business and turned it into a coffeehouse by day and cabaret by night. Like him, they enjoyed the company of other men and wanted a place where their fellow travelers could congregate without fear of judgment.

They renamed the business "Café Olé" and served coffee-based beverages, including café au lait during the day. At night, the café turned into a gay bar with a floorshow featuring a flamboyant array of singing and dancing drag queens.

The comandante had an eye for the androgynous young waiter and for the last year had tried unsuccessfully to woo him into a romantic relationship. The waiter did not lead him on, but he also did little to discourage him. They did develop a sort of friendship over time. The waiter teased him with an occasional double entendre while the comandante liked to brag about his involvement in the world of drug trafficking.

Norias stared at the waiter as he brought a cup of café con leche to the table. At first glance, the waiter could pass for a sleek female with a smooth complexion and reddish-brown hair. Like the other waiters at the café, he wore a white muscle shirt, black slacks, and a narrow belt. However, unlike the others, he wore his clothes skin-tight to showcase his curves.

"Are you dancing tonight, querida?" Comandante Norias asked flirtatiously as he tugged gently on his muscle shirt.

"Why?" the waiter replied, slapping his hand with his fingertips. "Are you coming to see me?"

Before the comandante could respond, his cell phone began to ring. He took it off the table and stepped away to take the call. He stared at the effeminate waiter as he spoke into the cell phone, making no effort to keep him from hearing his end of the conversation.

"Sí, jefe," he said as he glanced at the waiter. "I'll take care of everything."

The comandante smiled haughtily at him as he ended the call and walked back to the table.

"What are you so happy about?"

"That was my new boss," Norias replied as he sat. "I might be moving to Champotón soon."

"Are you retiring?"

"More like moving up in the world," he said cryptically as he laid his cell phone back on the table.

"Are you getting promoted?"

"You might say that."

"Tell me," the waiter said as he stomped one foot like a bratty teenage girl. "Don't play games with me."

The comandante chuckled as he watched the prissy young man. "You're looking at the future Norteño cartel plaza boss for Champotón," he said as he put his hands behind his head and leaned back in his chair. "Want to move there with me?"

"Hah!" The waiter covered his mouth and looked around, embarrassed by his outburst. "Why would I want to do that?" he whispered.

The comandante looked at the layout of the outdoor café nestled across the street from Norte Beach with an unlimited view of the Bay of Campeche. He looked at the marquee by the street advertising that night's floorshow. He turned to the waiter with a deadpan look on his face.

"How would you like your own place by the ocean in Champotón?"

"Don't toy with me," the waiter replied. "You know it's always been my dream to have my own place."

"I'm not toying with you," Norias insisted. "I can make your dream come true."

The waiter folded his girlish arms across his chest and stared at the comandante cynically. "You're not just saying that to get in my pants?"

"I'm serious," Norias replied. "We've already set our plan to take the plaza from the local gang in motion. It's just a matter of time before Champotón is ours."

The comandante stared lustfully at the waiter as he looked at him skeptically.

"When do I have to give you an answer?"

"Take your time, but don't wait too long," Norias replied as he put his hand on the waiter's hip. "So, are you dancing tonight?" Norias asked as he caressed him. "If not, maybe we can do something together."

This time, the waiter didn't slap his hand as they looked deeply into each other's eyes.

"I can ask for the day off," the waiter said as he glanced at Norias's phone on the table. "Call me this afternoon."

"I don't have your number."

"I'll enter it on your contact list," the waiter said as he picked up the cell phone and looked at the screen before working the phone expertly with both thumbs. "You'll find it under Café Olé."

Norias didn't realize that the waiter, who had an eidetic memory, had looked at the top number listed under recent calls and memorized it.

"Call me after you get off work," the waiter said as he returned the cell phone. "I'll let you know if they let me off."

The entrance to El Demonio's estate sat south of the hamlet of San Lorenzo well off the highway down a private road cut out of the thicket. Don Macario watched the scenery change dramatically from scrubby trees and underbrush to coconut palms as Quino drove the satin-colored Range Rover through the gates. He gazed at the impressive colonial-style house at the end of the drive. The marble columns, the Spanish-style red-tile roof, and the white stucco facade looked worthy of a prince. Across the lush green lawn sat a quaint little cottage, similar in construction but lacking the ornate trimmings of the old plantation house. Don Macario aimed his miniature camera at it and started taking pictures of it in rapid succession.

"See that house off to your left?" Don Macario said to Quino as he handed him the camera.

"You mean the servants' quarters."

"That's where Captain Donovan believes Itzél is being kept," he explained. "I want you to keep an eye on that cottage. Make note of who goes in and out. See if you can determine how many people are in there."

"Sí, Don Macario," Quino responded as they drove up to the colonial house. "Will you be long?"

"López agreed to let me see Itzél, to prove she's being treated well," Don Macario replied. "I don't expect that'll he'll let me be alone with her. This could be a very short visit."

"Sí, Don Macario."

Felipe, El Demonio's lawyer and lead sicario, stood on the red concrete veranda beside San Juana, the plump, silver-headed housekeeper waiting for the Range Rover to park. Quino opened the door for Don Macario, who stepped out of the sports utility vehicle dressed in a camel-colored tropical-weight suit, wearing a Panama hat.

"Bienvenidos, Don Macario. I am Felipe," he said graciously as he went to meet the old gentleman. "I will take you to Señor López."

"My driver has stomach problems," Don Macario said as he glanced at Quino. "Can he use your facility?"

Felipe turned to San Juana. "Take him to the servants' bathroom."

"Sí, Señor Felipe," she responded. She turned to Quino. "Ven, joven," she said, telling Quino to follow her.

"Sí, señora," Quino said as he glanced at Don Macario.

Don Macario removed his hat to block Felipe's view of him, signaling Quino to exercise vigilance with a tap of his finger to the side of his left eye.

Felipe escorted Don Macario through the house, down a corridor, and out a sliding door to the red concrete veranda that ran all along the back of the house under an overhang supported by white marble columns. El Demonio sat with Itzél at a rattan patio table with a glass top under a tropical-style ceiling fan.

"This way, señor," Felipe said to Don Macario.

The sicario showed him to the table and then went to stand by the patio door. Don Macario stood across from Itzél and Fausto holding his Panama hat by the pinch.

"Are you all right?" Don Macario asked Itzél.

"Yes," she said meekly.

"Have you been mistreated in any way?"

"No," she replied as she glanced briefly at Fausto.

"Poli's safe," Don Macario said to her. "He's with Benício."

"Gracias a Dios," she said as tears welled in her eyes.

"As you can see, she's fine," El Demonio said.

"I need to know she'll remain that way."

"You have my word."

"You'll understand if I ask for more than that," Don Macario countered.

"What do you have in mind?"

"Let me take her with me."

"Not on your life," Fausto replied. "You took advantage of my good nature the last time by moving her."

"You got what you wanted. Donovan went to Padre Island to get your guns," he explained. "You didn't need her anymore."

"But I *did* need her," Fausto countered. "I've yet to get my guns."

Don Macario glanced at Itzél and then turned to Fausto. "Can we speak privately?"

He put on his Panama hat as he stood and waited for Fausto, who waved Felipe over to the table as he stood.

"Make sure she doesn't get lonely," Fausto said to the sicario.

Fausto led Don Macario down the staircase to the lawn. Don Macario stared down the path into the coconut grove leading to the beach.

"Donovan is ready to bring your guns to you," Don Macario said. He turned around slowly to face the plantation house.

"When?"

"Tomorrow at midnight."

"Isn't that a bit melodramatic?"

The old gentleman panned his head slowly from one end of the porch to the other.

"He doesn't want to take a chance the police will interfere like at Padre Island," Don Macario explained.

"Then have him deliver them to my beach like he was supposed to," Fausto suggested.

"He prefers the warehouse," Don Macario responded. He made a slow turn to walk casually along the edge of the coconut grove. "He feels it's safer that way."

Fausto scoffed. "I'm hurt that he doesn't trust me."

Don Macario stopped and panned his head slowly until the servants' quarters came into view. He looked across the lawn at the small white stucco cottage and stared at it as he continued the conversation.

"Trust is a two-way street," Don Macario remarked. "Let me take the woman with me."

"That's out of the question."

"Then bring her to the warehouse," Don Macario countered. "He'll give you your guns after you hand her to him."

"No," Fausto said firmly. "So far, I've had to do all the compromising. He can pick up the girl here after he brings me my guns."

Don Macario turned his head slowly to look at El Demonio. "He wants a guarantee you'll release her unharmed."

"The only guarantee he's going to get is that I'll kill her if he crosses me again."

The young woman sitting alone at a small table at the back of the seafood restaurant buried her head in her menu to avoid the curious eyes of the male diners around her. She dressed modestly, and her clothes hung on her thin frame unremarkably. Even so, with the beauty of her face; the creamy, fair skin; eyes like an ocelot's; and the ash-brown hair she wore in a perky little bob, she turned every man's head when she walked into the restaurant. She had learned a long time ago to ask for a second menu and glass of water to discourage unwanted company whenever she dined alone. That day, however, she agreed to meet a special friend she hadn't seen in a while.

She had heard of Nico's Mariscos, the quaint seafood eatery on Champotón's coastal road, and looked forward to dining there. She wanted to sit outside to watch the sunset but decided against it when she saw a group of bikers sitting on the patio drinking beer and leering at her as she got out of her car. So, she decided to sit as far away as she could from them.

She glanced at the entrance when a man with a buzz haircut wearing a beard walked into the restaurant holding a motorcycle helmet under his arm. As the waiter went to greet him, she covered her face with her menu when she saw the man pointing in her direction. She used the menu as a shield as she watched the waiter leading the man toward her table out of the corner of her eye.

"Adelante, caballero," she heard the waiter say to the man as she continued to stare at her menu.

"Is this seat taken?" she heard the man say.

"I'm expecting somebody," she replied impersonally.

"Me, perhaps?"

She glared at the man curiously for a moment, and then her cat-like eyes widened.

"Alonso?"

"You look lovely today, *mí teniente*," Alonso said as he set his helmet on the floor to sit across from the lieutenant. "How are things at the Armada?"

Lieutenant Linda Maribal had met Alonso shortly after reporting for duty as a junior intelligence officer at the Third Naval Region in Ciudad del Carmen at a gun-trafficking conference hosted by the American Firearms and Explosives Administration. Like her, the handsome Carmen policeman had a fierce sense of duty and a positive outlook for Mexico's future.

She turned to look at the men staring at them and gave them an unfriendly sneer before reaching for Alonso's hands.

"I didn't recognize you," she whispered.

"You don't like my new look?"

She wrinkled her face like she had just bitten into a sour lemon as she looked at his beard and short-cropped hair. She shook her head subtly.

"It doesn't suit you," she replied. "Where have you been? I thought you were ..."

"Dead?"

She took Alonso by the chin and turned his head to look at the fresh scar on his cheek.

"What happened to your face?" she asked.

"I cut myself shaving."

"Don't give me that. I saw your car," she said crossly. "Who shot at you?"

Alonso's jaw tightened. "Cisneros."

"The Norteño?"

"Norias set me up."

Lieutenant Maribal handed her menu to the waiter as he came to the table while Alonso glanced at his.

"I'll have iced tea, a Cesar salad, and a small seafood soup," she said.

"Bring me a Corona and a dozen raw oysters," Alonso said as he smiled devilishly at the lieutenant.

"Con mucho gusto," the waiter said as he took his menu and left.

Lieutenant Maribal looked at Alonso sternly. Her cat-like eyes glared at him angrily.

"Why haven't you called me?" she asked.

"I've been in hiding," he replied. "I couldn't take a chance someone might be listening."

"That's not what I mean," she said bitterly. "I haven't heard from you since the last time we went out."

She glared at him as she watched him squirm uncomfortably.

"I meant to," he explained.

"Is it because I told you how I feel about you?"

"I—uh ..."

The lieutenant sighed and shook her head softly as a tear streamed down the side of her face. She sniffled and turned to face the wall.

Like most people with a single-minded focus on their career, Lieutenant Maribal had avoided a meaningful relationship until she met Alonso. She thought Alonso felt the same way about her as their romance blossomed. Then, she said what many men find difficult to say and what every woman wants to hear from the man she loves.

"I got scared," he explained.

"You're afraid of commitment," she said as she turned to him. "Why did you ask me to meet you here?"

Alonso glanced briefly at the other diners. "Cisneros and his sicarios are going to raid Champotón tomorrow."

She wrinkled her brow as her face started to turn red. She sniffled, dabbed her eyes with the back of her hand, and then breathed in sharply.

"How do you know?" she asked, her voice breaking slightly.

She would not look at Alonso, who stared at her uncomfortably.

"I have a source close to Comandante Norias," Alonso explained. "Can you alert the Marina?"

The lieutenant sat quietly looking at the wall as she regained her composure. She dried her eyes with her napkin and then turned to him.

"Is that all you wanted to tell me?"

"No," he said as he reached across the table to take her hand. "I know I've been unfair to you. The truth is, I just got scared."

"All I said was I love you," she said. "What's so scary about that?"

She glared at him as he looked back at her sincerely. He glanced at the other diners before turning to her.

"I got scared because I love you too."

She glared at him skeptically. "I don't believe you."

"If you want, I'll stand up and yell it out for everybody to hear."

She cocked her head and drew her cheek skeptically as she sat back. She stared at him dubiously as he looked back at her with the eyes of the truly penitent. The two continued to stare at each other, waiting for the other to flinch. Her expression changed suddenly when she saw him push his chair back, turn to face the other diners, and draw a deep breath. She lunged across the table to grab his hand and pull him back into his chair.

"Okay, I believe you," she said as he sat. "Do you know what time the raid is going to be?"

"No, but I can find out," he whispered. "The marines have to be ready at a moment's notice."

"I'll make sure of that," she replied. She smiled at him provocatively. "We're not through talking about this."

Alonso blushed as he chuckled nervously and looked at his watch. "I have to go." He started to get up to leave but let himself down slowly instead.

"What's wrong?" Lieutenant Maribal asked.

He turned his head slowly to look at her. "Do you think you can find someone to go to the caves at Punta Morro and check something out for me?"

"I can do it," she said confidently.

"No," Alonso said, shaking his head. "It's too dangerous. I don't want you getting hurt or worse."

"I'm not made of glass," she retorted sternly. "I'm an experienced spelunker and an expert diver. What do you want me to check out?"

She stared at Alonso, whose expression betrayed his reluctance.

"There's supposed to be a hundred AK-47 rifles hidden somewhere in the main cave."

"Are those the guns El Demonio was expecting?" she asked.

"You know about that?"

"Do you know who Simon Dónovan is?" she asked innocently. "The Armada issued a flyer on him and his ship, *Moonlight Runner.*"

"I saw the flyer," Alonso stammered. "Does the Armada think he's behind it?"

"He's one of the suspects."

"Who are the others?"

"There's only one. A man named Santos. He used to captain the Pemex supply boat to the Cantarell oil platforms out of the Port of Seyba Playa. He was transferred to Veracruz because of his ties to El Demonio," she explained. "He never showed up."

"Does the Armada think he went to work for El Demonio permanently?"

"Either that or he was killed for losing fifty kilos of El Demonio's cocaine he had hidden at Cayo del Centro. For now, he's listed as a missing person." She reached across the table to hold his hands. "What do you want me to do if I find the guns?"

"Nothing for now except to watch them to see if anybody comes to get them."

She caressed his hand as Alonso looked at her lovingly.

"I really wish you would consider sending someone else," he added.

"Why?" she asked as she smiled at him coyly. "Is it because you love me?"

She threw his hand back angrily when he began to stammer.

Chapter 9

The clouds over the mouth of the Sabancuy Channel looked like wispy strands of cotton suspended across a baby-blue sky. A pair of seagulls floated in the gentle breeze over the deck of the *Siete Mares*, watching Sandy adjust the position of the television monitor mounted on top of the main cabin. After removing the glare made by the midday sun, Sandy sat back on the deck to continue watching the dive on the mysterious sunken ship at the bottom of the channel.

A school of brightly colored fish swam around the professor and Donovan as they worked to separate the piece of coral believed to contain the ship's bell. The professor chipped away on the larger mass with a small rubber mallet and a dull chisel along a contour, loosening the piece he wanted. He slipped the end of a rubber-coated pry bar into a crack he had made and pried up on it while Donovan tugged on the coral with his gloved hands at different angles until it finally gave a little.

"Way to go, Professor," Sandy said as he watched the piece break off suddenly.

Augie stood halfway through the hatch at the stern of the ship to look across the top of the cabin at his nephew.

"You got any CDs we can listen to?" Augie asked as he set a portable CD player on the cabin top. "I forgot to bring some."

"The skipper's got a couple stowed in the drawer under the chart table," Sandy replied, never once taking his eyes off the screen.

The professor held the piece of coral they wanted while Donovan tied a barrel hitch around it. Sandy went to the davits on the starboard side to prepare to bring the bell to the surface. Augie rigged a pulley on the end of the boom of the forward davit and ran a rope through it to use to recover the bell. Sandy released the rope from the cleat on the gunwale and put both hands on it. He looked over his shoulder when he heard his uncle putting the CD player by the television monitor and watched him shuffle through the compact discs.

"*Banana Wind*?" Augie muttered as he read the title on the disc he had in his hand. "What's a banana wind? Is that like a monkey passing gas?"

Sandy felt the rope jerk several times.

"Can you give me a hand?" Sandy called to Augie. "They're ready to bring the bell up."

Augie set the disc on the cabin top and went to help his nephew. The pulley squeaked noisily with every tug as they worked to bring the bell to the surface. Sandy turned to his uncle when he heard his stomach growl.

"Are you hungry?" Sandy asked.

"I didn't have any breakfast," Augie replied.

"There are some bananas in the galley."

"No, thanks." Augie chuckled softly. "It might give me banana wind."

Sandy looked over his shoulder when he noticed something moving out of the corner of his eye. He immediately recognized the military vessel as it rounded Varaderos point.

"Uh-oh," he remarked. "Looks like trouble coming 'round the point."

Most people who dined at the Tucán restaurant never took notice of the structure at the center of the open-air restaurant. All they saw was the sprawling palapa roof supported by the highly polished hardwood poles and red concrete floor. Even those sitting at the bar that wrapped around the structure didn't realize that the swinging double doors led to more than just the kitchen. They also led to Doña Estér's office in a loft overlooking it.

Doña Estér sat behind her desk, working on a ledger when she heard a familiar rapping on her door.

"Come in, Fernando," she said as she removed her reading glasses.

Fernando walked into the office and closed the door behind him.

"Poli called," he said. "Dario left the house."

"Did he say where he was going?"

"He told Poli he was going to help his mother."

"Did he say how?"

"No, señora."

"Capitán Dónovan has to be told," she said as she set her glasses aside.

"One more thing, señora," Fernando added. "There's a man with a letter from Don Macario."

"It must be the answer to Simon's letter," Doña Estér said as she stood, pulling in the lapels of her blouse and fastening another button. "Show him in."

Fernando opened the door and stepped aside to let the messenger into the office. Doña Estér looked surprised to see the dapper little gentleman wearing a straw fedora. She hadn't expected to see him delivering such an important message, especially after seeing him with Comandante Norias the day the colonel and Cisco came to her restaurant. He removed his hat and dipped his head subtly.

"Buenas tardes, Doña Estér," he said as he handed her an envelope. "Don Macario asked me to bring this to you."

She undid the metal clasp on the envelope and pulled out a handwritten note to her, another one to Donovan, and a sealed envelope also addressed to Donovan. She glanced at her reading glasses on the desk but made no attempt to get them. Pablo and Fernando stood quietly as she read the letter addressed to her.

She looked at Fernando. "Get the panga ready."

"Right away, señora."

Doña Estér took the letter addressed to her and slipped it into the shredder behind her. She laid the note and the envelope addressed to Donovan on the desk and looked at Pablo.

"Is there anything else?" she asked Pablo, dismissing him.

Pablo looked offended.

"Do you have a message for Don Macario?"

"Just tell him I'll see that Capitán Dónovan gets his letter right away."

"Maybe I should wait to see if the capitán has anything to pass to Don Macario," Pablo suggested.

"Don't trouble yourself," she replied. "I'll send Fernando if he does."

"I don't mind waiting."

"There's no need. Fernando will handle it." She walked around her desk to open the door for him. "Now, please. I have work to do."

Pablo looked smugly at the doña as he put on his hat to leave. He stopped suddenly when he got to the doorway and turned around.

"Doesn't it worry you?" he asked.

"Does what worry me?"

"Having illegal weapons on your property?"

"I don't know what you're talking about," she replied sternly.

"What about the guns Capitán Dónovan brought back for El Demonio?" Pablo added. "Does he still have them on his ship?"

"I don't know anything about that," Doña Estér replied.

They both turned to look at the double doors into the kitchen below as they swung open suddenly. Fernando hurried to the foot of the stairs and looked up at Doña Estér and Pablo standing at the door.

"Señora," Fernando said urgently, "the Armada is boarding Capitán Dónovan's ship."

The crew of the *Siete Mares* stood amidships, watching the CB90 fast-attack patrol boat closing in on the starboard side of the *Siete Mares* as she cut her engines to come alongside the ship. About a half dozen marines dressed in camouflage battle dress uniforms, wearing navy-blue ballistic vests, stood about the deck holding HK 53 short assault rifles. Her deck didn't run as long as the *Siete Mares*'s, but she looked fast and mean.

"I'm gonna go help them tie on," Augie said to Donovan.

Donovan watched Augie go to the starboard side, where he caught a line thrown at him by a crewman dressed in navy-blue while another crewman deployed the fenders on the patrol boat's portside.

Donovan watched the marines board his ship as he and the professor removed their SCUBA tanks. He handed his to Sandy, who had just put the professor's tank in the locker.

"What do you think they want?" Sandy asked him.

"Could be they're here to check our INAH permit," Donovan replied as he undid his weight belt. "Why don't you go below and get it. Get our residency permits while you're at it."

"Aye, aye, Skipper."

Donovan and the professor turned their attention to securing the coral thought to contain the mysterious sunken ship's bell. Donovan undid the knot around the broken piece of rock-like material after helping the professor lower it carefully into a small cargo net placed in a washtub filled with seawater. The professor glanced at the marines boarding the ship.

"Do you want me to handle this?" the professor whispered to Donovan.

Donovan looked over his shoulder at Augie, who had his back to the last marine coming aboard as he mouthed, "That's Lieutenant Baeza."

"I've got this," he told the professor.

Donovan rose to his feet and went to meet the lieutenant.

"Good morning, Lieutenant. Welcome aboard," Donovan said to him. "I've sent a crewman to get our permits and documents. I'm sure you'll find everything in order."

"That won't be necessary," the lieutenant replied. He glanced at the coral sitting in the washtub. "Is that what you came to get?"

Donovan turned to the professor, who stepped up to answer the question.

"I believe so, mí teniente," the professor said. "I won't know for sure until we get it back to the institute."

"What's it supposed to be?"

"Hopefully, it contains a ship's bell identifying the shipwreck I'm studying," the professor replied as he looked down at the piece of coral.

"Hopefully?"

"Yes," he replied as he glanced at Donovan. "Underwater excavations are hampered not only by the aquatic environment but by such things as sediment, oxidation, and the formation of barnacles and coral that can conceal an artifact, especially when that artifact is made of a metallic substance as is the case with this bell. This specimen was extracted from a formation on the identifiable remains of the vessel where a bell would normally be found."

"How very interesting," the lieutenant said unenthusiastically.

Sandy came topside and handed Donovan several laminated cards resembling driver's licenses and an envelope with the logo of the National Institue of Anthropology and History on it. Donovan held them out for the lieutenant.

"Here are our permits, if you care to look at them."

"That won't be necessary," the lieutenant responded.

"I don't understand," Donovan said as he handed the documents back to Sandy. "Why did you board us?"

The lieutenant looked forward and then aft before turning to Donovan.

"Where have you been?" the lieutenant asked.

"Excuse me?"

"You left the Sabancuy Channel about a week or so ago. Your ship wasn't at its normal anchorage at the Paradise Lagoon during that time." He stared at Donovan suspiciously. "Where did you go?"

"I went to Tampico to meet the yacht race sailing from Corpus Christi," Donovan replied calmly.

"I saw that," the lieutenant remarked curiously.

Donovan frowned. "Saw what?"

"A picture, taken by the US Coast Guard of your ship off the coast of Tampico," he explained. "Did you make a declaration upon returning to Mexican waters?"

Donovan turned to Augie. "Do you remember ever leaving Mexican waters?"

"No," Augie replied. "We did go into the Tampico shipping lanes to meet the regatta, but I didn't think we were out of Mexican waters."

"The US Coast Guard is not in the habit of violating Mexican territory," he commented. "It's more likely that you were outside of Mexican territorial waters when the Coast Guard took that picture, therefore requiring that you make a customs declaration. You of all people should know that, Capitán."

"What do you mean by that?"

"Weren't you a shipping agent for an American shipping line in Panama?" Lieutenant Baeza asked.

"I used to be."

"Then you should be very familiar with customs regulations, shouldn't you?"

Donovan stared dryly at the lieutenant. "There's nothing to declare."

"Then you don't mind if I conduct an inspection?"

"What if I do mind?"

"You know very well you don't have a choice, Capitán."

"Then by all means." Donovan glanced at Sandy. "My crewmen will show you around." He turned to Sandy. "Make sure you show them the engine room."

"Aye, aye, Skipper," Sandy responded as he turned to the lieutenant. "Right this way," he said as he started aft.

The lieutenant turned to the petty officer standing by his side. "Take the men below, Maestre. Check her from stem to stern."

"A la orden, mí teniente," the petty officer said, acknowledging the order.

As Donovan watched Sandy lead the small contingent of marines aft, the lieutenant looked at the coral sitting in the washtub.

"Tell me, Professor," the lieutenant began. "How significant is this artifact?"

"If it is what I suspect it is, quite significant," the professor replied.

"Really?"

"If the wreck below is a coastal patrol vessel or even a cargo ship, it could enhance our knowledge of Mexico's colonial period."

"In what way?"

"A shipwreck like this is like a time capsule," the professor explained. "It's like a window into the past."

"It's that important?"

"Oh, yes," the professor replied. "Marine archeologists like myself get quite excited when we have an opportunity like this."

"Then why did you leave the Sabancuy Channel like you did?"

The question took the professor by surprise.

"The professor was called away," Donovan interjected.

"Yes," Dr. Ventura added. "I had some pressing matters to address."

"More important than this significant find?"

"Maybe not, but nevertheless requiring my immediate attention."

"What was that you said?" Donovan added. "About it waiting three centuries for someone to find it?"

"That's right." The professor chuckled. "I didn't want any distractions before I committed myself to the excavation."

"I see," the lieutenant said disinterestedly.

"We wanted to compete in the regatta," Donovan said. "But had to cancel because of the professor's charter. Right, Augie?"

"That's right," Augie agreed. "It was too late to sign up, so we decided to go meet the regatta when they got to Tampico."

"To network," Donovan interjected. "You know—make contacts, advertise, stuff like that."

The lieutenant stared at them suspiciously.

"How long were you in Tampico?" he asked them.

"In Tampico?" Donovan responded to give himself time to think. "We never put into Tampico."

"I thought you wanted to network?" the lieutenant countered. "I'm assuming you couldn't do that while your so-called contacts were in the middle of a race."

"As it turns out," Donovan began, "there wasn't time."

"That's right," the professor added. "I was through earlier than I anticipated."

"You know how it is, Lieutenant," Donovan continued. "We had an obligation to the institute, so we canceled our plans and headed back."

The lieutenant didn't seem to buy the explanation, and he glowered at them suspiciously as the professor turned his attention to the washtub.

"I'd better get the artifact in the stabilization tank before the air seeps through the encrustation," the professor commented.

"Let me help you with that," Augie volunteered.

The two men lifted the chunk of coral by the small cargo net wrapped around it and hoisted it out of the washtub. They carried it toward the forward hatch as the petty officer came topside to rejoin the lieutenant. He shook his head at the officer, who turned to Donovan.

"Are you certain you didn't meet the yacht race further out of the Tampico shipping lanes?" Lieutenant Baeza asked Donovan.

"Quite certain," Donovan replied. "We may have strayed a little further out from Tampico than I realized, but we were definitely in the shipping lanes when the Coast Guard showed up."

"So, you admit to seeing the Coast Guard."

"Why would I deny that?"

The lieutenant stared at Donovan like a nun listening to a Catholic schoolboy trying to explain what he had clutched in his hand behind his back.

"You didn't by any chance 'stray' close to Padre Island, just north of the Mansfield Pass?"

"Nope," Donovan said. "No reason to go there."

As the petty officer and Sandy came to the starboard side, the lieutenant looked at Sandy.

"Did this ship go anywhere near Padre Island?" the lieutenant asked him.

"No, sir," Sandy replied.

The lieutenant stared dubiously at him. Then, he glanced at Donovan before turning to the petty officer.

"Maestre," he said to the petty officer.

"Sí, mí teniente."

"Take the men back to the ship."

"A la orden, mí teniente," the petty officer replied. He turned to the boarding party, which had gathered amidships. "You heard the lieutenant—move."

In all the years that Donovan had worked as a troubleshooter for his shipping line, he had learned to maintain his composure. He had a lot of experience handling nosy customs officials, coast guard officers, and the police. Lieutenant Baeza, however, seemed more determined than most.

As the last of the marines returned to the fast-attack boat, the lieutenant stared at Donovan before hopping onto the patrol boat.

He continued to stare at Donovan as the patrol boat reversed its engines.

"Catch you later, Capitán," he said.

The patrol boat backed away from the *Siete Mares*, came about, and dashed off toward Punta Varaderos.

San Cristóbal de las Casas
Central Highlands
Chiapas, Mexico

The old Spanish colonial house Colonel Barca used as his headquarters sat high on a hill overlooking San Cristóbal de las Casas. From the modestly sized wrought iron balcony where he sat, he had a view of the historic center of town, which still maintained its old-days charm. Just about all the buildings had red-clay tile roofs, wrought iron balconies, and stucco facades painted in an array of pastels.

As he sat at a rustic wooden table drinking a cup of hot green tea and watching the street vendors push their carts along the narrow cobblestone streets around the main plaza, he thought about his childhood home in the mountains of Durango. His father worked as a cobbler in the center of the small town where his family lived in a building much like the ones in the town below his balcony. His father had hoped he would take over the business as his only son, but he longed for more and sought a career in the military instead.

He had set his cup on the table when he heard a soft knock behind him. Major Zamora stood in the doorway to the balcony holding a manila file. Like the colonel, he dressed in plainclothes suited for the cool, damp spring mountain air.

"I've completed the operational plan for tomorrow night, Colonel," the major said as he handed the file to him. "The advance team will don their PFP uniforms before bringing the pangas to the ship to commence the operation."

Colonel Barca opened it and glanced at the map of the general area surrounding the Port of Seyba Playa. He flipped the page and looked at the diagram of the area around the warehouse and at a diagram of the warehouse floor plan drawn by Dario.

"The colonel and I will ride in the first panga with Puma Uno to the back of the warehouse. The advance team, Pumas Dos and Tres will ride in the second panga and dock between the warehouse and the building to the west of it," the major said, summarizing the initial phase.

The colonel flipped another page and glanced at the bullet sheet highlighting the central aspects of the plan as the major continued his briefing.

"We will wait with Puma Uno on the dock behind the warehouse while Puma Dos takes its position on the roof and the advance team and Puma Tres take their position between the warehouse and the building to the west," the major continued.

The colonel turned the page back to the diagram of the floor plan of the warehouse as the major continued the briefing.

"The advance team will approach the guards at the front of the warehouse and neutralize them. Immediately afterward, Puma Tres will establish a security perimeter around the front door while Puma Dos makes entry through the roof to secure the warehouse floor and open the back door for Puma Uno and us to make entry," the major said, beginning the final phase. "Entry into the office will be made through the door from the warehouse floor by Puma Uno. We should be able to secure El Demonio and his men without firing a shot."

"Tell me more about these pangas we're using to approach the target," he said to the major as he looked at the picture of two sixteen-foot fiberglass launches.

"They are at Payucán Beach, two hundred and thirty meters north of the target area," the major responded. "Our advance team will bring them to a point west of Punta Morro and north of the target area where they will take-on our assault teams."

The colonel returned his attention to the operational summary as he took a sip of tea and flipped through the plan. He set his cup down and gazed pensively at the town square below them.

"I've been thinking about Donovan's plan to rescue his woman." The colonel turned to the major. "What if he gets caught? That could ruin the element of surprise."

"We'll be in before Donovan reaches the plantation grounds," the major responded. "Even if he were to get caught, it shouldn't affect the operation."

"I'm concerned about the extraction phase," the colonel retorted. "The Armada is just up the coast. If Fausto's men discover him, they might open fire and provoke a response by the Armada. We can't let Donovan jeopardize the operation."

The coral extracted by the professor from the larger piece looked different to Donovan sitting in the stabilization tank than it did at the bottom of the channel. Water, especially at a depth of seventy feet, affects the way the sun's rays play on an object. The sunlight coming through the forward hatch exposed what looked like solid coral at the bottom of the channel, showing it to be a composite of coral, barnacles, and a thick black mass.

"I still don't see a bell," Augie remarked as he stood in the forward hold next to Donovan and the professor.

"You're looking at it too hard," Donovan told him. He outlined the shape with his finger. "See it now?"

"All I see is a rock covered in barnacles and black stuff," Augie remarked skeptically.

"That black stuff you're seeing is ferruginous matter," the professor explained.

"English, Professor," Augie said.

"Rust—corroded iron."

"You think the bell was made of iron?" Donovan asked.

"No, I don't," the professor replied. "Bells are commonly made of bronze or brass."

"What if the bell *was* made of iron?" Augie inquired.

"Then, all we'll have after we give it an electrolytic bath will be concretion in the shape of a bell. If we break that open, all we'll find is an empty cavity." He smiled as he inhaled sharply. "Fortunately, that won't be the case."

"If the bell wasn't made of iron, how do you explain the black stuff?" Donovan asked.

"It could be that something else made of iron settled on top of the bell after the ship went down. Over time, it's possible that the rust from that object coated the bell."

Donovan looked up when he heard Sandy calling through the open hatch above him.

"Skipper, there's a launch approaching from the beach," Sandy called down the hatch. "It looks like Doña Estér and Fernando."

"We'll be right up," Donovan called up the hatch. He turned to the professor, who stared pensively at his dubious prize.

"You go ahead," the professor said. "I want to give this thing a harder look."

The hum of the outboard motor rumbled to a stop as Fernando guided the panga carrying Doña Estér toward the starboard side of the *Siete Mares.* Donovan smiled at the lovely doña from the deck as she sat daintily on the forwardmost thwart, holding a Ziploc bag containing a manila envelope. Sandy hung himself precariously over the side, waiting for Fernando to throw him a line while Augie hung the ladder on the gunwale.

Donovan stood over Doña Estér, offering her his hand. He turned his head to avoid looking down her blouse and the way she filled it so enticingly as he helped her board his ship. He did, however, glance at her long, lithe legs; deliciously rounded hips; and hourglass figure that could put a Barbie doll to shame once she set foot on the deck.

"Welcome aboard," Donovan said. "I'm sorry I'm not dressed for company."

Unlike Donovan, she made no effort to avert her eyes from looking at Donovan's bare chest and abs as she came aboard.

"I'm sorry I didn't call first," she said playfully. "We saw the Armada boarding your ship. Is everything all right?"

"No sweat," Donovan replied. "Just a routine customs inspection."

"Routine my … foot," Augie said. "I thought I was going to lay an egg when you told Sandy to make sure he showed him the engine room."

"You worry too much," Donovan remarked. He turned to Doña Estér. "To what do I owe this pleasant surprise?"

"Don Macario sent this for you." She handed him the Ziploc bag.

"It's very kind of you to bring it, but you could've given it to me when I came ashore."

"I also came to tell you that Dario left the house."

"Damn," Donovan said under his breath.

"He told Poli he was going to make sure nothing happened to his mother," she added.

"I wouldn't worry about him, Skipper," Augie commented. "Knowing how he feels about her, he was probably telling the truth."

"Why doesn't that make me feel any better?"

"Relax—you worry too much," he remarked mockingly.

"Remember what the professor said about Dario guessing we were going to trick his cousin into giving us Itzél?" Donovan retorted sharply.

"So?" Augie responded. "That just proves my point."

"It could screw things up for tonight."

"I think Augie is right," Doña Estér said. "I don't think he'll do anything that'll put Poli's mother in danger."

"I can't take that chance," Donovan retorted.

"You can't call it off," Augie argued. "You've got two very bad men expecting you. The colonel'll get suspicious and might back out of the plan, and I don't have to tell you what El Demonio will do if you don't show up."

The consternation on Donovan's face showed like a poor card player's tell. He had to agree with his first mate's assessment. The colonel could back out if Donovan changed the plan in any way or come up with a plan of his own. The ship had sailed, and he had no choice but to cast his fate to the wind.

"I'm afraid that's not all I came to tell you," Doña Estér added. "It's about Don Macario's messenger, Pablo."

"What about him?"

"He was asking questions about where you had the guns."

"That's just Pablo being curious," Donovan said.

"He's always sticking his nose where it doesn't belong," Augie added.

"He's harmless," Donovan said.

"Are you sure?" Doña Estér inquired skeptically. "I saw him with Comandante Norias that day the colonel and Cisco questioned you."

Donovan just looked at her, stunned by the revelation.

"I apologize for not saying something earlier, but I had forgotten about it until I saw him again today," Doña Estér added.

"What are we gonna do, Skipper?" Augie asked.

Faced with the possibility that Pablo might have ties with Comandante Norias, Cisco Cisneros's point man, Donovan's confidence in his plan had begun to waver. If Pablo told Cisco about the plan to set up the colonel, would Cisco warn him? Then he thought about the friction he witnessed between the colonel and Cisco the last time he came to the Tucán. They seemed to despise each other. He might not tell the colonel.

"What can we do?" Donovan turned to Augie. "Like you said, we can't call it off."

"Now you got me worried," Augie remarked.

"Why's that?"

"Because you agreed with me."

Donovan chuckled as he undid the Ziploc bag and took out the manila envelope. He opened it and read the handwritten note Don Macario wrote to him. He then took out the envelope addressed to him and opened it. He took out about a dozen photographs, a thumb drive, and a set of handwritten diagrams. He handed the thumb drive to Augie.

"What's this?"

"Video of the grounds around El Demonio's plantation," he replied as he sorted through the photos quickly before handing them to Augie.

He looked at the diagrams Don Macario made of El Demonio's property, the floorplan of the main house, and the cottage where El Demonio had Itzél sequestered.

"It looks like we're going to have to add master spy to Don Macario's list of talents," Donovan said as he handed the diagram to his partner.

CHAPTER 10

This time of year, the beach at Payucán hardly had a soul combing its sands or taking in the sun. Nevertheless, she decided not to make the kilometer-and-a-half trek across the rocky beach carrying a rucksack full of equipment. Lieutenant Maribal parked her Volkswagen Beetle convertible on the side of the Libre Road over the north end of the beach.

To prepare for the mission, she tucked the legs of her toughest pair of blue jeans into a pair of knee-high snake boots. She wore a thick cotton khaki shirt with the sleeves rolled up to her elbows and a pair of beige leather gloves. She took her rucksack out of the backseat, threw it over her left shoulder, and took the rocky path down to the Punta Morro caves.

The waves crashing against the large boulders sitting outside of the entrance sounded like cannon blasts. A light mist rolled off the broken rock and drifted mysteriously into the foreboding grotto. The sea breeze swirling in the caves made a deep moaning sound like the muffled groans of a wounded animal. Undaunted by an eerie feeling that had suddenly come over her, the lieutenant pressed forward, the waterlogged sand giving slightly under her boots with her every footstep.

She set her rucksack on the ground as she entered the cave to take out the gear she would need. She strapped on a red caving helmet and switched on the headlamp. She put on a utility belt and hung a large flashlight, a miniflashlight, a looped climbing rope, and a multipurpose tool on the safety hooks. She took an expandable metal baton out of the rucksack as she stood and extended it with a sharp flick of her right wrist.

The ambient light illuminated most of the larger cave as she advanced toward the back of the grotto. She took her flashlight off her belt and shined it into the corners and onto the ledges where the natural light did not reach. When she got to the back of the cave, she turned around to take one last look at the ledges she had passed, finding no sign of any rifles. She swung her light around and shined it into a narrow passage at the back of the cave.

To the best of her recollection, she had never had a claustrophobic experience in her life. However, the narrow passage made her uncomfortable as she moved through it, shining her light into the dark recesses of the intimidating passage.

She felt better as she stepped out of the passage into an adjoining cave. She looked out at the waves crashing against the fallen boulders as she filled her lungs with fresh air. She pressed forward toward the entrance, shining her light in the dark corners and onto ledges, looking for guns and as with the first cave, did not find any. She scoffed at the thought that she had embarked on a fool's errand as she came to the mouth of the second cave. Then, she caught a glimpse of what looked like an opening to a third cave. Had she not come upon it from the angle she had and at that precise moment of the day, she might have missed it.

The opening didn't look large enough for even her narrow feline-like body to squeeze through. The lieutenant retracted the baton and stuffed it into her back pocket. She took the miniflashlight off her belt and put it in her shirt pocket before unbuckling her belt and dropping it to the ground. She undid her helmet and set it next to her belt. She took several breaths before inserting herself into the craggy fissure.

She felt the baton pressing against her bottom and the flashlight cutting into her chest as she squeezed through the opening into a large room. Strangely enough, light found its way through the blocked entrance, illuminating the cavern in a dim twilight haze. She took the miniflashlight and shined its unusually bright light into the dark corners and onto the ledges of the cave as she advanced, finding no sign of any guns. The wind whined eerily through the gaps in the rocks blocking the opening and gave her a cold chill as she stared at the back wall of the room.

She turned her head when she caught a dark mass moving out of the corner of her eye. She shined her light at a rocky ledge where she saw it disappear. As she stared at the rocky overhang, waiting for the shadow to reappear, she heard what sounded like muffled laughter. Then she felt the sand giving under her boots. She looked down and saw water rushing around her feet. She hadn't realized that the ground had dropped below sea level as she had progressed into the grotto, and the tide rolling in had started to fill the cave. She took a last look at the ledge before turning to get out before the water got too high.

Then she heard a fearsome screech behind her like a woman screaming. As she turned to look, the dark mass swept down on her from the rocky ledge. She covered her face as she fell rump first into the rising water. With her heart pounding, she sat up and flailed her hands over her head to fend off the attack. As she quickly got to her feet, she pulled the baton from her back pocket and whipped out the rod to defend herself.

The screeching stopped suddenly, and she spun around, looking for the beast to return. Then she saw a shadow moving to her right and turned quickly to prepare for another attack. She saw the shadow moving gracefully against the cave wall as it closed in on the rocky ledge where she first saw it. The shadow brought in its wings as it landed and turned its horned head to look at the lieutenant. She brought down her baton and chuckled softly, relieved when she recognized her attacker as a great horned owl.

The cantina where the comandantes heading the gangs agreed to meet sat far from downtown Champotón in a part of town that even the most daring would hesitate to venture into. Comandante Antonio Briones, alias "El Chino," never liked coming to that part of town. It reminded him of where he grew up and the meager existence he once knew. He did, however, like coming to the cantina even if it did belong to Comandante Sánchez.

Comandante Briones had to wait for his eyes to adjust after entering the cantina. The only light in the dark den of insobriety came from the soft glow of the nervously flickering neon lights hanging unevenly on the cantina's dirty walls, which worked to the benefit of the *cantinera* who tended the bar.

The aging woman had developed a sharp-edged disposition over the years of waiting on the hard-edged men who came to the bar. Like most cantineras, she had a certain degree of raw sex appeal. She wore low-neck blouses to capitalize on her principal attributes. She relied on the low light, her busty brilliance, coquettish conversation, and above all alcohol to separate the machos and *borachos* from their hard-earned pesos. Unlike the rustic cantina, she had not aged well. Her bottom practically swallowed the stool she sat in, and she tended to wear far too much makeup, but in the dimness of the neon lights and the veil of an alcoholic stupor, she never wanted for masculine attention.

"Hola, Chino," he heard the cantinera call him by his sobriquet. "Highball?"

"Por favor," Comandante Briones replied. "Whiskey con soda."

"The others are in the back," she added as she poured a shot of Scotch and half a bottle of mineral water into a tall highball glass.

El Chino took his drink and headed for the back of the bar, where the other comandantes had put several tables together side by side to accommodate their number. At the head of the table sat Comandante Sánchez with his right-hand man, Comandante Prieto.

He despised Sánchez, who had betrayed the comandantes and the gangs they organized when he accepted a position as chief of security for the Campeche Growers Association to stop seizing their merchandise. He kept most of the monthly payoff while the comandantes did most of the work. If not for El Demonio showing the comandantes how to extort money more efficiently from the businesses operating in their plazas, the gangs would have broken up and reverted to fighting among themselves. Consequently, the wealth the gangs had since amassed had made them self-centered and fiercely independent. Only the threat of losing their plazas could bring them together once more at Sánchez's cantina.

Comandante Briones went to sit at the foot of the table with Comandante Tapia, who like him had turned to El Demonio for weapons and training, alienating Sánchez. Briones and Tapia worked hard to steer as many of the comandantes to El Demonio while Prieto did all he could to keep them reliant on Sánchez for weapons. Neither El Demonio nor Sánchez commanded the comandantes' complete loyalty. They didn't even share that among themselves.

"Have you seen Villegas?" Chino asked Tapia as he stared across the table at Sánchez.

"No. Was he supposed to come?" Tapia replied.

"I invited him," he said as he turned to Tapia. "He called to warn me when the Norteños came into town. It gave me time to get my people in place to protect the river warehouse."

"But they didn't come anywhere near it."

"Still, if he hadn't called, we would've been completely unprepared if they had."

"I'm a little surprised to see you here, Comandante Briones," Sánchez said across the table, interrupting his sidebar with Tapia. "I thought you were busy holding López's hand while he waited for his *guns* to come in."

Chino glared stone-faced at Sánchez as several of the comandantes broke out in laughter. He ignored their jeering as he waited for the laughter to subside.

"You said you had something important to tell us about the attacks," he said humorlessly.

"You mean the probe."

"I'd hardly call a handful of delinquents breaking bottles with gasoline a probe," Chino retorted. "Half of the bottles didn't even break. It hardly qualifies as vandalism."

"Your so-called delinquents were sent by the Norteños," Sánchez countered. "Still think it's vandalism?"

"Even if that's true and it was meant as a probe, the Marina made short work of them," Chino retorted. "The Norteños will think twice before they raid Champotón."

"Is that what you think, or is it something López told you?" Sánchez inquired sarcastically.

Chino could feel his face getting warm as the comandantes all turned to look at him.

"I happen to agree with Fausto."

"I think the firebombings were sent to lower our guard in preparation for a raid by the Norteños," Sánchez commented. "Tonight."

"That's unlikely," Chino said. "It doesn't make sense that the Thunderbolts would give up the element of surprise by sending amateurs to stir up the locals," Chino argued.

"Who said anything about the Thunderbolts?" Sánchez retorted. "I said the Norteños were coming ... led by Cisco Cisneros." He rose to his feet as he looked directly at Chino. "What does López say about that?"

Chino stared back at Sánchez as the table broke out in a hubbub of chatter between the agitated comandantes. He glanced at Tapia, who also looked to him for an answer.

"I don't speak for Fausto, but I do speak for Los Chinos," Chino responded firmly. "Tell me what you need us to do."

The subtle knock on the door made Don Rodrigo smile as he waited for his personal assistant, Emelia, to enter. The former Miss Campeche and valedictorian of her *prepartoria*, the Mexican equivalent of high school, had not lost an iota of her beauty since she came to work for Don Rodrigo over fifteen years ago. Like a fine wine, she had aged well. Her long legs still possessed a firm, muscular tone, and although her hips had broadened, they had done so wonderfully. She tried to understate her natural attributes to present a professional appearance by wearing unimaginative women's business attire that could barely contain her voluptuous bosom and the softness of her curves. She went as far as to wear her flowing brunette hair in a tight bun and don a pair of reading glasses she didn't need. Unfortunately for her, it only made her more desirable.

"Don Arturo and Señor Mendiola are here to see you," she said to Don Rodrigo as she opened the door.

He grinned triumphantly as he stood. The strong-jawed, barrel-chested, white-maned Campechano buttoned the middle button of his coat.

"Show them in."

"Adelante, caballeros," she said as she stood aside.

Don Arturo entered the room after giving her a gentlemanly tip of his head while Casimiro bowed more chivalrously as he watched her exit the room and closed the door.

"We should visit Rodrigo more often, Arturo," he said under his breath.

The spacious office looked more like an exclusive English gentleman's sitting room with oak-paneled walls, ornate molding, and a highly polished hardwood floor covered in part by an expensive Persian rug. His decorator had placed two wing-backed leather chairs in front of his elaborately hand-carved oak desk, which could have come from the study of an English lord. She had adorned his walls with antique flintlock pistols, muskets, sabers, and large paintings of the paternal heads of the house of De León.

"Sit down, gentlemen, and tell me what it is I can do for you on this fine afternoon," he said graciously.

"We missed you at our weekly luncheon," Don Arturo said as he sat in one of the wing-backed chairs.

"It's a good thing you brought that up, Arturo." He smiled capriciously. "I've believed for some time now that our weekly gatherings are of little use. I'm thinking that monthly or perhaps even bimonthly meetings should be enough." He chuckled softly to himself. "I'll put it to a vote with the members the next time I decide to attend."

"You shouldn't be so presumptuous, Rodrigo," Casimiro remarked as he sat in the other chair. "Such decisions are reserved for Arturo as the head of the association."

"That is a mere formality I intend to correct," Rodrigo said smugly. "I suppose I can attend the next meeting to put that issue to a vote as well."

"The issue has already been put to a vote at today's luncheon," Casimiro said as he stared unsympathetically at him. "You did not fare very well."

"I don't believe you," Rodrigo responded. "The members obviously prefer my leadership to handle this crisis."

"What crisis?" Casimiro retorted. He turned to Don Arturo. "Do you know anything about a crisis?"

Rodrigo glared at him. "Have you forgotten about the Norteño threat?"

"There never was a Norteño threat," Arturo responded.

"Of course, there is. What about the raid last Easter?"

"The Norteños had my permission to neutralize the Corsarios before they went to disarticulate the real threat—our common enemy, the Comisión."

"The Commission?" Rodrigo said softly.

"You see, Rodrigo," Casimiro said to the bewildered would-be usurper. "The Commission not only bought the merchandise Sánchez and his task force stole from us, but they also inspired Sánchez to emulate their organization, and they would have succeeded had it not been for the hiring of Fausto López."

"When you hired López, you unintentionally created a rift between the comandantes and their gangs," Don Arturo explained. "In a way, you kept Sánchez from making of his corrupt police commanders a carbon copy of the Commission."

"But you also played right into López's plan to take control of the gangs, thereby guaranteeing a response by the Norteños," Casimiro added.

"What about the New Order Cisco Cisneros spoke of?" Rodrigo argued.

"*That* was an invention of Cisco Cisneros's," Don Arturo replied. "Anastasio has directed Colonel Barca to reel him in."

"What about the firebombings in Champotón?" Rodrigo asked.

"Anastasio assures me the attacks were unauthorized," Arturo explained. "I spoke with him earlier this afternoon. Colonel Barca is almost done in Chiapas. The Norteños will be withdrawing their people from Ciudad del Carmen before the end of spring."

"Why was the association not informed of this?" Rodrigo inquired.

"Because, my old friend," Casimiro said, "the association had been unwittingly infiltrated by a deceiver who had so successfully implanted dissension among the members that we could not share what we were doing without tipping our hand to our real enemies."

Words failed the usually verbose Rodrigo. He suddenly realized that El Demonio had manipulated him, showing him what he wanted him to see, playing on his thirst for power and blinding him to the facts.

"The Marina knows about the guns López is expecting tonight," Arturo added.

"Excuse me?" Rodrigo said meekly.

"The guns your money launderer helped López to get," Arturo explained.

Rodrigo's face turned ashen.

"The PGR is investigating López in connection with the incident that occurred recently at Padre Island," Arturo explained further. "An American agent with evidence implicating him in the failed gun smuggling operation is coming to Campeche City to meet with a special prosecutor to investigate the matter."

"We also know about Comandante Sánchez's efforts to renew his arrangement with the Commission," Casimiro added. "The

CISEN intercepted a series of calls between Comandante Sánchez and the Comisión's chief of operations, Comandante Tercero, regarding a conspiracy to exchange guns for drugs."

"The CISEN?"

"The Center for Investigation and National Security," Casimiro explained. "Don't tell me you weren't aware of Sánchez's scheme."

"I had nothing to do with what Sánchez is doing," Rodrigo responded.

"You had to know that he wouldn't sit back and let López take the gangs from him. The key, it seems, to controlling the gangs depends on who can keep them supplied with guns and ammunition," Casimiro explained. "Knowing both men, you should have expected it would come to this."

"I was only doing what I thought was in our best interest," Rodrigo explained. "I hired Sánchez on Fausto's ..."

Again, he ate his words when he realized how El Demonio had played him from the start. He sat back in his chair, staring blankly at the wall.

"El Demonio is a deceiver, true to his namesake," Arturo said in closing.

Rodrigo sat listlessly on his self-styled throne. He did not turn to look as Arturo and Casimiro stood to leave.

"The Marina will be conducting an operation tonight to intercept López's guns," Arturo said as Casimiro opened the door. "You are not to warn him in any way."

The room where Naval Infantry Lieutenant Ramiro Baeza made his office looked like every other room at the headquarters building on the base in Lerma. All the furnishings except for the hardwood chairs he had in front of his desk were made of metal and painted battleship gray. Maps of the state of Campeche, the

Calakmul preserve, and the Cantarell oil platforms hung from the office walls not blocked by standing four-drawer metal cabinets.

"I'm sorry to inconvenience you, mí capitán," the lieutenant said as he poured his superior officer a cup of coffee from his thermos. "I didn't want to discuss it over the phone."

"No inconvenience," Captain Mendiola said as he laid his hat on the desk. "I still have several hours before I take my station off Punta Tonaché."

"That's south of Champotón," he commented.

"Correct, Lieutenant."

"I was wondering if you might consider positioning your ship slightly closer to the mouth of the river."

"May I ask for what reason?"

The lieutenant paused to choose his words carefully. "I have information that Fausto López is expecting his rifles tonight."

"I just spent a week patrolling the Campeche coast watching for your shipment of guns," the captain commented.

"I apologize, mí capitán. Dónovan had already made it to a safe harbor by the time we were alerted by the Americans," Baeza explained.

"Where did you say you boarded his ship?"

"In the Sabancuy Channel, off Santa Rosalia Beach, diving on an old wreck."

"Did he have the necessary permits?"

"He did," Baeza replied. "But he admitted leaving Mexican waters, so I inspected his ship for contraband."

"Did you find any?"

Baeza drew a long breath. "He undoubtedly moved the guns by the time I found him."

The captain looked at him skeptically as he took a long sip of coffee. Baeza looked into the senior officer's eyes for a window into his thoughts as he waited on the captain to say something.

"You said you had information about the raid we're expecting tonight?"

"Yes, mí capitán. I don't believe there will be a raid. I believe it's nothing more than a diversion initiated by El Demonio to cover the arrival of his shipment."

"Are you questioning the alert issued by Regional Command?"

"Not at all, mí capitán," the lieutenant responded respectfully. "Teniente Maribal is a very capable intelligence officer. I don't doubt that she presented a solid case to command."

"So, you don't believe Cisneros is raiding Champotón tonight?"

The lieutenant sat uncomfortably in his chair. The Third Naval Region had never issued an alert without cause. He had discussed the intel concerning the imminent attack with Lieutenant Maribal, who insisted on its accuracy despite contradictory information that Cisco's forces did not appear to be preparing for a raid of any sort.

"I've learned from a very credible source, that Arturo Farías, the head of the Campechano drug trafficking organization and Anastasio Noches are working together to eliminate the Commission. Cisneros is in Ciudad del Carmen with the Campechano's blessings. It doesn't make sense that he would defy his Norteño masters."

"He could be acting independently," the captain suggested. "You yourself told me Cisneros was brash and unpredictable. It could be the Norteños are unaware of his plans."

"From the reported inaction of his men, it appears that Cisco may be unaware of the plan himself."

"You may be right, Teniente," Captain Mendiola commented. "However, I prefer to err on the side of caution."

"That's understandable, mí capitán." Baeza put his finger through the handle of his coffee cup. "I'm just trying to reconcile the timing of the tip with the shipment of guns El Demonio is expecting."

"Your information regarding El Demonio's supposed gun shipment is highly speculative at best," Mendiola remarked. "How reliable is your source?"

"Reliable enough to keep me from getting ambushed by El Perro," Baeza countered. He stood and walked to the door leading to the hall. "Would you like to talk to him and evaluate his information for yourself?"

The lieutenant opened the door and motioned a neatly dressed man with a receding hairline to come to the office. The little man had an air of distinction about him as he removed his straw fedora, revealing the short, tightly bound ponytail he wore.

"Buenas tardes, Capitán," Pablo said upon entering.

The captain ran his eyes over the man's attire like he would a new seaman reporting for duty for the first time. He nodded in approval as he inspected him visually from the pointed tips of his spit-and-polished roan-colored shoes to the neatly pressed form-fitting white linen shirt he wore.

The captain squinted his eyes. "Do I know you?"

"Sí, mí capitán," Pablo responded humbly. "I'm the bar manager at the Paraiso Lounge."

"Ah, yes," Captain Mendiola said. "The lieutenant tells me you know something about a shipment of guns."

"It's like I told Teniente Baeza, mí capitán," the busybody barman began. "Surely you know that Fausto López, the one they call El Demonio, is here in Campeche."

"Go on," the captain replied.

"Sometime after dark, a ship will be bringing a hundred AK-47 rifles to him."

"How do you know this?" Mendiola's skepticism had not wavered.

"I overheard El Demonio say it himself."

Lieutenant Baeza looked at the captain, who glanced at him skeptically. "Who was he speaking to?"

"Forgive me for not being able to tell you, mí capitán," Pablo said respectfully. "I have my safety to consider."

"Capitán Mendiola," the lieutenant said. "It's obvious that he's come to us at great personal risk."

"The only thing that's obvious to me is that he's protecting somebody." The gunboat commander turned in his seat to face Pablo. "Let me ask you this. Is the somebody you overheard Fausto López tell the same person who told you about the attempt on the teniente's life?"

The balding barman nodded reluctantly.

"Do you know where the guns are being delivered?" Capitán Mendiola asked.

"I expect to know later tonight."

The captain turned to Lieutenant Baeza.

"I need a word with you."

Baeza went to open the door for Pablo. "Thank you, Don Pablo. I'll be waiting for your call."

"Remember, they won't come in if the Armada is in the area," Pablo added as he stepped through the door.

"I remember," the lieutenant said as he pushed him gently through the door. "Call me as soon as you know."

The officers waited quietly as they listened to the barman's footsteps fade into the distance.

"Do you think there's any chance he could be working for El Demonio?" Captain Mendiola asked. "I know he kept El Perro from killing you, but I don't like what he said about keeping the Armada away."

"With all due respect, Capitán, it makes sense that they wouldn't come in if they see your patrol boat in the area."

"Very well, Teniente. How do you intend to handle this?" Captain Mendiola pointed a finger at him. "Remember, you're on standby to help the Champotón detachment if the raiders come tonight."

"Of course, mí capitán." Baeza stood and walked to the map of the state of Campeche on the wall. "I'll be waiting here, off the road near La Joya between Villa Madero and Simochaca with a SandCat and a platoon of infantry. I can respond anywhere between Champotón and Lorenzo in half an hour or less."

Captain Mendiola retrieved his peaked hat from the desk, slipped it under his left arm, and walked to the door.

"I'll be moored at the community dock on the Champotón River," he said as he let himself out.

Late afternoons are not entirely unpleasant on the Isle of Carmen despite the heat and humidity. The sea breeze cooled the damp island air like a mother blowing on the skinned knee of a weeping child. To the west of the island, over the choppy waters of the Bay of Campeche, where the sun rushed to keep its appointment with the horizon, a band of clouds swirled ever upward in the afternoon sky, forming a magnificent anvil-shaped tower of wispy wonderment.

Cisco stood in his living room looking out the picture window across the swimming pool at the guests he invited to his pool party. He looked at his reflection, running his hands lightly over his slicked-back hair. He undid the buttons of his shirt, adjusting the gold chains around his neck, turning his head from side to side as he perched his sunglasses on the protruding ridge on his hooked nose. He had started to go out through the patio door when he heard a heavy knock on the front door.

He rushed through the hallway to the foyer where he saw Sergeant Reséndez push his way through Cisco's bodyguards as Colonel Barca and Major Zamora walked through the door.

"What are you doing here?" Cisco asked the colonel.

Sergeant Reséndez removed Cisco's sunglasses from his face and slipped them into his shirt pocket. He then grabbed Cisco's hand abruptly, twisting his wrist, and pushing it back unnaturally, forcing the brash Norteño crime boss to his knees. He looked up at Colonel Barca and Major Zamora, who stood over him dressed in black.

"I got an interesting call that you haven't given up on the idea of taking Champotón," Colonel Barca said calmly. He turned to Reséndez. "Release him."

Cisco stood slowly, massaging his aching wrist. "I don't know what you're talking about."

"Explain why Comandante Norias is bragging about being made the plaza boss of Champotón?" Major Zamora inquired.

"Where did you hear that?" Cisco asked.

"It doesn't matter," the colonel retorted. "What matters is that he seems to believe it."

"I don't know why he's saying that."

"You're to stay out of Champotón," the colonel said firmly. "Do you understand?"

Cisco took another look at the colonel's clothing, especially at his combat boots.

"Are you going on an operation?"

"That's not your concern," the colonel responded bluntly. "All you should be thinking about is packing to make the trip back to Nuevo León."

Cisco flexed his hand and then shook it to get the blood running in it again. "I was right about Champotón. They're unprepared. They're ripe for the picking."

"There will be no picking," the colonel said firmly. "The mission in Chiapas is almost complete. My men are tired. They're ready to get back to Nuevo León as soon as it's over. I don't want to have to come here to clean up your mess."

"I don't need your men to finish off the Campeche gangs," Cisco said defiantly.

The sound of water splashing and laughter filtered into the anteroom.

"Who else is here?" Colonel Barca asked.

"I'm throwing a pool party," Cisco replied.

"We've interrupted your party. Why don't you attend to your guests and leave the fighting to the professionals?" The colonel lowered his brow. "Stay out of Champotón."

Sergeant Reséndez pushed Cisco's bodyguards aside as he went to open the door for the colonel and Major Zamora. Cisco glared at them bitterly as he watched them leave. He glowered at his men.

"You're useless," he said to them angrily. "The next time somebody crashes through my door, I expect to see bodies lying in a pool of blood—yours if necessary."

"Sí, jefe," one of his men responded.

The lively sound of a cumbia playing flowed into the house. Cisco again rubbed his wrist and then ran his hands lightly over his hair.

"I'm going to the pool," he said as he put on his sunglasses, adjusted his chains, and fluffed the collar of his shirt. "I don't want any more disturbances."

"Sí, jefe."

Cisco walked through the house and out the back door. The pool took up most of the backyard and had a high wall surrounding it. Most of the guests sat close to the house by the outdoor bar at patio tables shaded by large umbrellas, except for three half-naked beauty queens lying facedown in a row of chaise lounges by the back wall.

The effeminate waiter from Café Olé brought a piña colada to Cisco as he looked across the pool at the current Miss Campeche, Daniela Henríquez, and the two runner-ups lying beside her. He gawked at her perfectly bronzed skin as she sunned her flawless back with her white bikini top undone.

Daniela Henríquez Santa Cruz was born an enchantress from the moment she drew her first breath with a smile so bewitching and a gaze so captivating that her doting father truly believed she had stolen their brilliance from the stars.

Armed only with overconfidence and a boat drink, Cisco strutted arrogantly to the opposite end of the pool, where he pulled a chair from a nearby table and set it squarely in front of the sunbathing beauty queen. He raised his sunglasses off his beak-like nose, propping them stylishly on his head.

"I'm glad you came to my pool party," he said in the sexiest voice he could muster.

He kept his eye on Daniela, ignoring the other stunning young ladies sunning next to her as they raised their heads to look at him. The pale-skinned plaza boss opened his shirt to show off the gold chains on his hairless chest. He grinned lasciviously as he took the bottle of tanning oil Daniela had next to her chaise lounge and squeezed some oil into his hand.

"Would you like for me to oil your back?" he asked.

Daniela lowered her sunglasses from her eyes to get a better look at the weasel-faced, pale-skinned young man. She glanced at his slicked-back hair, which gleamed in the sun.

"I think you could use it more than me," she remarked. "Your hair looks like it's a quart low."

Cisco fumed as Daniela's friends started to laugh. He resolved at that moment that he would have her. In his mind, he imagined ravaging her against her will on the lounge chair until she succumbed to the pleasure only he could give her. He glanced at the compressed sides of her breasts and at the roundness of her hips, imagining what he would like to do with them when his cell phone began to ring.

"Bueno?" he said into the phone.

"I see the colonel paid you a visit," he heard a voice he did not recognize say.

"Excuse me?"

"Did he tell you where he was going?"

"Who is this?" He stood up and stepped away to continue his conversation in private. "How did you get this number?"

"He's going to meet with his old friend, El Demonio, in Seyba Playa."

"What?" Cisco frowned. "Who is this?"

"Didn't you know?" he heard the voice say. "The colonel and El Demonio have decided to join forces and keep the isthmus for themselves now that he's eliminated the Commission."

"That's not true," Cisco countered.

"You can ask Comandante Norias, but he'll only lie to you," the voice said. "Who do you think has been keeping the colonel informed about your plans?"

"How do you know this?"

Cisco looked at his phone when the line went dead. He looked around the pool until he saw Comandante Norias flirting with the effeminate waiter. He caught his eye and waved him to come. A sudden unexpected thunderclap resonated across the party as a dark cloud swallowed up the setting sun. He glanced at Daniela, who raised her head to look at the darkening sky, exposing more than just the sumptuous side of her succulent sexuality.

"Sí, jefe," Norias said as he came to Cisco's side.

"Gather the men," he said. "We're going to Seyba Playa."

"Now?"

"Right now," Cisco said angrily. He looked at Norias's gold teeth. "You haven't been telling anyone about our plans for Champotón?"

"Of course not."

Cisco looked at him skeptically.

Just then, the rain began to come down in sheets. Daniela and her bikini-clad friends pounced to their feet like three alley cats trying to avoid a bucket of water. They stutter-stepped frantically around the pool to the house, holding their towels over their heads and their bikini tops to their naked breasts.

In the alley behind the back wall, Alonso jumped off the seat of his motorcycle after watching Daniela and the other kitty cats scurry into the house. He put his cell phone in his pocket and his helmet on his head. He started the motorcycle and drove down the alley to get out of the rain.

Chapter 11

After learning from San Juana that his cousin had gone for a run on the beach, Dario went into the coconut palms to look for him. As he walked down the path, he detected a faint odor in the breeze that he hadn't smelled since his time in the mountains of Michoacán. He wandered off the path, following the odor as it got stronger until he came to a clearing where he found a familiar sight and the malodorous stench of death hanging in the air like a burial shroud.

He gazed at the goat's head sitting on top of a four-foot-long pole over a cauldron containing a morbid soup of animal entrails, blood, and a partially submerged human skull with a policeman's badge wedged in its teeth.

"Are my eyes deceiving me, or are you a ghost?" Dario heard his cousin say behind him.

He turned to look at Fausto. "I am no ghost, primo."

Fausto stood glowering malevolently at him, holding a small-caliber pistol he normally carried in the pocket of his running shorts.

"Then you're an imposter," Fausto remarked. He pulled back on the hammer. "My cousin would have died at Padre Island rather than fail me."

Dario looked calmly into El Demonio's angry heterochromatic eyes, ignoring the pistol pointed at his head. "If I had done that, I wouldn't have been able to save your rifles."

The two men stared at each other as the sun hung over the horizon through the palms like a big red dot. Twice Fausto let his gun hand drop slightly, and twice, he snapped it back on target. Dario never flinched, never once showed fear or begged for his life.

Fausto brought the hammer home gently with his thumb and lowered his gun hand to his side.

"Tell me what happened."

Dario had to choose his words carefully. Since his cousin didn't put the gun back in his pocket, he knew he hadn't yet decided whether to kill him or not.

"We had just brought the rifles aboard when the police came. Dónovan used the distraction to take back the ship," Dario explained. "Nacho and Beto were killed."

"Why were you spared?"

"They had taken Nacho's and Beto's guns," Dario replied. "I couldn't do anything."

"You could have died trying."

Dario glanced at Fausto's gun hand as he tightened his grip on it. He looked at his face and saw the vein on his forehead getting bigger as he struggled to control his rage.

"If I had tried, they would have killed me, and I wouldn't have been able to bring you your guns," Dario explained.

He again glanced at Fausto's gun hand and saw that he had relaxed his grip. Although his cousin still looked at him suspiciously, the vein on his forehead no longer looked angry.

"You know about the delivery tonight?" Fausto asked.

"Sí, midnight at the warehouse."

"That's the plan, but ..." Fausto sighed.

"But what, primo?"

"It's Dónovan," he replied. "I can't help but believe he's up to one of his tricks."

"Like what?"

"I was hoping you could tell me," he replied suspiciously. "He didn't send you here as part of some scheme—did he?"

"How can you ask me that?" Dario asked resentfully. "I've been with you ever since Michoacán. I followed you to Tamaulipas. How can you question my loyalty?"

Dario used his indignation to mask the truth. Although he didn't really know, he knew Donovan had no intention of delivering the guns and surmised that he had some other plan to rescue Itzél.

"Have you've been with Dónovan all this time?"

"Sí, primo," Dario replied. "I had to make sure he followed through with the delivery."

"Why would Donovan keep you around?" Fausto asked curiously. "If it were me, I would have gotten rid of you long before I got back to Campeche."

"He wanted to but couldn't," Dario explained. "He had a wounded man he had to bring home to a doctor."

"Did he try to get any information out of you?"

"He tried, but I didn't give him anything he could use."

"What did he ask you?"

"He wanted to know if you would keep your word," Dario replied. "I told him you would."

"I thought you knew me better than that," Fausto responded as he grinned diabolically. "What else did he ask?"

"Many little things about what you might do," Dario answered. "I didn't tell him anything."

"Do you think he believed you?"

"I think so, but he made it obvious that he didn't trust me," Dario replied. "He tried locking me away at a house in Sabancuy, but as you can see, I got away."

"So, you wouldn't have any idea if he had some neat little trick planned for tonight?"

"No, primo. As far as I know, he plans to make the delivery. He's not going to do anything to put the woman in danger."

It looked like to Dario that his cousin had accepted his explanations. Then, Fausto asked him one more very significant question.

"Why did you come here?"

"To make sure you got your guns," Dario replied. "I thought you might be shorthanded and could use my help."

"As it turns out, you're right," Fausto said. "I want you to come with me to the warehouse tonight."

"I ..." Dario began as he felt the color wash from his face. "I was hoping to stay and watch the woman."

"Don't be silly," Fausto said. "Daniel can watch her. I want Dónovan to see you when he gets to the warehouse."

"I think you'd be better off taking Daniel instead and leaving me," Dario suggested. "I can keep her calm."

Dario swallowed as Fausto looked at him suspiciously. After a short while, he saw a fiendish smile come to his face.

"You're in love with her, aren't you?" Fausto said. "That's the real reason you came back."

"I can't hide anything from you, primo," he said a little awkwardly.

"Well," Fausto said as he drew a sharp breath, "you can have her after I kill Dónovan. Until then, I want you with me at the warehouse."

As Fausto led Dario to the plantation house, they did not notice Adán, the gardener, watching them from the palms.

The mix of mid-twentieth-century lounge music playing at the Paradise Lounge seemed fitting for the intrigue of the coming night. The soft lighting, the tropical setting, the French-Caribbean style furnishings, and the slow turning wicker-studded blades of the ceiling fans overhead would have brought a smile to Hemingway's weathered face.

Don Macario sat at his favorite table at the back of the lounge, enjoying his afternoon tea, when Dr. Ventura arrived dressed in a dark blue shirt with matching pants and not in his usual National Geographic photographer's garb. The hotelier had on a dove-gray tropical-weight business suit, a sky-blue dress shirt, and a narrow black tie.

"We may have a problem," the professor said as he sat. He had a severe look on his face. "Dario may have gone to see El Demonio."

"How long ago?" Don Macario inquired calmly as he set his teacup on the table.

"Two, three hours, maybe," the professor replied. "If he told El Demonio anything about tonight—"

"I don't think he has," Don Macario said, interrupting him. "If he had, El Demonio would have stormed in here by now."

"I suppose you're right," the professor said. "He did tell Poli he was going to make sure no harm came to his mother."

"Then, let's hope that's what he went to do," Don Macario concluded. "Are you ready for tonight?"

"I think so," the professor replied. He held out his hands. "How do I look?"

"Like Papa going marlin fishing."

"I thought you'd like it," the professor remarked as he sat. "Why was it important I dress like this?"

"It'll all become clear in a moment," Don Macario replied. He took a burner cell phone and a digital recorder from the side pockets of his suitcoat and set them on the table. "Listen carefully. You have a lot to do," he told the professor. "There's a fishing boat called *La Sirena* moored across from the front door of the warehouse. You're to board it after dark and watch the building."

"What am I watching for?"

"Any sign that the Thunderbolts have made entry into the warehouse."

"What then?"

Don Macario slid the cell phone across the table to him.

"As soon as you are certain that the Thunderbolts are in the warehouse, you're to make a call to Lieutenant Baeza. The number has been programmed into the phone. All you have to do is press any number to get the lieutenant."

"What do I tell him?"

"Nothing," Don Macario said as he slid the digital recorder to him. "As soon as he answers, press the play button on the recorder and put it up to the phone."

"What if the lieutenant doesn't answer?"

"He'll answer," Don Macario replied confidently. "Pablo is making sure of that."

"Pablo?" Dr. Ventura said disconcertedly. "He's going to take part in this?"

"Is that a problem?"

"Doña Estér told Simon that she saw him with Comandante Norias that day the Norteños came to the restaurant," the professor replied. "He could be working for them."

"Nonsense," Don Macario replied. "He was running an errand for an acquaintance of mine. I know all about it."

The professor sat quietly with his mouth open, digesting what Don Macario had just told him. After a moment, he looked at the controls of the recorder and started to depress the play button.

"Don't do that," Don Macario said. "The recorder is rigged to play the message only once. After you play it for the lieutenant, throw it and the cell phone into the water."

"What's on the recording?"

Don Macario reached into the inside pocket of his coat for Donovan's letter. He unfolded it, handed it to him, and waited for the professor to read through it.

"Oh, what a sinister prankster Simon is," the professor remarked as he handed the letter back to him.

After the squall, the skies over Isla Aguada cleared and the rays of the setting sun glistened on the wave tops like diamond chips on an Amsterdam diamond cutter's table. A light sea breeze blew across the deck of the *Siete Mares*, whistling softly through the rigging and swaying the ship lazily as the water lapped gently against the hull.

The *Siete Mares* sat at the end of the long pier in the calm waters beyond the white pristine sands and coconut trees of Isla Aguada. Augie stood on the pier by the gangplank on the portside of the ship with a hard-jawed man dressed in a black T-shirt, black cargo pants, and combat boots waiting on a group of men coming up the pier. He turned to Sandy, who lay on the main cabin top with his T-shirt over his eyes taking a nap.

"Avast you blasted sea-slug!" Augie called up to Sandy. "Make ready to take on passengers."

"Aye, aye, Mister Fagan!" Sandy said as he jumped to his feet.

The sandy-haired, blue-eyed boy slipped a faded green polo shirt over his head as he jumped on the deck and threw the slider back on its runners.

"They're here, Skipper," he called into the main cabin before going to the portside.

Donovan came topside, putting on a khaki shirt over the black V-neck T-shirt he wore. He buttoned it up, rolled the sleeves to the elbows, and tucked the tail into his black pants. He ran his fingers along the inside of the wide roan-colored belt as he went to join Sandy on the portside.

The men coming up the pier looked more like a soccer team on their way to a match than narco-paramilitaries on a mission. They all had muscular builds, short-cropped haircuts, and sunglasses. However, instead of dressing in sports attire, they dressed liked the hard-jawed man standing with Augie and instead of toting sports bags with name-brand logos, they carried military-style black canvas bags.

At the head of the group walked two older men, who by their gait and demeanor looked like the team's coaches. However, instead of that confident smugness common to coaches, they both walked with the formidable air of military officers.

"Request permission to come aboard," the colonel called up to Donovan as his men gathered around him.

"Welcome aboard, Colonel," Donovan replied as he made a quick head count.

"Thank you, Captain Donovan."

One by one, the narco-paramilitaries boarded the ship, gathering around the beam by the skylight forward of the main cabin where they set their bags on the deck.

Donovan looked at the colonel. "Didn't we agree on ten passengers?"

"We agreed to a ten-man team," Major Zamora responded for the colonel. "That didn't include the command staff."

Ordinarily, Donovan would have insisted on only allowing ten men to board his ship. Not that it made that much difference, but as the captain, he had to assert his authority or risk losing it. When confronted by twelve armed men, he found it wiser to assert his authority in some other way.

"They'll have to stay topside and keep out of the crew's way," Donovan said firmly. He looked sternly at the major. "Understood?"

"Understood," the major responded.

Donovan glanced at the black assault bags on the deck. He turned to Sandy. "Take them to the forward hatch and show them where they can stow their gear."

"That won't do," the major objected before Sandy could act. "The men need their bags with them at all times."

"I can't have your men cluttering the deck," Donovan countered.

"Please understand, Captain," the colonel interposed. "The men have to prepare for tonight's mission."

"And my crew needs clear access to the sails."

"You'll have it," the major responded. He turned to Sergeant Reséndez. "Put the teams where they'll be out of the crew's way."

"Sí, mí mayor," Reséndez said as he went forward.

Donovan watched the sergeant divide the Thunderbolts into three groups of three, setting one group amidships, one by the forward hatch, and one on the bow. The men settled into their spots neatly, keeping the areas around the masts clear. The discipline and efficiency the Thunderbolts demonstrated in executing the major's order impressed Donovan.

"Standby to cast off," Donovan said to Sandy.

"Aye, Skipper," Sandy replied as he went to join his uncle on the pier.

"The last time we talked, Capitán, you said you would find out if El Demonio has any guns in the warehouse," the major commented.

"I'm afraid all I could find out was that if he has any, they'll be in a crate at the very back of the warehouse."

"Do you know which crate?"

"Unfortunately, no, but if I had to guess, it'll be the easiest one to get to," he replied.

"Thank you, Captain," the major said.

"Prepare to cast off, Mister Fagan," Donovan called down to Augie on the pier.

"Aye, aye, Skipper."

"Help me with the gangplank," Augie said to his nephew.

"Please join me at the helm," Donovan said to the command staff as he went aft.

After helping with the gangplank, Sandy scurried down the pier toward the stern of the ship while Augie went toward the bow.

"How long will it take to get there, Capitán?" Major Zamora inquired.

"We should be there an hour or so after dark," Donovan replied. "I can take her further out and come in a little later if you'd like."

"That won't be necessary, Captain," the colonel replied. He turned to Donovan. "You haven't reconsidered selling me those Romanian rifles, have you?"

Donovan glanced at the Thunderbolts sitting amidships as they pulled their M-4 assault rifles out of their assault bags.

"Your men don't look like they're hurting for weapons," Donovan remarked.

"It's always a good idea to increase your inventory when the opportunity presents itself," the colonel responded. "Will you sell me those weapons?"

"Sorry, Colonel. Like I told you, those guns are going into the drink as soon as this is over."

"Ready to cast off, Skipper," Augie called to Donovan.

The water behind the transom burst into a churning wash of white and aqua when Donovan switched on the engine. He cupped his hands around his mouth.

"Cast off!" he yelled over the dull rumble of the ship's engine.

He turned to look when he heard the stern line hit behind him as Sandy tossed it up on the deck. He looked forward and watched Augie throw the bow line on the ship's deck. With the same grace of movement as two deer bucks gliding over a barbed-wire fence, Augie and Sandy jumped across the widening abyss to the retreating deck simultaneously as the schooner drifted slowly away from the dock.

The sun casting shadows through the thicket in the late afternoon can sometimes play tricks on a man's eyes, especially a man as tired as Cabo Muñoz, who routinely started his day at four in the morning. He sat behind the wheel of the Mini Commando not far from the town of La Joya, watching a tiny old man come out of the thicket dragging a sack behind him.

"Where did he come from?" Cabo Muñoz remarked as he turned to Lieutenant Baeza, sitting beside him. "It's like he popped out of nowhere."

"He probably lives somewhere nearby," the lieutenant replied.

The little old man lived in a tiny hut made of broken sticks and mud that a farmer had built for him to guard a field of corn he had cleared from the thicket many years ago. To appease the old man, the farmer had left him offerings of sweets and tobacco. After seven years, the field gave out, and the farmer abandoned the land without telling the tiny old man, who continued to use the hut since the farmer had left the door and window open.

"Is that a potato sack he's dragging behind him?"

"Poor old man," the lieutenant commented. "He's probably gathering aluminum cans to make ends meet."

"He looks like a dwarf." The corporal squinted his eyes. "A very old one at that."

"He doesn't look like a dwarf. He's just a very small man." The lieutenant took some money out of his pocket and peeled out several fifty-peso notes, which he handed to the corporal.

"What do you want me to do with this?"

"Go give it to him," the lieutenant replied.

"So much?" Muñoz frowned. "He'll just use it to buy cheap wine."

"What's wrong with that if it helps him wash down his dinner?"

"Nothing," Corporal Muñoz said, slamming the door as he got out of the truck. "If you consider a dead iguana or a feral cat dinner."

"Either should pair well," the lieutenant remarked as his cell phone began to ring.

Corporal Muñoz shook his head as he walked toward the old man. He nearly ran into him when the tiny man suddenly appeared right in front of him. He grinned at the corporal, exposing a mouth full of yellow teeth with several conspicuously missing.

The tiny old man's unexpected proximity so rattled the corporal that he stood speechless holding out the fifty-peso notes.

"What's this for?" he asked as he took the money.

"A donation from my lieutenant."

"Next time, tell him to send candy and cigarettes instead," the ungrateful little man said as he faded into the high grass before the corporal's eyes.

Darkness had yet to completely settle over the Bay of Campeche as the sky turned a deeper shade of blue. Cisco sat quietly in the lead vehicle of a large convoy of pickups and sports utility vehicles racing along the coast road toward Seyba Playa like rainwater rushing to a storm drain. As he listened to the lonesome whine of the tires on the roadway, he watched the soft glow of a large cargo ship's running lights lingering on the horizon. They looked like a taut string of white Christmas lights gliding along the edge of the world.

He thought about the gratitude he would earn from the Norteño cartel for foiling the colonel's plot to join forces with El Demonio. At last, he would prove his worth as a paramilitary leader. They would have to give him the Ciudad del Carmen plaza as his reward.

"Why are you slowing down?" Cisco asked his driver.

"We're approaching Villamar, jefe," the young thug responded. "If we run over somebody, the police might be called."

"Good thinking."

The road into the Villamar business district seemed uncharacteristically quiet as the convoy entered the tiny hamlet. Normally, the tightly packed buildings lining both sides of the road would have people on the sidewalks, sitting on the patios in front of the restaurants, or going in and out of the shops and hardware stores.

"That's strange," the driver remarked.

"What is?" Cisco asked.

"Where are the street vendors?"

Towns like Villamar normally had street urchins, cripples, and old people standing by the stoplights waiting to sell gum or mints, wipe windshields with a dirty rag, or beg for a handout. The Villamar business district had not seen such solitude since last Easter morning.

The driver stepped on the brakes suddenly, causing the rest of the convoy to slam on the brakes to keep from running into each other. Cisco put his hands out to keep himself from hitting the back of the front seat.

"Easy, pendejo!"

"Sorry, jefe, but there's a truck crossing the highway."

Cisco looked at the tanker truck moving slowly across the intersection until it came to a stop, blocking the road completely.

"What's he doing?" Cisco asked as the tanker's tires suddenly burst into flames. He looked out the side window and saw men with rifles taking positions along the roofs and second-story windows.

"¡Emboscada!" he yelled as he realized they had driven into an ambush.

A combined force of Campeche gang members, some dressed in police uniforms, attacked the trapped vehicles as they scattered like bumper cars looking for a way out of the deadly barrage of gunfire. The driver in the last vehicle in the convoy sped backward as another tanker truck emerged from an alley, crossing the concrete median and blocking both lanes of the road, forcing the driver to slam on the brakes. A man in a police uniform standing on a rooftop looking down on the vehicle tossed a Molotov cocktail, setting it ablaze.

Cisco dove to the floorboard as his driver backed the Tahoe, blindly striking the pickup behind him. He put the car in gear and drove on the sidewalk to his right before a high-powered rifle round pierced the bulletproof window, striking him under his left armpit. The Tahoe veered sharply to the right and crashed into a small building.

The road through the Villamar business district looked like the highway out of Kuwait during Desert Storm One. The gunmen who survived the initial onslaught abandoned their vehicles, leaving them strewn across both sides of the highway like Tonka toys at a day-care center. Several of the trucks burned spectacularly while others emitted vapor from their punctured radiators or smoke from their burning interiors. The bodies of dead sicarios littered the streets, median, and sidewalks.

Those sicarios who ran down the alleys on the west side of the road toward the rocky beach had their lives ended by the relentless gunfire coming from the bluff. Some sought shelter in the shops but met the same end at the hands of Sánchez's men waiting for them inside. A few ran wildly through the thicket behind the buildings on the east side of the road but couldn't outrun the guns of the Campeche gang's killers. Not a single man affected a successful escape. Those who fell wounded had their throats cut.

In the floorboard of the rear seat of the wrecked Tahoe, Cisco struggled to free himself from the dead sicario lying on him. He tried opening the right rear door, slamming his shoulder against it several times. He lay on the body of the gunman and kicked it open with his feet.

He opened the door and saw the lifeless body of a man dressed in a state police uniform pinned by the Tahoe against a counter. He could hear the gunfire subsiding, followed by an eerie silence. He heard men calling to each other in the distance, followed shortly afterward by a single gunshot.

Cisco fell as he got out of the Tahoe and noticed that his shirt had blood on it. He gasped and then checked himself for a wound. He sighed with relief when he realized the blood belonged to the dead sicario who had sat next to him. He held his breath as he rose to his feet to look out the window facing the street.

He realized that the gangs had annihilated his sicarios completely as he looked at the smoldering wrecks scattered haphazardly up and down the highway. At least two other vehicles had crashed into a building like his. He stared at the bodies lying motionless on the road as the voices he had heard earlier came closer. He had to make a run for it or face meeting the same fate.

He had a wild look in his eyes, like a cornered animal, as he moved quickly to the back of the shop. He opened the back door and made a mad dash through the thicket. He came out on a back street and looked to the left and right for pursuers. He spotted a state police car and watched it drive through an intersection, stop suddenly, and then back up quickly.

He ran between two houses toward a cedar fence. He jumped it, surprising a very large dog. He froze for a moment as he and the dog stared at each other. He then bolted toward the far fence with the dog literally on his heels. He struck the top of the cedar fence with his chest, rolling over it and dropping into the next yard. He listened to the dog barking frantically on the other side of the fence as he sat against it to catch his breath. His heart jumped when he heard his pursuers talking about the barking dog.

Without thinking, he ran to the next fence and jumped it and then to the next fence, jumping it as well, trying to get as far away from the ambushers as he could. After scaling several other fences, he finally found himself in another thicket. As darkness began to fall, he ran blindly through the brush and thornbushes, protecting his face as he crashed through the low-lying branches in his haste. Somewhere along the way, he had lost his pistol.

CHAPTER 12

The drive north from the Paradise Inn to the Port of Seyba Playa didn't take long, but it did give Dr. Ventura time to think. He had spent the greater part of his life with his head buried in books until he began doing fieldwork as an archeologist. His chosen area of study introduced him to spelunking, mountain climbing, and, when he moved into marine archeology, sailing and scuba diving. It had opened a whole new world to him, a world he never imagined he would ever see but nothing like the world he had seen since meeting Simon Donovan.

Dr. Ventura parked his BMW across the street from the *malecón* just outside the gate to the port as the sun's fading light began to dissipate gradually into night. He sat in his car for a moment looking through his binoculars for *La Sirena* among the shrimpers and fishing boats moored in the boat slips along the northside of the dock. He tried looking at the white plywood boxes at the foot of each slip to see if he could find the boat's name on it. When he couldn't, he lowered his binoculars and sighed.

As he prepared himself mentally for what he had to do that night, he gazed at the soft glow of the sky over the ocean and at the way the silhouettes of the booms on the cranes seemed to punch through the crimson brilliance. He stared at the forklifts and reach stackers huddled at the end of the dock where the larger ships put in to load or offload cargo as he thought about doing his part.

"Well, here goes nothing," the professor muttered to himself.

He put his binoculars in the cooler he had brought to transport the items Don Macario gave him and other things he might need. As he put on a ball cap with a fishing company's logo on it, he listened to the sounds of Seyba Playa buttoning up her streets for the night. The evening seemed relatively quiet except for the rumbling of a large truck somewhere nearby. Even the Tiburón, the dockworkers' bar just inside the gates to the port, seemed unusually quiet.

As the professor walked up the dock to where *La Sirena* sat in her moorings, the streetlights lining the northside came on suddenly. He felt panic shoot through him briefly when he noticed two thugs leaning against the outside of the warehouse across from the fishing boat. They looked like common street gangsters, and he worried that they might accost him or try to rob him. He kept calm and ignored them as he turned to walk up the finger pier to board *La Sirena*. He glanced briefly over his shoulder as he came alongside the wheelhouse before stepping over the gunwale to go aboard.

As soon as he entered the wheelhouse, he saw Pablo sitting on an overturned five-gallon bucket by the console, watching the warehouse through a pair of binoculars perched on the hub of the ship's wheel.

"Get out of the light, Professor," Pablo whispered. "There's somebody coming up the dock."

The professor moved into the shadows at the back of the wheelhouse, where he set his cooler on the deck to get his binoculars. He bent his knees to stay out of the light as he trained them on the warehouse.

"Has anything happened yet?" the professor asked as he sat on his cooler.

"I just got here," Pablo retorted curtly. "Try not to make any noise."

The professor played with the knobs on his binoculars until he got a clear picture of the taller thug standing by the door. He turned his binoculars briefly on the shorter thug and then at the plate-glass window. He adjusted the focus until he could see through the narrow slits in the blind.

"There are at least two people in the office," the professor commented in a low voice.

"Three," Pablo said curtly. "El Demonio, his cousin, Dario, and Felipe."

"You can tell all that by just looking through the blinds?" the professor asked as he put down his binoculars to look dubiously at Pablo.

"Felipe opened the door to talk to the guards before you got here," Pablo said in a subdued but impatient tone. "I saw El Demonio talking to Dario. Now, will you please be quiet and stop making so much noise?"

The professor stared at the back of the barman's head like a child after a good scolding. He mocked him by making a face and mouthing inaudibly as he thumbed his nose at him. He scoffed and then looked at the front of the warehouse where he noticed the thugs looking down the dock. He turned to see what had their attention and saw two policemen walking toward them at a brisk pace. He looked at Pablo, who held a cell phone to his ear.

"The police are here," he whispered to him.

Pablo looked back at him as he put an index finger to his lips.

The lieutenant looked at the bewildered corporal as he listened attentively to the caller. He motioned the petty officer sitting in the Mini Commando next to his to come. Petty Officer Lanceros stepped out of his vehicle and waited by the lieutenant's window.

"Are you sure?" Baeza nodded his head softly as he listened to the caller. "Keep me posted." The lieutenant closed his cell phone and turned to the petty officer.

"You wanted to see me, mí teniente," the petty officer said smartly.

"Fausto López is at the warehouse at Port of Seyba Playa."

"So, it's the warehouse then?"

"It could be," the lieutenant replied. "Two state police comandantes just got to the warehouse. One of them is none other than our friend Comandante Sánchez."

"I thought there was bad blood between López and Sánchez."

"There is, but with Cisco Cisneros expected to come to Champotón tonight, they could be working together," Baeza explained. "He is their common enemy."

"Do you really think Cisneros is coming?"

"I doubt it," the lieutenant replied. "Not this soon after the firebombings."

The lieutenant's cell phone started to ring.

"Baeza," he said into the phone. He listened carefully to what the caller had to say. "Entendido," he said as he closed his cell phone.

"¿Problema, mí teniente?" Petty Officer Lanceros inquired.

"That's the call I was hoping wouldn't come," Baeza responded. "There's a gun battle raging in Villamar. The detachment is responding, and command wants us to move to Champotón to be available to support them if necessary."

"What about the gun shipment?"

The lieutenant stared at Corporal Muñoz wandering through the high grass as darkness came. He knew the detachment had more than enough men to handle the situation in Villamar.

"Move us to the coast a little south of Haltunchén," he said to the petty officer.

"Are you sure, mí teniente?" Lanceros asked cautiously. "That's still a good distance from Champotón."

"I want to be close enough to Seyba Playa just in case."

"But your orders, mí teniente."

"We'll be close enough to Champotón if they need us."

"Wouldn't Paraiso be better?"

The lieutenant didn't normally disobey orders, but Comandante Sánchez suddenly showing up at the warehouse aroused his curiosity. He had to know why.

"I'll tell you what," the lieutenant began. He honked the horn and motioned Corporal Muñoz back to the Mini Commando. "We'll go to Paraiso, like you suggested," he continued as he punched in the number for the communications center on his cell phone. "But at twenty kilometers an hour."

The two thugs tried to block Comandantes Sánchez and Prieto from entering the warehouse by standing in front of the door. Neither looked like he had ever shaved or weighed very much. They looked like a pair of cheap bookends dressed in jeans and unbuttoned, lose-fitting shirts over white T-shirts. Each had a red bandana tied around his head with a red, flat-billed ball cap cocked to one side.

"Step aside," Comandante Sánchez barked at them.

The taller thug showed Sánchez the .38 revolver he had tucked in his waistband. Sánchez snatched the gun away by the butt, looked at the electrical tape wrapped around the grip holding it together, and scoffed. The shorter thug tried frantically to get his gun out of his pocket but froze when he felt the muzzle of Prieto's gun barrel pressed against his head.

"Quieto, mijito," Prieto said as he took the beat-up Saturday night special from him.

The warehouse door swung open suddenly as Felipe walked out of the office. Prieto tossed the weathered .22 revolver at him as he holstered his sidearm. Felipe stood quietly as Sánchez took his hand and slapped the .38 revolver he took from the taller thug into it.

Felipe stood in the doorway holding the cheap revolvers with his hapless sicarios standing dumbfoundedly behind him as the comandantes walked into the office. He turned to his sicarios and gave each back his gun.

"Get back to your posts," he said to them firmly. "We'll talk about this later."

Sánchez grinned at Fausto, who sat behind his desk glaring at him unpleasantly. He glanced at Dario, who stood quietly by the plate-glass window by the door. Comandante Prieto went to stand next to Dario as he stared at him like a cat about to pounce. The burly police commander went to sit in one of the wooden chairs in front of the desk, laying his crumpled policeman's hat in the chair next to him.

"Where did you find those car wash commandos?" Sánchez asked mockingly.

"They were all Chino could spare," Fausto replied.

"Oh? They aren't your men?" Sánchez chuckled faintly as he scoffed. "Where *are* your men?"

Fausto glared contemptuously at him. "What do you want, Sánchez?"

"I came to see if you got your guns, yet," he replied. "I believe you *were* expecting them tonight?"

Sánchez smiled widely as he watched the vein on Fausto's forehead swell. He looked over his shoulder at Dario, who remained stone-faced as he looked back at him.

"Why aren't you in Champotón waiting for Cisco with the others?" Fausto inquired.

"Oh, you know about that?" he asked as he turned to look at him.

"Chino told me about your little meeting."

"Did he also tell you about my brilliant plan?"

"You're just wasting the men's time," Fausto said confidently. "Cisco's not coming."

Sánchez stared arrogantly at El Demonio, grinning presumptuously. "Is that what you think?"

"It doesn't make sense that he would, not this soon after the firebombings."

"That's what Chino told me you said when I asked him why you weren't coming to witness my brilliant plan in action," Sánchez retorted.

"I'm telling you you're wasting everybody's time. He's not coming."

Sánchez's lighthearted mood changed suddenly as he settled back in his chair and stared sullenly at López.

"I almost wish that were true."

The twin Paxman diesel-electric engines churned in perfect balance as the Azteca-class coastal patrol boat backed away from her moorings into the middle of the Champotón River. The crew moved calmly about the deck performing their duties as the maritime patrol vessel prepared to get underway.

Captain Mendiola rested his left forearm along the top of the console while the executive officer calmly issued orders to the crew. Corvette Lieutenant Juan José Medrano had only recently graduated from the Naval Academy in Veracruz. For a boyish-faced young officer, the lieutenant seemed mature beyond his years and had already earned the respect of the crew.

"Maestre," the executive officer called to the petty officer on the bridge.

"Sí, mí teniente," the young petty officer replied smartly.

"It'll be dark soon. See that the searchlights are functioning properly before we get underway."

"Sí, mí teniente."

"Issue handheld spotlights to the forward and stern gun crews."

"Sí, mí teniente."

"Have the armorer issue automatic weapons and body armor to the rest of the crew when we clear the river."

"Sí, mí teniente."

The captain glanced at the young lieutenant before returning his eyes to the river ahead. The young officer reached over to the petty officer's tunic and buttoned the pockets on his shirt.

"That is all, maestre."

As the helmsmen headed the patrol boat slowly up the river, Teniente Medrano joined the captain at the console.

"This will be your first action. ¿No, teniente?" Capitán Mendiola asked the young officer as he watched a crewman coil the bow line.

"I count every ship we've interdicted as an action, mí capitán," the lieutenant replied stoically. "This will be my first combat action, if that's what you mean."

The captain turned to face a crewman holding a clipboard as he approached the console.

"Message, teniente," he said to the lieutenant as he handed the clipboard to Lieutenant Medrano.

The lieutenant glanced at the message, initialed it, and tore the top copy off the clipboard. He handed the message to the captain and returned the clipboard back to the radioman. He turned to the captain.

"Teniente Baeza is reporting suspicious activity at the Port of Seyba Playa," the executive officer informed him. "He requests permission to investigate."

"What is it now, Baeza?" the captain muttered to himself as he read the complete message. He turned to the radioman standing by to take a reply. "Marinero," he addressed the radioman directly. "Send the following to Teniente Baeza: You are authorized to go investigate. Ship will be off Villamar supporting Champotón detachment investigating gun battle between delinquents. Be prepared to deploy to Champotón at a moment's notice."

"We're clear, mí teniente," the helmsman reported as the ship came to the mouth of the Champotón River.

"Take us there, Teniente," the captain said to the lieutenant.

"Full ahead to Villamar," the executive officer commanded.

"Sí, mi teniente," the helmsman replied.

He threw the throttle forward, bringing the bow of the vessel down as it headed into the Bay of the Bad Fight.

The *Siete Mares* rounded Siho Playa Point as the twilight began to fade into a thick veil of darkness. Overhead, the royal blue of the sky deepened to cobalt as the stars began to show themselves, a sparkling speck at a time. Donovan took the ship well off the coast to avoid any curious eyes as Augie stood by his side waiting to take the helm.

The colonel and the major went below with Reséndez and three other Thunderbolts as Sandy sat on top of the main cabin watching the paramilitaries clean their weapons. They had the disassembled parts spread neatly on a large towel between them as they rubbed each metallic part with a soft cloth and applied a light film of oil afterward before reassembling the weapons.

Donovan looked across the water at the beacon flashing periodically on top of the dark hill overlooking Punta Morro. He thought about Itzél sitting in the cottage at Lorenzo. Thanks to Don Macario, he had a clear idea where to find her. He had committed to memory the photos the old gentleman had taken of the cottage, the beach, and the coconut grove leading to the plantation house. He had gone over his plan in his mind, anticipating contingencies and coming up with backup plans as he steered the ship toward the waters off Punta Morro.

"I hope you know what you're doing," Augie remarked. "I'm not so sure trusting those guys is a good idea."

"You want to stay at the Paradise Lagoon, don't you?" Donovan retorted.

"Of course."

"We can't do that with El Demonio around."

"I wish there was another way."

"I told you before I went to see the colonel what I had in mind," Donovan said. "I thought you were all right with it."

"It was just an idea then. Seeing it happen is … different."

They both turned to look as Reséndez swung open the doors to the hatch and looked viciously at Donovan.

"The colonel wants you at the briefing," he said.

Donovan turned to Augie. "Take the helm."

As Donovan came down the companionway, he looked at the Thunderbolt team leaders gathered around the captain's table.

"Please close the hatch behind you," Major Zamora said to him.

After throwing the slider forward, Donovan closed the doors to the hatch and went to sit near the bottom of the companionway. He watched Major Zamora finish going over the plan with the team leaders using the maps, diagrams, and aerial photos he had spread on the table. The major covered every aspect of the operation from boarding the pangas taken from Payucán Beach to breaching the warehouse to the extraction that would bring the teams back to the ship.

Donovan wondered where the major got the aerial photos and diagrams of the layout of the port and the warehouse. They all looked like official government documents. He concluded that Colonel Barca must still have friends in the army who helped him get such things.

Donovan glanced periodically at Colonel Barca, who sat quietly listening to the briefing. Every time Donovan glanced at Sergeant Reséndez, he always seemed to have his eyes on him.

"Any question regarding your assignments?" Major Zamora asked the team leaders.

The team leaders stood silently.

"Go brief your men." The major handed the diagrams and aerial photos to the senior team leader. "Dismissed."

Donovan went to throw back the slider and open the hatch for the Thunderbolt leaders to go join their teams.

"Would you please come here, Capitán?" the major asked politely. "I'd like to go over the extraction plan with you."

"I was listening," Donovan responded. "You want the ship to wait off Punta Morro for the pangas to come back."

"I need to discuss contingency plans in case of a problem."

"What kind of problem?"

"Just get over here and do as you're told," Sergeant Reséndez said sternly.

Donovan glared at the pit-bull-like noncom, who stared back at him viciously. He gave one last contemptuous glare at the sergeant before joining the major at the table.

"Most likely, there won't be a problem," the colonel said. "However, we must prepare for the unexpected."

"Like the colonel said," the major began, "there shouldn't be any problems, but in the unlikely event something does happen, I will need for you to bring your ship to the end of the dock to pick up the teams."

"You mean my first mate," Donovan said correcting him. "I'll be conducting an operation of my own in Lorenzo, remember?"

The major turned to the colonel, who took a step closer to the table.

"There's been a change in the plan," the colonel said. "The mission to take Fausto takes priority. I can't risk him being alerted by a reckless attempt to free a hostage."

"First of all—*Colonel*—I'm not reckless," Donovan said angrily. "I've found my way into a lot more heavily guarded compounds than Fausto's plantation house to repossess boats without being detected. Secondly, I know exactly where she is and that she's being guarded by an old couple I'm confident won't give me any trouble."

"I'm familiar with your exploits, Captain," the colonel responded. "However, I would be remiss in my responsibilities to the mission if I were to allow you to jeopardize it by some unforeseen variable." He sighed. "There's an old Prussian military adage, 'No plan survives first contact with the enemy.'"

Donovan glowered at the colonel. "I thought you were a man of honor," he said solemnly.

"In my business, there is no room for such indulgences," the colonel retorted.

As night fell over Campeche City, the bus making the last run to Champotón rumbled out of the terminal with José Luis aboard. He watched the bus driver adjust the round mirror over his head to better see the passengers and thought for a moment he had developed an unnatural interest in him, making him uncomfortable. To his relief, he determined that the lecherous bus driver had his eye on the immodest woman sitting in front of him wearing a low-neck blouse.

He lowered himself in his seat and tried to get some sleep as the bus turned on Old Mexico 180. He hadn't gotten much since leaving Houston in a fevered rush to avoid capture after murdering Billy Chávez and failing to silence Linda.

He presumed Linda would have gone to the police, who he also presumed would have issued a bulletin to look for Billy's Charger headed for Mexico. So, he decided to drive north on Interstate 45 to Conroe to find a less conspicuous vehicle to get him home.

Fortune had smiled upon him when he spotted a young girl getting out of an old white Chevy Cheyenne pickup after parking on the far side of the convenience store. The uniform smock she wore and her fresh demeanor told him she had just come to work. If his luck held out, that would give him at least eight hours before she would notice her truck missing, enough time to get to the border. He dumped Billy's charger at an apartment complex next to the convenience store and hot-wired the pickup to make good his escape. He shed his coat, pulled his hair into a ponytail using a rubber band he had found in the girl's glove compartment, and began the five-hour trek to the border.

The drive seemed too easy despite his uneasiness. He worried that the girl might notice her truck missing and report it stolen, prompting the police to issue a state-wide bulletin. His throat tightened every time he saw a highway patrol or a sheriff's car on the road. He made complete stops at traffic lights and signaled every time he changed lanes.

When at last he made it across the border, he watched the stoplight used by Mexican Customs to randomly inspect inbound vehicles with great apprehension. Although the odds he would trip a green light sided with him, the possibility that he would trip the red light obligating him to a secondary inspection loomed ominously.

After leaving customs, he sold the pickup to an old friend he knew in Reynosa who bought stolen trucks to sell to the cartel. With the cash he got for the truck, he caught a flight to Mexico City, where he connected to Mérida in the state of Yucatán. He got there just in time to catch the express bus to Campeche City.

As he made the long ride from Mérida, he thought about seeing Donovan's ship rising and falling beyond the surf as it headed into the full moon and the distinctive silhouette of a large man standing on the deck. He had no doubt that it belonged to Dario Róbles, and he couldn't wait to settle accounts with him.

The bus arrived at the terminal in Campeche City in the late afternoon, just in time to catch Domingo Figueroa's last run to Champotón. He expected the ride to Lorenzo would take just under an hour if the driver with the wandering eyes could keep the bus on the road as he stole glances of the big-bosomed woman sitting in front of him.

The coast between Punta Morro and Payucán Beach separated the dark of the night from the deep of the ocean like a humpback whale lying on its side under a moonless sky. The wake behind the pangas looked like two white ribbons spreading across the water as they glided toward the *Siete Mares*. The Thunderbolts waited quietly by the starboard beam for the high-bowed fiberglass launches to arrive. The black battle dress uniforms, helmets, and smudge on their faces made them look like shadow people on the haunt. They took a knee when Colonel Barca and Major Zamora turned to face the raiders to deliver the final briefing.

"You'd think they were going to a dance or something," Augie remarked to Donovan as they stood at the stern of the ship. "I've been with stage bands setting up that were more wound up. Look at 'em. Calm as bathwater."

Donovan didn't respond as he headed toward the starboard side.

"Where're you going?" Augie asked.

"To talk to the colonel."

"But he told us to wait here."

As the pangas cut their outboard motors to come alongside the ship, Major Zamora concluded the briefing and ordered the Thunderbolts to stand. The men lowered the stems from their radio headsets, positioning the mics close to their mouths. They put their hands on the pistol grips of their matte black M-4 rifles they had harnessed across their chests and formed two lines amidships in preparation to board the pangas.

Sergeant Reséndez saw Donovan coming and went to block his way.

"Go back," he said firmly.

"I want to talk to the colonel."

"He's busy."

"Let him through, Sergeant," Donovan heard the colonel say.

He looked at Sergeant Reséndez. "You're in my way, sugar cheeks."

Donovan looked down at the pangas as he went to talk to the colonel. It surprised him to see the men sitting at the stern wearing federal preventive police uniforms.

"I take it those are not real cops," Donovan commented.

"What can I do for you, Captain?" Colonel Barca asked him.

Donovan turned to look at the lighthouse perched on the top of the hill on Punta Morro.

"The plantation house is just beyond that hill. I can get Itzél and be back on the ship in under an hour." Donovan began. "Plenty of time to get the ship to the end of the dock to pick up your men in case there's a problem."

"I told you it's out of the question," Colonel Barca responded.

"What if I told you where I put Fausto's guns," Donovan said, playing the last chip he had in the game.

"You'd say anything to get what you want."

Donovan looked across the water at Punta Morro. He recalled the eerie sound of the wind blowing into the caves and the waves crashing against the huge boulders that night he came with the guns. If he told the colonel where he hid the guns, it could compromise his plan. He decided he didn't have a choice.

"They're in the warehouse," Donovan said. "In the crate, I told you about."

The colonel looked at the major who shook his head.

"Sergeant," the colonel called to Reséndez, "remove this man."

"With pleasure."

Donovan glared at the colonel disquietedly.

"I'm afraid you'll have to wait until we complete the operation," the colonel responded. "The Armada is also just up the coast, and I have to think about operational security. I can't have you mucking it up."

"I don't see how I could—"

"I'm sorry, Captain, but that's final," the colonel said interrupting him. "Your woman should be all right after we eliminate López."

"You don't know that," Donovan contended. "He could give the order to have her killed once he sees you coming."

"He won't see us coming," Major Zamora remarked.

"The odds are we'll have him neutralized before he can give such an order," Colonel Barca added confidently.

"I'm not willing to take that chance."

"It's not your choice to make," Sergeant Reséndez remarked.

"You can collect your woman after we secure from the mission," the colonel said.

"She could be dead by then," Donovan argued.

"I'm sorry, but there is no other way."

"You can't keep me from going."

"Sergeant Reséndez is staying aboard to see that you do." He looked at Sandy and then turned to the sergeant. "Shoot the boy if he attempts to leave this ship."

CHAPTER 13

The soft hum of the outboard motor went silent suddenly as the panga glided in the still water to the wharf behind the Campechano warehouse. The water trickled softly under the bow as the Thunderbolt sitting on the prow guided the launch alongside the dock until it came to a stop. The Puma Uno fireteam climbed out immediately and established a security perimeter on the dock while the colonel and the major tied down the launch.

Meanwhile, the second panga glided to a stop alongside the quay between the Campechano warehouse and the building just up the port from it. The Puma Tres fireteam jumped out to establish a security perimeter around the landing while the two paramilitaries dressed in federal preventive police uniforms tied down the second launch.

At the same time, the Puma Dos fireteam, each member carrying a rope over his shoulder with the grenadier also carrying an RPG-7 launcher strapped to his back debarked the second panga and rushed to the side of the Campechano warehouse. They tossed the grapplehooks tied to their ropes up to the roof, listened for the thud and then tugged on their ropes until the hooks caught. They scaled the side of the wall like cats climbing a chain-link fence.

On the ground, the Puma Tres fireteam leader led his riflemen quickly and stealthily along the west side of the warehouse with the pseudofederale policemen following close behind. The team leader held his fist up, stopping his riflemen just short of the front of the building. He let his M-4 assault rifle hang from its sling as he raised his pistol with both hands, pointing the silencer at the end of it in front of him as he side-stepped in a slow, deliberate arc until he had a view of the front of the warehouse. The team leader held his left hand to the side, signaling his team of the presence of two targets standing in front of the building.

On the roof, the Puma Dos grenadier lifted the trapdoor slightly while the fireteam leader lowered a miniature video camera by its cord into the warehouse. Meanwhile, the rifleman recovered his rope, secured the grapplehook to a heavy vent pipe, and waited by the trapdoor to drop the loose end down the opening. The fireteam leader looked at the miniature screen on his monitor as he turned the camera remotely to check the warehouse floor. He nodded at his team as he recovered the camera. The grenadier pulled the trapdoor open quietly as the rifleman dropped the rope into the warehouse and lowered himself to the floor while the fireteam stood by to support him if necessary.

On the wharf behind the warehouse, the Puma Uno fireteam leader stood to the side of the backdoor with his pistol in his hand while his riflemen trained their rifles in opposite directions. The fireteam leader stepped back when he heard movement behind the door and brought up the silencer at the end of his pistol. He holstered his weapon and brought up his M-4 after hearing two subtle knocks and a thud coming from the inside of the door. He knocked twice softly on the door, pointed his hand at the colonel and the major, and brought it back sharply in three rapid strokes signaling them to advance.

Colonel Barca and the major stepped out of the panga and followed Puma Uno and his team into the warehouse. The riflemen dropped to a knee and trained their M-4 assault rifles at the door leading into the office while the Puma Uno fireteam leader lifted the lids on the crates at the back of the room. After the third try, he looked at the colonel and nodded.

Colonel Barca went to look in the crate and nodded. He looked at the luminous dial on his watch and then summoned the major, who looked in the crate and nodded.

"Proceed, Major," he said softly.

The major turned to the Puma Dos rifleman. "Go back to your team," he said to him as he raised the stem of his mic to his lips. "Puma Tres—report."

"Two bandidos watching the door," the fireteam leader replied.

"Take them."

As the colonel and major stood by at the back of the warehouse, the two pseudofederales walked around the corner of the building with their hands behind their backs in casual conversation. The two thugs standing watch by the front door turned to look at them as one of the pseudoFederales waved harmlessly at them. When the thugs raised their hands to wave back, the other pseudofederale shot them with a silenced pistol.

As the pseudofederales dragged the dead gangsters to the side of the building, the Puma Tres fireteam leader shot out the streetlights around the warehouse with an air pistol. He started to signal his team to advance when a sudden splash coming from the boat slips got his attention.

The Puma Tres fireteam leader put the air pistol in his tunic, drew his pistol, and pointed the silencer at *La Sirena* as he stepped toward it. He looked up to the roof where the Puma Dos fireteam had moved to set up a sniper's nest behind the bulwark. He extended his arm out horizontally with the palm forward and waved his arm to his head and back several times to get the Puma Dos fireteam leader's attention. He pointed two fingers at his eyes and then at *La Sirena*. The Puma Dos fireteam leader pointed two fingers at his eyes and then at *La Sirena* and then held a thumb up. The Puma Tres fireteam leader turned to his team and signaled them to take their position around the front door.

"Front door secure," the Puma Tres fireteam leader said into his mic.

The colonel nodded at the major, who signaled the Puma Uno team leader to advance to the office. They followed the Puma Uno fireteam, who moved stealthily across the warehouse floor, where they stood by the door waiting for the order to make entry. Voices from within the office carried in the stillness, and the colonel gave the signal to hold fast as he listened to the conversation.

"I don't believe you," the colonel heard Fausto say to Sánchez.

"It doesn't matter what you believe," he heard Sánchez reply. "It's done."

"How did it happen?" he heard a third voice inquire.

"It was really quite simple," he heard Sánchez respond. "I set up an ambush at Villamar. Cisco led his men into town where we blocked in his convoy and the rest was like shooting fish in a barrel."

The colonel and the major looked at each other as they listened to Sánchez go on about how he set up and executed the ambush.

"Is that why you came here?" the colonel heard Fausto ask. "To gloat?"

"I told you," he heard Sánchez reply. "I came to see if you got your guns."

A long pause followed as the colonel continued to listen.

"You see, Señor López. Where you fail, I succeed," he heard Sánchez say arrogantly. "As we speak, Comandante Tercero of the Comisión is gathering a shipment of guns and ammunition for *my* men."

The colonel looked at the major and nodded, giving the go-ahead for entry.

The side door to the warehouse floor opened violently as the Puma Uno fireteam exploded into the office, pointing their silencers at the end of their pistols on the occupants.

Prieto and Dario instinctively raised their hands, while Sánchez tried to stand. The wheels on Fausto's swivel chair squealed strenuously as he pushed it back to get his gun from his desk. The fireteam leader slammed the drawer on his hand and kicked the chair away from the desk as a rifleman forced Sánchez to sit with the tip of his silencer against his head.

A sharp crack rang out as the major shot Felipe when he went for his gun, throwing him against the door. A streamlet of blood trickled out of a small hole in the center of his forehead as he slid slowly to the floor. Major Zamora brought the mic at the end of its stem close to his mouth as the colonel walked into the office behind him.

"Target secured," the major said into the mic and then picked up Felipe's pistol.

The colonel glanced at Dario and Prieto before turning to Comandante Sánchez and Fausto.

"Buenas noches, caballeros," he said greeting them politely. He went to Comandante Sánchez and held out his hand. "Your sidearm, por favor."

Sánchez glared at the colonel as he unholstered his pistol and gave it to him. Prieto raised his hands higher as the rifleman covering him took his pistol from his holster.

"I'm unarmed," Dario said, holding his hands out, inviting the paramilitary to search him.

The fireteam leader forced Fausto to his feet, spun him around rudely, and frisked him. He threw him back into his chair and pushed it away from his desk with his foot. He removed Fausto's gun from the top drawer and then opened the others to look for additional weapons. He found Fausto's cell phone and tossed it across the desk away from his reach.

"Sit down, Comandante," Colonel Barca said to Sánchez. "I believe you were saying something about Cisco?"

Sánchez didn't respond. The colonel took the comandante's pistol and pulled the slide back just enough to see the round sitting in the breech before releasing the slide. He pointed the gun at his head.

"We jumped a convoy at Villamar we believe was being led by Cisco Cisneros," Sánchez said.

The colonel stared at the comandante for a moment.

"Any survivors?" he asked.

Sánchez glared at him defiantly. "I'm told there were none."

The colonel glanced briefly at the major and then looked back at Sánchez. "What about Cisco?"

"He hasn't been found yet," Sánchez replied. "He might have got away."

The colonel drew a deep breath and then released it slowly. "That's unfortunate."

The colonel turned to Fausto, who chuckled obnoxiously. Major Zamora walked over to him and pointed his pistol at his forehead.

"What are you laughing at?" Zamora asked him.

"Sánchez—he was so proud of his little ambush," Fausto said through his sarcastic chuckling. He turned to the colonel. "Well played, Coronel. Only you would think of sacrificing a hundred men to buy you the element of surprise."

"I had nothing to do with ordering Cisco to do what he did," the colonel said. "He was supposed to stay in Ciudad del Carmen until we were done in Chiapas."

"Then what?" Prieto asked. "When were you moving against Champotón?"

"Never," the colonel replied as he looked at Prieto. "We were returning to Nuevo León."

"Then the Norteño cartel has no interest in Campeche?" Sánchez inquired.

"Of course not," the colonel replied. "Anastasio was never interested in Campeche. Only in settling with the Commission."

"Then what are you doing here?" Comandante Prieto asked.

"I heard Fausto was expecting a shipment of guns," the colonel replied. "So, naturally, I came to take a look."

"Then, I'm afraid you've wasted your time. There are no guns," Sánchez remarked sarcastically. "They're all in a police locker in Texas."

The colonel smiled affectedly. "What about the guns we just found in the back of the warehouse?"

"I don't have any guns here," Fausto said as he stared curiously at the colonel.

The colonel turned to Major Zamora. "Bring them to the office."

Major Zamora pointed at the rifleman covering Prieto and Dario and signaled him to get the guns.

Colonel Barca looked at Dario. "I'm surprised to see you here, Dario."

"Why wouldn't he be?" Fausto interjected.

The colonel turned to Fausto. "I was sure he wouldn't come back here after betraying you at Padre Island."

"He didn't betray me," Fausto retorted.

"But he did," the colonel insisted. "He helped Donovan set you up." He chuckled as he turned to Dario. "Isn't that right?"

"He would never do that," Fausto said as he looked at his cousin. "Dario would never betray me."

"Oh?" Colonel Barca remarked. "How do you think I was able to find my way into your office unimpeded?" He undid the button on his tunic and took out the diagram Dario had drawn of the warehouse's floor plan and tossed it onto Fausto's desk. "It seems your cousin and Captain Donovan pulled a fast one on you."

Fausto snatched it up, unfolded it, and looked at it. He turned to Dario.

"Did you draw this?"

Dario just stared at him.

"Donovan came to me with a proposition to—how did he put it? Oh, yes, 'Take you out' in exchange for my help to rescue his woman." He looked at Dario. "Dario helped with the plan."

Fausto looked at Dario angrily.

"I couldn't let you hurt Itzél," Dario explained.

The colonel saw Fausto glance at his cell phone on the desk but pretended not to notice.

"Donovan lured you here with the promise of delivering your guns," the colonel said. "Except, instead of delivering your guns, he delivered my team instead."

Fausto lunged across the desk to get his cell phone. The colonel snatched it before he could get it.

"Not so fast, *mí demoñito*," the colonel said affectionately. "I promised Captain Donovan I'd keep you from giving the order to kill his woman. Now what kind of man would I be if I didn't keep my promise?"

Fausto's odd-colored eyes stared angrily at the colonel.

The colonel looked at Dario. "What's this I hear about you wanting a normal life?"

Dario didn't answer.

"You know you can never do that," the colonel added. "There's a sizeable reward for your capture. You'll be hunted down—if not by the government, by the families of the people who died at the hands of the vigilantes or the Frontera cartel. Why don't you come with me?"

"I'll take my chances," Dario responded.

"Alone?" the colonel asked. "You can't roam like a lone wolf. You need the protection of the pack." The colonel looked sympathetically at his old friend. "Why don't you come with me?"

"If I go with you, will I be expected to kill?" Dario asked.

"You'll be expected to follow orders," the colonel responded firmly.

"I'm done with killing."

"There's nowhere you can go that's safe for you," the colonel added.

"I'll find someplace where nobody knows me."

"You'll be looking over your shoulder for the rest of your short life."

"All I ask for is a chance to try."

"Nonsense, you'll be dead inside a year."

"I'll take that year."

"Don't be foolish," the colonel said coldly. "Come back to Nuevo León with us."

The colonel waited for a response from Dario, who gave no sign that he would accept. His attention turned to the rifleman who came into the office holding a stack of new Romanian AK-47 rifles in his arms. Fausto's eyes widened with surprise as the paramilitary laid the rifles on the desk before going back to get the others.

Dario's sullen expression changed gradually to a smile as he recognized the guns.

"Dónovan," Fausto said bitterly under his breath.

The *Siete Mares* sat off Punta Morro with her bow pointed into the wind and her sails fluttering in the gentle breeze like bedsheets hanging on a clothesline. Reséndez stood by the hatch to the main cabin with his M-4 trained on the crew. To better watch them and keep them from talking to each other, he had Donovan stand by the steering box and Augie and Sandy sit several feet apart on the starboard bulwark.

Donovan looked at the assault rifle Reséndez had strapped to his chest and then at the pistol holstered to his hip. Although he knew he could make it over the side before Reséndez could get off a round, he had the colonel's order to shoot Sandy should he try anything to consider. He played out several scenarios in his head, none of which came to a satisfactory conclusion. He would have to wait for the right moment. So far, it didn't seem that it would ever come.

Then, Donovan saw Reséndez raise his hand to his right ear and take a sudden interest in the port. He looked across the water and noticed some of the streetlights no longer shining in the area around the warehouse. He looked at the sergeant, who had his head turned toward the port. He wondered if he could rush him before he could react but decided he couldn't—not by himself, not without help. Then an idea came to him.

"Looks like they've made it into the warehouse," he said to the sergeant.

He waited for Reséndez to shut him up as he had before, but he didn't. Instead, he kept focused on the warehouse. Donovan glanced at Sandy, who looked back at him. He made a rowing motion using his hands as he kept his eyes on Reséndez. He waited for Sandy to nod that he understood. He then brought his hands up like a batter holding a bat and brought them down sharply. Sandy again nodded that he understood. Donovan signaled him to wait with the palm of his hand as he looked at Reséndez.

"I didn't hear any gunshots," Donovan said to the sergeant, who continued to ignore him.

Donovan looked back at Sandy and then bent over slightly, holding his hands on his stomach. He held up two fingers and mouthed "number two." Donovan glanced briefly at the sergeant and then held up his left thumb. He used the index and middle fingers of his right hand to imitate a man walking up behind the thumb. Sandy nodded that he understood and then stood suddenly, causing Reséndez to look at him.

"Where're you going?" he asked Sandy.

"I have to go to the bathroom," Sandy replied.

"Do it over the side."

"I can't."

"He ate some bad oysters earlier this afternoon," Donovan interjected. "He's got the runs."

Sandy folded over, grunted, and covered his mouth.

"Looks like he's about to spew out of both ends," Augie remarked.

The sergeant looked suspiciously at the crew for a moment and then stepped aside.

"Make it quick," he said as he looked at his watch. "They're almost done."

"Thank you, sir," Sandy said as he hurried awkwardly to the hatch to sell the ruse.

Donovan looked up at the mainsail and then at Sergeant Reséndez.

"The wind is pretty light," he said to the sergeant. "It'll take us forever to get underway. We're going to have to use the engine."

The sergeant looked up over his shoulder at the mainsail fluttering gently. He looked at Donovan and nodded.

"I'm going to start it if that's all right," he said as he reached for the ignition key. "We've been having trouble with the starter. It may take a while to turn over."

Reséndez stared warily at Donovan, who had his hand on the ignition, waiting for permission.

"Go ahead," Reséndez said as he watched him carefully.

The engine churned sluggishly as Donovan turned the ignition on and off. The sergeant looked on with interest as Donovan tried half-heartedly to start the engine.

Sandy opened the forward hatch and slipped quietly to the deck. He had removed his boat shoes and hurried to the *Mona* sitting upright amidships. He took a wooden oar and stepped up gingerly on top of the main cabin.

Augie pushed Donovan aside. "Let me try."

Donovan stepped away from the steering box as Augie cranked the sluggish engine, causing it to whine incessantly.

"Starter's out," Augie commented, drawing the sergeant's interest. "I'm gonna have to go below and take a look."

"Stay where you are," Reséndez barked as Sandy closed in behind him.

"How do you expect to get out of here if we can't start the engine?" Donovan snapped angrily as Sandy raised the oar to his right side like a major league batter.

The sergeant's helmet sailed off his head, taking the earplug with it as Sandy brought the oar sharply against the side of his head. Donovan rushed the dazed sergeant and pinned him to the deck as Sandy jumped off the cabin to take his sidearm. Donovan raised his fist over his head and dropped it like a hammer on the bridge of the sergeant's nose, knocking him out. He released the rifle from its harness and slid it across the deck to Augie as Major Zamora's voice came over the radio.

"Reséndez—prepare for extraction."

Donovan ripped the radio off Reséndez's vest and looked at it as the major's voice crackled out of it.

"Respond," he heard the major call. "Repeat: Prepare for extraction phase. Please acknowledge."

Donovan glanced at Augie who looked at him like a reluctant accomplice. Donovan keyed the mic.

"Entendido," he said into it as he looked at his partner.

"I thought you said the marines would be here by now," Augie said anxiously. "Where are they?"

"I don't know," Donovan replied. "Don Macario said he'd have them here as soon as he knew the Thunderbolts were in the warehouse."

"Looks awful marine-less to me," Augie remarked. "How are we gonna keep them put till they get here?"

Donovan looked at the port and then at Reséndez and then at the port again.

"Get me the duct tape," he said to Sandy.

He got off the sergeant's chest and turned him on his stomach. Sandy brought the duct tape from the storage nook on the steering box.

"Get the *Mona* ready," Donovan told Sandy as he took the tape from him.

"Aye, aye, Skipper."

Donovan heard the radio pop, opening the channel as he rushed to bind the sergeant's hands behind his back.

"Bring the ship to the end of the dock to take on cargo, Sergeant," he heard the major say.

"Entendido," Donovan replied in a rush.

He winced with the realization that his second attempt to mimic Reséndez's voice had fallen short. He set the roll of tape on the deck as he stared at Augie.

"Reséndez?" the major called curiously over the radio.

Donovan drew a deep breath, this time concentrating on impersonating the sergeant.

"Sí, mí mayor," he said and then waited apprehensively for a response.

"We found the rifles," the major said. "There's not enough room in the pangas to bring them to the ship."

"Entendido," Donovan responded cautiously.

"What are we gonna do?" Augie said urgently. "If we don't show up, they'll run us down in those pangas."

Donovan set the radio on the deck.

"Wait here," he said to Augie as he hurried down the companionway into the main cabin.

Donovan went to the galley where he knelt on the deck to lift the hatch into the engine room. He worked his way around the engine to the bulkhead separating the engine room from the rest of the ship. He removed the panel covering the secret compartment where he had concealed the Barrett fifty-caliber rifle.

Augie looked nervously toward the port as Donovan came back on deck.

"What are you gonna do?" he asked Donovan when he saw the gun case.

"Making sure they can't run us down in those pangas," Donovan said as he set the case down on the main cabin to assemble the rifle.

"You sure like blowing up things," Augie remarked.

As Donovan slipped the locking pins into place, he thought briefly about the mortar rounds he blew up in Amalgamated warehouse on the Murindó River. He looked at Sandy as he tried dragging the *Mona* to the davits on the starboard side.

"Why don't you help Sandy get the *Mona* ready?" he told Augie as he extended the legs on the bipod.

As Augie and Sandy moved the *Mona* to the starboard side, Donovan climbed on top of the main cabin, where he pointed the rifle at the back of the warehouse and brought his eye to the scope. He could just make out the panga tied to the wharf in the available light. He brought the muzzle to bear on the outboard motor as he sighted in on it. He put his finger on the trigger, drew a breath, and held it until the crosshairs drifted to where he wanted to place the shot. He pulled the trigger and saw the stern of the panga burst into a fireball through the scope as the round pierced the outboard motor.

As Donovan watched the fireball climb into the night, he spotted a Ford F150 Mini Commando pickup stop suddenly on the backside of the parking lot.

"The marines are here," he called back to Augie and Sandy.

Donovan knew he had to act fast. He hoped the fireball would hold the marines' attention long enough for him to get off a shot and disable the last panga the Thunderbolts had left to make their getaway. He put his eye back on the scope and used the light from the fireball to look for the second panga. He spotted it moored to the quay between the warehouse and building just up the port from it. He sighted in on the outboard motor, drew a breath, and put his finger on the trigger while he waited for the crosshairs to drift onto the target.

"Damn!" he said as he pulled the trigger and watched a molten glob of light streaking just above the water toward the target. "Not another tracer."

Donovan knew that the marines in the Mini Commando must have seen the tracer giving away the ship's position like an accusing finger as the outboard motor on the second panga exploded into another brilliant fireball.

"Wow!" Sandy exclaimed as he hooked the stern chains to the *Mona*.

"Yeah, wow," Donovan said under his breath. "I'm sure that wowed the marines as well."

"They'll be sending the Armada to board us for sure," Augie remarked after hooking the bow chain.

"Not if we're not here," Donovan said as he got off the main cabin. "Let's get rid of the guns and get out of here."

"I hope there's time," Augie said.

"There's time," Donovan said as he began to disassemble the Barrett rifle.

Augie took the sergeant's M-4 off the deck and swung it out to sea by the barrel. The assault rifle spun horizontally into the darkness, making a faint splash as it went into the water. Sandy jumped off the top of the cabin to get Reséndez's pistol to throw into the ocean.

"Give me that," Donovan said, taking the gun and tucking it into his belt.

Sandy pointed at the helmet rocking back and forth as the ship swayed.

"What about that?" he asked.

"Fill it full of water and sink it," Donovan replied. "Get rid of any sign that the Thunderbolts were on this ship; then finish getting the *Mona* in the water."

"Aye, Skipper."

"What are you gonna do about him?" Augie asked about the sergeant. "You gonna throw him over the side too?"

"That's not a bad idea," Donovan remarked as he picked the duct tape up off the deck and handed it to him.

"I wasn't serious," Augie said as he snapped the tape from his hand. "I'll bind his feet."

"You're no fun," he said facetiously.

As Sandy ran to the side to sink the helmet, Donovan disassembled the Barrett rifle and put the upper and lower receiver in the case, using the foam padding to keep the gun case from closing completely. He went to the side and waited for Sandy to finish sinking the helmet before dropping the gun case into the water. Both he and Sandy stood on the starboard side watching the headlights of the marines' vehicles roll slowly up the ramp onto the dock and then stop suddenly.

"Why'd they stop?" Augie asked as he finished wrapping duct tape around the sergeant's ankles.

"They must know the Thunderbolts are in the warehouse. They're probably waiting for backup," Donovan said.

"A lot of marines are gonna get killed if they try taking that warehouse with the Thunderbolts dug in there," Augie remarked as he joined Donovan on the side.

"We've got to get them out of there," Donovan said.

"How do you propose to do that?" Augie asked skeptically.

"The colonel ordered Reséndez to bring the ship to the end of the dock. If he sees the ship moving toward it, he'll think Reséndez is coming to get them," Donovan replied. He turned to his partner. "I'm going to get Itzél, so—"

"You want me to take the ship to the end of the dock," Augie said. "Are you nuts?"

"Just make it look like you are, and then take her out to sea before the Armada shows up."

"You think there'll be time before they get here?"

Donovan turned to look at Sandy cranking the forward davit lifting the stern of the *Mona*. He looked at his partner.

"I don't know," he said softly.

"I'm not sure you fooled the major the last time you impersonated the sergeant," Augie added as he followed Donovan amidships to help Sandy with the *Mona*. "What if he calls on the radio?"

"Don't answer it," Donovan replied as he took the crank on the stern davit to raise the *Mona*'s bow off the deck.

"Don't answer it?" Augie said apprehensively over the clanking of the gears. "Sure, why wouldn't that work?" he added sarcastically.

"I don't think it's a good idea taking Itzél to the Paradise Lagoon," Donovan said as he and Sandy swung the *Mona* over the water. "That'll be the first place Fausto's people will come looking for us if they somehow get away from the marines."

"You want me to go get you at Lorenzo Beach?" Augie asked.

"I don't know. It could be risky with the Armada around," Donovan said as he and Sandy worked the cranks lowering the *Mona* to the water. "We need a rally point." Donovan bit down on his lip as he gave the problem some thought. "I'll tell you what—take the ship out to sea. I'll take Itzél and hide in the caves at Punta Morro. You can come get us when the coast is clear."

"Are you sure you want to do that, Skipper? The water's awfully rough around the point."

"Poli says the caves are supposed to be haunted," Sandy added.

Donovan turned to Sandy as he removed his khaki shirt and tucked his black T-shirt into his black slacks.

"Right now, the ghosts of Punta Morro are the least of my worries."

CHAPTER 14

The smoke from the burning vehicles drifted across the road like a dense sea fog creeping ashore in a light breeze. The stench of burning rubber, melting fiberglass, and incinerated corpses hung in the air like a wet blanket. The thunderous roar of gunfire that had rattled Villamar had fallen silent save for an occasional gunshot that echoed through the eerie stillness, delivered unceremoniously to the head of some unfortunate survivor.

Comandante Tápia emerged through the thick haze to join Chino and the other comandantes standing around the driver's side of a burned-out sports utility vehicle. Their faces did not look like those of the triumphant but of men standing somberly around an open grave.

"Did any of your men find Cisco?" Chino asked Tapia.

Comandante Sánchez had charged the comandantes with several tasks before he left for Seyba Playa, which included gathering weapons and ammunition and any valuables, a head count of the dead, and Cisco's corpse. Tapia asked for the honor of bringing in the corpse.

"They're still looking," Tapia replied.

Tapia looked inside the smoldering vehicle at the remains of a sicario whose cindered hands still clutched the steering wheel with his head turned outward and his jaw hanging in a final gesture of agony. The flames had consumed his eyelids and cheeks, making his eyes look like cooked golf balls sitting in two bony cups. The fire also burned off the skin around most of his mouth, giving the sicario a morbid grin.

Comandante Tápia had never seen such a sight, having spent his career in the administrative office of the Campeche Municipal Police. He gagged and covered his nose and mouth with his hand as he gawked stupidly at the incinerated remains of the dead sicario. One of the older comandantes broke off the filters of a couple of cigarettes and handed them to Tápia.

"Put these in your nose," he said to him.

"What a horrible way to die," Tápia remarked as he screwed them into his nostrils.

Another shot rang out, snapping Chino from his trance-like gaze.

"We need to go before the Marina gets here," the older comandante said to him.

"Not until we find Cisco," Chino responded firmly.

"Maybe he wasn't with them," Tapia suggested. "My men have looked everywhere."

"We have to be sure," Chino retorted. "If we can't give him his body, Sánchez will want proof he wasn't with them."

"There isn't time," the older comandante said urgently. "The Marina will be here soon."

Almost as if on cue, a booming voice bounced off the walls of the small hamlet.

"Armada! Bajen sus armas y entréguense," the voice said, reverberating between the buildings. "Throw down your arms and surrender," it said, repeating the order.

Panic swept through Tapia, who turned to Chino. "What do we do?"

Chino looked all around him. "Where's it coming from?"

"It's coming from offshore," another comandante said.

"Listen!" the older comandante said in a low but urgent voice.

The dull hum of heavy trucks approaching grew louder as a mechanical voice pierced through the smoky haze from the road north of town.

"Marina!" the voice called through a bullhorn over the hum of the approaching convoy of trucks. "Tiren sus armas. Están detenidos."

Tapia looked toward the sound of the bullhorn as several marines in camouflage BDUs wearing navy-blue bulletproof vests advanced cautiously through the smoky haze.

"It's the marines!" Tápia said in a panic.

He turned to look for a place to run when he saw the faint forms of fleeing men filtering through the clouds of smoke like the fleeting images of ghosts seen out of the corner of the eye. Tapia backed away slowly from the group of comandantes as they watched their men flee in panic from the advancing marines. Another blast from the marines' bullhorn sent him running in the opposite direction, turning down an alley toward the beach road that swung behind the Villamar business district.

He ran down the embankment where he had left his patrol car parked on the strip of rocky beach. He stopped when he saw the other police cars, pickups, and sports utility vehicles trying to go around each other like bumper cars at a carnival. Some tried to drive on the soft sand at the water's edge, sinking their tires almost immediately. Others tried to climb the rocky embankment only to get high-centered on a rock outcropping or be unable to get enough traction to make the steep climb.

"¡Armada! ¡Bajen sus armas!" the voice thundered all around him.

Tapia stared at the intimidating superstructure of the Azteca-class patrol vessel, while men dressed as policemen and regular street thugs swarmed past him. He turned his head when he heard a shot fired and looked at several of the men firing at the ship. He looked back at the gunboat and saw her cannons and machine guns coming to bear on the shore.

"Madre de Dios," he muttered just as the machine guns opened fire.

The men on the beach threw themselves on the ground as the rounds ricocheted off the rocks along the water's edge.

"¡Estan detenidos!" Tapia heard the voice thunder over his head. "Throw down your arms!"

He looked up when he heard a pickup engine starting. He saw several men in state and municipal police uniforms jumping into the only pickup with a realistic chance to climb the steep slope to the main highway. A single burst from the ship's twenty-millimeter Oerlikon gun struck the engine compartment, raising the front end off the ground and sending the pickup rolling backward slowly. The state and municipal police impersonators jumped out of the pickup with their hands raised over their heads.

A platoon of marines swarmed the ridge of the embankment, trapping the Campeche gang members on the beach. The gangsters threw down their weapons, raised their hands, and then lay facedown on the ground as the marines moved down the slope to detain them.

Tapia jumped to his feet and threw his hands up high as he walked up to the nearest marine.

"I'm not one of them," he said loudly. "I'm not one of them. I was caught in the crossfire. I'm glad you got here so soon. ¡Viva la Marina!"

Sweat-soaked, bleeding, and insect bit, Cisco made his way through the thorny underbrush to the edge of the thicket on the east side of the highway just south of Villamar. He looked up and down the road for police cars or pickups full of armed men as he struggled to catch his breath. As he rubbed the sweat stinging his eyes from his face, he looked at the thorn pricks and abrasions stinging the tops of his arms. A thin red film of blood coated his arms like sweat. He turned to look back toward Villamar when he heard heavy machine-gun fire followed by a booming voice echoing over a public address system in the distance.

When he finally caught his breath and could listen to his surroundings without hearing his own breathing, he heard what sounded like an engine idling nearby. He moved closer to the road but remained hidden in the thicket. He saw a Lincoln Town Car parked about twenty meters up the road with the lights off and the engine running. He went back into the thicket to get closer to the car without the people inside noticing. He swatted at the insects stinging him and pushed away the branches slapping against his face and body as he worked his way to within a few feet of the back of the car.

He crouched low, got his folding knife from his pocket, and moved quietly out of the thicket to go to the back of the car. He felt the exhaust stinging his nose and eyes as he listened to the car's engine humming softly. He looked through the far-right side of the rear window and saw a man sitting behind the wheel who looked asleep. He extended the blade as he moved slowly to the left side of the vehicle. He focused his eyes on the door handle as he took several rapid breaths before rushing the driver's door to open it.

The door swung open suddenly before he could grab the handle, and he found himself looking down the barrel of a police revolver.

"Drop the knife, pendejo," the man in the Carmen municipal police uniform said.

The knife clanked dully as it struck the asphalt. Cisco's eyes crossed as he stared down the barrel. The officer grabbed his arm, spun him around, threw him against the car, and kicked his feet apart as he pressed the muzzle against the back of his ear.

"I thought you were someone else, Oficial," Cisco said as the officer patted him down.

The putrid smell of smoke carrying in the sea breeze filled Cisco's nostrils as he listened to the bullhorn blaring in the distance.

"Do you know what's going on?" Cisco asked over his shoulder.

He felt himself spun around violently by the arm. He stumbled and nearly fell as the officer pushed him to the back of the car. A faint gunshot rang out to the north followed by the much louder sound of an M-4 rifle firing a short burst as he stared at the officer.

"I was in my backyard when the shooting started," Cisco said anxiously. "Men running down the street shooting at people. I got scared, so I ran." He swallowed sharply. "I thought you were one of them."

"Is that the best you can do, Cisco?"

It surprised Cisco that the officer called him by his name. He looked at his short-cropped hair and clean-shaven face and the thin scar running down the left side.

"Do I know you?" Cisco squinted his eyes to read the name plate on the officer's chest. "Officer Andrade."

"We've never met, but I think you know who I am," Alonso replied. "You tried to kill me last Easter on the south side of Carmen."

"I think you have me mistaken for someone else," Cisco said. "I'm just a shop owner … in Villamar."

"Your name is Cisco Cisneros. You go by Cisco," Alonso retorted. "Until recently, you worked for the Norteño cartel as a minor functionary."

Cisco glared angrily at Alonso. "What did you call me?"

"A minor functionary. A boot polisher for Colonel Barca," Alonso replied and smiled derisively. "Tell me, Cisco. How does it feel being the colonel's butt boy?"

Alonso's words cut deep into Cisco's pride, his greatest weakness.

"I know who you are too, Officer Andrade," Cisco said acerbically. "You're the one they call the Crusader Cop." He breathed in and exhaled sharply. "I should have made sure you were dead."

"That's the problem with drive-by shootings," Alonso remarked. "You seldom hit what you're shooting at, especially if you're a bad shot like yourself."

"I won't make the same mistake next time."

Alonso brought his revolver up and pulled back on the hammer.

"There won't be a next time," he said.

"You won't shoot me," Cisco snickered unsavorily. "You can't kill in cold blood."

"You killed my friend, Corporal Camilo Carvajal," Alonso said.

"I don't know who that is."

"You had him assassinated at Isla Aguada," he explained. "He worked for the Carmen municipal police for over thirty-six years. He was known by everybody and respected for his fairness, kindness, and honesty. He had a wife, two sons, a daughter, and two grandchildren."

"Who gives a damn?"

"A lot of people do," Alonso said solemnly. "He was a good man and no danger to you."

"He was just another worthless parasite in uniform."

It startled Cisco when Alonso pushed the revolver toward him. He watched Alonso anxiously as he started breathing deeply, expelling the air heavily through his nostrils. He looked at his gun and saw it moving unsteadily as Alonso's hand started to shake. Cisco grinned sarcastically at him.

"I knew you couldn't shoot me in cold blood." Cisco snickered sardonically. "Why don't you put the gun down before it goes off accidentally?"

He winced when he saw Alonso take a step forward to backhand him with his revolver. He closed his eyes and turned his head waiting for the blow to strike. As he waited for the gun to slam against the side of his head, he thought he heard Alonso sniffling. He opened his eyes and saw that he had lowered his gun hand to wipe a tear from his eye with the back of his free hand.

As Cisco lunged to get the gun, a shot rang out that faded slowly into the night.

The light from the burning pangas shined on Major Zamora's face as he stared blankly at them from the backdoor of the warehouse. The rumble of a diesel engine accelerating nearby attracted the major's attention. He turned to look as the SandCat pulled ahead of the Mini Commando pickups full of troops. He looked out to sea for the *Siete Mares* and saw it heading toward the end of the dock. He lowered his mic to the side of his mouth and closed the door.

"Puma leaders, the Marina is at the port. The pangas have been disabled," the major said as he hurried across the warehouse floor to the office. "Hold fire and stand by for instructions."

When he entered the office, the major saw Colonel Barca sitting on the edge of the desk looking down on Fausto and Dario, who sat in the chairs in front of him as the Puma Uno fireteam leader stood behind them with his pistol in hand. The two Puma Uno riflemen stood watch over Comandantes Sánchez and Prieto, whom they had kneeling on the floor facing the west wall.

"How many troops?" Colonel Barca asked Major Zamora.

"Looks like a platoon with a SandCat," he replied.

"Where are they now?"

"Sitting on the ramp waiting to advance. They could be waiting for a larger force to arrive. We must leave soon," the major replied. He glanced at the AK-47 rifles on the desk and leaning against the back wall. "There won't be time to take the rifles."

As the major waited for the colonel to order the extraction, he glanced at the prisoners and put his hand on the butt of his pistol. Only Dario noticed the gesture.

"Has Reséndez brought the ship to the dock yet?" the colonel asked.

"I saw it heading this way, but ..."

"But what, Major?"

"Something's not right," the major replied. "Reséndez didn't sound like himself. I'm not sure it was him I was talking to," the major said warily. "I asked for the countersign, but he wouldn't respond."

"The Marina could be jamming communications," the colonel suggested.

"*Or* whoever answered the radio didn't know the countersign."

The major glanced briefly at Fausto when he heard him chuckle.

"But you saw the ship headed for the end of the dock?" the colonel asked.

"Sí, mí coronel."

"Then we must assume that the Marina has identified our frequency and is jamming it," the colonel concluded. "Prepare for extraction."

"Sí, mí coronel," Major Zamora replied. He turned to the fireteam leader. "Take the prisoners to the back and execute them."

"I need to have a word with Fausto and Dario first," the colonel said.

The major looked concerned. "The Marina, Coronel—"

"I'll be brief," he replied tersely. "You can execute the others."

The major looked at the Puma Uno fireteam leader. "You have your orders."

"Sí, mí mayor," the fireteam leader responded. He turned to his team. "Adelante."

The riflemen forced Comandantes Sánchez and Prieto to their feet and pushed them toward the door leading into the warehouse.

"You won't get out of here alive," Sánchez taunted. "That SandCat will blow your ship out of the water before it reaches the end of the dock."

"¡Silencio!" the rifleman behind him said.

"I can help you get out of here," Sánchez added.

"Let him talk," the colonel said.

Again, the major glanced disapprovingly at the colonel as Sánchez held out the palm of his hand, grinning presumptuously.

"Give us back our guns and let us take your men into custody," Sánchez said. "Once we're away from the port, I'll make it easy for you to escape."

The major watched anxiously as the colonel sat quietly, staring curiously at the presumptuous state police commander.

"Your proposal is ... intriguing," Colonel Barca said. "However, I think I'll take my chances with the SandCat." He turned to the rifleman escorting Sánchez and cocked his head sharply toward the door to the warehouse floor.

"Wait," the comandante blurted as he tore his arm out of his escort's grasp. He stared solemnly at the colonel.

"Will you at least spare me the indignity of being shot in the back of the head?"

"Did you serve?" Colonel Barca asked.

"Five years in the infantry," he replied proudly.

"There isn't time for this, Colonel," Major Zamora said.

The major watched the colonel and Sánchez stare at each other as he listened to the Puma Dos fireteam leader report on the marines' position in his headset. He had never known the colonel to dally with the enemy about to advance. He started to say something when he saw the colonel point the pistol in his hand at Sánchez.

"I hope you don't mind if I shoot you with your own weapon," the colonel said as he aimed it at Sánchez's chest. "Think of it as poetic."

The major looked at Comandante Sánchez, who never broke eye contact with the colonel. He pushed his chest out, calmly removed his policeman's peak hat, and tucked it under his arm as he stood straight and proud.

The colonel fired once.

The major looked on as Sánchez neither flinched nor batted an eye as if the bullet had missed him. He watched him take his hat, brush it with the back of his hand, and then place it on his head. A trickle of blood oozed slowly out of the corner of his mouth as he saluted the colonel. He coughed once and then collapsed to the floor.

With that, Comandante Sánchez's dream of reinstating his personal money-making relationship with the Comisión in Chiapas had come to an inglorious end. He died not as a dedicated public servant fallen in the line of duty nor as the rich man living comfortably in a majestic hacienda, as he had envisioned for himself. Instead, he died a corrupt police commander on a cold concrete floor in a damp warehouse.

Major Zamora turned to the Puma Uno riflemen escorting Prieto. "Get him out of here."

Unlike Sánchez, Comandante Prieto had no grand illusion about his future. He had long accepted the possibility if not the likelihood that his criminal activity would result eventually in at least his imprisonment and quite possibly his death. He knew that very well when he first accepted Comandante Sánchez's invitation to join his illicit money-making venture. He could have pursued an honorable career, taken a meager pension, and lived a humble existence like most of his brethren. With a little luck and the right contacts, he might have even have parleyed his experience into a lucrative postretirement job in security. Instead, he chose to betray his oath, integrity, and honor only to come to an ignoble end.

Comandante Prieto's escort pushed him toward the door into the warehouse. Shortly afterward, a sharp crack rang out, and Comandante Prieto had met the fate he had long anticipated.

Major Zamora turned his head to listen to Puma Dos report in from the sniper's nest on the roof. He put his fingertips gently on the mic by his mouth.

"Entendido," he said, acknowledging the report. He looked at the colonel. "The Marina is gathering at the foot of the dock. They'll be advancing soon. We must leave before the Armada arrives and blocks our escape."

"Order a withdrawal," the colonel said calmly. He looked at Dario before turning to the major. "I'll be with you in a moment."

"Please hurry, Colonel," the major said as he put his fingers on his mic. "Atención, Pumas. The colonel has ordered a withdrawal. Puma Tres—prepare to move to point alpha on my order. Puma Dos—cover Puma Tres." Major Zamora turned to the Puma Uno fireteam leader. "When I give the order, have your team set up a perimeter outside the door to cover Puma Tres and our retreat."

"Entendido, mí mayor." The Puma Uno team leader turned to his men. "Listos."

As the Puma Uno fireteam gathered around the door, Major Zamora covered Fausto and Dario with his M-4 assault rifle, waiting for Colonel Barca.

"We're ready, Colonel," the major said. "Please hurry."

The major watched anxiously as the colonel sat calmly on the corner of the desk, looking down at Fausto and Dario with Comandante Sánchez's pistol in his hand.

"Thank you again for providing us with the floor plan," the colonel said to Dario. "This operation would not have been possible without it."

"I'll get you for this," Fausto said menacingly to Dario.

"I didn't mean for this to happen," Dario said to him.

"You helped Dónovan double-cross me."

"That was not my intention."

Major Zamora turned an ear when he heard a heavy diesel engine drawing closer. He put his hand on his headset and listened to Puma Dos report on the marines advancing.

"Slow them down," he said into his mic. He turned to the Thunderbolt. "Please, Colonel—the Marina's advancing."

"When Donovan came to see me with his proposal, he told me about what happened at Padre Island and that you came back with him," the colonel said to Dario. "I told him that I wanted to offer you a chance to come back with me to Nuevo León, but he refused to tell me where you were. When I saw you tonight, I had hoped to change your mind."

Outside the front door, Puma Tres opened fire on the advancing marines. The marines responded immediately. The bullets striking the building sounded like a sledgehammer against the stucco-and-cinderblock wall.

"We have to go, Colonel," Major Zamora said sternly.

"Come with us," Colonel Barca said to Dario.

"I'm surprised, Colonel, that you trust him," Fausto remarked. "If Dónovan could persuade him to turn against me, his own blood, what makes you think he didn't persuade him to turn against you?"

The major started to take his pistol out of its scabbard to shoot the prisoners and end the colonel's dalliance, but his respect for the colonel trumped his concern for his men. He sighed in frustration as he listened to Fausto weave a twisted tale of betrayal.

"Doesn't it strike you a little strange, Colonel, that the Marina showed up just as your men got here?" Fausto said. "Dónovan set us both up." He turned to Dario. "Isn't that right, primo?"

"I don't know anything about that," Dario retorted.

"You didn't come to Lorenzo to see that I got my guns," Fausto added. "You came to make sure I was at the warehouse when the colonel got here."

"I went to Lorenzo to make sure you didn't hurt Itzél."

The major glanced at the colonel and then at Fausto, who looked bewilderedly at Dario.

"You're in love with her, aren't you?" Fausto remarked as if he realized it for the first time.

Dario didn't respond.

"It all makes sense now," Fausto commented. "You set us all up, Dónovan included. You planned to cash in on the rewards for the colonel and myself and run off with Dónovan's woman." He laughed wickedly. "Bravo, primo. What better way to start a new life than with a beautiful woman and thirty pieces of silver in your pocket."

Another volley raked the front of the warehouse, shattering the plate-glass window. The major shielded his face with his arm as glass shards flew into the office.

"Now, Colonel," Major Zamora said emphatically as he joined Puma Uno at the front door. "We have to go."

"You love this woman?" the colonel asked Dario, ignoring the major.

The major looked at the colonel when Fausto's cell phone began to ring. He watched the colonel take the cell phone out of his pocket, look at the screen, and then show it to Fausto.

"Someone named Daniel is calling you," he said to him.

The major looked at Fausto, who glared bitterly at the colonel.

"Is he the one you have watching the woman?" Colonel Barca asked.

"He has a knife against her throat," Fausto replied as he turned to look at Dario malevolently. "Waiting for me to give the order to cut it."

"Colonel, I must insist," the major said as the cell phone stopped ringing.

He watched the colonel set the cell phone aside, remove the clip from Comandante Sánchez's pistol, and slip it into the side pocket of his tunic. The major drew his pistol and aimed it at Dario and Fausto as the colonel walked around them with

Sánchez's pistol in one hand and Fausto's cell phone in the other. As he joined Major Zamora and the Puma Uno fireteam at the door, Fausto and Dario turned in their chairs to look at him.

"Thank you, Colonel," Majora Zamora said.

He aimed his pistol at Fausto's forehead when he felt the colonel put his hand on his forearm and stop him from shooting. He looked at the colonel, who turned to Dario.

"I don't know if you're responsible for what's happening tonight," the colonel said to Dario. "I may never know."

"With all due respect, Colonel, we're wasting time," Major Zamora said firmly.

He watched the colonel set Fausto's cell phone on the broken plate-glass window frame as he turned to Dario.

"If Fausto gets this phone, he'll give the order to have the woman's throat cut."

"*That* I can promise you," Fausto said as he glared at Dario.

"Life is about choices," the colonel said sympathetically to him. "Including sometimes who lives and who dies."

"I've made my choice," Fausto said sinisterly.

The major watched impatiently as the colonel walked to the other end of the broken plate-glass window and laid Sánchez's pistol on it.

"You said you're through with killing," the colonel said to Dario. "There is a single bullet in the chamber. You're going to have to kill your cousin if you want to stop him from making that call." He turned to Major Zamora and nodded.

Major Zamora put his fingertips on his mic. "We're coming out."

By the time Domingo Figueroa's bus pulled into the Lorenzo *paradero*, José Luis had fallen into a deep sleep.

"Villa Lorenzo," the bus driver called to him over the rhythmic clanking of the diesel engine.

José Luis did not stir and could not see the bus driver's impatient eyes glaring at him in the big rearview mirror. An old man sitting behind him shook his shoulder gently.

"I think this is your stop, señor," the old man said to José Luis as he turned to look at him.

José Luis grabbed the rail to steady himself as he walked to the front of the bus.

"Drop me off at the next dirt road on the right, por favor," he said to the driver as he handed him his last 100-peso note.

The bus driver looked at José Luis bitterly as he took the bill and put it in his shirt pocket. José Luis looked up the road, trying to shake the sleep from his eyes as the bus rounded a curve and eased down a hill to the next dirt road. The driver pulled back on the lever, opening the accordion-style door to let him out.

After José Luis stepped out of the bus, it pulled out to continue its run to Champotón. He looked at the majestic entrance to the plantation house. The tall, rectangular pillars made of white stucco supporting the wrought iron gate each had a small Spanish-style red-clay tile roof with a rounded rectangular window near the top that made them look like the watchtowers on an old Moorish castle. He thought he saw a silhouette of a little man looking down on him from one of the windows as he punched in the code to open the gate. He rubbed to clear the last vestiges of sleep from his eyes as he stared at the window, waiting for the shadow to reappear as the gate opened slowly.

He looked at the plantation house sitting at the end of the caliche road ahead of him and then began to walk. The balmy night air didn't do much to take the edge off the humidity. José Luis threw his jacket over his shoulder, hoping to get some relief. He felt his shirt sticking to his skin like a sweat-soaked film and the three-hundred-dollar shoes he bought in Houston, unlike Nancy's boots, were not made for walking.

When at last he got to the plantation house, he heard his name called as he started up the steps to the front door. He turned to look at the servants' quarters across the lawn and saw Daniel standing in the doorway.

"Over here, José Luis," Daniel called again.

José Luis threw his jacket over his forearm and hurried across the lawn.

"We thought you were dead," Daniel said as he stood aside to let him into the cottage.

"It's only luck that I'm not," he said as he shook his hand. "Where's Fausto?"

"At the warehouse, waiting to get his guns."

"What guns?" José Luis responded disconcertedly.

"The guns he sent Dónovan to Texas to get."

"But Dónovan betrayed us at Padre Island."

"We heard," Daniel said calmly. "Dario told us all about it."

"Dario?" José Luis looked at him curiously. "He came back?"

"Come," Daniel said as he led him to the kitchen. "I'll tell you all about it over a beer."

José Luis followed Daniel through the small living room to the kitchen, where he saw Itzél sitting at the table with San Juana and Adán standing around her.

"I see how Fausto got Dónovan to bring him the guns," he remarked.

"Sit down," Daniel said.

As Daniel got the beer out of the refrigerator, José Luis threw his jacket on an empty chair and sat next to Itzél, smiling lasciviously at her.

"Hola, hermosa," he said to her.

Itzél looked at him reluctantly, the tears in her eyes making them glisten like emeralds as she trembled like a frightened child.

"No wonder Dónovan is so taken by you." He glanced at her cleavage. "You're so … healthy."

Itzél folded her arms across her chest and turned her head as Daniel handed José Luis a beer and sat on the other side of her. José Luis winked at Daniel as he reached to brush away a lock of hair that had fallen over her eye.

"Leave her alone," Adán said sternly.

"Shut up, old man," Daniel snapped at him.

"Can't you see she's scared?" San Juana added.

"She has nothing to be afraid of from me," José Luis said as he sat back. "Relax, querida. I think we can have a lot of fun together."

"You look hungry, Señor José Luis," San Juana said. "Let me make you something to eat."

"No, gracias, señora," he responded. He rubbed the sweat from his forehead with the back of his hand. "It's hot enough in here already."

"I'll open a window," Adán said.

"Let the girl do it," José Luis said as he continued to stare at her.

Itzél glanced at him and then turned to look nervously at Adán and San Juana. She got up slowly and walked around the table to open the window over the sink. As she stood on her toes to undo the latches, José Luis stared at the way her pants found the creases in her perfectly shaped bottom.

"Um, um," José Luis remarked lecherously. "I see very clearly why Dónovan's bringing the guns."

"Show some respect," Adán said.

"I told you to keep your mouth shut," Daniel snapped at him. He turned to José Luis and chuckled sarcastically. "The old man says he used to be a wrestler."

"Really?" José Luis said as he looked at the old man. "Were you any good?"

"Good enough to handle a pair of *mocosos* like you two with no trouble."

"That must have been a very long time ago."

"Let me run a bath for you, Señor José Luis," San Juana said to defuse the situation.

"No, gracias, San Juana," José Luis responded. "But I would like a shower."

"I'll go get everything ready for you."

"I've changed my mind about eating," he added.

"I'll make some taquitos," San Juana said as she started to leave. She turned to Itzél. "Would you like to come help?"

"She stays here," Daniel said sternly. "Take the old man with you."

"I'm staying here," Adán insisted.

"Go with her," Daniel said. "Before I sweep the floor with you."

Adán looked at Daniel defiantly, determined to stay and watch over Itzél.

"I'll be all right," Itzél said to him as she returned to her chair. "It's okay."

The old man glanced at José Luis and then turned to glare at Daniel. Daniel grinned fiendishly as he blew a kiss in Itzél's direction.

"I'll be back soon," Adán told Itzél as he glared angrily at Daniel.

José Luis sat quietly, waiting for the old couple to leave the cottage. He turned to Daniel when he heard the screen door slam.

"What did Dario say about Padre Island?"

"Not much," Daniel replied. "Only that he was lucky to get out of there alive."

"What about Nacho and Beto?"

"He said they were killed," Daniel responded.

"Did he say why *he* wasn't killed?"

"They must have overpowered him," Daniel surmised.

"Four unarmed men?" José Luis said. "I think he threw in with them. I saw him standing on the deck. Nobody had a gun on him."

"What are you saying?"

"I'm saying he was probably working with Dónovan all along," he replied. "I don't see how they could have killed Nacho and Beto without his help."

"Maybe they got lucky."

"Luck had nothing to do with it," he insisted. "When I tried calling Dario, he signaled me that his radio wasn't working."

"Maybe it wasn't."

"I don't believe it. I don't see how they got the sails up with only three men when one of them was steering and another one was shooting the antitank gun."

"Three men?" Daniel said as he drew down his brow. "I thought you said there were four."

"I saw Chato kill one," José Luis explained as he turned to look contemptuously at Itzél. "Before he was killed by your lover."

The blood rushed from Itzél's face as she turned to him.

"Do you know who was killed?" she asked apprehensively.

"It was dark. All I saw was a shadow."

"Was he tall or short and heavy?"

José Luis looked at her as he tried to recall what he saw that night. He remembered seeing the sails flying up almost simultaneously as the ship rose and fell beyond the surf against a full moon. He recalled seeing the man steering the ship lower his head. He then tried to make out in his mind's eye the shape of the man falling backward as a bullet from Chato's machine gun struck him.

"Like I said, it was dark. All I could see were shadows," José Luis concluded. "He could have been short or tall. I couldn't tell."

A tear slid down the right side of Itzél's face.

"My husband was on that ship."

"Well ... with any luck, it might have been him," José Luis said as he grinned cruelly. "That should make things easier for you and Dónovan."

He winked at Daniel, who burst out in laughter. He looked at Itzél, who cradled her head in her arms on the table to cry. Unmoved, he pulled on his shirt and took a sniff.

"I need a change of clothes," José Luis said to Daniel.

"My room is the last one down the hall on the left before you go out into the patio," Daniel said. "I have some clothes in the closet that should fit you."

"Better than the ones you have on?" José Luis remarked sarcastically.

"Ha, ha, very funny," Daniel said. "At least they're dry and clean."

"I need to let Fausto know I'm here," José Luis said as he stood.

"I tried calling him when I saw you walking up the road," Daniel said. "He didn't answer."

CHAPTER 15

The Puma Dos and Tres fireteams unleashed a savage barrage of gunfire to cover Puma Uno coming out of the office. The fireteam leader and a rifleman dropped to the ground and opened fire while the other rifleman ran across the dock to jump in the prow of *La Sirena* as the bullets pinged and clanked off the fishing boat's hull around him.

"Puma Tres—fall back," the major yelled as he ran out the door and took a knee to lay cover fire.

The Puma Tres fireteam rose from their prone positions and fell back halfway up the dock where they set up a defensive perimeter to cover the retreat.

Dario looked at the colonel, who stopped at the door to look back at him. The colonel raised his right hand and gave Dario a subtle salute.

"Adiós, mí coronel," Dario said under his breath.

As the colonel ran out the door, the major stood and fired a long burst from his M-4 rifle before falling back to join the colonel at the Puma Tres defensive position.

Fausto and Dario both sprang out of their chairs to run to the broken plate-glass window. Dario threw his shoulder into Fausto's side, knocking him off balance to get the cell phone. Fausto regained his balance and got Comandante Sánchez's pistol.

"Give me the phone," Fausto demanded as he pointed the gun at Dario.

As the battle raged outside, the Puma Uno fireteam began their withdrawal to the Puma Tres defensive perimeter up the dock. A forty-millimeter grenade exploded in the prow of *La Sirena*, killing the rifleman taking cover there. Dario glanced outside when he saw the Puma Uno rifleman take a round to the head as he jumped to his feet to withdraw. Meanwhile, in the sniper's nest on the roof, the Puma Dos grenadier readied his RPG-7 launcher for firing.

"Let's get out of here," Dario said to Fausto.

They both glanced out the window when they heard the Puma Uno fireteam leader fire a burst next to the broken window before retreating up the dock.

"Give me the phone first."

Dario watched a string of bullets impacting the asphalt behind the fireteam leader's feet as it chased him to the Puma Tres defensive perimeter. A round found its mark, knocking him off his feet. A second one thudded into the back of his helmet as he tried to stand.

"No time to argue," Dario said defiantly as the SandCat's engine revved up suddenly. "The marines are almost here."

The turret mounted on the SandCat's roof rotated slowly to the right as the barrel of the forty-millimeter grenade launcher rose gradually to take aim at the sniper's nest. The launcher burped out a grenade as the grenadier aimed his RPG-7.

"It may already be too late," Fausto said morosely.

They both turned away to shield their faces as the forty-millimeter grenade exploded over their heads. They looked outside as the rocket-propelled grenade fired by the Puma Dos grenadier swooshed harmlessly in an arc over *La Sirena*, exploding in the water in the distance.

"Now give me the phone," Fausto said forcefully as a marine called for an advance outside through a bullhorn.

"I won't let you kill her."

"Why do you care what happens to her?" Fausto retorted bitterly. "She's in love with Dónovan, not you."

"That's not important," Dario replied. "She doesn't deserve to die."

"I can't let Dónovan have her. He took from me. Now I have to take from him."

"I can't let you do that," Dario said firmly.

A round ricocheted off the window frame, nearly hitting Dario in the head. He didn't flinch as he stared into Fausto's odd-colored eyes.

"For the last time," Fausto said as he pulled back on the hammer, "let me have the phone."

Dario stared at him for a moment. He looked at the cell phone and then held it out for Fausto to take. El Demonio grinned as he lowered the pistol to reach for the cell phone. Before he could put his hand on it, Dario tossed it out the broken window with all his might. He turned to Fausto, whose eyes bulged out of his head. The vein on his forehead swelled.

"That was very foolish," Fausto said as he raised the pistol to shoot Dario.

Just then, the front door flew open suddenly as a marine burst into the office, pointing his M-4 rifle at the cousins. Fausto shot the marine in the cheek, throwing him back-first against the open door. Dario punched Fausto in the face before turning to get the marine's rifle. Fausto pushed Dario hard against the wall and wrapped his forearm around his neck. Dario pushed back, throwing them on the floor as he tried to break the deadly chokehold.

Dario rolled onto his side, trying to force Fausto's arm from around his throat. As he felt himself losing consciousness, he looked at the marine sitting against the door bleeding from a hole on the side of his face. He saw the marine take an M-84 stun grenade from his harness and remove the pin. As he watched the dying marine slide sideways to the floor, he saw him open his hand, releasing the grenade. The spoon pinged free as the grenade rolled slowly away from his body.

Dario tapped Fausto's arm twice and then pointed at the grenade. As he felt Fausto's grip loosen, he rolled him over his shoulder, putting his body between himself and the grenade.

The blast deafened Dario as he felt the wave shoot over Fausto's body. He felt seriously disoriented but did not lose consciousness. As he pushed himself off the floor, he saw Fausto rolling back and forth with his hands over his ears. He climbed over him to get on his feet and get the fallen marine's rifle. By then, Fausto had raised himself to his hands and knees. Dario stood over Fausto and smashed the rifle butt into his head, knocking him unconscious.

Dario went to check the marine's pulse. He opened his eye to look at the pupil that stared back at him like a lifeless bead. He raised his head when he heard the marines approaching the warehouse. He had to move quickly.

He propped the dead marine back up to a sitting position against the door. Then he dragged Fausto's body and laid him in front of the marine. He got Comandante Sánchez's pistol off the floor and put it in Fausto's hand with his finger wrapped around the trigger.

Still shaken by the effects of the grenade, he staggered to the door leading to the warehouse floor and opened it. He took a last look at Fausto lying by the dead marine and at Comandante Sánchez's mortal remains. He turned to look at the stack of new Romanian AK-47 rifles on the desk and against the back wall. He closed the door when he heard a marine's voice just outside the door.

Dario rushed to the back of the warehouse as an explosion threw the office door open behind him. He opened the trapdoor on the floor, lowered himself into the opening, and let go of the trapdoor as he dropped into the water.

As Donovan used the lights of the plantation house to guide the *Mona* to Lorenzo Beach, he thought about the heavily guarded compounds he had penetrated before to repossess boats and other equipment. He had learned to suppress his fear and apprehension by staying focused on the job. He accepted the consequences if he made a mistake, but he had never had to face losing someone he loved before. That made everything different.

He switched off the outboard motor as the *Mona* slid onto the sand short of the high-tide line. He felt the sand give under his boat shoes as he got out to push the *Mona* to the beach. In his haste, he didn't notice the pistol he had tucked into his pants fall out as he pushed the boat past the tide line.

He looked up the coconut grove at the plantation house as he took a can of black shoeshine out of his back pocket. He thought of the sketch Don Macario had made of the path leading through the palms to the lawn behind the house as he dabbed shoeshine on his cheeks, forehead, and arms. He hurried to the tree line for cover and worked his way up the beach until he found it. He lowered himself behind a tropical shrub to listen for people moving about or talking or the sound of a radio or television set blaring. He heard nothing, except for the chirping of crickets. He needed to get closer.

In the dimness of night, he moved cautiously through the palms, pausing now and again to listen and check his surroundings. He could feel the sweat running down his back as he stared at the lights behind the plantation house. He turned his head when he caught a glimpse of something moving to his right. He lowered himself to look through the palms for the threat but couldn't see anything.

He started to push ahead when he heard rustling to his left. He again lowered himself to look and again saw nothing. Then he heard something running behind him, so he jerked his neck around but not in time to see anything. He felt his heart pounding in his ears as he looked to his left and then to his right and back left again. He felt for his pistol as he dropped to a knee and realized he had lost it. He inhaled sharply and held his breath to listen. The sweat on his face felt cold as did the air on his upper lip coming out of his nose.

Then he saw a shadow of what looked like a small man low-crawling through the palms toward the path ahead of him. He held his breath as he waited for it to emerge.

A large iguana came out from under the palms and stopped in the middle of the path to look at him with its large, bulging eyes. After a moment, the beast slipped into the underbrush beneath the coconut palms, where it seemed to vanish.

Donovan moved swiftly up the path to the edge of the lawn, where he took a knee behind a large palm to look at the back of the house.

In the stillness, he heard the clattering of dishes and a woman muttering something. He knew through talking with Dario and Don Macario's scouting report to expect three people at the plantation house besides Itzél. The old housekeeper, her gardener husband, and one sicario. The breeze blowing gently through the coconut palms felt good against his sweat-soaked skin as he watched the old woman through the kitchen window.

He darted across the lawn and ran up the steps to the veranda, nearly losing his balance as his shoes slid on the concrete. He lowered himself as he approached the kitchen window to look inside and saw the woman making taquitos. The smell of mixed peppers and onions she had roasting in one pan made him hungry as she warmed shredded chicken in another. He watched her take the tortillas off the griddle and slap several more on as she finished making about a half dozen taquitos. She wrapped them in aluminum foil and tucked them into an insulated lunch bag.

Donovan lowered his head suddenly after he heard his stomach growl unexpectedly just as San Juana turned to look. She wiped her hands on her apron, walked carefully to the window, and made the sign of the cross before she looked out at the coconut grove.

San Juana truly believed that the ghosts of long-dead pirates, victims of bloody Mayan sacrifices, or travelers killed by bandits on the old royal road haunted the coconut grove. She also believed that demons dwelled under the palms behind the house. Of all the entities of the netherworld, she feared the mischievous little goblin-like Mayan spirits known as the Alux the most.

"Adán?" Donovan heard her call out of the window over his head.

Donovan listened to the electric shrill of the crickets chirping as she waited for her husband to answer.

"I need a towel," Donovan heard someone say as San Juana let out a shrill of her own.

Donovan duck-walked away from under the window and went to hide behind a marble column with a view into the kitchen. There he saw San Juana panting deeply as she stared at a man of about thirty in a sweaty linen shirt and unruly hair. He recognized him as the narco he had met at the beach at the Devil's Elbow.

"Aye, Señor José Luis," San Juana said as she caught her breath. "You scared me."

"I need a towel," he repeated himself as an old man walked up behind him and stood in the hall. The old man's limp made him recall Grandpa McCoy of the old television sitcom.

"Can you get Señor José Luis a towel, Adán?" San Juana asked her husband.

As the old man went to get the towel, Donovan watched José Luis go into the kitchen and make himself a quick taquito out of the frying pan. He took a man-sized bite and turned to San Juana.

"Muy bueno," he said to her as he exited the kitchen.

By then, Adán had returned with a towel and a washcloth, which he handed to José Luis as he went into the hall.

"I started the shower for you to warm up the water," Adán told the narco.

José Luis took another bite of the taquito as he grabbed the towels and went down the hall. Donovan pulled his head back behind the marble column when he thought he saw San Juana look back toward him. He peered around the column carefully and saw her looking down the hallway. Donovan heard a door slam shut and watched San Juana pull her husband back into the kitchen. She handed him a bundle of taquitos wrapped in aluminum foil.

"Take these to Daniel, and don't let him run you off this time," she said to him.

"He didn't run me off. I left because Señora Itzél told me to go," he said bitterly as he took the bundle.

"Ándale, ándale, ándale," she said, giving him a push between the shoulders.

As Donovan watched San Juana go back into the kitchen to continue making taquitos, he heard something moving behind him and turned to look. He barely got a glimpse of something running into the brush under the palms. He thought of the large iguana he had seen earlier and brushed it off as he turned to look back into the kitchen. He saw San Juana looking out the window and guessed she had heard the disturbance as well.

"I thought you went to check on the señora." San Juana said out the window as Donovan ducked behind the marble column. "Adán?" he heard her call nervously.

Donovan lowered himself and low-crawled across the lawn below the veranda to the next column away from the window when he heard the patio door sliding open.

"Adán?" he heard her call again.

Donovan raised his head to peer over the edge of the veranda at San Juana as she stood nervously by the patio door. She reminded him of a child frightened by a bump in the night who despite a fear of the dark had to peek from under the covers to take a look. He watched her cross herself before switching on the porchlight. Donovan raised his head a little higher and saw her looking at the muddy footprints he had left when he went to look in the window. He ducked his head when he saw the old man come to the sliding door.

"What are you doing?" Adán asked her.

San Juana shrieked as she turned around and then slapped him on the chest.

"I told you never to do that," she said angrily.

"What are you afraid of?" Adán took her by the hand and dragged her to the edge of the porch a few feet from where Donovan had pressed himself against it. "I told you, there's nothing out there."

"No, Adán!" Donovan heard her say nervously.

Donovan raised his head and saw her looking through her fingers. She gasped as she pointed to the far edge of the lawn.

"Over there!" she exclaimed.

Donovan rolled onto his back to watch her husband limp down the steps, muttering something under his breath as he went to check the coconut grove.

"It's probably just an iguana," he said to her over his shoulder.

Donovan smiled as he watched San Juana walk nervously to the staircase. He stepped up on the veranda without her noticing as she watched her husband go into the coconut grove.

"You'd better take something to give the Alux," she said in a loud whisper. "I'll go get some candy," she said as she spun around into Donovan's arms.

Donovan put his hand over San Juana's mouth to keep her from shrieking again. The old housekeeper's eyes bulged out of her head with fear as he shushed her gently like a parent shushing a whimpering child after skinning a knee. He looked for the old gardener, who had disappeared into the coconut grove.

"Don't be afraid," he said to her calmly. "I'm not going to hurt you."

The old housekeeper's eyes relaxed, and she nodded her head. Donovan removed his hand and released her.

"You're Capitán Dónovan," she said as she smiled at him. "You came for Señora Itzél the last time she was brought here."

"Is she in the house?" Donovan asked as he glanced over his shoulder.

"No," she said as she pointed to her cottage. "She's in my house over there."

"Is anybody with her?"

"Right now, only Daniel," she replied. "There's another one in this house taking a shower."

Donovan looked over San Juana's shoulder at Adán, emerging out of the coconut grove. The old man with the bad leg dressed in khaki walked briskly across the lawn toward the veranda.

"Is that your husband?"

San Juana turned to look at Adán. She waved him over in a frantic manner. Donovan watched the old gardener limp up the steps with his eyes fixed solidly on him.

"This is Capitán Dónovan," San Juana said to him.

"I know who he is," Adán said impatiently. He looked at Donovan. "You've come to rescue Señora Itzél. Come—there's no time to waste."

Donovan followed the old man to the steps at the end of the veranda leading to the cottage he shared with his wife. He looked at the windows on the side of the plantation house as he followed Adán and saw a light shining out of only one of them.

"That's Daniel's room. José Luis will go in there to dress after he's done with his shower," Adán whispered as he led him to an old cart under a tree near the front of the cottage. He pointed at the kitchen window. "Your lady is in the kitchen with Daniel."

Donovan put his foot on a divide in the trunk and pulled himself up to get a better view of the kitchen. He could see Daniel leering at Itzél as he sipped on a beer. Itzél sat facing away from him with her arms crossed. He jumped off the tree and turned to Adán.

"Can you draw his attention to give me time to rush him from behind?" he said to Adán.

"I can get him to …" he said as he looked past Donovan at his wife. "What's she doing?"

Donovan turned to look as San Juana walked up behind them, holding an insulated lunch bag.

"What are you doing, vieja?" Adán whispered angrily at his wife.

"I came to help."

Adán scoffed. "This is men's work."

"I've got José Luis's taquitos," San Juana said. "I can distract Daniel for you."

"That's my job," Adán said as he took the lunch bag from her. He turned to Donovan. "Do you have a gun?"

Donovan looked at him. "No."

"We'll have to take him by surprise. He's been drinking so I don't think it'll be too hard. We'd better move quickly before José Luis is done with his shower."

"I'll go hide his clothes," San Juana whispered. "It'll take him a while to find them."

Donovan smiled. "That'll be a great help, señora."

"The screen door is very noisy," Adán said. "I'll undo the spring and leave it open, so you can get in without him hearing you."

Donovan followed the old man to the cottage, where he opened the screen door and held it open as he undid the spring.

"José Luis?" he heard Daniel call.

Adán slammed the screen door and then pushed it open for Donovan.

"It's me, Señor Daniel," Adán said as he entered the cottage. "I've got more taquitos."

Donovan followed Adán into the cottage and waited outside as he went into the kitchen. He pressed himself against the outer kitchen wall as he listened to Adán drop the insulated lunch bag on the table. He heard the refrigerator opening.

"What are you doing?" he heard Daniel ask.

"I'm getting you a beer," he heard Adán reply as he closed the refrigerator.

Donovan stepped back to get a better angle to run into the kitchen. He walked in an arc until he could see Itzél sitting at the table. He motioned her to look away when she turned to look at him.

"What were you looking at?" Daniel asked her.

"Nothing," she said as she turned to face him.

Donovan heard a chair slide back and then the click of a handgun hammer cocking.

"No!" she screamed.

Before Donovan could react, he heard a gunshot followed by a man gurgling and then another gunshot. He rushed through the doorway and saw Adán with his arm around Daniel's neck in a chokehold as he took him down to the floor.

Itzél ran to Donovan and wrapped herself around him as he watched Adán release the unconscious sicario, pick up the revolver, and stand.

"I told you I used to be a wrestler," Adán said to Itzél.

San Juana burst into the kitchen and gasped as she looked at her husband standing over Daniel holding the gun.

"What did you do, *viejo*?"

"Don't worry," Adán said proudly. "He's just sleeping."

Donovan took Itzél by the hand. "We'd better get out of here. I've got a boat waiting on the beach."

"Take the gun," Adán said to Donovan.

Donovan opened the five-shot revolver to look at the cylinder. He closed it and looked at Daniel passed out on the floor.

"What about him?" Donovan asked.

"He won't be a problem," the old gardener said as he got a nylon cord. "I make a real tight knot."

"Go, before José Luis is done with his shower," San Juana said anxiously.

Itzél hugged San Juana and then kissed Adán on the cheek.

"See that," Adán said as he turned to his wife pointing at his cheek. "That's what I mean by appreciation."

"That's going to have to last you a long time, viejo," she retorted.

Donovan winked at San Juana as he turned to Adán. "Hasta luego, luchador."

"Hurry," San Juana said.

Donovan took Itzél's hand and ran out of the cottage across the lawn toward the back of the plantation house as quickly as he could with her in tow. He looked at the window to Daniel's room and saw José Luis looking out, wearing only a towel around his waist.

"We've been spotted," he said to Itzél as he pulled her around the back of the house.

He glanced over his shoulder as they ran across the lawn toward the coconut palms and saw a shirtless José Luis struggling to unlock the patio door holding an AR-15 rifle.

José Luis almost slipped when he ran out to the veranda in his bare feet, wearing only his sweat-soaked pants. He brushed back his damp hair, aimed the rifle, and fired a burst at the fleeing couple as they ran out of the light and vanished under the palms.

The bullets glanced off the trees over their heads as Donovan threw Itzél to the ground. He crouched behind a palm and fired a shot at José Luis, hitting the marble column next to his head and causing him to lose his balance. Donovan watched José Luis run down the steps and take aim as he helped Itzél off the ground.

The bullets impacting the ground threw sand up around their feet as Donovan and Itzél ran deeper into the palms. Donovan threw Itzél down and covered her panther-like body with his as another burst flew just over their heads. The warmth and roundness of her hips cradled against his inner thighs and the tenderness of the side of her breast on the inside of his upper arm distracted him for a moment as he listened to José Luis running into the coconut grove.

He heard José Luis moving slowly through the palms as he felt Itzél quaking softly beneath him. Donovan looked through the ferns at José Luis's bare feet stepping cautiously down the path. He reached for a coconut lying close to his head and waited until he saw José Luis move further down the path before he raised himself off Itzél and hurled it as far as he could across the path.

Almost as soon as he heard it thud against a palm tree, he heard José Luis fire a burst. He looked up and saw the narco running toward the thud. Donovan pulled Itzél up by the hand and ran deeper into the coconut palms in the opposite direction until he found a fallen tree. He set her behind it and put the revolver in her hand.

"There're two shots left," he told her as he started to leave. "Keep your face hidden and don't look up no matter what."

"Don't leave me," she said apprehensively.

"I'm going to circle behind him," he cupped her face in his hands and kissed her. "I'll be right back."

Not far from where Donovan left Itzél, he saw José Luis come back to the path and hurry down it toward the beach. He continued to watch him as he stopped running suddenly to look to his left. He could almost hear the narco struggling to catch his breath as he stared into the ferns under the palms.

Donovan strained to see what had caught José Luis's attention. He rubbed the sweat from his forehead with his hand as he continued to watch the narco's silhouette staring into the ferns.

Then, out of nowhere, a sudden wisp of cold air blew across Donovan as he saw a blue glow rising in the ferns a few meters in front of José Luis. A sickly sweet scent of licorice laced with a hint of menthol carried in the cool breeze along with a faint whisper of a child-like voice calling José Luis's name.

"Who's there?" he heard José Luis call out as the whisper turned to a soft, barely audible chuckle.

Donovan lowered himself when he saw the narco swinging the rifle around frantically as he looked for the person whispering his name. José Luis turned suddenly to look at the ferns behind him.

"Show yourself, coward," José Luis called out angrily.

He saw José Luis dart suddenly into palms to chase something Donovan could not see. He watched the narco weave through the palms in a full circle before coming back to where he started. He stopped to look at the blue glow. Donovan turned his eye on the mysterious light as it, the cool air, and the sickly sweet scent faded away gradually. So did the coolness and the scent of licorice and menthol.

Donovan rubbed his eyes as he tried to explain to himself what he had just witnessed. He knew from experience that the light of the waning moon can play tricks on the eye, especially as it casts shadows of the clouds rushing across its face in a high wind. Donovan recalled a weed in Texas that smelled of mint when cut. He reasoned that José Luis must have disturbed some tropical plant as he ran through the bush chasing moon shadows. As for the blue glow … he would have to think more about that later.

As Donovan watched José Luis lower his rifle to change magazines, he heard a twig snap to his right. He saw the narco bolt in that direction after the sound. Donovan caught sight of a shadow that appeared to dart between the palms. He saw José Luis fire a burst after the shadow before running after it. He wondered if Adán had sneaked into the palms to draw his fire.

Then he heard another twig snap and turned in time to see another shadow weaving through the palms in the opposite direction. He grinned as he watched José Luis fire another burst at the moon shadow. Then he caught a glimpse of still another shadow moving away from the narco in yet another direction. This time, he saw José Luis give chase.

Donovan followed José Luis from a safe distance, watching him run haphazardly through the coconut grove, changing directions suddenly and often as he chased the shadows. He tried to maneuver into a position where he could jump him, but José Luis's erratic behavior confounded his efforts. At one point, he came close enough, but again the narco changed directions suddenly. He felt the blood run from his face when he saw José Luis running to where he had left Itzél.

Afraid that he had seen her, Donovan decided to risk running up directly behind him. The palm grove made it difficult for him to make headway as the two men zigged and then zagged through the palms toward the fallen tree where he had left Itzél. Just as Donovan caught up to him, he stumbled on something and fell. He saw José Luis look over his shoulder and stop to look at him.

"I've got you now!" he heard José Luis say.

Donovan heard Itzél scream as he watched the narco running back toward him with his rifle pointed at him. Then, out of the ferns, he saw a shadow grab José Luis by the ankle, sending him headfirst to the ground. The rifle flew out of his hands as he put them out to break his fall. Donovan pounced on José Luis, pummeling his fists on his face like a pair of jackhammers until he lost consciousness.

Itzél stood up from behind the fallen tree and embraced Donovan. He heard something rustling through the ferns and saw Adán walking up to them seemingly out of nowhere with a length of rope in his hands. He watched him curiously as he turned José Luis on his stomach and began to tie his hands behind his back.

"Thanks for knocking him off his feet like that," Donovan said to Adán.

"I didn't do that," Adán said. "He must have tripped on a vine."

"No, it wasn't a vine. I definitely saw a hand reach out and grab his ankle."

"Your eyes must have been playing tricks on you."

Although he didn't think so, it made sense to Donovan that he could have mistaken a vine for a hand in the darkness. After all, he had attributed the shadows he saw José Luis chasing through the palms to the moon, so it seemed reasonable that the moonlight could have played on a vine protruding from the ground. He looked up through the palms at the sky.

"What are you looking for?" Adán asked him as he bound the narco's hands behind his back.

"The moon," Donovan replied.

"We're in a new moon," Adán said. "You can't see it at night."

He stared curiously at the worldly old gardener as he finished tying José Luis. Without the moon to explain the shadows he saw running through the palms or the hand he saw trip up José Luis, only one other explanation made sense.

"You're pretty quick on your feet for a man your age," Donovan remarked.

"Not me, Capitán," Adán said as he stood over José Luis. "I haven't been able to run since a rattlesnake bit me when I was a boy. One of my legs is shorter than the other."

It confounded Donovan how the crippled old man had found them so quickly with José Luis running haphazardly all over the coconut palms and underbrush.

"How'd you get here so fast and how'd you know we'd need a rope?" Donovan asked.

"I was watching from the veranda. I came as soon as I heard you call me to bring a rope," he replied.

Donovan just stared at him.

"I didn't call you."

The streetlights over the port went out in segments in step with the Thunderbolts' retreat to the end of the dock. Not even the darkness could protect the paramilitaries as they fell one by one to the punishing barrage of fire laid down by the marines' guns. The muffled pop of a flare igniting overhead brought the shooting to a momentary halt as the flare descended over the dock. The light from the sparkling flare swung from left to right and back again, casting floating shadows, silhouetting the paramilitaries running between the abandoned forklifts and reach stackers like rats running from the light.

The colonel and Major Zamora were running to the end of the dock under the swaying shadow of a large crane when a string of bullets splattered the asphalt around them, knocking them off their feet. Major Zamora grabbed the colonel by the load-bearing straps and dragged him behind the rear tires of a tractor-like reach stacker. He sat the colonel on the asphalt and let himself drop next to him.

"How bad?" Major Zamora asked the colonel between pants.

"I can't feel my legs," he replied as he removed his helmet and let it drop. "You?"

The major put his hand on his side and looked at the blood in his glove in the unsteady light.

"I'm all right," he lied.

"What about the men?"

The major took a deep breath, gritted his teeth, and lowered himself to look under the vehicle used to stack containers. He saw the SandCat advancing cautiously toward the end of the dock. As far as he could see, only the two Thunderbolts dressed like policemen had made it to the end of the dock and taken cover behind a forklift. Both looked badly wounded with only one able to return fire.

"Only a couple left," he said as he breathed deeply.

"How far is the ship?" Colonel Barca asked.

Major Zamora looked out at an empty sea. He panned his head from left to right and saw the sails of the *Siete Mares* fading beyond Punta Morro. He closed his eyes and let out his breath.

"Reséndez is staying out of range of the SandCat," Major Zamora lied.

"Puma Dos has the RPG," the colonel said as he struggled to get a satisfying breath. "Why haven't they taken out the SandCat?"

"Puma Dos is ..."

The major wrapped himself around the colonel to shield him after hearing a grenade bounce nearby and then detonate. He could feel the blast rushing around him from under the reach stacker. He looked around the tire he and the colonel had hidden behind to check on the remaining men. The grenade had killed them.

"What about the RPG?" the colonel asked again.

"Puma Dos never got off the roof, mí coronel," the major explained.

"Use ... the ... 203," the colonel said weakly as he struggled to breathe.

The major loosened the collar on the colonel's tunic to make him more comfortable as he watched him fade in and out of consciousness. He turned an ear when he heard the gunfire slow to a stop. He listened to the clanking of the SandCat's diesel engine idling nearby as he undid the strap on his helmet and let his hand drop. He looked down at the pool of blood puddling by his left side and felt himself getting weaker.

He grimaced in pain when he felt the weight of the colonel's head against his shoulder. He felt his throat go dry and closed his eyes as he turned his head to the right. In his mind's eye, he pictured himself and the colonel at a press conference standing between two marines wearing hoods. He saw camera flashes bursting like muzzle blasts as a horde of reporters fired off questions over each other.

He looked at the sails of the *Siete Mares* rounding Punta Morro as the salty taste of blood in his mouth made him cough. He removed his pistol from its holster and stared at it as he listened to the SandCat advancing slowly toward his position.

He turned to look at the colonel, who had lost consciousness. He pointed the pistol at the colonel's temple and pulled the trigger. He heard the SandCat brake to a stop and listened to the rumbling clank of its engine. He lowered the colonel's body slowly to the ground and then rested his head on the reach stacker's tire.

He took a deep breath and turned his head to get a last look at the *Siete Mares* as it disappeared behind the point. He released the air in his lungs slowly, put the muzzle of the pistol in his mouth, and pulled the trigger.

It didn't take long for Donovan to find his ship even on a moonless night like that night when the sea looked as dark as tar and the horizon was lost to the night sky. The *Siete Mares* sat 150 yards off the beach at Villa Lorenzo. Her hull reminded Donovan of a piece of chalk sitting on a blackboard.

The ordeal had drained Itzél. She had her head nestled into Donovan's shoulder as she slept. He tried not to disturb her as he reached back to shut off the outboard motor and guided the *Mona* alongside the *Siete Mares*'s starboard side, where Augie and Sandy waited to make a quick recovery of the boat.

Donovan took Itzél to the boarding ladder hooked to the gunwale, where Augie waited to help her aboard.

"Welcome aboard, pretty lady," Augie said as he took her hand.

"Gracias, Señor Fagan," she replied demurely. "I'm not feeling very pretty right now."

"Send down the chains," Donovan called up from the bow.

Augie and Sandy released the bow and stern chains as Donovan waited to hook them to the rings. He heard a faint rumbling hum coming from the north and turned his head to look. In the distance, he could see the bioluminescent glow of the water breaking before the bow of a fast-moving vessel about 500 yards off the coast.

"There's something headed this way—fast," Donovan called to the deck.

"Must be the Armada headed to the port?" Augie remarked.

"Let's not stick around to find out," Donovan said as he climbed up the boarding ladder in two steps. "I don't want to explain what we're doing with a Thunderbolt tied up in the hold."

Augie and Sandy hurried to turn the cranks in unison to get the *Mona* out of the water on a level plain.

Donovan smiled at Itzél as he walked over to her. Despite what she had said to Augie, she had never looked more beautiful to him. Her clothes had worked out of place but fetchingly so and her hair had come undone. A lock covered the right side of her face, prompting an unwanted memory Donovan quickly purged from his mind. He looked into her green cat-like eyes, which gleamed even in the low light. Tears welled in them like twin limestone pools in the Texas hill country.

"What's wrong?" he asked her.

"I was told somebody was shot at Padre Island," Itzél said nervously. "Was it …"

Donovan glanced at Augie and Sandy, who had turned to look at him after they swung the *Mona* over the deck.

"He's going to be all right," Donovan said to her reassuringly. "A spent round punctured Benício's lung."

A tear streamed down her face, and Donovan tried to comfort her by taking her into his arms, but she pulled away and gave her back to him. He just stood there gawking at her like a child who had just dropped the ice cream from his cone as she wept into her hands.

"Go get the anchor," Augie said to Sandy as he went to offer Itzél his handkerchief.

"Aye, aye, Mister Fagan," Sandy said.

As he started to go forward, Sandy stopped suddenly and pointed at a dark figure running up behind Donovan with his hand high over his head, holding a galley knife.

"Watch out, Skipper!" Sandy yelled.

Donovan spun around barely in time to catch Reséndez's wrist with both hands. Augie grabbed Itzél by the shoulders and handed her to his nephew before going to try to help his partner. Reséndez and Donovan twisted and turned their bodies at odd angles as they fought along the starboard side. Donovan threw him over his hip, and they both went over the side.

Augie and Sandy ran to where they had gone overboard and watched the air trapped in their clothes rising to the surface in a churning fountain of bubbles. Augie looked to the north at the white glow of the wake looming larger as it approached. He grabbed Sandy who had put his foot on the bulwark and stopped him from diving into the water to help Donovan.

"Get the anchor," he said to him.

'But the skipper—"

"We can't help him now," Augie said coldly. "We got to get out of here. Now get going."

Donovan and Reséndez continued to twist and roll as they sank deeper and deeper in a roiling column of bubbles. Reséndez put his free hand on Donovan's throat, tearing at his larynx. Donovan released his left hand to break the paramilitary's grip. Reséndez twisted his body, freeing his knife hand from Donovan's grip. He lunged it at Donovan, who grabbed him by the forearm, bringing the knife directly between them.

A dark plume rose from between them as they sank to the bottom.

CHAPTER 16

The burned-out panga floated just beneath the surface of the water, hanging by the bow line tied to the dock behind the warehouse. Lieutenant Baeza shined his flashlight on the ghostly outline of the partly sunken fiberglass launch, studying the flotsam suspended in the rainbow-like halo of fuel floating over the wreck. He ran his light from stem to stern and back again, looking for the reason it had exploded and burned until he spotted a piece of broken fiberglass floating on the outer edge of his light.

He walked to the end of the dock to get a closer look, shining his light on the broken fragment. His driver, Corporal Muñoz, went to stand by the rail beside him.

"What is it?" he asked the lieutenant.

"It looks like the cowling of the outboard motor," he replied. He looked behind him and shined the light on the dock. "I need something I can use to fish it out."

"I saw a fishing gaffe in the warehouse," Corporal Muñoz said.

"Get it for me."

As he waited for the corporal, he walked back up the dock next to the stern of the sunken launch and shined his light into the water. He could barely make out the mangled remains of the powerhead sitting three feet underwater. The blast had sheared off the cylinder head, starter drum, and fuel tank.

Corporal Muñoz walked out to the dock holding a long pole with a hook on the end. He reached over the rail, striking the water several times before hooking the broken piece of fiberglass and pulling it out of the water as Petty Officer Lanceros walked out of the warehouse to the dock.

"There's a *ministerio publico* in the office wanting to see you, mí teniente," the petty officer said.

"What's a public ministry agent doing here?" Lieutenant Baeza inquired curiously. "This is the navy's purview."

"The ministerio publico is with the SIEDO."

"How did he get here so quickly?" Baeza asked himself. "There's no direct flight until tomorrow afternoon."

The SIEDO, the Assistant Attorney General's Office for Special Investigations on Organized Crime, had jurisdiction on all matters that related to drug cartels in Mexico. Their authority superseded the distinction between civilian and military courts. Based in Mexico City, their agents traveled at a moment's notice to the four corners of the republic. They generally traveled by commercial airline but had used private and military aircraft to reach remote areas.

"Here you go, mí teniente," Muñoz said as he handed the broken cowling to the lieutenant.

Baeza looked at the half-inch-sized hole cut perfectly into the fragment. He flipped it over, looked at the blackened surface, and sniffed it.

"The ministerio publico is waiting, mí teniente," the petty officer said politely.

The lieutenant handed the fragment to Corporal Muñoz before walking across the warehouse floor to where a marine stood guard outside the inner door to the office. Like all his marines, he wore a navy-blue ballistic vest over the tunic of his camouflaged battle dress uniform with "Marina" stamped proudly across it. Dirt had occluded the middle part of the M, making it look more like an H. He stood in front of the marine and stared at his bulletproof vest.

"How do you explain this, Maestre?" he asked his petty officer.

"There's no excuse for this, mí teniente," Petty Officer Lanceros apologized as he wiped the offending substance from his marine's vest.

"That's better," Lieutenant Baeza said. He turned to the marine. "Now you don't look like a label for a sack of flour."

"Sí, mí teniente," the marine said as he clicked the heels of his boots and opened the door for the lieutenant.

"I'll deal with you later," the petty officer said to the marine in a low voice before walking into the office.

Inside the office, a woman with a stern look on her face standing nearly as tall as the lieutenant dressed like a university brat in frayed jeans and a loose-fitting sweatshirt stood by the desk photographing the AK-47 rifles. She wore horn-rimmed glasses and no makeup and had her auburn hair in a tight bun behind her head. Despite her shabby attire, she had an alluring feminine appeal.

"Where is the public ministry agent?" Lieutenant Baeza whispered to the petty officer.

"*That is* the public ministry agent," he whispered back.

Generally, in the Mexican judicial system, it was the prosecutors and not the police who investigated crime. They collected evidence, directed forensic specialists to conduct tests or studies, interviewed witnesses and suspects, and otherwise prepared the case for submission to a judge.

The prosecutor finished taking her pictures, put her cell phone in her hip pocket, and walked over to the lieutenant as she picked up her notepad and pen off the desk.

"Licensiada Lourdes Santiago Rosas with the Assistant Attorney General's Office for Special Investigations on Organized Crime," she said, introducing herself.

"Teniente Ramiro Baeza, Naval Intelligence," he said, a little disconcerted by the SIEDO's presence in Campeche but more surprised by the firmness of her handshake. "If you don't mind my asking, Licensiada, how were you able to get here from Mexico City so fast? We just informed command of the incident."

"Strictly good fortune, Teniente Baeza," she said over the top of her Buddy Holly glasses as she wrote on her notepad. "I was vacationing at the Hacienda Paraiso."

The lieutenant glanced at her left hand, noting that she had no wedding ring as she scribbled on her notepad.

"With your husband, I presume," he commented.

"I'm not married," she responded flatly. "Where is Colonel Barca's corpse?"

"His and Major Zamora's bodies are at the end of the pier by a container stacker."

"Were any of the Thunderbolts captured?"

"They all fought to the death."

"Was any video taken of the gun battle?"

The question annoyed the lieutenant. "We were a little busy at the time."

"In the future, you might consider taking a video." She looked over her glasses at him. "It refutes any claims of excessive force."

She raised her notepad and pen to resume her line of questioning. "What happened here?"

The lieutenant cleared his throat. "From what we have determined so far, the Thunderbolts raided the warehouse to intercept a gun shipment El Demonio was receiving tonight."

"You mean Fausto López?"

"Yes."

"Where is he now?"

"I had him transported to the holding cell at the base in Lerma," he explained.

"I want to question him," she said.

"Of course," the lieutenant responded. "But you might find him reluctant to talk."

"I'll get him to talk," she said confidently. She turned to look at Comandante Sánchez's corpse on the floor. "What was the state police doing here?"

"That's Comandante Sánchez, the man who united the Campeche gangs," the lieutenant explained.

"I know who he is," she said dryly. "What's he doing here? I thought he and López were at odds."

"They might have been working together to prepare for the raiders—"

"Might?" she remarked pointedly. "Are you speculating, or do you have facts to back it up?"

Although Lieutenant Baeza preferred directness, he found the prosecutor's directness a little too direct.

"For weeks, there have been rumors that Cisneros planned to raid Champotón."

"The SIEDO has information to the contrary," the prosecutor said, interrupting him. "It is our understanding that he was placed in Ciudad del Carmen as a rearguard for Colonel Barca while he conducted a campaign against the Commission in Chiapas. Nothing more."

"The Armada is aware of that information," the lieutenant retorted. "However, the incident at Villamar would seem to contradict that information. Cisneros being their common enemy, it's reasonable to *speculate* that López and Sánchez put aside their differences to work together to stop Cisneros."

"What's behind Cisneros's attempt on Champotón?" she asked. "Do the Norteños plan to expand their influence to Campeche?"

"The situation is still fluid," the lieutenant replied. "I won't have an *opinion* until I review the debriefing reports submitted by the Champotón detachment and Capitán Mendiola."

"Why do you think he launched a raid all of a sudden?"

Lieutenant Baeza glanced at the petty officer before responding.

"Are you asking me to speculate?"

The prosecutor's face showed signs of blushing as she smiled subtly. Lieutenant Baeza wouldn't let her off the hook as he looked at her coldly, waiting for an answer.

"Please do," she said humbly.

"From my understanding, Cisneros's raid was poorly planned and may have been spontaneous," Baeza said as he glanced at the agent scribbling feverishly on her notepad. "The fact that the gangs were waiting to ambush them at Villamar leads me to conclude that they were tipped off that the raid was coming."

"By whom?"

"We may never know. None of Cisneros's men are available for debriefing," Baeza replied as he looked at the rifles on the desk and against the back wall. "It could be that Colonel Barca sent Cisneros to raid Champotón as a diversion to intercept López's gun shipment."

"You don't think he tipped off the gangs?" she asked.

"I understand the colonel had a low regard for Cisneros," Baeza retorted. "He's not above it."

He watched her scribble on her pad, waiting to field her next question. She stopped writing and looked back at the desk.

"Are these all the guns?"

The lieutenant turned to Petty Officer Lanceros. "Maestre?"

"I believe so, Licensiada," the petty officer responded. "We're waiting for the divers to search the bottom behind the warehouse."

"Why do they have to search the bottom?" she asked.

"Like I said, Licensiada," Lieutenant Baeza interjected. "We believe the Thunderbolts came here to take López's guns. His men might have loaded at least a part of the guns before their pangas were destroyed."

"Who authorized the destruction?"

"We didn't fire on them, Licensiada," he replied.

"Then who did?"

"We don't know," the lieutenant replied. "I saw a tracer coming in from the ocean."

"What's a tracer?"

The lieutenant again glanced at the petty officer before replying.

"It's a specially designed round with a pyrotechnic charge at the base that ignites after being fired, making the round visible from the moment it is fired until it strikes the target."

"Might it have come from one of the Armada's ships?"

"Neither of our vessels was in the area at the time. Capitán Mendiola had his gunboat at Villamar, and the fast attack boat didn't respond until after we had engaged the Thunderbolts."

"Then who fired on those pangas?"

"We don't know," the lieutenant admitted. "We're checking the port's surveillance cameras to see if they caught anything."

"Do you know what kind of weapon was used?"

The lieutenant turned to Petty Officer Lanceros. "Have Muñoz bring the broken cowling we found."

"Sí, mí teniente," Lanceros said as he opened the inner door to send the marine standing in the warehouse to fetch the corporal.

The lieutenant looked at the hard-charging public ministry agent. "We found a piece of the engine cowling to one of the outboard motors on the pangas. It has a clean circular perforation on it I believe was made by a high-powered rifle."

"A rifle round can cause an explosion like that?"

"With the right ammunition, it can."

"What kind of ammunition?"

"An incendiary or explosive incendiary round."

A subtle knock on the door to the warehouse drew both their attention. Corporal Muñoz walked into the office and handed the fiberglass fragment to the lieutenant, who handed it to the public ministry agent.

"What am I looking at?" she asked.

"That's the piece of the engine cowling I was telling you about," he explained. "Take a look at the hole in the middle of it."

The agent went to her bag to get a small cardboard ruler she used to measure the bullet hole.

"Twelve point seven millimeters," she said.

She set the fragment on the floor as she reached for the cell phone in her back pocket. She laid the ruler across the perforation and took a picture with her phone.

"Bag it and transport it with the guns to your evidence locker in Lerma," she said to Baeza.

"See to it, Maestre," the lieutenant said to Lanceros.

"A la orden, mí teniente," the petty officer said as he picked up the broken cowling off the floor.

"I want to know who fired on those pangas," the agent said firmly.

"We will do our best to identify the responsible party," the lieutenant responded.

The hard-charging prosecutor walked over to where Comandante Sánchez lay sprawled on the floor. She stared at the wound in his chest.

"I need a postmortem performed on all the bodies," she said.

"A medial forensic team is already on the way."

"The comandante looks like he was shot at point-blank range," the prosecutor commented. "Who do you think shot him?"

"It could have been López," Lieutenant Baeza replied. "He was found unconscious holding Sánchez's gun."

"How do you know it was his gun?"

"The comandante's scabbard is empty, and the gun López was holding had a state police stamp on it," he explained. "We'll verify it through the army's inventory records."

She turned to look at the dead marine by the front door.

"Did López also shoot your marine?" she asked him.

"It appears he did," the lieutenant replied. "His hands were swabbed with paraffin. An examination will confirm it."

Donovan emerged from the water holding the gash on his side to slow down the bleeding. He fell to his knees a couple of times as he waded the rest of the way to the caves at Punta Morro. The swim and blood loss had exhausted him despite a favorable current. He turned to look at the searchlights sweeping the water from a ship off the coast as he entered the cave. He scanned the horizon for the *Siete Mares* and nodded in approval when he didn't see anything. He lowered himself carefully to lie on the sand as he held his side. He closed his eyes as he regained his breath and listened to the surf.

The swells crashing against the rocks comforted him like a mother's lullaby as he struggled to breathe. He felt the waves carrying him away not to another place but across time as his vision began to blur. He fought to keep from losing consciousness but slipped in and out as the waves ebbed and flowed outside of the cave.

As he felt himself slipping off to sleep, he listened to what sounded like the faint sound of tires screeching and several short bursts of machine-gun fire coming from above the cave. He closed his eyes tightly and opened them again several times trying to regain his vision but seeing only the blurred image of a pickup rolling down a ravine. He saw flashes of lights swinging wildly down the ravine and two bodies covered with a tarp lying side by side beside a stack of assault rifles.

As the images faded, the sound of the surf carried him off to a time where he saw feathered priests, painted in bright colors plunging obsidian knives into the chests of half-naked brown-skinned men tied to a bed of rocks fashioned into an altar. The sound of their screams transcended time as they echoed from within the cave.

The waves then washed him to the shores of another time where he saw a longboat with many oars coming up into the mouth of the cave. He saw men dressed in flowing shirts, faded breeches, and dirty leggings dragging a heavy chest into the back of the cave where he watched them dig a hole to bury their prize. He saw one of them take a knife and run it across the throat of an unsuspecting crewman, throwing him into the hole before burying the chest. He saw this play out several times with different men, at different parts of the cave, but each time with an unsuspecting crewman succumbing to a knife drawn across his throat or plunged into his back or felled by a single shot to the back of the head or into his back.

The surf ushered in another time where he saw men and women condemned to death for some petty transgression or alleged heresy left to drown in the cave with their hands and feet bound, screaming in horror as they watched the tide rising slowly.

Seyba Playa
1665

The Royal Road from Campeche City to Champotón ran along the ocean through the thicket and the limestone hills that rolled gently along the coast. It had existed long before the first Spanish ships came to the Yucatán. The Maya had carved it out of the jungle connecting the villages of Ah Kin Pech and Chakanputon the Spanish would later rename Campeche and Champotón respectively.

It's not certain when Seyba Playa came into existence, but it happened sometime after the final pacification of the Maya and the last pirate attacks in the middle of the seventeenth century. The English pirate Henry Morgan used to anchor off nearby Siho Playa beach between attacks on Spanish shipping leaving Campeche City up the coast.

Fishermen from Campeche City and Champotón most likely settled the area between the points of Punta Siho Playa and Punta Morro to exploit the bountiful fishing off Payucán Beach. In time, a small fishing community formed along the Royal Road, and travelers going between Campeche City and Champotón used Seyba Playa as a waypoint.

Over the years, the villagers of Seyba Playa had learned not to trust strangers traveling the Royal Road. They endured raids by bandits who took their food and forced their unwanted attention on their wives and daughters during bouts of drunkenness. They had also suffered similar abuse from the Spanish soldiers patrolling the roads who behaved no better than the bandits they sought to apprehend. Runaway slaves came to Seyba Playa asking for refuge, forcing the townspeople to suffer the retribution meted out by the bounty hunters hired by their masters. The road also brought beggars, thieves, and charlatans seeking to rob them of their meager possessions.

For all the trouble strangers brought to the tiny seaside hamlet, no one took notice of the old woman with the tortured face who came knocking on their doors, looking for a handout and a place to spend the night. Shortly afterward, the children in the village started to disappear mysteriously. The authorities believed that the youths had merely run off to Campeche City to escape their dull existence as many young people had done in the past. However, that did not satisfy their mothers, who knew their children and couldn't believe that they would leave so abruptly, especially when many of them had not yet seen their tenth birthday. They believed some evil had come to the village, and they turned to the parish priest for help.

The padre stood before the parents of the missing children sitting in the pews of the church. He pulled nervously on the frayed end of the cord tied around the tattered brown robe he wore. The newly ordained priest had only recently arrived at Seyba Playa from Spain and knew little of the ways of the world. He knew even less of witchcraft and the dark arts. He had heard the older priests in the diocese talk of the dark tales and mysterious happenings along the coast but could hardly believe what he heard that afternoon as he listened to the villagers recount their tales.

"It has to be a coincidence," the padre suggested as he listened to one woman tell her story.

"It's no coincidence, Padrecito," the woman insisted. "We all allowed the old woman to spend the night in our homes, where she befriended one of our children. Each time, that child disappeared a day or two later."

"My husband followed her into an alley one night," another woman said. "He saw her turn into a *lechuza*."

"A barn owl?" the priest said, frowning skeptically.

"Just her face, Padre," the woman explained. "Witches change forms when they feed."

"I've seen this unfortunate woman," the priest responded. "She's old and may have suffered burns to her face. In the dark, I could see how your husband might have thought she looked like an owl."

"He saw her spit out pieces of bone," she retorted. "Human bones. She let out a vile screech when she noticed him. He was so frightened, he wet himself."

The padre knew her husband and had seen him on more than one occasion stumbling through Seyba Playa in a drunken stupor after celebrating a good catch. That could easily explain a hallucination and certainly his urine-soaked breeches.

"Was that the day he brought in all those fish?"

"The Bible warns about witches," the oldest woman there remarked.

The young priest looked curiously at the old woman. The older priest he replaced had warned him about her, the village *curandero*, the faith healer. The villagers went to her to heal their illnesses and deliver their babies. She used native remedies and pagan religious practices, often incorporating elements of the Catholic religion and prayer to heal the sick, calm the nervous, and counsel the confused. The villagers believed she had mystical power and turned to her not only to heal their bodies but to ward off evil spirits and curses. Back in Spain, a woman like her would surely have found herself brought before the tribunal for witchcraft.

The people respected her, and because of that, she stood between them and the church. She had one foot firmly planted in the shadow world of the curanderos. What she and the other townspeople attributed to the handiwork of a witch, he chose to dismiss as superstition.

The *curandera* stepped into the aisle holding a rope as she walked up to the padre.

"Bless this for us, Padricito," she said, handing the crudely made rope to him.

"What do you intend to do with it?" the padre asked. "The church will not condone murder."

"Nobody's going to get murdered, Padrecito," the curandera said dryly as she coiled the rope. "We just want to bind the evil she conceals."

Donovan listened to his heartbeat throbbing in his ear like the slow rhythmic cadence of a distant drum coming toward him as he struggled to open his eyes and his consciousness ebbed and flowed like the tide rising ever closer to him. The dampness of the sand felt cool against his face as he opened his eyes slowly and looked at the shadowy blurs walking toward him.

A young boy dressed in ragged white clothing and a tattered straw hat beat the bass drum hanging from his shoulders in a slow measured cadence as he led the procession past Donovan into the caves at Punta Morro. Behind him walked the old woman with the tortured face escorted by two Spanish soldiers standing behind her holding the flared ends of their blunderbusses aimed at her back.

The old crone had her hands tied to the ends of a weathered yoke balanced on her neck and shoulders like the ox that used it. The priest dressed in his vestments stood by the cave entrance holding an aspersorium as the soldiers prodded the old woman to enter the cave.

"Ayudame, hijo," the old woman pleaded for help from the young priest.

"¡Silencio! Bruja maldita!" one of the soldiers said as he pushed her past the priest with the sole of his boot.

"Don't let them take me into the cave," she cried. "They're going to drown me."

The padre looked at the procession that had gathered around him at the entrance. "This is wrong," he said to them.

The curandera stepped forward from the crowd, holding the homespun rope the padre had blessed. She pointed at the old crone with her free hand.

"She doesn't deserve your pity, Padre!" the curandera said to the priest. "She is a servant of the evil one."

"Use the holy water," a woman yelled from the back of the crowd. "Make her tell you what she did with our children."

The young priest held his arms up to quiet the villagers, who expressed their anger by hurling insults and cursing at the old woman.

"You have no proof she's behind the disappearance of your children," he said to them. "Send her to Campeche and let the *corte* decide if she's guilty of any wrongdoing."

"She's a witch!" someone in the crowd yelled.

"You have no proof of that," he argued.

"Sprinkle her with holy water," the curandera said. "You'll have your proof."

The villagers also urged the padre to use the aspersorium to force the old crone into confessing.

"This is not a tool of interrogation," the priest said, quieting the villagers. "It is for bestowing God's blessing. I brought it to give the condemned her last rites."

"Then give her the rites or step aside," the curandera said fiercely.

The crowd began chanting, "Bless her, bless her," repeatedly, growing louder with each chant. The padre lowered the aspersorium as he hung his head. The curandera walked over to the old woman with the tortured face, holding the consecrated rope out in front of her for protection. She made a noose like a lasso, threw it over the yoke, and tugged on it.

The old woman straightened her back cursing angrily. Her face changed before the priest's eyes into a cadaverous, hollow-eyed crone's with a hideous scowl.

"Help me tighten the noose!" the curandera exclaimed.

The soldiers laid their blunderbusses on the sand by the old crone and pulled tightly on the consecrated rope. The witch screamed and began to mutter incoherently in Latin as she lowered herself slowly to the sand. The priest, astounded by what he saw, doused the old crone with holy water.

"Be gone from this woman, unclean spirit!" the padre said as he doused her again. "In the name of God, I command you to leave this child of the Lord!"

The old crone let out a hideous screech as the holy water burned her face. She hardened her eyes and ignored the priest as she leered hatefully at the villagers gathered around her. The soldiers wrapped the consecrated rope around her several times, tightening it harder with each pass. The soldiers picked up their blunderbusses and dragged the old crone by the yoke to the back of the cave, where they threw her facedown into the sand.

The villagers watched from the mouth of the cave as the soldiers kicked and beat her with the stocks of their short-barreled blunderbusses. The soldiers stopped beating her when she fell silent. They spat on her before turning to walk out of the cave.

The padre watched in horror as the woman lay silently in the sand. He crossed himself.

"Forgive me, God," he muttered under his breath.

The villagers watched the witch quietly as the waves crashed against the rocks behind them. The old crone did not move as the wind blew into the cave and swirled around her, raising a cloud of sand like a dust devil. Then, a low guttural sound rose from her, growing weaker as the dust devil of wet sand settled back to the floor of the cave.

The old crone struggled to lift herself off the sand, using the yoke to help her sit. She turned to look at the villagers watching silently from the mouth of the cave. Her face had taken the pallor of sun-bleached leather, and her eyes turned as big as a barn owl's. With what strength she could manage, she parted her withered lips, and in a deep, gravelly voice, she spoke her last words.

"From beneath the waves and the bowels of the sea, I will haunt all thy future progeny," she moaned balefully. "From the depths of darkness, from the pit of despair, I will return to this place, so beware. This rope that binds me was made by man and will rot with time, strand by strand. When at last the final strand has broken, your progeny will heed the words that I have spoken."

The images in Donovan's mind faded to a soft blur as he fought to regain consciousness. He could hear the air rushing in and out of his lungs like the rhythmic beat of the surf rolling to the shore. He tried to open his eyes as the seawater ebbed and flowed into the cave, coming closer to his face each time. He struggled to clear his vision and felt the sensation of floating as the soft blur turned into a whirling wisp of white light that changed gradually into a dust cloud, swirling in the rearview mirror of his convertible as he drove down a caliche road.

He could feel the sun against his face and the wind whipping around him. The white had cooled to sky blue as he drove his classic convertible down the backroads of the Texas hill country.

"You shouldn't be on this road," he heard a familiar voice say.

He turned to his right and saw Xóchitl sitting beside him wearing a sleeveless white summer dress, a white lace scarf, and a large pair of sunglasses. The skin on her bare shoulders looked like cinnamon.

"I know where I'm going," he said to her as he reached over to brush away the lock of rich black hair that had fallen across her face.

She grabbed his hand, stopping him.

"I wonder if you really do."

She released his hand and then swept hers across the left side of his face as she smiled at him dolefully. He reached over and brushed the lock of hair hanging over the right side of her face back under her scarf.

"Hmm," she muttered softly. She turned on the radio and sat back to look up the road.

Donovan continued to look at her as she sat quietly listening to the music playing. Donovan recognized the song immediately. The last time he heard it, he and Xóchitl were sitting in her apartment on an antique Italian sofa, watching the lights of Old Town Veracruz through the open french doors to her balcony.

"Do you remember that song?" she asked him as they listened to the sultry melody of the jazz saxophone playing.

"Of course, I do," he replied. "It was playing the night I proposed to you."

"Do you remember what we talked about?"

He put his arm around her and turned to look up the road as he thought about that night. He remembered how she had buried her head in his shoulder as he held her hand out to look at the diamond ring he had given her.

"I remember talking about loving each other forever."

"Till death do us part," she said.

He looked at her as she raised her head to look at him. Her face looked sad somehow as she stared at him through the large sunglasses on her angelic face.

"I remember telling you I'd love you forever," he said solemnly.

She smiled and then rested her head back on his shoulder.

"Do you remember talking about finding someone else if one of us was to die first?" she asked him.

Donovan gazed pensively at the road as it cut through a limestone hill before dropping into a valley. He remembered her calling him a liar when he said he could never marry anybody else.

"I remember telling you that I could never find another you," he said.

"But you tried anyway," she said softly.

Her tone alarmed Donovan. He had never heard her admonish him for something he did. She had scolded him for not taking care of himself or driving too fast, but she had never spoken to him that way. He turned to her as she looked up at him and removed her glasses. Her doe-like brown eyes had changed to emerald-green.

"I told you to find a woman to love for who she is and not because she reminds you of me."

"But I do love Itzél," Donovan said softly as if trying to convince himself.

"No, you don't," Xóchitl said as she shook her head gently. "You love that she looks like me."

Donovan felt his heart sink as he faced the truth for the first time. He saw the emerald in her eyes change back to the doe-like brown that had captivated him so thoroughly. He lost himself in their warmth and could feel her undying love for him.

"There's a good woman out there waiting for you to love," she said sincerely. "Go find her. In the meantime,"—she dropped her scarf of white lace on her shoulders—"you shouldn't be on this road."

"I get it," Donovan retorted. "You want me to move on."

"No," she said as she smiled at him with her eyes like only she could. "I want you to wake up. You're not ready to be on this road."

He looked at her curiously as she raised the scarf over her head, turning everything around her into a bright white light.

"I will always love you, Simon," he heard her say as she faded into the whiteness.

The images in his mind faded once again as he started to regain consciousness. He felt a pair of hands roll him over and then slap him on the side of the face repeatedly before splitting his right eye open and shining a light in it.

"He's alive," he heard Augie say to someone with him.

He struggled to look at the two men as they lifted him off the beach by his underarms and the back of his knees and set him down on an olive-drab blanket spread out beside him.

Chapter 17

Sunrise came to the Paradise Lagoon a little later than the rest of Campeche, thanks to the hills that overlooked the grounds of the Paradise Inn. Jack sat on the patio outside the restaurant watching the effects of the sunlight on the bluff across the lagoon. The cabañas nestled on the bluff seemed to hang in midair as the red-tile roofs and white stucco walls emerged out of the relative darkness of the predawn light. As the sunlight spread to the lagoon, he turned his attention to the perfectly horseshoe-shaped body of water, the beach around it, and the beauty of the coconut palms and tropical flora that surrounded it.

He looked at the boats moored in the marina, admiring each for its unique character. The older motor-powered yachts had teak or mahogany trim on their simply designed cabins and decks while the modern ones that lacked such detail made up for it with stylish wind-swept cabins and shiny fiberglass hulls. The sailboats varied in size and design with no two alike. He never paid much attention to the differences before. However, he developed an interest since the incident on Padre Island and learned to tell them apart.

The sloops and cutters reminded him of racing dogs. Built for speed, they had low profiles with a single lightweight aluminum mast, a barely discernible cabin, and a sleek fiberglass hull. The twin-masted ketches, yawls, and schooners looked more elegant. To the untrained eye, they all might look the same. The difference lay in the rigging and position of the main and mizzenmast on the deck. Ketches and yawls had the taller main mast set forward on the ship. Ketches had a shorter mizzenmast set forward of the steering post while a yawl had a tiny mast set aft of it. Schooners had the larger main mast set aft of the slightly lower mizzenmast with the steering station set squarely in the stern.

The schooner he had his eye on sat at the end of the pier. Her highly polished masts, cabin tops, and deck gleamed in the early morning light that glimmered off her white hull like light dancing off a glass windchime in a light breeze.

"Enjoying the view, Jack?" Agent Tom Gebhardt asked him.

"Just admiring the boats," Jack said as he turned to look at the younger agent who had a naval officer wearing a dress white uniform with him.

"This is Teniente Ramiro Baeza, the intelligence officer who's been helping us with your case," Tom said.

"Jack Lyons, Firearms and Explosives Administration," Jack said, introducing himself with a handshake. "It's a pleasure meeting you teh—teh ..."

"Teniente," the lieutenant said. "You may call me Lieutenant or Ramiro if you like."

"I'm sorry—Lieutenant. I don't have an ear for Spanish, and I can't roll my *r*'s," Jack said.

"Fortunately, I don't have a problem speaking your language."

"Please have a seat," Jack said as a waiter came to the table to pour coffee in the coffee cups.

"Did you have a pleasant trip from Mérida?" Lieutenant Baeza asked.

"We did," Jack replied. "Aside from a heavy dosage of Bob Seger," he said as he glanced at Tom, who chuckled to himself. "I got a good look at the countryside. In many ways, it reminds me of my hometown in Central Texas. I didn't see any rivers or lakes, though."

"That's because they're all underground," the lieutenant explained. "The Yucatán Peninsula is made of limestone, and the rain seeps through it, forming huge lakes and rivers beneath the ground."

"Sort of like the springs around Central Texas," Jack commented.

"Lieutenant Baeza and his counterpart at the Ciudad del Carmen Naval Region attended the gun trafficking school we held in Mérida last year," Tom said. "Since then, we've been tracing all the guns the Marina and the Armada seize in Campeche."

"Excellent," Jack said. "Tracing is an important tool for us. It's the starting point of all our investigations."

"Teniente Maribal, my associate in Ciudad del Carmen, designed a database we use to analyze the information we collect," the lieutenant said. "We enter as much detail as we can relating to the guns we decommission, including where they were seized, from whom, and their criminal affiliations. Using that information and the trace results we get from your agency, Teniente Maribal developed a mapping program which allows us to analyze supply sources, supply lines, and hot zones. We've even been able to link seizures, identify Mexican-based gun traffickers, and in some instances predict when and where to expect a gun load headed for Campeche."

"In fact, an analytical report using tracing data prepared by Lieutenant Maribal was used to interdict a large gun load at Punta Morro a couple of months ago," Tom added.

"That's very innovative," Jack remarked.

"Teniente Maribal is an expert programmer, a skilled analyst, and an expert shot," Lieutenant Baeza added.

"I'd like to meet him."

"Her," Tom corrected Jack. "Lieutenant Maribal is female." He turned to Baeza. "The best-looking naval officer I've ever seen."

"Brains, beauty, and good with a gun," Jack commented. "My kind of gal."

"Teniente Baeza delivered a copy of the case report you sent to the SIEDO agent handling the case."

"SIEDO?"

"The federal prosecutor investigating the gun seizure at the Port of Seyba Playa last week," Tom explained.

Jack glanced at the lieutenant. "I thought the marines were conducting the investigation."

"The Marina doesn't conduct a formal investigation," Tom explained. "That's handled by the Judge Advocate General or the Federal Public Ministry agent."

"I'm not sure I follow."

"The Mexican judicial system isn't like ours," Tom explained. "It's based on Napoleonic Law and Civil Code. The prosecutor conducts an inquest, gathers all the evidence, and prepares the case for submission to a judge. The judge reviews the prosecutor's case and the defense prepared by a defense attorney and then renders a judgment. No juries, no cross-examination, and no presumption of innocence. Here, you're guilty until you prove your innocence."

"Tom's correct," the lieutenant said. "There is an effort to modernize the system to be more like yours, but I'm afraid that's still a number of years away."

"I had no idea," Jack commented.

"Agent Santiago, the agent handling the investigation, reviewed your report and believes there is enough probable responsibility to charge José Luis Ortega and Fausto López with the illegal introduction of firearms into the territory of the republic," the lieutenant added.

"Since the guns you tied to Ortega were found in López's possession, you can use the public ministry agent's case report to add to the list of defendants in your case," Tom added. "I'll get a copy of the report, slap a consular certification on it, and you're good to go in district court back in Houston."

"Well ..." Jack scoffed. "Fat chance of getting him extradited."

"I don't know, Jack. When they extradited Chapo Guzman, that set a precedent."

"I'm sure Mexico has a better case against him. The most he'll get is ten years in the US."

"What about extraditing Ortega?" the lieutenant asked Jack. "How much time would he face in the US?"

"We tied him to a murder, so he could get as much as life in prison," Jack replied. "But I'm sure he's probably hiding out somewhere where he'll never be found."

"What if I were to tell you I have José Luis Ortega in a cell at the base in Lerma?" the lieutenant said. "We found him and another man tied to a coconut tree at López's house in Lorenzo. One had a handgun stuffed in his pants and the other an AR-15 across his lap."

"It'll be a test case for us," Tom told Jack. "But I'm willing to jump through the hoops if you are."

"The man he killed was no saint, but he still deserves to have his killer brought to justice," Jack said as he noticed the lieutenant staring at the *Siete Mares*. "Do you still believe that ship was the one I saw at Padre Island?"

"I'm almost certain of it," the lieutenant replied. "I read the transcript of the recording you included with your report. The one of someone telling José Luis about putting the guns on a ship."

"That was Billy Chávez, the man José Luis is suspected of murdering," Jack said. "He was trying to guess how José Luis was going to get the guns to Mexico."

"It looks like he guessed correctly," the lieutenant remarked.

"Unfortunately, that doesn't constitute evidence unless it can be tied to something substantial," Jack said.

"Didn't Ortega admit to Chávez that he was meeting a ship at the Devil's Elbow?"

"He admitted to having run drugs there in shark boats from the Playa Bagdad," Jack replied.

"Too bad they didn't get into who they were meeting," Tom commented.

"Could we be mistaken about Donovan being at the Devil's Elbow?" Jack proposed.

"I believe he was there," the lieutenant said unequivocally. "I had solid information he went to Texas to get the guns. Very reliable. Highly placed."

"Highly placed where? The military?" Tom inquired.

Lieutenant Baeza sat quietly, obviously reluctant to identify his source.

"You might say it was insider information from a competitor," the lieutenant said cryptically. "Beyond that, it is not wise to say."

"I've heard that drug traffickers often pass information on their rivals to the authorities," Tom said.

"I've heard that too," the lieutenant added.

"I've found that even insider information can be wrong," Jack commented. "Especially if passed on by a rival."

"You don't seem anxious to believe Donovan was at the Devil's Elbow, Jack," Tom commented.

"It's not that. If Donovan brought guns to Mexico, he deserves to answer for it. It's just ..." Jack drew a long breath. "Whoever was on that ship kept us from driving into an ambush."

"How do you know the shots came from the ship?" the lieutenant asked. "Maybe it was a hunter. I've read where hunters in the United States have shot people to help policemen on the highway."

"It's not likely that a hunter would have used a fifty-caliber rifle and next to impossible that he would have incendiary ammunition," Jack countered. "Besides, I saw a round streak in from offshore before hitting one of the trucks."

"You mean a tracer?" Tom said.

"Something similar to that happened to me," Lieutenant Baeza said. "The night we came to the port, somebody offshore destroyed the launches the Thunderbolts used to get to the warehouse. Whoever did it made it impossible for them to escape."

"Did you determine the caliber of the gun that was used?" Tom asked.

"We fished out the engine cowling from one of the launches," the lieutenant replied. "It was made by a twelve-point-seven-millimeter incendiary round."

"That's fifty-caliber," Tom said.

"More circumstantial evidence, Agent Lyons?" the lieutenant asked rhetorically.

"Does Donovan have a history of doing something like that?" Tom asked the lieutenant.

"Nothing in his file," Baeza replied. "But I wouldn't put it past him."

"Where would he have gotten the gun? There's no record of a fifty-caliber rifle being bought by any of the straw purchasers Ortega used," Jack pointed out to Baeza. "Incendiary and tracer ammunition is next to impossible to get."

"Not for someone like Dónovan. He's made a lot of connections over the years he worked out of Panama," the lieutenant retorted. "That may be a circumstantial fact as well, but you have to admit, the circumstances are piling up."

"That may be," Jack responded. "However, without literally a smoking gun, we haven't got a case against him."

"There may not be a case in a US court, Agent Lyons," the lieutenant said. "But this is Mexico. Tom is correct. If a charge is brought against you, it is up to you to prove your innocence. The prosecutor has a reputation for being aggressive and will most likely charge Dónovan, based on the evidence we discussed, circumstantial or not."

Donovan tried to ignore the faint droning in his ear as he willed himself to stay asleep. On any other day, he would have enjoyed waking to the rhythmic hum of the ceiling fan over his bed but not today. Xóchitl had come to his dreams again, and he wanted to bring her back but could only manage the drive through the Texas hill country in his convertible. The sky had turned to gray, and the music had faded to static. Every time he turned to look for Xóchitl, he couldn't find her. She had slipped away and taken with her the joy he felt in his heart, leaving a hollow ache in its place. He found himself driving down the backroad utterly alone until the subtle yet enticing scent of a woman's perfume coaxed him into opening his eyes. He looked at the soft blur looking back at him as the woman put her hand against his face.

"Xóchitl?" he said barely audibly.

Slowly, the blur began to sharpen as the delicate features on the woman's face came into focus. She had the face of an angel but not the one he had hoped to see.

"The fever has broken," he heard Doña Estér say to someone standing behind her.

Don Macario came to Donovan's bedside and sat in the chair next to the lovely doña as he tried to raise himself up in his bed.

"Easy, Simon," Don Macario said. He helped Donovan sit up in his bed. "You'll tear your stitches."

Donovan looked at the white band wrapped around his ribs and ran his hand gently along his left side. He turned to look at Doña Estér as she got up suddenly.

"That bandage needs to be changed," she said as she went to get her medical bag from the small table across the room.

Not even the tantalizing sight of Doña Estér's pants catching in the creases of her teardrop-shaped bottom could shake the hollow heartache Donovan had felt since he woke. He thought about the dream, but the details kept slipping away with every waking moment until only the heartache remained.

He watched Doña Estér take her distressed brown medical bag off the table and start back to Donovan's bedside. He tried to say something, but the dryness in his throat made him cough.

"I'll get some water," Don Macario said.

"You've been a very sick boy," Doña Estér remarked as she sat. "I'm going to remove the bandage to air out the wound." She set her bag on the nightstand. "Lift your arms."

He winced as he raised his hands over his head. As she removed the dressing from around his ribs, he took the glass of water Don Macario brought to him and sipped from it slowly.

"You gave us quite a scare," Don Macario said to him. "You've been out of your head with fever these last couple of days. Do you remember what happened?"

Donovan stared aimlessly out the window at the lighthouse sitting on the hill at Punta Morro as he tried to remember. He recalled twisting and turning in a cascade of bubbles and someone tearing at his throat as they sank toward the bottom. He recalled the cold, tingling sensation he felt slicing down his left side as a dark cloud enveloped them. He remembered holding on to his assailant's feet as he tried to swim to the surface after cutting him. He recalled the kicking and the twisting as they continued to sink until it finally came to a stop. Then, he recalled watching his assailant's lifeless body sink slowly into a dark abyss below him.

He looked down at his wound and at the stitches, which reminded him of a long zipper.

"Fifty," Doña Estér said to him.

"Fifty?" he said as he watched her drop the dressing in the trash can next to the nightstand.

"I thought you were counting the stitches," she explained. "The wound was twenty-five centimeters long. It took me fifty stitches to close it."

"You lost a lot of blood," Don Macario added.

"How long have I been out?"

"Several days now," Don Macario replied. "We've been taking turns sitting with you since we brought you to the cabaña."

"Who's we?"

"Mostly Itzél, Augie, and me," the old gentleman replied. "Estér's been kind enough to drop in from time to time to check on you and Benício."

"Itzél's been pulling double duty watching over you and her husband," Doña Estér added.

Hearing the word *husband* used to describe Benício's relationship to Itzél unsettled Donovan much like hearing Poli refer to him as his father had at the Tucán restaurant. It made him feel like an interloper, a homewrecker, an outsider. He believed he had won Itzél's love fair and square, unlike Benício, whom, by her own admission, she did not love. He felt he had built a strong father-and-son relationship with Poli every bit as solid as the boy had with Benício. Still, something didn't feel right. He couldn't shake the consuming heartache that had come over him since he woke.

"How did I get here?" Donovan asked.

"We found you in the witch's cave at Punta Morro," Don Macario replied.

"The witch?" Donovan said softly. He tried to recall what he saw as he lay in the sand at the mouth of the cave, but the images would not come clearly. He remembered hearing screeching, groaning, and people yelling angrily.

"It's a good thing you told Augie to look for you there," Don Macario added. "The Armada was sweeping the coast after the shootout. Augie had no choice but to leave you or risk getting boarded."

"That's what I expected him to do."

"He said that, but I could tell he didn't like doing it," Don Macario commented. "Too bad Dario didn't tell anyone where to find him."

"What are you talking about?"

"Itzél said Dario went to see Fausto the day of the delivery," Don Macario replied.

"Dario went to see Fausto?" Donovan said.

"To protect Itzél," Doña Estér explained. "He risked his life going there."

"It's evident that Fausto didn't trust Dario," Don Macario added. "He probably forced Dario to go to the warehouse with him."

"Dario was at the warehouse?"

"The professor and Pablo saw him with Fausto through the door just before the Thunderbolts got there," he explained. "They never saw him come out."

"What do you think happened to him?"

"No one knows," Don Macario replied. "He was not listed among the dead. Fausto was the only one taken alive."

Donovan turned to the door when he heard it opening. He felt a chill run through him when he saw Itzél come into the cabaña. He couldn't take his eyes off her, spellbound by her beauty as if seeing her for the first time. She had on the same red blouse and buff-colored slacks she wore the first time they made love.

Don Macario and Doña Estér walked to the door to leave them alone.

"You have an appointment at the Federal Attorney General's office downtown this afternoon," Don Macario said as he held the front door open for Doña Estér. "The SIEDO and some people from the American consulate want to talk to you."

"I'll be back to wrap your wound later," Doña Estér said as she stood in the doorway. "Try not to exert yourself."

"Augie'll be by at two to take you," Don Macario said as he followed Doña Estér out the door.

Donovan gazed into Itzél's eyes as she looked down on him lovingly. She looked beautiful to him but somehow sadly so.

"Is there something wrong?" he asked her.

Itzél walked to his bedside and took his hand in hers as she sat. As he reached to brush away a lock of her hair that had fallen over her right eye, the dream he had tried so hard to recall suddenly came back.

The dust swirled in his rearview mirror like jet wash behind an airliner coming in for a landing. The sun beat down on his uncovered head as he barreled down a caliche road in the hill country in his vintage convertible. He reached over to tune his radio as he turned to look for Xóchitl, who had moved from his side to sit by her door. She had her head turned away, looking off at the distant hills that looked like blue clouds rolling along the horizon.

"Beautiful, aren't they?" he commented.

She took the white lace scarf off her shoulders and put it over her head. He saw his reflection in her sunglasses as she turned to look at him.

"Don't let your love for me blind you from finding true love," she said. "Don't look for me in her."

A single tear trickled down the right side of Itzél's face. Donovan wiped it off with his thumb. She kissed his hand and then put her face on the back of it.

"There's something I have to tell you," she said softly.

He swallowed the lump in his throat and drew a deep breath, anticipating the worst.

"I love you so, so much," she said softly.

"And I love you."

She smiled at him sadly as she put her hand on the side of his face.

"No, you don't," she said. "You love Xóchitl."

He looked at her curiously. "How ...?"

"You talk in your sleep, mí amor," she said as she released his hand. "You must love her very much, but ... I'm not Xóchitl."

"I love you now."

"You love that I look like her," she said, again surprising him.

Donovan felt the blood run from his face.

"We were going to be married," he heard himself confess. "You know she's dead."

She kissed his hand again.

"Not to you," she said as she stood still holding his hand. "In a way, I'm haunted by the dead too."

Donovan looked at her sullenly.

"Poli's father," Donovan said.

Itzél nodded sadly as she released his hand. He felt his heart sink as he watched her walk to the door.

"Please don't leave," he said to her softly.

Itzél stopped as she started to open the door and hung her head. Donovan winced as he sat on the edge of his bed to wait for her to come back.

"I'm moving to Ciudad del Carmen with Benício," she said without turning to look at him.

"Stay here—with me," he said.

He felt his heart sink when he heard the knob turning.

"I can't," she said as she turned to face him. "A woman's place is by her husband."

"I want to be your husband."

She scoffed softly as she smiled sadly. "I've already got one. He's replacing the pastor at his old church on Norte Beach. Poli's enrolling in an art school in Ciudad del Carmen."

He heard the knob turn and held up a hand to block the sun as she opened the door to leave.

"What about us?" he asked as he watched her walk out the door.

She turned to look at him as she stood in the doorway.

"Was there ever really an us?"

Donovan didn't answer. He just stared at her hopelessly as he felt his insides go numb.

"Adios, Simon," she said as she tried to keep from crying. "Mí amor."

"Wait," he said fruitlessly as he watched the door close behind her.

CHAPTER 18

Donovan couldn't recall the last time he rode in his convertible as a passenger. He basked in the warmth of the sun's rays flickering through the trees overhead, the smell of the ocean carrying in the sea breeze, and the wind in his face, but it did little to ease the pain of losing Itzél. It felt like losing Xóchitl all over again.

If he had only listened to Augie, he might have avoided feeling the way he did. He turned to him as he drove the big convertible down the hill from Punta Morro to Seyba Playa. The self-proclaimed saltwater channel rat and jack-of-all-trades had more to him than just that crusty, rough-edged persona he presented. With a mere glance of a picture, he had seen what he refused to see. He had fallen in love with the ghost of a woman he would always love and not Itzél. His experience with Itzél had taught him one thing: that he would never find another Xóchitl but, more important, that he shouldn't try.

"The ocean looks greener than usual," Augie remarked as they rounded the curve overlooking Seyba Playa.

Donovan looked at the water and thought instantly of Itzél's eyes and how they would always haunt him. She may have looked like his lost love, but she had traits of her own worth falling for. He had no doubt that he would have fallen for her had she not looked like Xóchitl but wondered if he would have given her a second look otherwise.

"Drive down the malecón," Donovan said as they entered town.

"The seawall is a little out of the way, don't you think?" Augie commented.

"We'll get there on time."

Augie turned the big Oldsmobile off the road and headed down the hill toward the seawall. Most of the fishermen had gone for the day after selling their catch. A few remained to mend nets or clean out their pangas. Donovan looked at the line of boats on the narrow beach until he found the one that until recently had belonged to Benício. He looked at the outboard motor that still looked new and at the young fisherman drying the hull of his newly bought panga with a chamois.

"I'm sorry things didn't work out for you and Itzél," Augie said as they drove by Benício's old launch.

Donovan turned his head to look across the street at the Cocina Maya. He stared pensively at the "SE VENDE" sign taped to the plate-glass window advertising it for sale. He looked up at the second-story window to Itzél's bedroom and recalled the coquettish way she teased him while wearing his Panama hat before taking him up to her room to make love for the first time. He turned to look up the road.

"I guess it just wasn't meant to be," Donovan said regretfully.

The office of the Attorney General of the Republic sat on the principal thoroughfare that ran through downtown Seyba Playa.

The two-story building looked cold and uninviting as government offices tended to do.

After getting through security, Donovan followed the federal agent through the building with sterile walls past the offices of the Federal Agency of Investigation, the AFI, Mexico's equivalent of the FBI. They continued down the hall to the offices of the Federal Public Ministry, where the organized crime taskforce agent from Mexico City waited for him in the conference room. The agent knocked on the door before entering.

"Señor Dónovan is here," the agent announced.

The room looked like a typical government conference room with the attorney general's logo dominating the principal wall along with pictures of the president, the attorney general, and the local head of the office. Donovan stood by the door with his Panama hat in his hands as he looked at the people sitting at the far end of the table.

"Sit down, Capitán," the woman at the head of the table said.

The federal agent pulled out the chair at the foot of the table for Donovan to sit. He glanced at the small microphone propped up in a small tripod on the table in front of him as he sat. He set his hat down and looked across the table at the public ministry agent.

The woman, who was dressed in a gray business suit with a white blouse buttoned to the top, had her face buried in the file in front of her. He looked at the faint creases around her mouth and wondered if she ever smiled. She wore her auburn hair pulled back so severely in a tight bun it looked like it hurt. She had lush eyebrows and cat-like gray eyes she hid behind a pair of Buddy Holly–style horn-rimmed glasses she wore on her elf-like nose. He looked at the ominous-looking digital recorder on the table in front of her as she read through the file, sorted through a stack of photos, and jotted notes on her notepad.

He looked at Lieutenant Baeza, sitting to her right in his dress white naval infantry uniform and at the two Americans in business suits sitting across the table from him. He looked at the Mexican federal agent standing behind her, waiting to assist her. They all stole glances at him as they waited on the prosecutor to begin the interview.

"We're ready to begin," she said abruptly as she raised her head. She turned on the digital recorder. "Interview of Capitán Simón Xavier Dónovan recorded this day at the office of the Seyba Playa Sub Delegado. My name is Lourdes Santiago Rosas, Federal Public Ministry Agent for the Assistant Attorney General's Office for Special Investigations on Organized Crime. The following interview relates to the illegal introduction of one hundred and ten firearms into the territory of the Republic of México." The public ministry agent looked across the table at Donovan. "Please state your name and occupation."

Donovan glanced at the mic on the table and cleared his throat. "Simon Xavier Donovan, master of the schooner *Siete Mares*."

"Capitán Dónovan, this is an informal interview. You will be questioned about your knowledge of a gun shipment recovered by the Marina at the Port of Seyba Playa earlier this week. A statement regarding your responses will be prepared for your review after which you will sign. Do you have any questions?"

"A couple," Donovan replied. He pointed at the Americans. "Who are they?"

"They're from the American consulate in Mérida," the public ministry agent replied. "They're here as observers."

"They don't look like State Department."

The public ministry agent turned to the Americans for a response.

"We're from the Justice Department, Captain Donovan. I'm Special Agent Thomas Gebhardt assigned to the consulate in Mérida, and this is Special Agent Jack Lyons from our Houston office."

"You guys with DEA or FBI?"

"Firearms and Explosives Administration," Tom replied.

"The F-E-A," Donovan said, spelling out the acronym. "La FEA. Are you aware of what that translates to in English?"

"Yes, I am," Tom said, unimpressed with Donovan's pointing out the unfortunate circumstance of his agency's acronym translating to "ugly woman."

"What made you say we didn't look like State Department?" Jack asked.

"You don't have pasty skin, and you both look like you know what you're doing,"

Donovan replied.

"What's your other question?" the public ministry agent asked.

"I don't understand why I'm here," Donovan replied. "I don't know anything about any guns."

As the public ministry agent dropped her cat-like eyes to review her notes, Donovan looked at Lieutenant Baeza, who stared at him with cold, analytical eyes. He turned to the Americans, who also looked at him studiously.

"On the night when Fausto López, alias El Demonio, received an unauthorized shipment of one hundred and ten Romanian AK-47 rifles in violation of Mexican law, your ship, the *Moonlight Runner*, was sighted off Punta Morro in close proximity of where the delivery was made," the public ministry agent stated factually.

"My ship is the *Siete Mares*," Donovan corrected her. "She no longer sails as *Moonlight Runner*."

Donovan waited for the agent to continue as she looked down on her notes.

"I apologize for the mistake," she said as she looked up at him. "What was the *Siete Mares* doing so close to the Port of Seyba Playa at the time of the incident?"

"It's on the way to my anchorage at the Paradise Lagoon just on the other side of Punta Morro," Donovan replied. "I was headed in from the Sabancuy Channel."

"What were you doing at the Sabancuy Channel?" she asked.

Donovan glanced at Lieutenant Baeza. "I was hired by the National Institute of Anthropology and History to help recover a ship's bell from a wreck at the mouth of the channel that may have historical significance."

The prosecutor wrote feverishly on her notepad as Donovan waited for her to ask the next question.

"Your ship was spotted off the Texas coast a day after the American police interrupted an attempt to smuggle illegal firearms out of their country at Padre Island, specifically at a place known as the Devil's Elbow," the public ministry agent continued. "What was your ship doing off the Texas coast?"

"I was not off the Texas coast and nowhere near the Devil's Elbow," Donovan said firmly. "I went out to meet the yacht race coming into Tampico from Corpus Christi."

"The sponsors of the yacht race have no record of your ship listed as a participant," she added.

"That's because I didn't enter the race," Donovan explained. "I did what a lot of other skippers do—sail with the regatta as a noncompetitor."

The prosecutor took a document out of the file in front of her and looked at it carefully. Donovan recognized it as the diving permit issued by the Mexican government.

"By your own admission, you were on a charter for the institute," she said as she examined the document. "Do you customarily break a charter to go on a pleasure cruise?"

"I wasn't on a pleasure cruise. The head of the dive had to go to Campeche City on business, so we took advantage of the break to make the run to Tampico," Donovan explained.

"For what purpose?"

"To drum up business," Donovan said offhand. "Get the word out that we're available for charter. You now—network. Most people don't think about Campeche when looking for somewhere to vacation. You know—honeymooners, romantic getaways, that sort of thing."

The prosecutor stared coldly at Donovan as she waited for him to continue.

"Diving," he added abruptly. "There are a lot of stateside divers that don't know about all the great diving in Campeche."

"And did you?"

"Did I what?"

"Network?"

"I—uh, no."

"Why not?"

"As it turns out, there wasn't enough time, so we had to get back," he responded lamely. "I miscalculated how long it would take. The wind doesn't always cooperate."

He held his breath, hoping she would move on to another question as he watched her go through her notes and shuffle through the photos she had on the desk before turning to the lieutenant to confer privately with him.

He watched the prosecutor summon the federal agent assisting her and hand him an eight-by-ten photograph as she whispered something to him. The federal agent walked over to Donovan and gave him the photo.

"That photograph was taken by the US Coast Guard in the waters off the Texas coast precisely where a ship that rendezvoused with the gunrunners at the Devil's Elbow would be if they went to hide among the yacht racers."

"Or," Donovan said as he slid the photo on the table away from him, "where somebody would be if they sailed from the Bay of Campeche to meet the regatta like I did."

Donovan crossed his arms as he watched the prosecutor confer quietly with the lieutenant. He watched the lieutenant point at the Americans and then watched the prosecutor confer with them in the same secretive manner as she took notes.

"Mister Dónovan—"

"*Captain* Donovan," he corrected her.

"Forgive me," she said as she glanced at her notes. "At the time of the incident at the Devil's Elbow, a ship with two masts like yours was seen leaving."

"A lot of ships have more than just one mast, and they're not all sailing vessels," Donovan retorted. "Shrimpers and fishing boats have radio masts and outriggers to drag their nets that when stowed could look like the masts on a sailing vessel."

"The Coast Guard reported that the only ships in the area at the time were a flotilla of sailboats like yours."

Donovan felt his face turn red as he glared at the prosecutor. He drew a long, deep breath to keep himself from losing his cool.

"My ship's a schooner," he said almost calmly. "It has two masts and runs sixty-five feet along the deck. She carries a crew of four and can sleep ten. She's a blue-water ship and has the capability of circumnavigating the globe." He let out his breath slowly. "A sailboat is what you play with in a bathtub."

He looked at the prosecutor's cat-like eyes as she stared back at him unemotionally. She removed her reading glasses and resumed the questioning.

"Let's talk about your schooner, Capitán," she said. "The *Moonlight Runner* was seized for running drugs."

"She's not the *Moonlight Runner* anymore," Donovan said firmly. "I rechristened her *Siete Mares*."

"To hide her past?"

"To purge her karma," Donovan replied. "Once a ship is christened, it develops a personality. It becomes a living entity with a soul and mind of its own. The *Moonlight Runner* had bad karma. I needed to exorcise it from the ship by renaming it."

"How do you do that?" the prosecutor asked, returning her reading glasses to the bridge of her elfin nose.

"You have to perform a de-christening ceremony," he explained. "I took the *Moonlight Runner* out to where I estimated was the center of the Gulf of Mexico, wrote her name on a piece of paper, and put it in a wooden box."

"Is that all it takes to exorcise your ... ship?"

"I'm not finished," Donovan replied. "I put the box in a metal bowl and set it on fire. I said a dechristening prayer over the ashes, asking that the *Moonlight Runner* be allowed to rest in peace, and tossed the ashes over the side."

"Are you a superstitious man, Capitán Dónovan?" the prosecutor asked.

"I believe in tradition," Donovan sat back in his chair. "Yes, to a certain extent, I guess I am superstitious. I'm a sailor, and superstition is part of the sailing tradition."

"You sound like a romantic and adventurous man," she remarked.

"To quote a seafaring legend," Donovan added, "I am what I am, and that's a sailor man."

"Then you are an adventurous man?" she added. "Perhaps, adventurous enough to smuggle guns for Fausto López?"

Donovan stared at her curiously. She had made him drop his guard and struck when he least expected it.

"I'm no gunrunner—and there's no amount of money that could entice me to take a load of coconut husks much less guns to a drug trafficker."

"Let's talk about that," she said as she pulled a document out of the file in front of her. "You have been detained in Costa Rica, Panamá, the Dominican Republic, Haiti, French Guyana—"

"Colombia, Ecuador, Venezuela, and Surinam, among others," Donovan said interrupting her. "What's your point?"

"The charges include misrepresenting cargo, smuggling, fraud, forgery of official state documents—the list is quite extensive."

"I was never formally charged in any of those instances."

"That's curious," she commented. "How do you explain that?"

"They were just misunderstandings," Donovan replied.

"Then you must be the most misunderstood man in the hemisphere," she countered.

In all the years Donovan had worked as a shipping agent, he had heard countless remarks made by customs officials and policemen about his brushes with the law across the Americas but never one as well-delivered. It had the perfect blend of subtlety, incredulity, and suspicion laced with sarcasm.

"I found that customs officials in the Caribbean basin either don't read English well or get nervous with anything out of the ordinary," Donovan explained. "Their way of handling it is to lock you up until they figure it out."

"And they always manage somehow to *figure it out*," she commented dryly.

"That's right."

"Have you ever paid a bribe?"

Donovan had to think about how to answer that question. He knew nobody would believe him if he said he hadn't.

"Paying off officials to expedite permits and approve cargos comes with the territory. You don't work the Gulf and Caribbean without paying 'departure taxes,' 'inspection fees,' or 'overtime' for overworked and underpaid customs officials," he explained. "It's the price of doing business."

"So, you admit to committing bribery?"

"*Bribery* is such a subjective term."

"For the record, Capitán Dónovan has admitted to committing bribery to avoid prosecution," she said formally.

"I didn't say that," Donovan objected. "I never paid off anyone to get out of getting thrown in jail. I didn't have to. My paper was always good, and I never handled contraband," he explained. "I simply said I paid to grease the wheels to avoid delays. Time is money in the shipping business."

"If what you allege is true, those officials are corrupt," the prosecutor commented. "Did you report them?"

"I know you don't really believe it would have done any good," Donovan retorted. "I can't control the direction of the wind, only the trim of my sails."

There was a long pause. The public ministry agent wrote extensively on her notepad.

"Do you know Fausto López?" she asked as she held up a picture of him standing on the deck of his ship, talking to Fausto standing on the dock.

"We've met. He tried to charter my boat, but I turned him down," Donovan said as the prosecutor looked through the other photographs on the table.

"What about Aníbal Barca Rayos?" she asked as she picked up another picture and looked at it.

"Can't say that I know who that is."

"You may know him as El Rayo—the Thunderbolt."

Donovan had hoped she would drop the question and move on to the next one, but with her looking at another picture, he couldn't take the chance that she didn't have a picture of him with the colonel. He didn't want to have to explain how he knew the colonel much less that he had offered him protection.

"Oh, him," Donovan said. "We've met."

The prosecutor continued to look at the picture before showing it to Donovan. He scoffed when he recognized it as the one taken by the Coast Guard of him standing at the helm of the *Siete Mares.*

"Nice picture of you," she said as she looked at it again. "A friend of mine thinks you look like Gardner McKay, but I don't know who that is." She set the picture down. "Tell me about how you met the Thunderbolt?"

"There's not much to tell," Donovan began. "I was having dinner ashore on the beach off the Sabancuy Channel when he came to the restaurant. I was called to his table, and he asked if I had been approached by El Demonio to hire out my ship. I told him the truth, and he warned me not to accept any other attempts by him to charter my ship."

"Is that all?"

"Pretty much," Donovan replied.

"Have you ever run contraband of any sort?"

In an instant, Donovan thought about the work he had done for his parent company in Houston under government contract. He also remembered the mortars he delivered tragically for Amalgamated Industries to Murindó, Colombia. He chose to believe that the cargo had the approval of his government at least tacitly.

"No," he answered.

He watched the public ministry agent review her notes and then continue to write extensively on her notepad as the lieutenant and the Americans also watched her. She would stop occasionally to check her notes before resuming her writing. Time dragged on for Donovan, who reviewed in his mind what they had discussed. She never once accused him of helping El Demonio get the rifles the Marina recovered at the warehouse, but her line of questioning clearly demonstrated to him that she suspected him of it. She got him to admit that he paid bribes and that he knew both El Demonio and the Thunderbolt and concede that his ship was near the Port of Seyba Playa when the Marina recovered the guns they seized at the warehouse. After what seemed like an eternity, the prosecutor stopped writing and looked across the table at Donovan.

"To conclude," the public ministry agent said, "your vessel was photographed a day's sail from the incident at the Devil's Elbow and could have been the ship the American police saw fleeing the scene. You claim that you were innocently participating in a yacht race to Tampico to network, but you never did. Is this correct?"

"Yes, but—"

"Your vessel was near the Port of Seyba Playa the night Fausto López received a clandestine shipment of one hundred and ten Romanian AK-47 rifles that had been illegally introduced into the territory of México," she added. "You claim that you were—and I emphasize—*coincidentally* heading to your home at the Paradise Lagoon after completing a charter to the Sabancuy Channel. Is this correct?"

"Yes."

"You also admit that you know and have spoken with both Fausto López and Colonel Aníbal Barca Rayos concerning specifically the hiring of your ship," she added. "You claim that you turned down López and later heeded Colonel Barca's warning not to hire out your ship to López. Is that correct?"

"Yes," Donovan said uneasily.

"On the night in question, both Fausto López and Colonel Aníbal Barca Rayos were at the Port of Seyba Playa to contend for the ownership of one hundred and ten Romanian AK-47 rifles. Again, you claim that your proximity to the port at the time of the delivery and subsequent conflict between López and the Thunderbolt was incidental to your approach to your anchorage. Is this correct?"

"Yes, definitely."

The prosecutor took another long, uncomfortable pause to review her notes, and Donovan looked at the lieutenant and the American agents, who also hung on her every word, waiting for her to render a decision whether to charge Donovan or not.

"I have to ask you one last time, Capitán Dónovan," she said, looking directly and firmly at him. "Did you go to the Devil's Elbow in the territory of the United States of America, collect one hundred and ten Romanian AK-47 rifles, and deliver them to Fausto López at the Port of Seyba Playa in the state of Campeche, México, in violation of Mexican law?"

"No," Donovan said.

"Has all the testimony you have given today been truthful without any reservations, exclusions, or omissions?"

"Yes."

"Is there anything you would like to add, Capitán Dónovan?"

Donovan sat back, put his right elbow on the back of the chair, and looked directly at the prosecutor.

"I came to Campeche about two years ago to run a charter service. I partnered with Duncan Augustus Fagan and incorporated his dive shop into the business." He looked at the public ministry agent as she scribbled feverishly to keep up with him. "We're struggling but far from starving. My ship is available for cruises and diving trips."

The public ministry agent finished writing her notes and laid her pen gently on her notepad. She looked up at Donovan, unsmiling and stern. "Do you understand that if it is determined that you have lied, omitted any fact relevant to this investigation, or misrepresented the truth in any manner that you will be held accountable to the fullest extent of Mexican law?"

Donovan looked at the stern-faced public ministry agent before answering.

"I do."

"This concludes the interview of Capitán Simón Dónovan," the public ministry agent said abruptly. She looked at the lieutenant and the Americans. "I'm done here."

She turned off the digital recorder and began gathering the pictures, permits, and other documents and put them in the file she had on the table. Donovan looked at the lieutenant as he turned to the public ministry agent.

"What about Duncan Augustus Fagan?" Lieutenant Baeza asked. "Aren't you going to question him?"

"There's no point in it," she told the lieutenant. "I'm sure he will only repeat what the capitán has said."

"He will because it's the truth," Donovan insisted.

"I'm sure you'll agree that the truth can have many shades, Capitán," the prosecutor said to him cryptically. "You and Señor Fagan are free to go."

EPILOGUE

Until recently, Alonso thought he had his career mapped out perfectly. He would join the Carmen Municipal Police to get experience, work several years for the Federal Agency of Investigation assisting investigations, and then apply for a management position. He hadn't counted on unexpected variables getting in his way. He thought about how those unexpected variables changed his life forever as he stood on the banks of the Terminos Lagoon in his police uniform, staring pensively across the tranquil waters, watching a perfect blue sky and listening to the wind in the palms.

Much had happened to him since last he wore his police uniform officially. He discovered that the world no longer existed in black and white but in varying shades of gray. Donovan taught him that. He had seen friends turn against him and turned to strangers for help. He learned to bend with the wind to keep from breaking, not to accept things at face value or take anything for granted. He had come to this isolated spot in the botanical gardens on the southeast side of Carmen to take care of something he had taken for granted for too long. The time had come to settle the matter once and for all.

He turned around when he heard the soft rumble of a car driving up behind him on the crushed limestone rock. He smiled when he saw Lieutenant Maribal behind the wheel of her Volkswagen convertible, driving down the palm-lined road to park next to his motorcycle.

"You're late, Teniente Maribal," he said as he went to meet her and open her door.

"Are you putting me on report?" she asked playfully as she swung her long, lithesome legs out of her car.

She looked fetching in her dress white naval uniform skirt and blouse. Her slender body and subtle curves might not compare with those of a more voluptuous woman, but her grace and exquisitely beautiful face would make even Sophia Loren envious.

"I think I can let it go this time," he said as he closed the car door.

"Did you have any trouble persuading Comandante Norias to make a statement at the attorney general's office?"

"He made a full confession," Alonso replied. "He confessed to everything, from helping the Thunderbolts plan the Easter raid, to setting me up, and to Camilo's murder."

"And you thought making him confess would be like pulling teeth," she remarked.

"Oh, that reminds me," he said as he put his fingers in his shirt pocket to get something. "I thought it wise to get that part over with before we went downtown." He opened his hand and showed her a pair of gold teeth.

"Ah," she moaned. "You didn't."

"I guess we won't be calling him Comandante Dientes anymore," he said as he bounced the teeth in the palm of his hand. "How does the saying go? An eye for an eye ..." He turned and tossed them as far as he could into the lagoon. "I forget the rest."

"Did you speak with the *delegado* at the AFI?" she asked.

"He thinks he can get me in the next academy in January."

"That's wonderful, Federal Agent Andrade," she said, chuckling softly. She looked around her at the tropical setting. "Why did you ask me to meet you here?"

"To give you this," he replied as he reached into his pocket.

He set a knee on the ground and opened the black velvet box with the engagement ring in it.

The meeting with the special prosecutor had exhausted Donovan, and he went to his cabaña to try to get some rest before meeting his friends for cocktails but couldn't manage to fall asleep. He kept on thinking about the way the public ministry agent itemized each of the circumstances in her summation pointing to his suspected involvement in the delivery of the cache of guns recovered at the port. She made it clear she had him, and he fully expected her to file charges against him. He couldn't understand why she had let him go.

He thought about Itzél on the walk down the bluff and around the beach from his cabaña to the Paradise Lounge. Maybe he *had* transferred his love for Xóchitl to her after all. He felt he truly loved Itzél but wondered if he would have pursued her if she hadn't looked so much like Xóchitl. He had never pursued a married woman before, especially a mother.

He felt the stitches on his side pull a little when he opened the front door to the Paradise Inn. Doña Estér had done such a crackerjack job closing his wound he kept forgetting about it. He slid his hand down his side as he listened to the soft jazz sounds coming from the Paradise Lounge.

It surprised him when he saw Lieutenant Baeza, who had changed into street clothes, sitting near the entrance at a table with the two agents from the US consulate. He tipped his crumpled captain's hat at them cordially as he headed to Don Macario's table at the back of the lounge, where he got an even bigger surprise, one he had not expected.

He didn't recognize Lourdes Santiago, the public ministry agent, at first as she and Don Macario stood around the table, listening to Augie spin some yarn. She had a nice smile, he thought, far more pleasing than the stern, judicious expression she had had on her face earlier that afternoon. She had lost the horn-rimmed glasses and wore her luscious auburn hair Emma Peele style, curling in on her bare shoulders. She had on a floral print summer dress that looked absolutely stunning on her light caramel skin. She smiled at him coyly as he got to the table.

"I still don't know what this Gardner McKay you knew looked like," she said to Don Macario as she smiled at Donovan. "But he must have been a very handsome man."

"You knew Gardner McKay?" Donovan asked Don Macario.

"I met him in Pape'ete in sixty-two on my third round-the-world sail," Don Macario said. "Charming man. He was there filming location shots for his television show."

"It's a good thing you invited me to bring my mother to spend the week at the Paradise Inn," Lourdes said to Don Macario. She glanced at Donovan. "Otherwise, Mexico City might have sent another public ministry agent to handle the gun seizure and capture of Fausto López."

Donovan looked stupefied as he turned to Don Macario for an explanation. The old gentleman ignored him as he kissed Lourdes's hand.

"It's a shame you have to go back to Mexico City so soon," Don Macario said to her.

"Duty calls," she said. "I just stopped by to thank you again before going to the airport."

"Can I drive you there?" Augie offered graciously.

"No, thank you. I rented a car," she replied. She turned to Donovan. "Try not to upset any more drug lords while you're in México, Capitán Dónovan. It'll be the death of you." She kissed Don Macario on the cheek and winked seductively at Donovan. "Ciao, bello."

Donovan stood with his mouth open as he watched her head for the exit, swaying her hips playfully to the beat of the lively jazz song playing.

"You know, she's not married," Don Macario remarked as he invited Donovan to sit. "It might be something you'd like to change."

"No, thanks," Donovan responded as he sat along with Don Macario and Augie, never taking his eyes off the public ministry agent's swaying hips. "Marrying a lawyer is like getting in a sleeping bag knowing there's a rattlesnake in it."

"No rattlesnake ever looked like that," Augie remarked.

Donovan chuckled as he watched Lourdes walk out the exit just as Dr. Ventura walked into the lounge. The professor stopped to take in her seductive walk.

"It looks like Conrad just got snakebit," he remarked as he watched the professor coming to the table.

"What an incredibly beautiful woman," the professor said as he sat across from Donovan.

"Don't get in a sleeping bag with her," Augie remarked.

"Excuse me?"

"Never mind," Augie said as he grinned at the others.

Donovan laughed softly. "What brings you here, Conrad? I thought you were headed back to the institute to check on our bell?"

"I already did," he responded. "Using a mechanical process, the lab was able to remove enough of the encrustation to reveal the ship's name. It looks like it may have been commanded by El

Tiburón, one of several brothers who led the defense of Campeche City against the pirates." He chuckled giddily. "You'll never guess who his descendant is."

"The suspense is killing me," Donovan quipped sarcastically.

"Arturo Farías."

"The narco?"

"For our purposes, let's just call him the chairman of the Campeche Grower's Association," the professor responded. "The institute notified him of the tentative assessment, and he promised to fund any further research."

"I see why you're making the distinction," Donovan commented.

"That should keep you busy for a while," Augie remarked.

"I handed it off to Professor Covarrubias," the professor responded surprisingly. "The reason I came back here is to see if you want to help me investigate the wreckage of a twin-tailed aircraft they found near San Enrique."

"Don't tell me you're still chasing down that old legend?" Donovan scoffed. "It's probably just a fairy tale."

"I agree there are aspects of the legend that are most likely exaggerated, but it's no fairy tale," the professor responded. "Like most legends, it has a basis in fact."

"Next to Amelia Earhart's airplane, that's got to be one of the most famous lost aircraft in history," Donovan remarked.

"And like Earhart's airplane, it too is a Lockheed 10 Electra," the professor commented.

"How long has it been lost, Conrado?" Don Macario inquired.

"It took off from Mérida on November 4, 1939, with a cargo of priceless Mayan artifacts including what might have been an original copy of the Popul Vuh."

Augie frowned. "Popul who?"

"The Popul Vuh. That's the sacred book of the Maya," Don Macario explained. "It was thought that the Spanish destroyed all the existing copies. If the one believed to be aboard the Electra is an original version in the Mayan language, it would be a priceless find."

"The sacred book aside," the professor added. "The plane itself has a great deal of historical significance for Mexico. The Mexican government loaned it to the Republican government during the Spanish Civil War before it was brought back to Mexico. It was bought by Mexico's most illustrious aeronautical pioneer before he was killed in an aviation mishap on the Potomac River. If we were to find the aircraft in reasonably good shape, it would be a boon for the nation's aeronautical museum."

"There's no guarantee the plane they spotted is your legendary Electra," Donovan said. "Lots of planes have been lost in the Campeche jungle."

"With twin tails?" the professor countered.

Before Donovan could respond, he noticed the two agents from the US consulate and Lieutenant Baeza walking toward their table.

"I wonder what they want," he said.

"Who are they?" the professor asked.

"My accusers," Donovan replied softly as Agent Lyons walked up to him while Agent Gebhardt and Lieutenant Baeza stopped just short of the table.

"I wonder if I could have a word with you, Captain Donovan," Agent Lyons said as he glanced at the others sitting at the table. "In private."

"Go ahead and speak your mind," Donovan said. "These are my friends."

"Very well," Lyons said. "That night at the Devil's Elbow—"

"Like I told the prosecutor, I wasn't there," Donovan said, interrupting him.

"Well, whoever it was that blew up those pickups kept us from driving into an ambush," Jack said. "He saved our lives, and I just wanted to convey my thanks."

Donovan nodded his head subtly. "I have no idea why you're telling me."

"I think you know why," Jack retorted as he turned slowly to leave.

"Oh, Agent Lyons," Donovan called, stopping him. "I'm glad none of your people were hurt."

The seasoned agent scoffed as he smiled and then headed for the exit. Agent Gebhardt dipped his head once at Donovan and then followed Jack out of the lounge. Lieutenant Baeza watched the agents leave before approaching Donovan.

"By the way, Capitán Dónovan," he began, "I compared notes with Agent Lyons regarding the weapon he suspects was used to destroy the trucks at Padre Island. The similarities to the weapon used to destroy the Thunderbolt's launches are … interesting. The same caliber and likely the same type of explosive incendiary ammunition," he said as he stared at him suspiciously.

"That *is* interesting," Donovan commented.

"I'm thinking it was the same gun and probably the same man who fired it," the lieutenant said as he pointed at him. "In fact, I think you may even know him."

"I can't imagine who that might be," Donovan responded.

"Perhaps not," the lieutenant said. "Whoever he was, he did help bring an end to the Thunderbolts—but he also violated Mexican law." He looked at Donovan and his friends. "Enjoy your celebration," he said as he turned to leave.

"By the way, Lieutenant," Donovan said as he started to leave, "that was some haul, bringing in El Demonio and eliminating the Thunderbolts like that. Think there's a promotion in it for you?"

"Probably," he said. He smiled at him enigmatically. "I'll catch you later."

"You sure like stirring hornets' nests, don't you?" Augie remarked as they watched the lieutenant leave.

"Sometimes, I just can't help myself," Donovan replied.

Donovan looked at Pablo as he set a bottle of twenty-one-year-old El Dorado rum on the table along with several glasses.

"Now you're talking," Donovan said.

"I thought a toast would be appropriate," Don Macario said as Pablo poured rum into the glasses.

"Here, here," the professor remarked. "El Demonio is finally out of our hair, we solved the mystery of the shipwreck at the mouth of the Sabancuy Channel, and we have a new mystery to investigate."

"I was thinking more of wishing Donovan and Benício a speedy recovery," Don Macario said.

"Here, here," the professor added. "And to Itzél's safe return home."

Donovan shifted his eyes uncomfortably.

"Here, here," he said along with the others.

"Doña Estér tells me Alonso got his old job back and is planning to ask his girl to marry him," Don Macario commented.

"Here's to Alonso," the professor toasted.

"Here, here," they all said almost in unison.

"I wonder whatever happened to Dario," Augie commented. "No one seems to know what became of him."

The sun hung low in the sky as the multi-pastel-colored minibus named Rosita came to the end of the paved road at a small fishing village sitting on the banks of the Naranjo River, a stone's throw from the Pacific Ocean in southwestern Guatemala.

Dario stepped out of the minibus wearing a pair of cheap sunglasses and holding a potato sack he used as a duffle bag over his shoulder. He looked at the line of pangas tied below the palms and banana trees running along the opposite bank as he walked into town. He smiled when he saw the "SE VENDE" sign painted on the bow of a weathered old panga with the well-worn outboard motor tied to a dilapidated dock.

FIN

Lightning Source UK Ltd.
Milton Keynes UK
UKHW011128200820
368549UK00006B/593